BY SHEER PLUCK

Also by Roger M. Kean

Storm Over Khartoum
Avenging Khartoum
Winning His Spurs
A Storm of Peril
Felixitations
Thunderbolt: Torn Enemy of Rome

Non-fiction
The Complete Chronicle of the Emperors of Rome
Forgotten Power: Byzantium – Bulwark of Christianity
Exploring Ancient Egypt
The Fantasy Art of Oliver Frey
Pirates: Predators of the Sea

About the author

Roger M. Kean has been writing for many years, but only in the past three as an author of published fiction. He has written five action tales based on a core of late-Victorian boys' adventures, available for the Kindle from Amazon and other eBook formats from Smashwords.

Having spent a stint at Hornsey College of Art studying painting, Kean attended the London Film School, where he began writing film scripts and his first attempts at full-scale novels. For eight years he edited film documentaries for the BBC before moving into full-time journalism. In the 1980s, as co-founder of magazine publisher Newsfield, he created and edited the best-selling CRASH magazine for the Spectrum home computer and then ZZAP!64 for the Commodore 64. Since then, Kean has authored several history reference titles, including the well-reviewed *The Complete Chronicle of the Emperors of Rome*. Now he spends his time inventing new scenarios to populate with characters from the imagination. He lives with his partner in the the Welsh Marches of Shropshire, England.

By Sheer Pluck

Roger M. Kean

RECKLESS BOOKS

First published as an ebook in Great Britain in 2011 by Reckless Books
and in the U.S.A. as a Smashwords ebook edition

First published in paperback in 2012

© 2012 Roger M. Kean
The right of Roger M. Kean to be identified as the author of this Work has been
asserted by him in accordance with the Copyright,
Designs and Patents Act 1988.

All rights reserved. No part of this publication may be reproduced or transmitted
in any form or by any means, electronic or mechanical, including photocopying,
recording or by any information storage and retrieval system, without written
permission from the publisher.

Typeset in Minion Pro by Reckless Books
Ludlow, Shropshire, England

Cover design and internal illustrations: Oliver Frey / http://oliverfreyart.com
Map: Roger M. Kean

Contents

	Prologue	9
1	A Fishing Trip	14
2	Angry Farmer, Mad Dog	21
3	A Tale with 'Bellishments	31
4	The Rising and Ebbing Tide	41
5	Alone in the World	51
6	The First Step	61
7	An Old Friend	71
8	To the Dark Continent	83
9	The Start Inland	92
10	Lost in the Jungle	103
11	Tribal Trickery	113
12	Stolen and Sold	125
13	A Fugitive Slave	135
14	Abeokuta Under Threat	144
15	Amazons of Dahomey	152
16	Kumasi Captives	165
17	Invading the Fanti	178
18	Assault on Elmina	191
19	They Come to Fight	203
20	Enter the Newsmen	212
21	Advance to the Pra	225
22	The Battle of Amoaful	235
23	Kumasi Captured	245
	Epilogue	259
	Historical Notes	264

Maps

6	West Africa: Ivory, Gold, and Slave Coasts and the Gabon
8	Routes of explorers mentioned in the text
229	The march on Kumasi, 1874

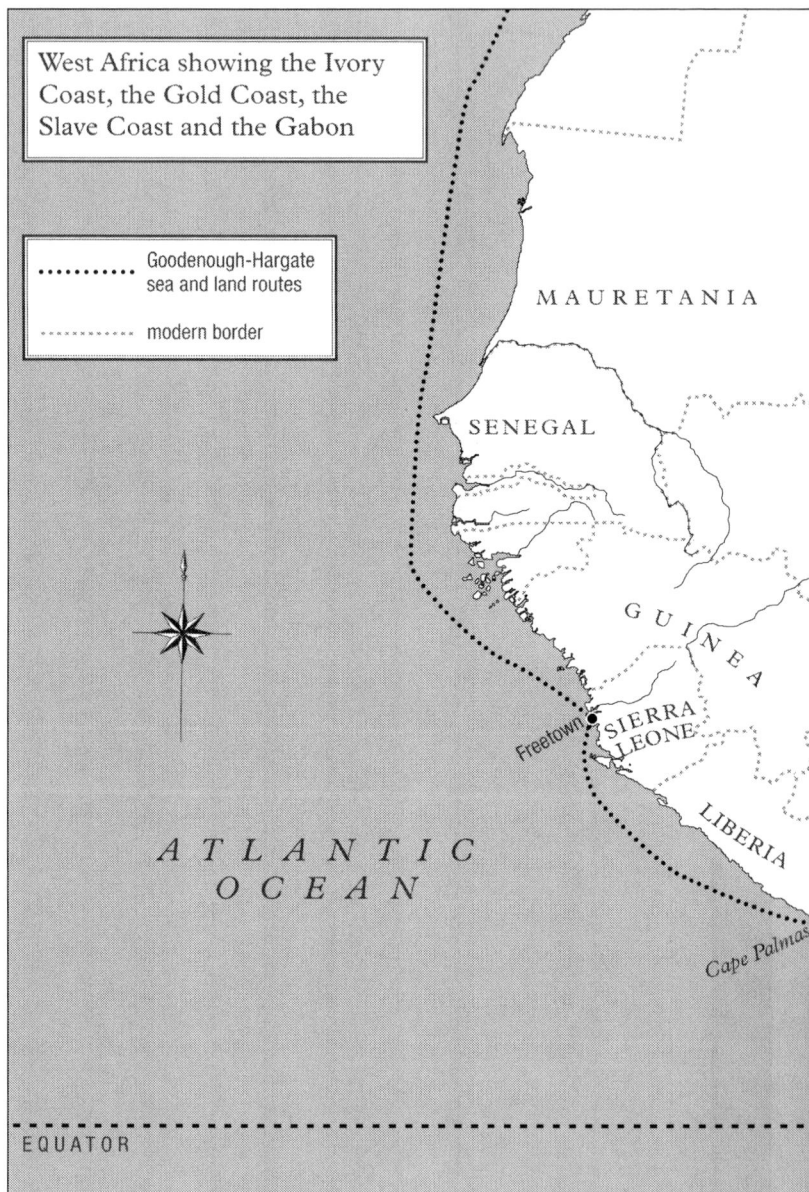

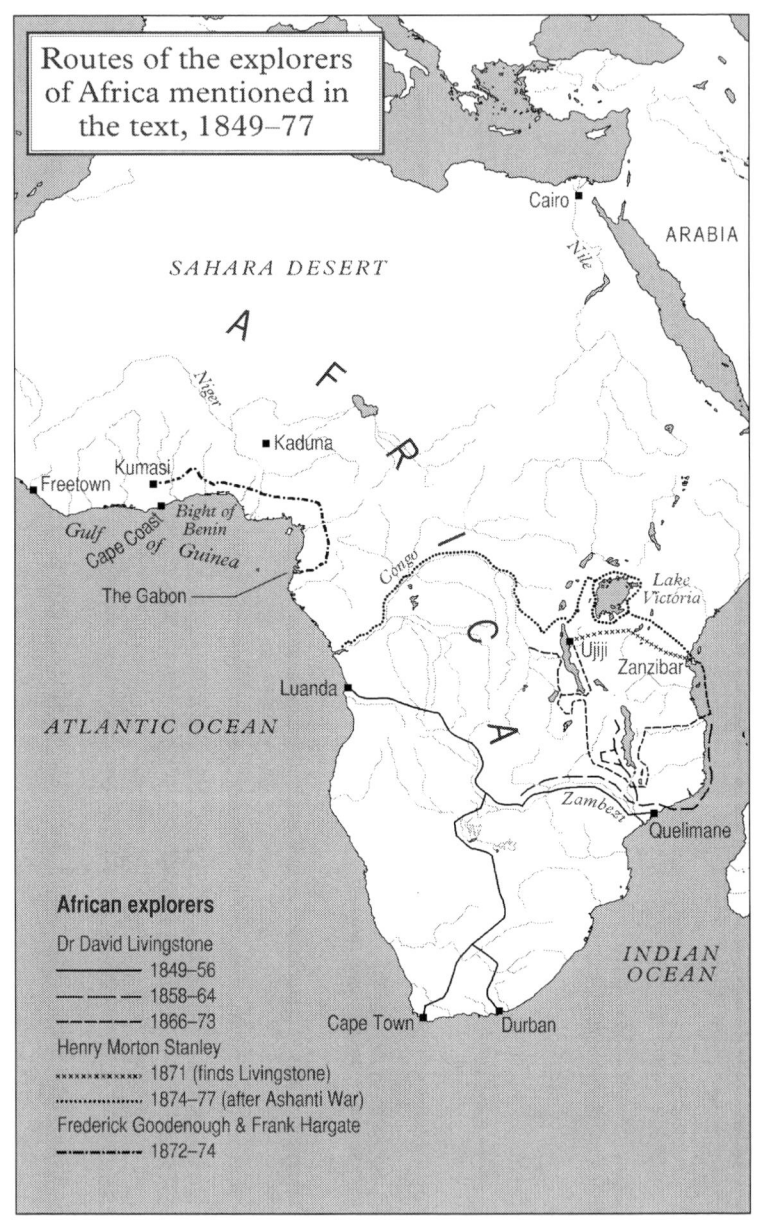

Prologue

London, 1896

It is named Kumasi in the Ashanti language, which means Place of Death, and it is an abode of obliteration for thousands of slaves every year.

Frank stirs in his sleep, but he's deep in the darkest heart of Africa's Guinea Coast. At a languid pace—which is not relaxing, but inexorable—he moves through the wide space, not so much of his own volition but as though some force is pressing him gently but firmly from behind.

In the gloomy light, the squat buildings around the square form a black backdrop of solid shapes, gapped in front to frame the ghostly fingers of the great ju-ju fetish cottonwood. Frank finds himself propelled in a slow curve until the dread tree fills his frozen vision. In the twilight, the great mountain of human skulls glows dimly with a sickly paleness, silhouetting the massive trunk of the ritual tree, its branches draped with magic talismans. The skulls fill the sacred grove behind the fetish tree, blank eye sockets and gaping jaws seemingly trying to engage Frank in a conversation in a language he understands but whose meaning is confused.

Now he sees a line of kneeling men, pathetic figures, hands brutally bound behind their backs, their mouths squeezed grotesquely into figures of 8 as a result of the thin-bladed knives like skewers driven through their cheeks to secure their tongues. There is a practical reason for this cruelty, but it eludes Frank, who is now being guided toward a large brass bowl, stained darkly around its edges. Even though he knows, somewhere deep inside his mind, that he is dreaming this nightmare, he can begin to smell the fetid stench coming from the bowl. The vessel is about five feet in diameter. It is ornamented with four small lions, and a number of round knobs all around its rim, except at one part, where there is a space for the sacrificial victim's neck to rest snugly on the edge.

Suddenly he reels as an unseen force pushes him to his knees and twists his head down, the bowl's rim biting into his Adam's apple. Frank tries to struggle free but he realizes his hands and arms have been lashed behind his back. Beneath him he can see the bowl is inches deep in blood, sloshing sluggishly from side to side, hot and fresh mixed with old and rotting, from which rises a putrid stink, the smell of death, of countless deaths, a smell of Africa which he cannot get out of his head, a scent of decay so awful his head reels.

His hands are useless, but his mouth is free. Frank screams, filling his lungs with a shuddering gasp, and screams again…

Chapter 1: A Fishing Trip

Deal, south of England, 1871

"Frank Hargate, what a pain you are! I've been looking for you all over. Have you forgotten you're supposed to be in your cricket whites and down on the field?" Dick Ruthven glared at the miscreant and saw a boy of his own age, just fifteen, but tall for his years and with a slender frame, although finely muscled. Brown eyes glared back penetratingly at Ruthven from a slightly triangular face set in a typically determined expression, accentuated by the strong eyebrows under a thatch of light brown, almost straw-colored hair on a well-rounded head.

Frank Hargate relented slightly and managed a contrite look, somewhat spoiled by his response.

"Oh, dammit. I can't come now—"

"It's the boarders against the day boys, and it's as well that House got the first innings and Town is fielding—we began batting a quarter of an hour ago, but you won't get out onto the field to bat for a little bit, but that may not be long. Now c'mon, quickly—what's so important anyway?"

"I was watching something fascinating here. Can you see this little chaffinch nest in the hedgerow... No! Don't touch it, there's a newly hatched brood in it. Anyway, there was a small black snake threatening the nest, and the mother was defending it with quivering wings and open beak. It was amazing. I sat quite still and neither of them seemed to notice me. I suppose I would've scared the snake off if I'd seen it getting what it wanted. When you came running up like a cart horse, the snake slid off in the grass, and the bird flew off."

He turned. "I'm sorry. I forgot all about the match."

"As I said, Hargate, you're a pain in the backside. Here's the opening meeting of the season, and you—one of our best batsmen—poking about after the birds and the bees—"

"Birds and snakes," Frank corrected with a grin.

"Well you'd be better off concentrating on the *birds and the bees*, still… come on now, for God's sake, our captain isn't very pleased with you. Thompson sent me and two or three others off in all directions to find you."

Frank Hargate leaped to his feet and, laying aside for the moment all thoughts of his favorite pursuit, set off at a fast run with Ruthven to the playing field. His arrival there was greeted with a mingled chorus of welcome—for his skill—and indignation—for being late. His game was steady rather than brilliant, and he was noted as a good sturdy player. Had he been there, Thompson would have put him in to bat first in order to frustrate and upset the House team's bowling.

As it was, the disappointments had piled up rapidly. The House bowlers were on top form and the Town boys weren't making many runs off the balls. Thompson himself had gone in when the fourth wicket fell, and was still in, although two wickets had since fallen for only four runs and the seventh wicket fell just as Frank arrived, panting, on the ground.

"You screw-up, Hargate! Where've you bloody well been?" Thompson raged from the crease, barely avoiding more foul language. "And not even in your flannels yet."

"Keep your hair on," Frank shouted back cheerfully, "I'm sorry, and never mind the flannels for once. Shall I come on now?"

"No," Thompson shouted back. "You'd better get your wind first. Get Fenner out here next."

Fenner stayed in for five overs, adding three single runs as his share, while Thompson put on a three and a two. Then Fenner was caught.

Thirty-one runs for eight wickets. Frank took the bat and walked onto the pitch. Thompson came across to him. "Hargate, you've completely ballsed up my game plan, and the match looks about as bad as can be. Whatever you do, play carefully. The best thing is to upset their bowling a bit. They're so cocky now, that pretty much every ball is straight on the stumps. Be content with blocking for a bit, and Hancock's eye will soon go off. He always looses his cool if his bowling is obstructed."

Frank obeyed orders. In the next twenty minutes he only scored six runs, all in singles, while Thompson, who was also playing very carefully, put on thirteen. The game looked more hopeful for the Town boys. Then there was a shout from the House, as Thompson's middle wicket was sent flying. Childers, who was the last of the team, walked out.

"Now, Childers," Thompson said as they passed, "don't you hit at a ball. You'll only get bowled or caught if you do. Just lift your bat and block every ball. Now, Frank, it's your turn to score. Put them on as fast as you can. It's no use playing carefully any longer."

Frank set out to hit each ball in earnest. His eye was well in, and the stand he and Thompson had made together had taken the sting out of the bowling. The ball which had taken Thompson's wicket was the last of the over. Consequently the next came to him.

It was a little wide, and Frank, stepping out, drove it for a four. A loud cheer rose from the Town boys. So far in the innings, there had only been one boundary score. Off the next ball Frank made two runs, blocked the following one and drove the last of the over past long leg for another four.

Childers obeyed orders in the next over, blocking each ball. Then it was Frank's turn again, and seven more went up on the board. They remained together for just fifteen minutes, but during that time thirty-one had been added to the score. Frank was caught at cover point, having added twenty-eight since Thompson left him, the other three being credited to Childers.

The total was eighty-one—not a bad score in a school match.

"Well, you've redeemed yourself," Thompson said grudgingly, as Frank walked back to the pavilion with him. "You played a great game—once you graced us with your presence. If we do as well next innings we'll be safe. House won't average eighty. Now get on your wicket-keeping gloves. Green and I will bowl."

In fact the boarders scored rapidly at first before their pace slowed, and the end result was a draw, but both sides were equally satisfied and declared that no one had ever seen a better match played at Parker's School for quite a while. Inside the pavilion, Frank checked the time and decided against changing out of his whites. Without waiting to join in the traditional post-game dissection, he shoved his school pants, shirt, and tie in his bag, put on his jacket, and started at a run for home.

Frank Hargate was an only son. His mother lived in a tiny cottage on the outskirts of Deal, a small fishing village on the Kentish coast. She was a widow. Her husband, Captain James Hargate, had died the year before. Mrs. Hargate had only her pension as an army officer's widow, a pittance that barely covered even the modest needs of herself, Frank, and her little daughter Lucy, now six years old.

"I hope I've not kept tea waiting," Frank said as he ran in. "It's not my beetles and butterflies this time. We had a cricket match."

"You're only fifteen minutes late," his mother replied, smiling, "which is far more punctual than you usually are when you're out with your net. We were just about to start—I know you too well to hang about for more than a quarter of an hour."

"I always go out promising myself to be on time for things, but somehow there's always something that drags me away."

"I don't mind, Frank. If you're happy and amused I'm content, and if the tea's cold it's your loss, not ours. Now, my boy, wash your hands and we'll eat."

As Frank stood over the sink, his mother said, "You weren't out with your blowgun. I know because I near tripped over the thing in the hallway."

"It's dangerous," Lucy said with a pout.

"Sorry, Mother. I might take it out tomorrow, though. I need a few new specimens."

"That reminds me, Mr. Potter from the hotel called in to pay me for making those cakes for their tearoom and he admired the arrangements in the front room."

As he dried his hands, Frank suffered a pang of regret for his father. His loss was a terrible blow. When off duty his father had been his constant companion. Intending his son to enter the army one day, he'd educated Frank himself when he was at home. Frank inherited his father's devotion to field sports and zoology. The offending blowpipe had come from India, where the family lived when Captain Hargate's regiment was stationed there until it returned to home service four years before he left for New Zealand. Frank had been child of ten when they came to England, but he still retained vivid memories of the lovely butterflies and bright birds of the great sub-continent.

His father brought back a large collection of preserved birds which he'd shot there. These he had stuffed and mounted, and so masterly was he at the work, so natural and artistic were the groups he created, that he found a ready market in one or two specialist shops in London, which added considerably to his income. In India his father instructed Frank in taxidermy, and gave him one of the long blowguns some of India's northern hill tribes used. Frank became so skilled in its use that now he could bring down sitting birds with clay pellets with almost unerring accuracy. These he stuffed, mounted, and arranged in groups with a taste that delighted the few visitors to his mother's cottage.

"Did Mr. Potter wish to buy something?" he said as he sat at the table.

"He only commented how lifelike they looked." She began to pour tea into their cups. "But I expect he might be persuaded. The larger arrangement would like fine on the dresser in the tearoom."

The simple meal—slices of bread and butter and a cup of tea—reflected Mrs. Hargate's situation. She could only afford to serve the cheapest cuts of meat once or twice a week, though vegetables were more plentiful and some fish when the weather was fine and the fishing boats returned well laden. Fortunately, Frank cared very little what he ate, and what was good enough for his mother was good enough for him.

In his father's lifetime things had been different, with a captain's pay and his supplementary income from the stuffed birds. Frank, Lucy, and their mother lived with him in barracks until his regiment went out to the Antipodes and he settled his family in the little cottage they now occupied. He had fallen in an attack on a Maori *pah* only a fortnight after landing in New Zealand.

"And how did the match go?"

Frank finished a mouthful of bread and butter. "It ended in a draw, but most of the fellows were happy at the result. We might easily have lost, if it weren't for Ruthven and Thompson."

Frank was ready to join in almost any sport when wanted, and could hold his own in any. But he much preferred long walks with his blowgun, butterfly net, and collecting boxes. At home, the moment homework was done, he spent every minute in mounting and arranging his collection. He was quite ready to follow the course his father proposed and to enter the army, but not for any love of military matters. Frank based his desire for a military life chiefly on the fact that it would enable him to travel to many parts of the world, and to indulge his taste for geography and natural history to the fullest. His father had been at pains to teach him that a naturalist must be more than a mere collector, and that like other sciences it must be methodically studied. He possessed an excellent library of books on the subject, and although Frank might be ignorant of the name of any bird or insect shown to him he could instantly name the family and species.

In the year following his father's death that Frank had been a day boy at Parker's School he made few intimate friends. His habits of solitary wandering and studious indoor work hindered his becoming close to any of his schoolfellows. Then, too, their financially straightened circumstances made him reluctant to ask anyone home, and since he felt he was unable to return any hospitality, he declined invitations to visit the homes of the other boys. He was too proud to eat and drink at another's house when he could not ask them to do the same at his own.

"Well, you're honest," Ruthven told him once. "You always say you can't afford anything, which stops you seeming stand-offish I suppose."

And the fact I'm the son of an officer killed in battle gives me a standing among the best in the school in spite of my lack of money. Not that he capitalized on the sad fact. Frank preferred others to make mention of his father's service.

Frank's interest in natural history extended to the sea and its denizens, and he made friends with many of Deal's fishermen who often brought him strange sea creatures caught in their nets, instead of throwing them back.

During the school vacations he often went out with them for twenty-four hours in their fishing-boats. His mother made no objection to this. "The exercise and sea air is good for you," she always said. Frank himself was so fond of the sea that he was half minded to opt for the navy, but his mother was strongly opposed to the notion.

"You think you'll get to see more of the world, but although a sailor may visit many ports he doesn't stay long at any of them. The few hours of shore-leave you might get sometimes wouldn't be enough to go chasing after the local wildlife."

Frank saw the wisdom in this, and decided against a life on the ocean wave, although events were about to suggest that the sea would not let him go so easily.

"Hargate," Ruthven said a few days after the match, "the headmaster's given Hancock, Jones, and myself permission to take a boat and go out this afternoon. We'll be set off after lunch, with some rods and bait. Do you want to come with us?"

"Thanks, Ruthven," Frank replied, "I'd like to, but you know I'm short of money and I can't pay my share of the boat hire, so I'd rather leave it, if you don't mind."

"Oh, stuff it, Hargate!" Ruthven answered hotly. "We know you're not exactly rolling in it, and anyway, there's a selfish motive… you can manage a boat better than any of us, so you'll be doing us a favor if you'll go with us."

Frank hummed and hahed a moment, and then agreed with a cheerful grin as he looked up at the sky. "I don't think the weather looks very settled. However, if you don't mind a soaking, I don't."

"That's agreed then. We'll meet next to the pier at three o'clock?"

"All right. I'll be there."

Ruthven and his two companions wanted to choose a light rowing boat, but Frank strongly urged them to take a much larger and heavier one. "In the first place," he said, "the wind's blowing off shore, and although it's calm here it will be rougher farther out. And, unless I'm mistaken, the wind is getting up fast. Besides, it will be much more comfortable to fish from a good sized boat."

His comrades grumbled at the extra work they would be put to row the larger skiff, however, they finally gave in.

"Look out, young Hargate," the boatman said as they started. "Don't get too far out—the wind's freshening fast and we're in for a nasty night."

The boys thought little of the warning—the sky, gloomier earlier, was now bright and blue, broken only by a few gauzy white clouds, a fine late June day in fact. They rowed out about a mile and then, laying in their oars, lowered the anchor and ran out the lines. The haul was good. The fish bit freely and the boys rapidly pulled them on board to be gaffed. Soon, the keel planks disappeared under a quicksilver of scales. Even Frank was so absorbed in the activity that he paid no attention to the sky's changing aspect, the sea's increasing choppiness, or the rapidly rising wind.

Suddenly a heavy drop of rain fell in the boat. All looked up.

"We're in for a squall," Frank exclaimed, "and no mistake. I told you that you might get a ducking, Ruthven."

He had scarcely spoken when a deluge of rain swept down, driven by a strong weather front. "Sit in the bottom of the boat," Frank shouted to the others. They all slumped down unhappily amid the fish.

For ten minutes no one spoke, by which time they were all drenched to the skin. With the rain a sudden darkness had fallen, and the land was entirely invisible. Frank looked anxiously toward the shore. The sea rose fast and soon had the boat straining at the anchor rope. Frank shook his head worriedly. *It looks bloody awful. If this storm doesn't pass quickly we're really in for a bad time.* He kept his thoughts to himself to avoid alarming the others.

After quarter of an hour the rain changed into an unseasonal sleet. The thick leaden clouds covering the sky made it unnaturally dark. The boat yawed at the head rope and dipped her bow heavily into the growing waves.

Frank shouted to make himself heard above the howling wind. "Look, we must start rowing. We could ride it out if we had a longer anchor rope, but this one's too short. If the sea gets up much more we'll be dragged under the waves, so we've got to raise the anchor. We'd better get out the oars and row to shore, if we can, before the sea gets worse."

The pale-faced boys, alarmed at the sea's threatening aspect, soon got the four oars in the water and hauled up the anchor. A few strokes were enough to show them that with all four rowing flat out the skiff's bow could not be headed toward the shore. The wind kept taking it and turning the little vessel broadside on.

"This will never do," Frank said. "I'll steer and you row, two oars on one side and one on the other. I'll take a spell after. Row steadily, Ruthven," he shouted. "Don't rush it and knock yourself out. We've a long way to go, so save up some energy."

For the next thirty minutes no one spoke. They didn't have the energy to waste breath. Frank saw the dimly visible shore at times through the driving mist, but his heart sank as he recognized that it was farther off than it had been when they first began to row. "Here, Ruthven, you take a spell now," he said.

The rowers, plying themselves to the oars, had little idea of their true position through the drizzly mist. It was only as Ruthven took the helm he realized, and exclaimed, "My God! The shore's gone. We're being blown out to sea."

"I'm afraid we are, Frank shouted back, "but we must keep on rowing. The wind may die or shift and give us a chance of making for Ramsgate. This is a good sea boat. It should stay afloat even if we're driven farther out. Or if we're missed they may send the lifeboat out after us. That's our best chance."

In another quarter of an hour Ruthven's turn at the steering oar came around again. Exchanging places had become easier since more than half their catch had been washed overboard. "It's no good," Frank yelled in his ear over the roaring gale as he climbed over the seat. "There's no chance whatever of making shore. All we can do now is row steadily and keep her head to the wind. Two of us will do for that. You and I row now. Hancock and Jones can steer and rest by turns. Then when we're done in they can take our places."

In another hour it was quite dark, save for the grey light reflected from the foaming water. The gale blew stronger than ever, and it required the greatest care on the part of the steersman to keep the boat dead in the eye of the wind. Hancock was steering now and Jones lay at the bottom of the boat, where he was sheltered, at least from the wind. Frank did his best to keep a bright expression on his face to buck up his companions' good spirits, but he could see that in all their hearts they knew their position was desperate.

Chapter 2: A Mad Dog

In the English Channel, June 1871

"Hargate!" Ruthven shouted in Frank's ear. "Don't you think we'd better run before it? It's as much as Hancock can do to keep her head straight into the wind."

"Yes," Frank shouted back, "if it were not for the Goodwin Sands. The banks lie right across ahead of us."

Knowing only too well the bank's evil reputation as a graveyard of shipping, Ruthven looked aghast but said nothing more, and for another hour he and Frank rowed their hardest. Then Hancock and Jones took the oars. Ruthven lay down and Frank steered. After another hour Frank was too exhausted to keep the boat into the wind. They were shipping several heavy seas and Ruthven was baling continuously, using the tin can that had held their fish bait. All the caught fish were long gone.

"Ruthven, we must let her run. Put out the other oar, we must watch our time. Row hard when I give the word."

The maneuver was safely accomplished and in a minute they flew before the storm.

"Keep on rowing, but take it easily," Frank said. "We must try and make for the tail of the sands. I can see the lightship." But the wind refused to co-operate, changing to blow along the line of sands and pushing them away from the lightship. Already, far ahead, a grey light glimmered, marking where the angry sea broke over the dreaded shoal.

"Sod it! It's no use," Ruthven shouted. "There's no hope for us."

All semblance of cheerful spirit had waned as the four boys contemplated their fate, cast into the violence of the breaking seas over the treacherous sands. Suddenly, there came a flash of light ahead, followed directly afterward by the boom of a gun. Then a rocket soared up into the air.

"There's a vessel on the sands," Frank exclaimed. "Let's make for her. If we can get on board we'll have a better chance than here."

The boys again bent to their oars, and Frank tried to steer exactly for the spot from where the rocket had gone up. A moment later there came a second flash.

"There she is," he said. "I can see her now against the line of breakers. Take the oar again, Ruthven. We must get in under shelter of her lee."

In another minute or two they were within a hundred yards of the ship. A large vessel, she lay just at the edge of the broken water. The waves, as they struck her, flew high above her deck. As the rowing boat neared the stricken ship a bright blue light suddenly sprang up, followed by a faintly heard cheer.

"They've seen us," Frank told Ruthven. "But they must think we're the lifeboat. What a disappointment for them. Now, steady, men. Prepare to pull her around the instant we're under the stern. I'll get as near as I dare."

Frank steered the skiff to within a few yards of the ship. Then Jones and Ruthven, who both had oars on the same side, rowed for their lives, every sinew strained, while Frank pushed with the steering oar. A minute later they lay in the comparatively still water under the stranded ship's lee. Two ropes snaked down and the four boys speedily climbed on board.

"We thought you was the lifeboat at first," the captain shouted, as they reached the deck, "but, of course, they can't be out here for a couple of hours yet." He looked gloomily at his new passengers. "Which means, me lads, you've only stretched yer lives a few minutes, for she'll no hold together much longer."

The ship presented a pitiable appearance. Her masts already gone, the bulwark to windward carried away, and the hull lay heeled over at a sharp angle so her deck to leeward sat level with the raging water. The crew and passengers huddled down near the lee bulwarks, sheltered somewhat by the sharp slope of the deck from the force of the wind, but as each wave broke over the ship, tons of water cascaded over them.

Suddenly there was a great crash, and the vessel parted amidships. "A few minutes will settle it now," the captain barked stoically. "God help us all."

At this moment Frank heard a faint shout to leeward above the gale, immediately answered by yells of joy from those on board the wreck. And there, close alongside, lay the lifeboat, whose approach had been hidden by the listing hull. In a few minutes the fifteen crew, three passengers, and the four schoolboys were on board her.

"Am I glad to see you, Frank Hargate," the sailor who rowed one of the stroke oars shouted. Under his sou'wester, Frank recognized the sailor they had hired the boat from. "I were up in the town and clean forgot you until it were dark. Then I ran down and found the boat hadn't returned, so I got the crew together and we came out to look for you," he gasped in the intervals between gusts of wind. "Though we had little hope of finding you. It were just luck we happened to be only half a mile off when the ship fired her first distress rocket, just as we'd given you up and decided to go back. We're making for Ramsgate now. We'd never beat back to Deal in this weather. I don't know as I ever saw it blow much harder."

"Will we make it?"

The sailor shook his head gloomily. "Maybe. Maybe not…"

When Frank hadn't returned, Mrs. Hargate threw on her rain wear and ran all the way through the storm to the beach. One of the fishermen took her arm. "It's impossible for anyone to reach shore here in the teeth of such a storm, missus."

She gnawed at her knuckles in terror.

"The lifeboat's just put out in search of them."

"What are the chances?"

He shook his head uncertainly. "Got to be honest. In this sea, finding them? Not so good. You shouldn't be out here, missus. Go home. If they're found someone's bound to send word there."

She had long given up hope when the school headmaster, Mr Parker, himself knocked at her door to bring her the news of her son's safe return to land. "They made it to Ramsgate," he told her. "Even with the wind behind them they say it took two hours to make shore. A man came to Deal on horseback to let us know and the lads have been put to bed at the Kentish Sailors' Home for the night. Your Frank will be back home tomorrow."

Overcome by emotion, she staggered and the schoolteacher just managed to catch her before she fell in a faint. He got her to the sofa and seated, but she waved away his concerns for her health. "I shall be right as rain when I see Frank," she insisted when he offered to fetch out her doctor. It was with evident misgivings that he left her in peace and returned to the school. She never moved from the couch, and when he returned, Frank found his mother still asleep there.

Frank and Hancock took the first train to Deal alone because Ruthven and Jones, too exhausted by their ordeal, had been ordered by the doctor to remain in bed for another day.

The incident raised Frank to the status of school hero when the other three were unanimous in saying that it was his coolness and skill which alone kept up their spirits, and enabled them to keep the boat afloat during the gale, and to make the wreck in safety.

Frank's natural modesty took something of a beating amid his newfound popularity, which even extended to his naturalist pastime. In the general enthusiasm Frank's hobby, which had previously found few followers, now became the school fad. The boys formed a field club, of which he was elected president, and long rambles in the country in search of insects and plants were frequently organized.

However, a newsflash which electrified the whole civilized world overshadowed his fame. An obscure American journalist called Henry Morton Stanley had found Dr. David Livingstone, the famous explorer-missionary, who had disappeared in the unexplored depths of central Africa many months before. Livingstone's wellbeing had been on everyone's minds, fearful of what dreadful things may have happened to him. Now the world knew he was alive. Frank thrilled to the newspaper account of Stanley's amazing trek through the African jungles to find the Scottish explorer. He imagined doing the same thing, catching and cataloging immense quantities of strange and wonderful insects, birds, and small mammals on the way to rescue of some lost missionary.

While many avid readers shuddered at Stanley's description of the Dark Continent's inhospitable interior, Frank found himself spellbound with wonder. *If only I could go to Africa for myself,* he thought. *Now that would be a marvellous thing."*

The countryside around Deal was nothing like Frank imagined Africa to be, but it would have to do. So on Saturday afternoon he set out with Charlie Goodall, a younger boy who was one of his most devoted followers, acting as his African bearer-cum-porter for a long country walk. As Frank strode ahead with his blowgun, hacking aside imaginary parasitic creepers, Charlie struggled along in the explorer's wake carrying all the bottles and tin boxes to hold their captured prey, and the large butterfly net. This was about a foot in depth, made of canvas, mounted on a stout brass rim and a strong wooden pole.

They had passed through Eastry, a village four miles from Deal, when Frank exclaimed, "There's a green hairstreak. The first I've seen this year."

He approached the butterfly, sunning itself on the top of a thistle, cautiously. But as he prepared to strike, it suddenly flew off over a hedge. In a moment the boys had scrambled through a gap and were in full pursuit. The butterfly flitted here and there, sometimes allowing the hunters to approach within a few feet and then fluttering away again for fifty yards without stopping. The chase continued, the explorer and his porter paying no heed to where they were going, until a sudden shout startled them to halt.

"You little buggers, how dare you run over my wheat!"

Frank saw what, in his excitement, he had failed to notice, and looked back guiltily at the two trails they had trampled through the grain field, which reached to his knees. "I'm very sorry, sir," he stammered. "I was so excited than I really didn't see where I was going."

"Not see?" the angry farmer fumed, going beetroot red in the cheeks and neck. "I'll break every bone in your bodies." He raised the heavy stick he carried.

Not unreasonably, Charlie Goodall began to cry.

"I've no right to trespass on your wheat, sir," Frank said firmly, "but you've no right to strike us. My name's Hargate, Frank Hargate, and you can easily find me at Parker's School in Deal. Tell me what the damage is and I'll pay for it."

"You'll bloody well pay for it now," the farmer shouted and advanced with his staff uplifted.

Frank slipped three pellets into his mouth. "Leave ush alone or it'll be worsh for you," he slurred either side of the clays as he put the blowgun to his lips.

The farmer took two more threatening steps forward, and Frank sent a bullet with all his force, and with so true an aim that he struck the farmer on the knuckles. It was a sharp blow and the farmer, with a cry of pain and surprise, dropped his weapon.

"Don't come a step nearer!" Frank warned, speaking more easily around two pellets. "If you do, I'll aim at your eye next time." He pointed the tube at the enraged farmer's face.

"I'll have the law on you, you young hoodlum. I'll make your backside smart for this."

"You can do as you like about that," Frank retorted. "I fired in self defense and let you off easily. Come on, Charlie, wipe your eyes and let's get out of this."

In a few minutes they were again on the road, and it seemed the farmer was making no attempt to chase them. They walked silently along, Frank angry with himself at his carelessness in running over grown crops. He wondered how he could pay the fine without having to ask his mother. It occurred to him that his father had earned extra money selling his stuffed creatures and thought he might do the same—more modestly—at a shop in the town. He had seen stuffed birds in its window, which were, he was sure, inferior to his own both in execution and naturalism. Or perhaps he might persuade Mr. Potter at the hotel to buy a piece.

After walking a few hundred paces along the road they met a pretty little girl of seven or eight years old strolling along alone, humming cheerfully to herself. Frank, engrossed in working out how many cases of stuffed birds he had, scarcely spared her a glance when she waved at them. But at that moment he heard a ruckus in the distance and saw some men shouting and running along the road toward them. For an instant he thought that the farmer had sent some of his men to stop them, but quickly dismissed the idea, as they were coming from the opposite direction. They disappeared from sight as they ran into a dip in the road and, as they vanished, something else appeared on the road on the near side of the hollow.

"It's a dog!" cried Charlie with some alarm at its size. "It's a *really* big dog..."

Frank muttered, "What are they shouting at?"

The dog was within fifty yards of them when the men reappeared over the brow of the road. Frank could now make out their cries.

"Mad dog! Mad dog!"

Their words galvanized Frank into action. "Christ, Charlie, get through the hedge, quick. I'll help you over, never mind the thorns." The hedgerow was low and well trimmed. Frank bundled his young porter over and then threw himself across. He struggled to his feet and peered over its top. The dog was within ten yards of them and Frank could see immediately what the alarm was about. A prickle of fear ran through his frame at the sight of the huge crossbreed, somewhere between a mastiff and a bulldog. Its rough hair bristled. The animal loped along with its head down and foam churned from its black lips. Frank looked the other way and gave a shout. Twenty yards off, the little girl had stopped in the middle of the road and turned to see who was causing the fuss. She seemed oblivious to any danger and watched the distant men, not the advancing dog.

Frank placed the blowgun to his mouth, and in a moment his pellet struck the animal smartly on the side of the head. It gave a short yelp and paused. Another shot struck it, and then Frank, snatching the butterfly net from Charlie, threw himself back over the hedge and placed himself between the child and the ravening animal. It shook its head, flecks of foam flying in all directions and then, with a savage growl, rushed at him.

Frank stood perfectly cool and, as the dog powered forward, thrust the net over its onrushing head. The net's rim was just large enough to allow its head in. Frank sprang forward and twisted around behind the dog, keeping a strain on the handle, which locked the net tightly around its neck. The massive beast gave a furious flurry of snarling barks and his powerful muscles bunched as he struggled to get away, dragging Frank behind him. Then he stopped, backed, and tried to withdraw his head from the restraint. Frank held on grimly, digging his heels into the road's surface and managed to keep the net in place long enough until the men, armed with pitchforks, ran up and speedily dispatched the unfortunate beast.

"Tha's bravely done, son," one of them said. "You've saved missy's life surely. The savage brute rushes into the yard and bites a young colt and a heifer, and then, as we comes running out with forks, he takes to the road again. We chases him along, not knowing who we might meet, and it give us a rare turn when we see the master's Bessy standing alone in the road, wi' nowt between her and the beast. Where've you been, Bessy?"

"I've been to auntie's," she said, "and she gave me some strawberries and cream, and it's wicked of you to kill the poor doggie."

"Her aunt's farm lies next to our employer's," the man explained, "and little miss often goes over there. The dog was mad, missy, and if it weren't for this young gen'leman here, it would have killed you as safe as eggs. Won't you come back to the farm, sir? The farmer and his wife would be main glad to thank you for having saved their daughter's life."

"Thanks, but no. We're late and must be getting back. I'm glad I happened to be here at the time." So saying, Frank waved a cheery farewell and strode off, carelessly tossing the net over his shoulder for Charlie, still encumbered by the naturalist's baggage, to catch, and headed in the direction of Deal.

"Did you really do these yourself?" the shopkeeper said in surprise, as he examined four of Frank's best cases of stuffed birds. "They're beautifully done. Like living pictures, I call them. It's a pity that they're homely birds. There's no great sale for such things here. I can't give you more than five shillings each, but if you had them in London they would be worth a great deal more."

Frank gladly accepted the offer and, feeling sure that the pound would cover the damage done and the fine, which might be five shillings apiece for trespassing, went home in good spirits. The next morning Mr. Parker was called out in the middle of a lesson, and shortly returned accompanied by a man Frank knew only too well. *Oh, no!* He felt his cheeks flush as he anticipated what was about to come—in front of the whole school too.

"This is Mr. Gregson, boys," Parker said. "He tells me that two of you were out near his place at Eastry yesterday. One of them gave him his name, which he has forgotten."

Frank rose from his seat with embarrassment. "It was me, sir." In spite of his feelings, Frank spoke up firmly. "I was there with Goodall. We ran on this man's field after a butterfly. My fault, sir, we ran through his wheat—"

Frank broke off in bewildered surprise as the big farmer stepped briskly forward and grabbed him by the hand, shaking it vigorously. He smiled broadly. "You're welcome to trample on my wheat for the rest of your born days."

Frank snapped his jaw, which had dropped open in surprise, firmly shut.

"I haven't come over here to talk about the wheat. I owe my child Bessy's life to you. There aren't many men who would have thrown themselves in the way of a rabid dog for the sake of a child they don't even know. God bless you, son."

The result of this unexpectedly happy circumstance was that the farmer and his wife invited the whole school over to their farmhouse in Eastry for a feast of huge pies, cold chicken and duck, hams, and piles of cakes, and every kind of fruit tart. As the boys stuffed themselves to the point of illness, Mr. Gregson amused them by telling them of the battle with Frank, and especially of the threat to send a bullet into his eye if he attacked him.

"Y'know, Hargate," Dick Ruthven muttered in his ear, "I always thought you were a pain in the ass, now it seems I have to watch out for my eyes as well."

Chapter 3: A Tale with 'Bellishments

Deal, south England, June 1871

"You had a close shave the other night," one of the local fishermen remarked to Frank, as he strolled along the front with Dick Ruthven and Hancock a few days after their sea adventure. "I had one out there meself when I were about your age. I went out for a sail with my father in his fishing boat, and I didn't come back for nigh on three years. That was the only long voyage I ever went on. I've stuck to fishing ever since."

"Why were you away three years?" Hancock asked.

"Well, it's rather a long yarn," the boatman said, drawing out his words.

"Well, your best plan, Jack," Ruthven said, laughing and putting his hand in his pocket, "will be for you to go across the road and get something for that dry throat before you begin." He handed the boatman a sixpence.

"Why thankee kindly. I will take some grog."

Jack went across to the pub, and soon returned with a large tankard in his hand. Then he sat down on the shingle with his back against a boat, and the boys threw themselves down close to him.

"Now," he began, after taking a long swig and wiping his lips appreciatively, "this here yarn as I'm going to tell you ain't no gammon. Most of the tales which gets told on the beach to those sucker visitors as comes down here and wants to hear of sea adventures is just lies from beginning to end. Now, I ain't that sort. I don't say, mind you, that every word is gospel. My mates as has known me from a boy tells me that I've 'bellished the yarn since I first told it, and that all sorts of things have crept in which wasn't there first. That may be so. When a man tells a story a great many times, naturally he can't always tell it just the same, and he gets so mixed up atween what he told last and what he told first that he don't rightly know which was which when he wants to tell it just as it really happened."

Jack's weatherworn face was as honest as the day was long, and the boys winked at each other as much as to say that after such a foreword they must expect something rather staggering. The boatman took two or three hard swigs at his tankard and then began.

"T'was toward the end of September in '32—that's just forty year ago now—that I went out with my father and three hands in the smack, the *Flying Dolphin*. I'd been at sea with 'im off and on ever since I was bout nine, and a smarter boy wasn't to be found on the beach. The *Dolphin* was a good sea boat, but she wasn't, so to say, fast, and I dunno as she was much to look at, for the old man wasn't the sort of chap to chuck away his money in paint or in new sails as long as the old ones could be pieced and patched so as to hold the wind. We sailed out pretty well over to the French coast, and was turning for home when the old man remarked we was in for a gale. There was some talk of our running in to Calais and waiting till it blew itself out, but the fish would've spoiled, so we made up our minds to run straight into Dover and send the fish up from there.

"The night came on wild and as dark as pitch. It might be about eight bells, and I'd turned in, when father gave a sudden shout down the hatch, 'All hands on deck!' I was next to the steps and sprang up 'em. Just as I got to the top something grazed my face.

"I caught at it, not knowing what it was, and the next moment there was a crash, and the *Dolphin* went away from under my feet. I clung for bare life, scarce awake yet, not knowing what had happened. The next moment I was under water. I still held on to the rope and was soon up again. By this time I was pretty well awake to what had happened. A ship running down channel had walked clean over the poor old *Dolphin*, and I'd got a hold of its bobstay.

"It took me some time, but at last I swarmed along the bowsprit and got on board. There was a chap sitting down fast asleep there. I walked aft to the helmsman. Two men paced up and down in front of him. 'You're a nice lot, you are', says I, 'to go running down the Channel at ten knots without any watch, a-walking over ships and a-drowning of seamen. I'll have the law on ye, see if I don't'.

"'Jee-rusalem!' says one, 'who have we here?'

"'My name's Jack Perkins, and I'm the sole survivor of the smack, the *Flying Dolphin*, as has been run down by this craft and lost with all hands'.

"'Darn the *Effin' Dolphin*, and you too', says the man, and he begins to walk up and down the deck a-puffin' of a long cigar as if nothing had happened.

"'Oh, come', says I, 'this won't do. Here you've been and run down a smack, drownded me father and three hands, and your lookout fast asleep, and you does nothing'.

"'I suppose', says the captain, all sarcastic, 'you want me to jump over to look for 'em. You want me to heave the ship to in this gale and to invite yer father perlitely to come on board. P'raps you'd like to be chucked overboard yourself. I reckon the wisest thing you can do is to go for'ard and turn in'. There didn't seem much for me to do else, so I went to the fo'csle. Most hands was asleep, but a couple was yarning. I told 'em my story and what this captain had said.

"'He hasn't a soft place about him', said one. 'Well, my lad, I'm sorry for what's happened, but talking won't do it any good. You've got a long voyage before you, and you'd best turn in and make yourself comfortable'.

"'I ain't going a long voyage', says I, beginning to wipe my eye, 'I wants to be put ashore at the first port'.

"'Well, my lad, I daresay the skipper will do that, but as we're bound for the coast of Chile from Hamburg, and ain't likely to be there for about five months, you've got, as I said, a long voyage ahead. And then again, he may not want you free with stories about the watch asleep and running down another vessel. He wouldn't care next time he entered an English port to have a claim fixed on his ship for the value of the smack'.

"I saw what the sailor said was right enough, and blamed myself for having let out about the watch. However, there weren't no help for it, and I turned into an empty bunk and cried myself to sleep. What a voyage that was, to be sure! The ship was a Yankee—the *Potomac*— and so was the master and mates. The hands were of all sorts, Dutchies and Swedes and English, a Yank or two, and a sprinklin' of blacks. It was one of those ships they call a hell on earth, and the three mates' cussing and kicking and driving went on all day.

"I hadn't no regular place to bunk, and helped the cook, pulled ropes, swabbed the decks, and got kicked and cuffed all around. The skipper didn't often speak to me, but when his eye lighted on me he gave an ugly sort of look, as seemed to say, 'You'd better ha' gone down with the others. You think you're going to report the loss of the smack and to get damages against the *Potomac*, do you? we shall see'.

"The crew was a rough lot, but the spirit seemed taken out of 'em by the treatment they met with. It was a word and a blow with the mates, and they would think no more of catching up a handspike and stretching a man senseless on the deck than I should of killing a fly. Two or three among the crew was of a better sort than the others. The best of 'em was Jans the carpenter, an old Dutchie. 'Leetle boy', he used to say to me, 'you keep yourself out de sight of de skipper. Bad man dat. Me much surprise if you get to de end of dis voyage all right. You best work vera hard and give him no excuse to hit you. If he do, by gosh, he kill you, and put down in de log: *boy killed by accident*'.

"I felt that this was so myself, and I worked as well as I could. One day, though, when we was near the equator I upset a tar bucket. The captain was standing close by. 'You young dog', he barked, 'you done that a purpose', and afore I could speak he caught up the bucket by the handle and brought it down on my head with all his might. The next thing I remember was lying in a bunk in the fo'csle. Everything looked strange to me, and I couldn't raise my head. After a time I made shift to turn it around, and saw old Jans sitting on a chest mending a jacket. I called him, but my voice was so low I hardly seemed to hear it myself.

"'Ah, my leetle boy!' he said, 'Good to see you back. Two whole weeks you say nothing except talk nonsense. De captain meant to kill you, I haf no doubt, and he pretty near do it. After he knock you down he said you dead. He sorry for accident, not mean to hit you so hard, but as you dead, better be tossed overboard. De mates they come up and take your hands and feet. Den I insist you was only stunned and carry you here.

"'You haf fever and near die. Tree days after de captain he swear you shamming and come to look at you hisself, but he see that it true and tink you going to die. He go away wid smile on his face. Every day he ask if you alive, and give grunt when I say yes. Now best keep you here as long as we can, de longer de better. He make you come on deck and work as soon as he tink you strong enough to stand. Best get pretty strong before you go out'.

"For another three weeks I lay in me bunk. The captain came several times and shook me and swore I was shamming, but I only answered in a whisper and seemed as faint as a girl. All this time the *Potomac* was making good way, and was running fast down the coast of South Americy. The air was getting cool and fresh."

Jack paused to take another long pull on his ale before continuing.

"'I tink', Jans said one evening to me, 'dat dis not go on much much longer. De crew getting desperate. Dey talk and mutter among demselves. Me tinks we haf trouble before long'.

"That night I heard the men whispering and judged from what they said that they intended to wait for another week, when we expected to be in the Magellan Straits, and then to attack and throw the mates and captain overboard. Nothing seemed settled as to what they'd do after. Some wanted to continue the voyage to port, and tell the authorities that the captain and officers had been washed overboard in a storm.

"The others insisted that someone would be sure to welch. They said sail on west and beach on one of the Percific islands, where they could live comfortable like and take wives among the native women. If we was ever found we'd tell how the natives killed the captain and officers. Seemed to me that this lot were the strongest.

"For the next week I was thrashed and kicked every day and if'n I'd been as weak as I pretended, I'm sure the mates would've killed me. Then, on the night watch it all broke open. I saw the whole crew come out, and joining the watch on deck they went aft quietly in a gang. They'd all got marlinspikes. Then there was a rush. Two pistol shots was fired, and then a splash, and I knew that the officer on watch was done for. Then they burst into the aft cabins. There were more shots and shouts, and for three or four minutes the fight went on. Then all was quiet. Then I heard three splashes—that accounted for the captain and the two other mates—then the crew got at the spirit stores and began to drink.

"Morning was just breaking when I suddenly woke. There was a great light, and running on deck I saw the fire pouring out from the cabin aft. They'd all drunk themselves stupid, upset a light, and the fire had spread and suffocated them all. Anyhow, there was none to be seen, even poor ol' Jans was gone. I found a water keg and put it in the bumboat, which luckily hung out on its davits so it hadn't got burned up. I rowed off some two or three miles from the ship, which was now a mere smoking shell. Two miles north lay land, and getting out an oar at the stern I sculled her to shore.

"I s'pose I'd been seen, or that the flames of the ship had called down the natives, for there they was in the bay, and such a lot of creatures I never set eyes on. Men and women alike was pretty much naked, and dirt is no name for them. Though I was but a boy, I was taller than most. They came around me and jabbered and flabbered till I was deafened.

"Well, young gentlemen, for upward of two years I lived with them critters. My clothes soon wore out, and I got as naked and dirty as the rest of 'em. They was good hands at fishing, and could spear a fish by the light of a torch wonderful. In other respects they didn't seem to have much sense. Law, what a time that was! I had no end of adventures with wild beasts. The way the lions used to roar and the elephants—"

"I think, Jack," Ruthven interrupted, "that this must be one of the embellishments which have crept in since you first began telling the tale. I don't think I should keep it in if I were you, because the fact that there are neither lions nor elephants in South America throws a doubt on the accuracy of this portion of your story."

"It may be, sir," Jack said, with a twinkle of his eyes, "that the elephants and lions may not have been in the first story. Now I think of it, I can't recall that they were. But, you see, people wants to know all about it. They ain't satisfied when I tell 'em that I lived two years among these chaps. They wants to know how I passed my time, and all about the wild beasts, and a lot of such like questions and, of course, I must answer them. So then, you see, naturally 'bellishments creeps in. But I did live there for two years, that's gospel truth, and I did go pretty nigh naked, and in winter was pretty near starved to death over and over again.

"When the ground was too hard to dig up roots, and the sea was too rough for the canoes to put out, it went hard with us, and very often we looked more like living skelingtons than human beans. Every time a ship came in sight they used to hurry me away into the woods. I s'pose they found me useful, and didn't want to part with me—leastways, there was a host of girls that wasn't willing to part with any part of me, begging your young pardons. At last I got desperate, and made up my mind I'd make a bolt whatever came of it."

"What, Jack," Ruthven asked seriously, "and leave all those willing girls behind?"

"As I said afore, they was a dirty bunch, and I fancied getting back to civil-ation an' a good wash. Anyways, they didn't watch me when no ships came close. I expect they thought there was nowhere for me to run to, so one night I steals down to the shore, gets into a canoe, puts in a lot of roots which I'd dug up and hidden away in readiness, and so makes off. I rowed hard all night, for I knew they'd be after me when they found I'd gone. I'd chosen a time when the tide was with me and soon after morning I managed to cross a narrow bit of the strait to the mainland and came to a river mouth.

"Well, gents, would you believe me, if there wasn't two big allygaters sitting there with their mouths open ready to swallow me, canoe'n'all, when I came to shore."

"No, Jack, I'm afraid we can't believe that. We would if we could, you know, but alligators are not fond of such cold weather as you'd been having, nor do they frequent the seashore."

"Ah, but this, you see, was a straits, Master Ruthven, just a narrow straits, and I expect the creatures took it for a river."

"No, no, Jack, we can't swallow the alligators, any more than they could swallow you and your canoe. Besides, they're creatures of the North American continent, not the South."

"Well," the sailor said with a sigh, "I won't say no more about the allygaters. I can't rightly recall when they came into the story. Anyways, I landed, you can believe that, you know."

"Oh yes, we can quite believe, Jack, that—if you were there, in that canoe, in that backwater, with the land close ahead—you most certainly did land."

Frank hid a smile behind his hand.

The would-be Crusoe looked searchingly at Ruthven and then continued. "I hauled the canoe up and hid it in some bushes, and it were well I did, for a short time afterward a great…" and he paused. "Does the hippypotybus live in them waters, young gents?"

"He does not, Jack," Ruthven said firmly.

"Then it's clear," the sailor said, "that it wasn't a hippypotybus. It must have been a seal."

"Yes, it might have been a seal," Ruthven agreed amiably as he nudged Frank's arm. "What did he do?"

"Well he just took a look at me, gents, winked with one eye, as much as to say, 'I see you', and went down again. There warn't nothing else as he could do, was there?"

"It was the best thing he could do anyhow," Ruthven said, nodding his head and winking at the others.

"Well, gents, I lived there for about three weeks, and then a ship comes along, homeward bound, and I goes out and hails her. At first they thought as I was a native as had learned to speak English, and it wasn't till they'd boiled me for three hours in the ship's copper as they got at the color of my skin, and could believe as I was English. So I came back here and found the old woman still alive, and took to fishing again. But it was weeks and weeks before I could get her or anyone else to believe as I was Jack Perkins.

"And that's all the story, young gents. Generally I tells it a sight longer to the suckers as comes down from Lunnun in summer but, you see, I can't make much out of it when ye won't let me have 'bellishments."

"And how much of it is true altogether, Jack?" Frank asked. "Really how much?"

"It's all true as I've told you, young masters," the boatman said. "It were every bit true about the running down of the smack, and me being nearly killed by the skipper, and the mutiny, and the burning of the vessel, and my living for a long time—no, I won't stick to the two years, but it might have been three weeks, with the natives before a ship picked me up. And that's good enough for a yarn, ain't it?"

"Quite good enough, Jack, and we're much obliged," said Frank.

"But I should advise you to drop the embellishments in future," Dick Ruthven added.

"It ain't no use, Master Ruthven, they will insist on 'bellishments, and if they will have 'em, Jack Perkins isn't the man to disappoint. And, Lord bless you, sir, the stiffer I pitches it in the more liberal they is with their tips. Thank ye kindly all around, genl'men. Yes, I do feel parched again after the yarn."

"A load of cobblers," Ruthven said with a laugh as they strolled off, another sixpence lighter. "But well told cobblers."

"I wish I could travel the world," Frank mused.

"Better watch out for the allygaters, then."

Chapter 4: The Rising and Ebbing Tide

Deal, south England, July 1871

The eventful summer term drew to its close. On the Saturday before breaking up for the long vacation Frank, with Ruthven, Charlie Goodall, and two of the other neo-naturalists, Childers and Jackson, were strolling along the seashore looking for anemones and other marine creatures among the rocks and pools at the foot of the South Foreland. Between Dick Ruthven and Frank Hargate a strong feeling of affection had grown since their boating adventure.

They were constantly together now. As Ruthven had every intention of going into the army, and would probably obtain his commission about the same time as Frank, they often talked over their futures. They hoped that they might often meet and that, in their campaigns, they might enjoy adventures together in far-off places—allygaters notwithstanding.

The tide was out when they set out on the three-mile walk. They had regularly searched through the tidal pools near Deal and Walmer, but Frank hoped that around the Foreland they might discover different specimens to those they had found so far. For some hours they inspected the pools before retiring to the foot of the cliffs to sit down and examine what they'd collected. For a long time they sat comparing their samples. Then Frank said, "It's time to be moving."

As he rose to his feet he uttered an exclamation of dismay. Although the tide was still well out from where they were sitting, it already lapped at the cliffs extending out at either end of the bay. A brisk wind blew on shore and the waves crashed against the foot of the rocks.

The others jumped up and, seizing their cans, ran off flat out to the end of the bay. "I'll check and see how deep it is," Frank shouted over his shoulder as he ran full tilt into the incoming waves. "Perhaps we can wade around."

The water soon reached his waist, and then his shoulders, and he had to leap as each wave broke over him. "I could see around the point," he said, returning to his friends on the beach, "and I think I could get around, but the problem is that the bottom's rocky. I stumbled several times and would have gone under if I couldn't swim. You can't swim, Dick, I know," he said to Ruthven. "What about the rest of you?"

Goodall and Jackson, it turned out, could swim.

"Now, Dick," Frank said, "if you put your hand on my shoulder and keep quiet, I think I can carry you. Charlie, you and Jackson take Childers between you."

But neither had much confidence in their swimming. They managed thirty or forty strokes, but then felt there was little else they could do to help Childers. In fact they were frightened of rounding the point on their own, let alone drowning their companion. For some time they debated the question.

"Look, Frank," Ruthven said at last, "you aren't sure you can carry me. The others are quite certain that they can't take Childers. We must give up. The best thing is for you three who can swim to go, and if Goodall or Jackson struggles you can help them a bit. Childers and I must take our chances here. When you get to the farther beach you can send a boat as soon as possible."

"I'm not going desert you, Dick." Frank looked indignant at the very thought. "I'm not likely to find a boat until I get near Walmer Castle, and long before we could get back the tide would be fully in. Jackson and Charlie Goodall can swim off if they like."

These lads, however, expressed their concern at the risk of swimming alone, but said they would go if Frank would go with them.

"All right, it's warm enough, thank god. Chuck off your boots and jackets." Frank proceeded to strip rapidly to the skin. "I'll take them around, Dick, and come back to you. See if you can find any sort of ledge or projection that we can take refuge on. Now, then, come on you two, quick as you can."

The sea had already reached within a few feet of the foot of the cliff all around the bay. "Now, mind," Frank said sharply, "no struggling and nonsense, you guys. I'll keep quite close and stick to you, so you needn't be afraid. If you get tired just put one hand on my back and swim with the other and your legs."

The three boys waded out as far as they could go and then struck out. Jackson and Goodall were both poorer swimmers than they had admitted to and would have managed badly alone. Their confidence in Frank, however, gave them courage, and they were well abreast of the point when first Jackson and then Goodall put their hands on his shoulders. Thanks to the instructions he had given them they did not weigh down on him. But every ounce tells heavily on a swimmer, and Frank gave a gasp of relief as at last his feet touched pebbles and sand. "You two run off now, or you'll get chilled, I just need a minute or two to get my breath back. I'll get your things back to you," he yelled after them.

He found the return swim even harder work than it had been to come out from the bay with the tide race against him. At last he stood beside Dick Ruthven and Childers. "Grab their shoes and jackets, would you, Dick, while I get back in my pants at least."

As soon as he finished buttoning up his fly, he gathered up the rest of his own things and, taking the other items from Ruthven, pushed the bundle into a crevice in the rocks as high up as he could reach.

"We've only found one place, Frank, and that's only large enough for one. See!" Childers pointed up at a projecting block of chalk, whose upper surface, some eight inches wide, was reasonably flat. "There's a cave here, too, which may go beyond the tide. It's not deep but it slopes up a bit."

"That will never do," Frank said firmly. "As the waves come in they'll rush up and fill it to the top. Can you see, it's all rounded by wave action? Now, Childers, we'll put you on that stone. You should be safe. It's two feet above the tide mark there and these aren't like spring tides, so though you may get a splashing there's less risk of your being washed off."

The water was already knee deep at the foot of the cliff, and the wave crests reached up almost to their shoulders. Ruthven did not attempt to dispute Frank's allotment of the one place of safety to Childers. Frank and he placed themselves below the block of chalk, which was a bit over six feet from the sand. Then Childers scrambled up on to their shoulders, and from there stepped on to the ledge.

"I'm all right," he said, uncertainly. "I wish you were too."

"We'll be fine," Frank shouted up at him. "Mind you hold tight. You'd better face the cliff. It will be easier to grip on in case the waves come up high. The tide will turn in three quarters of an hour at the outside. Now, then, Richard my man, let's make a fight for it."

"What are we doing, exactly?"

"We'll wade along here as far as we can toward the point, and than we must swim for it."

Dick looked alarmed. "Isn't it possible to stay here?" he said quickly. "If the tide's going to turn so soon…?"

Frank shook his head firmly. "Quite impossible. I've been nearly knocked over twice already, and the tide's still got three feet in at least. We'll be smashed against the rocks, even if we weren't drowned. C'mon, Dick, there's no other way. We've a longer way to go now than if we'd set out earlier, but distance isn't so much of a problem. We've only got to go out a little way, and the tide will soon take us around the point and back in to the beach. Everything depends on you. I can take you and land you safely enough, if you lie quiet. If you don't, you will drown both of us. So it's entirely in your hands."

"Look out!"

At this moment a larger wave than usual took both boys off their legs and dashed them with considerable force against the cliff face.

Frank seized his friend, hauled him to his feet, and dragged him away from the sharp rocks with the receding water. Both boys fell into the heaving sea.

"Now, stay on your back. I'm going to backstroke with one hand—you lie on me and I'll tow you along with the other under your chin. For God's sake don't struggle. Don't move. Above all, don't try and lift your head. And don't mind if a little water gets in your mouth. Now, here we go."

For a moment Dick panicked when his head went under water and he had to make a great effort to restrain himself from struggling to come to the surface. Then he felt himself lying on his back, held up by Frank. The motion was not unpleasant as he rose and fell on the waves, although now and then salty seawater splashed over his face and made him cough and splutter for breath.

He could see nothing but the blue sky overhead, could feel nothing except that occasionally he received a blow from one or other of Frank's knees, who swam beneath him. His friend kept Dick's head pressed against his chest. It was a dreamy sensation, and looking back on it afterward Dick could never recall anything that he had thought of. It seemed simply a drowsy pleasant time, except when occasionally a wave broke over his face.

His first sensation was that of surprise when he felt the motion change, and Frank lifted his head from the water and said, "Stand up, Dick. Here we are, safe."

Dick rolled over onto his knees and staggered upright. "You saved my life, Frank."

"That's a bit dramatic. It's been a close thing, but you owe your life as much to your own coolness as to me."

"Well, I won't forget it," Dick said quietly. A great welling of emotion choked off anything else he might have said. They stood for a few minutes without speaking. "Now, what do we do? Run home?"

"I can't." Frank laughed and waved a hand at his lower half reminding Dick that his friend had nothing on but his soaking pants, which now clung to his hips and legs in a manner too revealing for public display. "You'd do better to strip off as well and lay your clothes out to dry in the sun. The others will have a boat here in half an hour. I wonder how Childers is getting on?"

Childers was utterly exhausted; the sea had risen so high that the waves were breaking against his feet, throwing the spume far above his head. Sometimes the lashing spray was so dense it made it hard to breathe and the brine stung his eyes. He could not wipe them clear because both hands were grimly engaged in hanging onto the ledge he had found about eighteen inches above his head. This position was, in itself, tiring, and he was beginning to think he would not be able to hold on much longer, for the ache in his arms was becoming punishing.

Nevertheless, the ledge had saved him when three times his feet were swept off the rock by the rush of water. The boy was on the point of true despair when he sensed a decline in the force of the incoming waves. He prayed. He wasn't deceived that the water level was dropping. The tide was just on the turn, but he was exhausted and uncertain that he could hold out for another half hour's buffeting. It would surely take that time to recede sufficiently to leave him safe in letting go and jumping down.

When will help come? he thought.

Half an hour after gaining the beach, Dick Ruthven spotted a boat rowed by four men approaching. "They're putting effort into it," he noted. "They couldn't row harder if they were in a race. But if it hadn't been for you, Frank, they would have been too late."

As the boat approached, the cox waved his hat to the boys. Frank motioned with his arm for them to row on around the point. The four put their backs into it again. Frank and Dick watched them breathlessly. As it went around the point they saw the cox stand up and say something to the men, who glanced over their shoulders as they rowed. Then they faintly heard the him shouting. "Hold on. We're nearly with you."

"Thank God," Frank said with a long sigh, "Childers must be all right."

In another quarter of an hour, the boat edged into the shallows where they waited and it turned out that the rescuers had arrived barely in time. "He just fell into his our arms, completely at the end of his strength," the cox said. "Here, I think these are yours." He held out a wringing wet package of the clothes they had jammed in fissures of the cliff.

From his prone position under a blanket on the planks of the boat, Childers gave a weak smile as his schoolfellows jumped over the gunwales, relieved to see them also safe.

"You've made quite a stir in the town." The cox of the boat nodded his head at the shore as they neared it. "Look, there's half Deal and Walmer coming along to gawp."

Frank groaned when he saw the number of people streaming along the beach. He put on his things as they approached Walmer, shivered at the clammy feel, and then shivered again at the impending reception. His shoes were lost, as were Dick's, and he had difficulty in getting his arms into his wet and shrunken jacket. Quite a crowd was gathered near the castle as the boat rowed to shore, and a hearty cheer went up as it ran up on the shingle and the boys were helped out. Frank and Dick Ruthven needed no assistance, none the worse for the adventure, but Childers was so weak he couldn't stand. Two of the rowers carried his limp form up and laid him across the seat of a hansom cab. Frank and Dick piled in opposite. As they were all still very damp, the cabbie had taken the sensible precaution of first removing his precious seat cushions.

Among the crowd were most of the boys from Parker's School. Goodall and Jackson had arrived nearly an hour and a half before, and the news had spread like wildfire. Bats and balls thrown down, everyone had hurried to the beach. By this time, the story of their being cut off by the rising tide and how Frank Hargate had guided them to safety was known to everyone.

Dick Ruthven's added tale raised the general mood of enthusiasm to boiling point and Frank had difficulty in taking his place in the cab amid hand-shakes and patted shoulders. Had it not been for his anxiety to get home as soon as possible, and his urgent entreaties, they would have carried him on their shoulders in triumph through the town.

Frank was quite oppressed by the fuss made over the affair, especially by the thrilling description of it which appeared in the local papers. And he received letters of heartfelt thanks from his four schoolfellows' parents.

On the following Wednesday the school broke up for the summer vacation. Frank had several invitations from the boys to spend time with them, but he knew how lonely his mother would feel if he went, and he declined all the appeals. Mrs. Hargate was far from strong, and had suffered several fainting fits, which worried him. But the doctor always seemed calm and unconcerned and she forbade him to make a fuss.

One day toward the end of the vacation, on returning from a long walk he saw a carriage standing outside the cottage. Just as he arrived the door opened and the doctor came out. On seeing Frank he spoke in a neutral tone. "Come in here, my boy."

Frank followed him and, seeing that the blinds were down, went to draw them up. The doctor laid his hand on his arm.

"Never mind that," he said gently. "Frank do you know that your mother's been very ill for some time?"

"No…" Frank said with a gasp of pain and surprise.

"Well, it's the case, my boy. I've been attending her for some time for an increasing weakness of her heart's action. She has obliged me to say nothing of alarm to you about it. Two hours ago your neighbor called me out, but when I got here I found her unconscious. My poor boy, you must prepare yourself for the worst news. Your mother passed away quietly half an hour ago, without recovering consciousness."

Frank gave a short cry, and then sat stunned by the suddenness of the blow. The doctor took a small phial from his pocket and poured a few drops into a glass, added some water, and held it to Frank's lips. "Drink this," he said firmly.

Frank turned his head from the offered glass.

"Drink it," the doctor repeated. "It will calm you. Try and be strong for Lucy's sake. She only has you now."

The thought of his little—orphaned—sister made him burst into unchecked tears. The doctor left him alone with his grief for some minutes, then said, "Now drink this. We can't be having you ill, you know."

Frank gulped down the contents of the glass and, passive as a child, allowed the doctor to place him on the sofa before taking his leave.

For an hour Frank lay there sobbing, and then, remembering the doctor's words, sat up and prayed for strength to carry him into the future.

A week passed. Sunlight bathed the cottage rooms from blinds raised again. The funeral over, Frank sat alone again in his parlor thinking over what had best be done. The outlook looked bleak, more than enough to shake the courage of one much older. His mother's pension, he knew, died with her. The War Office had informed him that—as a male, now fifteen years old—he was not eligible for a pension, but that twenty-five pounds a year would be paid to his sister until she married or reached the age of twenty-one.

The doctor had made an arrangement with a lady he knew, who kept a small school, and who was willing to take Lucy in and to board and clothe her for that sum. She was a very kind and motherly person, he told Frank, and he was sure that Lucy would be well treated and cared for by her.

His own future, however, needed considerable thought and, to be brutal, he had little time left to contemplate his options. There were a few pounds in the house, but the letter from the War Office enclosed an order for twenty pounds—his mother's final quarterly pension payment. The furniture would fetch a small sum, not more, Frank thought, than thirty or forty pounds.

There were a few debts to pay, and after everything had been settled he reckoned on being left with about fifty pounds. Of this he determined to place half in the doctor's hands for Lucy's needs.

"She will want," he said to the doctor, "a little pocket money. It's hard on a girl having no money of her own to spend. Then, as she gets on, she may need lessons in something or other. Besides, half the money rightly belongs to her, The question is, what am I to do?"

Chapter 5: Alone in the World

Deal and London, September 1871

What indeed? A difficult question to answer for a boy of fifteen, with about twenty-five pounds and without a friend in the world. Was he without a friend, he asked himself, or was he simply wallowing in self-pity? There was his headmaster, Mr. Parker. But he had gone on a trip to France the day after the term ended, and would not return for six weeks. Besides, was it right to impose on his head teacher for the next four years or so when few boys stayed on at Parker's past fifteen, going elsewhere to finish their education?

No, Frank felt, he could not live on school charity.

Then there were the parents of the boys he had saved from drowning. But even in his own company his face flushed at the very thought of trading on their gratitude. He accepted that pride was his chief fault. Not the kind of vanity that came from overcoming poverty, he had felt no shame at being poorer than the rest of his schoolfellows. No, it was rather a pride which led him unduly to rely on himself, and to shrink from accepting favors from anyone. Frank could well, without any belittlement, have written his friends, tell them of his loss and the necessity for him now to earn a living, and ask them if their fathers might use their influence to find him a job. But this he could never do. He had to fight his own battles without asking for the help of others, especially those who might feel they owed him a debt.

As far as he was aware, he had no relations to appeal to either. He knew nothing of his parents' families. His father was an only son, orphaned at a young age. His mother, too, had lost both her parents, and he'd never heard her speak of aunts, uncles, brothers, sisters, or cousins.

So, no friends in the world—at least in the practical sense of the situation he faced. And no future now in Deal. Frank had already cast a desultory eye over job offers in the locality, but no one wanted anyone of his age or qualifications… sorry, lack of them. It seemed to him that it must be easier for a strong, active lad to find employment of some sort in London. He didn't care what. He had no pride of that kind. So long as he could earn his bread, anything would do.

Already preparations had been made for the sale of the furniture, to take place next day. Everything was to be sold except for his father's library of scientific books. These he had packed in a large box until the time when he might place them on shelves of his own, and the doctor kindly offered to keep the books for him until such time should arrive.

Frank wrote a long letter to Dick Ruthven, telling him of his loss, and his reasons for leaving Deal, and promising to write some day and tell him how he was getting on in London. However, he had no intention of posting it until the last thing before leaving Deal. Lucy had already gone to her new home and Frank felt confident that she would be happy there.

As the brakes squealed, steam spurted from between the locomotive's wheels, echoing loudly from the steel and glass roof arching high overhead London Bridge Station. The reverberation of the train's stopping mingled with an astonishing amount of general noise such as Frank had never experienced before. The rattle of luggage trolleys, the barking huffs of other engines getting up steam, the clank of connecting rods, shouts of porters, guards, and passengers threw the country boy into a dizzy confusion. He knew he had to master this pretty quickly, or go under.

On getting out of the carriage he felt lonely amid the bustle and confusion of the platform. The doctor had suggested asking a porter or a policeman to recommend him to a quiet and respectable lodging. Gathering his bruised senses, he waited until the departing passengers had cleared off and then went up to one of the porters and asked if he knew of anywhere he might stay.

"What sort of lodgings do you want, sir?" the man asked, looking at him rather askance, with, as Frank saw, the thought that he was a runaway schoolboy.

"I only want one room," he answered, "and I don't mind how small it is, so long as it's clean and quiet. I'll be out all day, so I shouldn't be much trouble."

The porter nodded. "Wait here while I goes an' asks a few mates—and watch yerself around here. Station's no place for a young lad like you to hang around. There's many gets themselves picked up by kindly-seeming gentlemen an' dragged off for… well, nuffin' good, that's fer sure." After a last dark look, he went off to talk to some of the other porters, shortly returning with one of them.

"You're wanting a room I hear, young sir," the man said in a similar accent to the first porter, which Frank knew he would have to get used to. "I've a little 'ouse down the Old Kent Road, and my missus lets a room or two. It's quiet and clean, I'll guarantee, and I know we've one room vacant now."

Relieved at so quick a resolution to his first problem, Frank responded quickly. "I'm sure that would suit me very well. How much is it a week?"

"Three-'n-six, if you don't want any cooking done."

Frank took the address, and leaving his small trunk in charge of the porter, who promised, unless he heard to the contrary, to bring it home with him when he left work, he set off from the station.

After Deal, one of the quietest places on the coast of England, Frank was astounded at the crowd and bustle which filled the street when he left the station approach at the foot of London Bridge. The porter had told him to turn left and keep straight ahead until he reached the Elephant and Castle. Although he had no clue as to what elephants had to do with castles, with such otherwise simple instructions he was able to give all his attention to the sights about him. For a time the stream of buses, cabs, heavy wagons, and light carts completely befuddled him, as did the throng of people who pushed, bustled, and hustled along the sidewalks.

He was depressed rather than exhilarated at the sight of this busy multitude. He seemed such a solitary item in the midst of this great moving crowd. After a while, though, the thought that where so many millions gained their living there must be room for one boy more, went some way to cheering him.

He was a long time getting to his destination because he stopped to stare into every shop window he passed, but eventually arrived at the porter's house in the Old Kent Road. Like most of the houses seemed to be, it was part of a dark-brick terrace, small but clean and respectable, and Frank found that the room would suit him well.

"I don't wait on the lodgers," the porter's wife said, "'cept to make beds and tidy in the morning. So if you wants breakfast and tea at home you'll have to shift for yerself. There's a separate place downstairs for your coals. There are some tea things, plates, and dishes in this cupboard, but you'll need to buy a small tea kettle and a fryin' pan, in case yer wants a chop or a rasher." She frowned. "Can you cook?"

Frank, who had never considered the notion of cooking anything, was amused at the thought and said boldly that he would soon learn.

His landlady eyed him doubtfully. "You're very young to be settin' up on yer own. I mean," she said, seeing Frank's puzzled look, "settin' up on yer own account. You'll have to be p'ticler careful with the fryin' pan, because if you was to upset the fat in the fire y'might have the house in a blaze in a jiffy."

Frank said that he would certainly be careful with the frying pan.

"Well, as yer a stranger to the place I don't know as you could do better than get tea 'n sugar 'n things at the grocer's at the next corner. I deals there meself, and he gives every satisfaction. The baker will be around in a few minutes, and, if yer likes, I can take in yer bread for you. Same with milk."

Frank paid his rent in advance and found himself alone in his new apartment. It was a room about ten feet square. The bed occupied one corner, with a washstand at its foot. A small table stood in front of the fireplace with two chairs. A piece of carpet half covered the floor, and these with the addition of the articles in a small freestanding cupboard constituted the room's furniture.

Feeling hungry after his journey and the walk, Frank decided to go out and get something to eat, and then to lay in a stock of provisions.

He decided on two Bath buns for the time being and to have something more substantial later in his room. He laid in a supply of tea, sugar, butter, and salt, bought a little kettle and a frying pan. Then he hesitated as to whether to get a mutton chop or some bacon. In the end the bacon won out. He felt confident of checking to see whether bacon was properly frizzled up, while with a chop he wouldn't know if it were properly cooked until he cut into it.

He returned carrying all his purchases, then asked his landlady where he could get coal.

"Greengrocer's around the corner. Tell him to send in a hundredweight of the best, that's a shilling, and you'll want some firewood too."

The coal arrived in the course of the afternoon, and at half past six the porter came in with Frank's trunk, pausing only briefly to announce that his name was Jekks, though whether that was his first or last name, Frank never discovered. He had by this time lit a fire, and while the water came to the boil he got some of his things out of the box. By hanging some clothes on the pegs on the back of the door, and by putting the two or three favorite books he had brought with him on the mantelpiece, he gave the room a more homelike appearance. He enjoyed his meal all the more from the novelty of having prepared it himself—and the bacon ended up nicely frizzled.

Frank's arrival in the big smoke had gone remarkably smoothly, all things considered. But that was the end of his good luck. On checking the newspapers, he was dismayed to discover how many people actually advertised their services for employment rather than employers advertising for prospective workers. All those advertising were older than himself, and possessed various accomplishments he lacked. Many had warm references from their last employers or certificates from their schools. The prospects did not look hopeful. He ran his eye down the columns to see if any required errand boys, but found no such job offers.

Well, I suppose I shouldn't expect to find a place waiting for me on the very day after my arrival. If it came to the worst he reckoned he could live for a year on his twenty-five pounds.

After the first week he answered many job-seeker ads, but received not a single reply. In the middle of his second month in London he wrote to one firm which wanted a lad who could write a good fast hand; wages to begin with eight shillings a week. Frank decided to call in to the place two days after writing. It was a small office with a solitary clerk sitting in it. He, on learning Frank's business, replied exasperatedly, "My mind is being worried out by boys. We've had four hundred and thirty letters," he snapped. "About a hundred of them must have called in. We took the first who applied, and all the other letters were chucked in the fire."

Frank returned to the street greatly disheartened.

That many others on the lookout, just as I am, for a place as a junior clerk, and lots of them, no doubt, with friends and relations to recommend them. The lookout seemed to be a bad one."

He walked disconsolately homeward. When he had gone some distance he saw a glare in the sky ahead, and then a steam-powered fire engine clattered past him at full speed. "Something's on fire," he muttered to no one, and broke into a run. Others were headed at speed in the same direction. As he passed the Elephant and Castle public house the crowd became thicker. He could see the flames now rising high in the air. A horrible fear seized him. "It must be," he exclaimed to himself, "either our house or the one next door."

He immediately examined his memory. *Could this be my fault?*

Had he not damped down his small fire properly? A dreadful sense of guilt attacked him, even though he was certain of his carefulness.

A line of policemen drawn up across the road kept a space clear for the firemen. No one could clearly see what was happening. After a bit the flames began to die down, and the crowd to disperse. At length Frank reached the first line of spectators. "Can you tell me which houses burned down?" he asked a policeman.

"Two of 'em, mate," the policeman replied crisply. "One-oh-four and one-oh-five. "Undred 'n four went up first, and they say a woman and two children died."

"That's where I live," Frank cried. "Oh, please let me through."

The policeman nodded, and led him forward to where the hoses still played on the smoldering embers. "Is it true, mate, that a woman and two children have died?" the constable asked a fireman.

The fireman confirmed it was. "Can't be sure as yet, but it looks like a frying pan caught light in the kitchen out back. Her husband only came back from work a quarter of an hour ago, and he's been going on like a madman, poor sod." He pointed to Jekks, slumped on the doorstep opposite, head in his hands.

Frank was dreadfully torn between pity for the man and relief that it had not been his upper-floor room where the fatal fire began. And neither did the irony of the landlady's warning about frying pans, fat, and fire escape him. Frank and Jekks had chatted on many an evening and become friendly. He went and sat down beside the distressed porter, but could find no words to say.

"I can't believe it," Jekks said huskily. "Just to think. When I went out this mornin' there was Jane and the kids, as well and as 'appy as ever, and there, where are they now?"

"Happier still," Frank said gently. "I lost my mother just as suddenly only five weeks ago. I went out for a walk, and when I came back, there she was, dead."

"I would've given my life for 'em."

"I'm sure you would," Frank answered.

"There's the home gone, with all the things it took ten years' savings of Jane and me to buy. Not that it matters one way or t'other now. And your things are gone, too, I s'pose."

"Yes," Frank said quietly, "I've lost my clothes and twenty-three pounds in money. Every penny I've got in the world except for half a crown in my pocket."

For a brief moment, the porter was roused from his own sorrows. "An' you don't say nothing much about it. But, there, p'raps you've friends as will make it up to you."

"Like you now, I've no one whom I could ask."

"Well, you're a plucky lad, I'll say that. That would be a knock-out blow to a grown man, let alone a boy. What're you going to do now?" For a moment he seemed to forget his own loss.

"I don't know," Frank replied. "Perhaps," he added, seeing that interest in his condition roused the poor man from his own deep sorrow, "you might give me some advice. I was thinking of getting a place in an office, but of course that's out now. At the moment I'd be thankful to get anything to earn some cash for food."

"You come along with me," said Jekks, rising. "You've done me a heap of good. It's no use sitting here. I'm going back to the station and turn in on some sacks. If you've nothing better to do, and nowhere to go to, you come along with me. We'll talk it all over."

Jekks's offer relieved Frank of having to fend for himself that night and he happily accompanied his friend to London Bridge. With a word or two to the night men on duty, Jekks led the way to a shed on one of the side platforms.

"Now, if you're not sleepy, would you mind talking to me? Tell me something about yourself, and how's you come to be alone here in London. It does me good to talk. It stops me from thinkin'."

"There's not much to tell." But then Frank related the circumstances of the deaths of his father and mother, and how he needed work to earn a living.

"You're in a fix." The porter stated the obvious.

"Yes, I can see that."

"You see you're young for most work, and you never 'ad no practice with 'orses, or you might've got a job driving a light cart. Then, again, yer knowing nuffin of London is against you as an errand boy. And what's worse than all this, anyone can see with 'alf an eye that you're a gentleman, and not accustomed to 'ard work. However, we'll think it over. I'd better try'n get some kip. I'm on again at six. Tomorrow I've got to look for a room, and when I gets it there's half of it for you, if you're not too proud to accept it. You'll be doing me a kindness, I can tell you, for what am I to do alone of an evening without Jane and the kids, Gawd knows. I can't believe they're gone yet."

Then he threw himself down on the sacks, and broke into sobs. Frank listened for half an hour until these gradually died away, and he knew by the regular breathing that his companion had dropped off. Sleep for Frank, however, was slow in coming.

His position did, indeed, appear hopeless. Thanks to the kind offer he would have a roof over his head. But that could not last. *I was wrong not writing to Dick and my schoolfellows. In fact I know now I was stupid, but it would be ten times harder to write now.* Frank might be a country boy, but in his weeks in London it hadn't escaped his attention that many boys his age earned a living by selling their bodies to men who liked that kind of thing. Many of them right there on that railroad station.

I'd rather starve than do that. How am I to earn a living? I shall try—at least for a few days—to get a job as an errand boy. If that fails, I'll sell my clothes and get a rough working suit. I'm sure I'll have more chance of getting work if I don't look as elegant as I do now.

At last, Frank slept. He woke to the noise of trains, suggesting a late hour, and no sign of Jekks. His thoughts returned to last night's talk and he spoke aloud to the deaf walls. "I've done one wise thing, anyhow, leaving my father's watch safe with the doctor. It would so easily be stolen here. It's my only worldly possession, except the books, and I would rather go into the workhouse than part with any of them."

Getting to his feet, he made his way into the station, where he found Jekks at his usual work.

"I didn't wake you," the porter said, "you was sleeping so quiet, and you didn't have to get up early. I'm going out in my break to get a room. If you come here at six o'clock we'll go together. The mates have all been very kind. They took a collection to bury my poor girl and the kids. The guvnor's offered me a week off, but I'd rather be here where there's no time for thinking, than hanging about with nothing to do but to drink."

Chapter 6: The First Step

London, October 1871

All that day Frank tramped the streets. He went into many shops where he spotted notices that an errand boy was required, but everywhere without success. He began to accept that his well dressed appearance was against him, and he either received the abrupt answer of, "You're not the sort for my place," or an equally firm refusal on the grounds that he did not know the locality, or that they preferred a boy whose parents lived close by and could speak for him.

At six o'clock he returned to London Bridge and found Jekks, who led him to the new lodging he had secured, a neat room with two small beds in it. He brought with him some bread and butter and a piece of bacon and was initially surprised at the reaction as he opened his parcel.

"Don't you do that again, young Frank. You're just coming to stop with me for a bit till you see your way, and I'm not going to have you bringing food in. Jekksie's money's good for two months, and your living here with me won't cost three shillings a week. So don't you hurt my feelings by bringing stuff home again. There, don't say nuffink more about it."

Frank, seeing that his friend was serious, kept quiet and accepted the other's kindness. He saw that his being around in the evenings was really a great relief to the man in his trouble. After the simple meal they went out to a second-hand clothes shop. Here Frank sold his outfits, and received in return a suit of clothes fit for a working-class lad.

"I don't know how it is," Jekks wondered as they sat together afterward, "but a gentleman looks like a gentleman put him in what clothes you will. Now, if you go into a factory or workshop, I'll bet a crown to a penny that before you've been there a week you'll get called Gentleman Jack, or some such name. You see if you ain't."

Frank laughed. "I don't care what they call me, so long as they take me on."

"All in good time, don't you hurry yourself. Unemployment figures are as high as anyone can remember. But as long as you can stay here you'll be heartily welcome. Just look what a comfort it is to have you sitting here being sociable. You don't s'pose I could sit here alone in this room if you wasn't here? I'd be in a pub making a mess of myself, and spending as much money as would keep the pair of us."

Day after day Frank went out in search of work. In his tramps he visited scores of workshops and factories, but without success. Either they did not want boys, or they declined to hire one who had neither experience in work nor references. Then, one night, thinking matters over in bed, Frank made up his mind to do something that had been an unformed plan from the start.

I always had a liking for the sea. Why don't I go down to the docks and see if I can get a place as a cabin boy? After all, I might get the chance of seeing one of Jack's famous allygaters!

It was not that he was afraid of the roughness of the life. He had put the idea aside because a job ashore would be more likely in the end to offer the upward mobility he needed. Now that was as far off as ever, cabin boy looked more attractive than wagoner's lad.

The streets on the north side of the Thames, after Frank crossed London Bridge, were as crowded as those to the south. He turned down Eastcheap, heading for the docks and soon found himself in Ratcliff Highway, made infamous, as he knew from his reading, by the terrible killings of 1811. As he recalled, a Mr. and Mrs. Marr, shop keepers, were murdered along with the shop boy and an infant. Twelve days later, the landlord of the King's Arms, his wife, and a female servant also met brutal ends. A man named Williams, the only suspect, later hanged himself in prison. The authorities had his corpse removed for upright burial in a hole dug specially where New Road crossed Cannon-Street Road, after driving a stake of wood through his breast for good measure.

Enjoying a brief shudder over these gruesome thoughts, Frank wandered along, part amused at the nautical character of the shops, part alarmed at its thronging denizens, tars of all races, all colors, and in all kinds of dress. While the Highway itself clung to some shred of respectability, the alleyways running off it suggested portals to hell. Frank fixed his eyes on the shops instead. One, simply called Horton's, particularly attracted his attention and he found himself staring into a window full of foreign birds, for the most part alive in cages, but among which were a few cases of stuffed birds. He stared hard.

And then it hit him.

"How stupid I've been," he said aloud. "Why on earth didn't I think of it before? I can stuff birds and beasts at any rate a deal better than those wooden looking things on display here."

The obvious course was to get hold of a directory and find all the naturalist shops in the city, take down all the addresses and then go around. As he was considering this exciting idea he became conscious of a conversation going on in the shop doorway between a little old man with a pair of thick horn-rimmed spectacles and a sailor who had a parrot and a cat in his hand—both dead.

"I really can't do them," the old man was saying. Frank assumed he must the shop owner, Mr. Horton. "Since my daughter's death I've had little time to attend to taxidermy. What with buying and selling, and feeding and attending to the live ones, I've no time for stuffing. Besides, if the things were poisoned, they wouldn't be worth stuffing."

"It isn't the question of worth, skipper," the sailor argued, "and I don't say, mind you, that these here critters was poisoned, only if you looks at it that this was the noisiest bird and the worst tempered thievingest cat in the neighborhood—though, Lord bless you, my missus wouldn't allow it for worlds. Why, you know, when they were both found stiff and cold this morning people does have a sort of a suspicion as how they've been poisoned." He winked one eye in a portentous manner, and grinned hugely.

"The missus, she's in a nice fit, screeching, and yelling as you might hear her two cables' length away, and she turns around on me and will have it as I'd a hand in the matter. Well, just to show my innocence, I offers to get a glass case for 'em and have 'em stuffed, if it cost me a couple of quid. I wouldn't care if they fell all to pieces a week afterward, so that it keeps the old bint quiet, like. If I can't get 'em done I shall ship at once, for the place will be too hot to hold me. So, Mr. Horton," he wheedled, "you can't do it fer me nohow?"

The old man shook his head, and the sailor was just turning away when Frank went up to him. "Will you please wait a moment? Can I speak to you, sir, a minute?" he asked, turning to the older man. The naturalist went into his shop, and Frank followed him.

"I can stuff birds and animals, Mr. Horton, sir," he said. "I think I do a fine job. Some I did for amusement were sold at ten shillings a case, and the man who bought them told me they would be worth four times as much in London. You will find me hard working and honest. Let me stuff that cat and parrot for the sailor. If you're not satisfied, I'll go, and charge nothing for it."

Horton looked at him keenly. "Who are you, boy, and where from?"

"Frank Hargate, late of Deal in Kent, sir."

Well," Horton said eventually, "you look decent enough. I'll probably regret it but I think I will give you a go."

The nautical poisoner took an interest in this curious development and pushed back through the door with a broad grin. "There's a lad! Let him stuff 'em."

"I know nothing about him," the naturalist protested, "but I'm inclined to believe him. As you heard, if you're not satisfied you won't have to pay anything."

The sailor placed the corpses on the counter. "There you go, one dead moggie and a parrot as was." Then, with a piratical grin, he stumped off up Ratcliff Highway.

"Now," the old man said to Frank, "you can take these out into the backyard and skin them. Then you can go to work in that room back there. You'll find arsenical soap, cotton wool, wires, and everything else you require there. This was a fine cat," he said, looking at the animal.

"Yes, a splendid creature," Frank answered. "It's a magnificent macaw also."

"Ah. You know it's a macaw," Mr. Horton said with some surprise.

"Of course, it has the tail."

Mr. Horton scratched the back of his head, paused a moment, and then ducked his head in the direction of the back door.

Taking the bird and cat, Frank went out into the yard and in the course of an hour had skinned both animals. Then he returned to the shop and set to work in the room behind.

"May I make a group of them?"

"Do them just as you like."

After settling on his design, Frank set to work for the remainder of the long day. Horton came in several times to check on progress, but each time left without making a remark. At six o'clock Frank stopped. "I'll come again tomorrow, sir," he said.

The old man nodded, and Frank went home in high spirits. At last he was doing something he enjoyed and with the prospect of finally earning some cash.

"I won't interrupt you today," Mr. Horton said when Frank turned up early the following morning. "I'll wait patiently to see them finished."

Working until the evening, Frank finished the group to his satisfaction, and wrapped them with around several times with fine thread to keep them in precisely the attitudes in which he had placed them. "They are ready for drying now, sir," he said. "If I might place them in an oven they would be dried by morning."

Horton led the way to the kitchen, where a small fire burning in a grate under a large range. "I won't put any more coals on the fire, and it will be out in quarter of an hour. Put them in there and leave the door open. I'll close it in an hour when the oven cools."

The next day Frank was again at work. It took him all day to get fur and feather to lie exactly as he wished them. In the afternoon he asked the naturalist for a piece of flat board, three feet long, and a perch, but said that instead of the piece of board he should prefer mounting them in a case at once. There wasn't a case sufficiently big enough in the shop, so Frank arranged his group temporarily on the table. On the board lay the cat. At first sight she seemed asleep, but it was clearly only seeming. Her eyes were half open, the upper lip curled up to partly reveal sharp teeth. The hind feet were drawn slightly under her as though tensed for effort. Her front paws were taut in front of her, the claws were a little stretched and one paw was curved. Her ears lay slightly back. She was evidently on the point of springing.

The macaw's perch, which had been cut down to a height of two feet, stood behind the cat. The bird hung by its feet and, head leaning down, stretched with open beak toward the tip of the cat's tail, which was slightly uplifted. On a piece of paper Frank wrote, *Dangerous Play*.

Evening draped the Highway in shades of grey before he had finished to his satisfaction. Then he called the naturalist in. The old man stopped at the door and surveyed the group. Then he entered and examined it carefully.

"Wonderful," he said. "Really wonderful! You could almost imagine they were alive. There's not a shop in the West End where it could have been turned out better, if as well. But I can offer you nothing fit for your efforts. With such a genius, you ought to be able to earn a good income. Not one man in a thousand can make a dead animal look like a live one. You have the knack of the art."

"I'll be very content with anything you can give me," Frank said.

"For the moment I only want a living. If later on I can, as you say, do more, all the better."

The old man stood for some time thinking, and then said, "When I had my daughter with me I did a good deal of taxidermy. There's a good trade hereabouts. The sailors bring home skins of foreign creatures, especially brightly colored birds, and want them stuffed and put in cases as presents for their wives and sweethearts. You work fast as well as skillfully. I've known men who would take a fortnight to do such a group as that, and then it would be a failure. I don't know how it will go yet, but to begin with I will give you twelve shillings a week and a room upstairs, if you want it. If it succeeds we'll make other arrangements."

Still staring in some wonder at Frank's artistry, Mr. Horton spoke more to himself than to Frank standing beside him. "I'm an old man, and a very lonely one. I shall be glad to have someone else to talk to now and then, and one who, despite the evidence of his clothing, is clearly a well educated lad."

Frank joyfully embraced the offer, and ran all the way to his digs to tell Jekks of the change in his fortunes.

"I'm very glad, heartily glad. I'll miss you badly. I don't know what I would have done without you when I first lost poor Jane and the kids. But now I can go back to my old ways again."

"He's got the space. Why don't you arrange to have a room in the house as well," Frank suggested. "It wouldn't be a very long walk, not above twenty minutes, and I'd be so glad to have you with me."

Jekks sat silent for a time. "No," he said at last, "I thank you all the same. I should like it too, but I don't think it would be best in the end. Here, all my mates live nearby, and I'll get on in time. The Christmas holiday season will soon be coming on and we shall be up working late and picking up good tips. If you was always going to stop at that place, it would be different. But you'll rise, never fear. I'll be seeing you in gentleman's clothes again one of these days. I'll come over sometimes and have a cuppa tea and a chat. Now, look here, I'm going out with you now, and I'm going to buy you a suit of clothes, something like what you had on when I first saw you. They won't be altogether unsuitable in a shop. This is a loan, mind. You can pay me back when you get flush."

Frank saw he would hurt his friend's feelings by refusing, and so off they went, and next morning he turned up for work at the shop in a quiet suit of dark grey tweed, and with his other clothes in a bundle.

Mr. Horton took in the new apparel with a sly glint. "Aha! You look more as you ought to do now, though you're a cut above an assistant in a naturalist's shop in Ratcliff Highway. Now, let me tell you the names of some of these birds. They're all exotic foreigners. Some of them I don't know myself."

"I can tell you the family names," Frank said quietly, "and the species, but I don't know the varieties."

"Can you?" Horton said in surprise. "What's this now?"

"That's a mockingbird, the great black capped mockingbird, I think. The one next to it is a golden lory." So Frank went around all the cages and perches in the shop, pointing and naming.

"Right in every case," said Horton enthusiastically. "I shall have nothing to teach you. The sailor has been here this morning. I offered him two pounds for the cat and bird to put in the window, but he wouldn't take it, and paid me that sum for your work. Here it is. This is yours, you know. You weren't in my employment then, and you will want some things to start with, no doubt. Now come upstairs, I'll show you your room. I'd intended at first to give you the one at the back, but now you can have my daughter's. I think you'll like it."

Frank did. It was on the second floor, at the front. Old Horton's daughter had evidently been a woman of taste and refinement. The room was well papered, a quiet carpet covered the floor, and the furniture appeared neat and in good condition. Two pairs of spotless muslin curtains hung across the windows.

"I put them up this morning," the old man said, nodding. "I've got sheets and bedding airing in the kitchen. They've not been out of the drawer for the last three years. You can cook in the kitchen. There's always a fire there.

"Now, the first thing to do," he went on when they returned to the shop, "will be for you to mount a dozen cases for the windows. These drawers are full of skins of birds and small animals. I get them for next to nothing from the sailors, and sell them to furriers and feather preparers, who supply ladies' hat-makers. In future, I propose that you stuff and mount them and we sell them direct. We'll get far higher prices than we do now. I seem to be putting most of the work on your shoulders, but you won't need to help out in the shop. I'll look after the stock and buy and sell as I used to do. You can have the back room to yourself for the taxidermy work and mounting."

Frank was delighted at this allotment of labor, and was soon at work rummaging through the drawers and picking out specimens for mounting. He soon made a selection sufficient to keep him employed for weeks. That evening he sauntered out and spent some of his two pounds on underwear, which he definitely needed. Mr. Horton ordered glass-domed showcases for the window of various sizes and shapes as they were required, getting the backgrounds painted and arranged as Frank suggested.

Frank did not get on as fast with his window display work as he had hoped, for the fame of the sailor's cat and macaw spread rapidly in the neighbourhood. A sudden rush of sailors and their wives anxious to have birds and skins, which had been brought from abroad, mounted overwhelmed him. The cat-and-macaw pirate himself looked in one day.

"If you'd like another two pounds for that 'ere cat, guvnor, I'm game to pay you. It's the best thing that ever happened to me. Every one's wanting to see 'em, and there's the old woman dressed up in her Sunday clothes a-sitting in the parlor as proud as a peacock a showing 'em off. The house ain't been so quiet since I married. Them animals would be cheap to me at a ten pound note. They'll get you no end of orders, I can tell you."

The old salt was right. The orders flooded in much faster than Frank could fulfill them, even though he put in regular twelve-hour days.

Chapter 7: An Old Friend

London, December 1871

For three months Frank passed a quiet, pleasant life with the old naturalist in Ratcliff Highway. Mr. Horton quickly took a great liking to him, and treated him more like a son than a taxidermist and shop assistant.

The two took their meals together—occasionally joined by Jekks, who got on well with the old man in spite of the great differences in their backgrounds—and Frank's salary had been raised from twelve to eighteen shillings a week. So attractive had the cases of stuffed birds in the window proved that quite a little crowd gathered in front of the window every day, and as a result Horton's business expanded.

Surprisingly, the proprietor was less happy about this than might be supposed. Before Frank came along, the naturalist had dropped into a comfortable groove. He had no dependants and had been content to jog along, covering the expenses of his shop and living. The extra bustle and push worried rather than pleased him.

"I'm elderly," he told Frank one day over their evening meal. "I've no reason to make pots of money. I did it because I liked your face and appreciated your talent. Now I'd be glad, if I thought that you would succeed me here as my son might have done—if I had one. I'd happily take you into partnership, and you'd inherit the business after I've gone. But I know that's not going to work, the time's coming when you'll want to stretch your wings. No, don't protest," he interrupted Frank's response with an upraised hand. "You will either get an offer from some West End house which would open up much better prospects, or you'll wander off as a collector, somewhere unexplored and exciting, Africa perhaps, like that Stanley chap you go on about.

As it is, I don't want to see you waste your life here in this backwater."

"Well, you're right about Africa, I'd love to go, but I've no clue when that might be… if ever." Frank, however, accepted the basic truth of Mr. Horton's words.

Once he had settled at his new work, Frank had sent a letter to his friend the doctor, at Deal, telling him that he was making at least a comfortable living and doing something he was passionately fond of. He wrote to ask after his sister, but insisted the doctor not tell anyone his address. "I'm not ashamed of where I am but I would rather my old schoolfellows didn't know my whereabouts until I've made another step up in life."

He had also written to Dick Ruthven a bright chatty missive, telling him of his adventures in London, the loss of his money, and that he was now employed at a naturalist's with every chance of doing well.

"When I'm a bit better off," he concluded, "I'll be so happy to see you again, and will let you know where I'm living. For the moment I'd rather keep it to myself. Write to me at the General Post Office, telling me all about yourself and the others. It will cheer me up to hear. I suppose school's breaking up for Christmas in a few days."

Frank received no reply, as Christmas came and went, but afterward he did get a big surprise. One morning a week after the festival he heard somebody come into the shop. As Mr. Horton was out, he went through the passage and into the front.

"I knew it was!" shouted a voice. "Dr. Hargate, I presume. How are you?" and he found his hand warmly clasped in that of Dick Ruthven.

"Good Lord, Dick," was all Frank could say, weakly.

"I had intended," Ruthven exclaimed, "to punch your lights out as soon as I found you, but I'm too glad to see you to do it, though you deserve it fifty times over. What kind of a friend are you? I wouldn't have believed it, running away in that secret sort of way and letting none of us know anything about you. I was furious, and sorry too, when I got the letter you wrote me from Deal. When I went back to school and found that not even Mr. Parker, not even your sister, knew where you were, I was mad. So were all the others. However, I said I'd find you wherever you'd hidden yourself."

"But how *did* you find me?" Frank asked, actually moved at the warmth of his friend's greeting.

"Oh, it wasn't so very difficult once I got your letter saying what you were doing. The very day I came up to town I began to hunt about. I found from the London Directory there were not such a great number of shops where they stuffed birds and that sort of thing. I tried the places in Bond Street, Piccadilly, Wigmore Street, and so on to begin with. Then I began to work east, and the minute I saw the things in the window here I felt sure I'd found you at last. You tiresome bloke! Here I have wasted nearly half my vacation looking for you."

"I'm sorry, Dick."

"Sorry! You ought to be more than sorry. You ought to be ashamed of yourself. But, there, I won't say any more for now. Can you come out with me?"

"No, I'm responsible for the shop while Mr. Horton is out, I can't go out now, but come into my room."

Frank pushed aside whatever he was working on to make some space, and they sat at his work table for the next hour chatting. Frank quickly filled Ruthven in on all he had gone through since he came to town, who in return gave him the gossip of the months at school.

"Well," Dick said at last, "this old Horton of yours must be a nice guy. Still, you know, you can't stop here all your life. You must come and talk it over with my father, who's very interested in your health."

"Oh, no, I'm getting on very well here. I'm very contented with my lot, and I couldn't think of troubling your father."

"Well, if you don't come you will trouble him—a great deal," Dick snapped out with a short laugh. "You'll trouble him to come all the way down here. He was worried when he first heard you'd vanished, and encouraged me in the search for you. I feel like that Yankee chappie, what's his name, Stanley, finding Livingstone, in the deepest, darkest dens of London's East End. Ratcliff Highway, for God's sake. What you don't see—because I know you're stiff with your foolish pride—is that you've put my father under a tremendous obligation."

"Oh, Dick, that's rubbish—"

"Come on, you save the lives of five schoolfellows—"

"Four, there were four of you."

Dick frowned. "Well, yes, you made the fifth, I know, but don't try and change the subject, and don't interrupt me when I'm in full flood. And then you run away and hide yourself as if you were ashamed. I know you. It would be a weight on your mind if you couldn't repay a heavy debt. That's just the position in which you've placed my father."

"I'm not sure I see what that's got to—"

Again, his friend cut off Frank's protest. "Well, anyhow, you've got to come and see him, or he's got to come and see you. I know he has something in his mind's eye which will just suit you, though he didn't tell me what it was. For the last day or two he's been particularly anxious about finding you. Only yesterday when I came back and reported that I'd been to half a dozen places without success, he said, 'Damn the young delinquent, where can he be hiding? Here are the days slipping by and it will be too late. If you don't find him in a day or two, Dick, I'll set the police after him—say he's committed a murder or broken into a bank and offer a reward for his arrest'. So there you are, Frank: you must either come home with me this afternoon, or you'll be having my father down here tonight."

"No, Dick," said Frank, finally getting a word in, "I wouldn't put your father to such trouble. He's very kind to have taken so much interest in me, only I hate—"

"Oh, nonsense. I hate to see such stuck-up pride, putting your own dignity above friendship. For that's really what it comes down to, if you face it."

Frank flushed a little and was silent for a minute.

"I suppose you're right, Dick—"

"Of course I am! Young Goodall, who lives over at Bayswater, has been over four or five times to ask me if I've found you, and I've had letters from Hancock, Childers, and Jackson. Just as if a man about town like me had nothing better to do but to write letters back."

"Ah, that's Mr. Horton just come in," Frank said, jumping to his feet in evident relief. "I'm sure he'll let me go at once."

At the Mansion House the boys caught an omnibus heading west through to Knightsbridge, where they got off and walked to Eaton Square and the London residence of Sir James Ruthven. He was not in at that time, so Frank accompanied his friend to what he called his sanctum, a goodly sized room littered with books, model sailing ships, cricket bats, insect boxes, and a great variety of interesting rubbish of all kinds. Here they chatted until a servant came up to announce that Sir James had returned and wished to see them.

"Come on, Frank," Dick said, running downstairs. "There's nothing of the ogre about the governor."

Frank followed his friend into the study with a hollow feeling of trepidation in the pit of his stomach.

"I've caught him, father, at last. This is the culprit."

Sir James Ruthven was a pleasant looking man, with a kindly face. He stepped forward with a smile and held out his hand. "Well done, Richard. Well, troublesome Master Frank Hargate," he said, shaking Frank's hand, "where have you been hiding all this time?"

"I'm not sure that I've been hiding, sir," Frank said.

"Not exactly hiding," Sir James smiled broadly, "only keeping away from those who wanted to find you. Well, and how are you getting on?"

"Very well, thank you sir. I'm earning eighteen shillings a week and my board and lodging, and my employer will make me a partner when I come of age."

"I am glad to hear that. It says you must be clever as well as industrious."

"Yes, father," Dick broke in, "and the place was full of these fantastic cases of things Frank has stuffed. There was quite a crowd peering in at the window."

"That's what I wanted to hear. I wonder, Frank, would you do me the favor of writing a note to your employer asking him to send down half a dozen of the best cases. I want to show them to someone who's dining with me here this evening, and who has an interest in taxidermy. When you've written the note I'll send a footman off at once in a cab to fetch them."

"And, father," Dick continued, "if you don't mind, might Frank and I have our supper quietly together in my room? You've got a dinner party on, and Frank won't enjoy it half as much as he would eating quietly with me."

"By all means," Sir James said, and then wagged an admonitory finger. "But mind, he's not to run away without seeing me."

"Thanks for that Dick. I couldn't have faced a full dress dinner party wearing these clothes," said Frank as they climbed again up the stairs.

"Oh for God's sake, Hargate the High and Mighty. No one would care about that, except for you, of course. No, I just want you to myself for a bit. I have a horrible suspicion that what my governor's got in mind for you means we may not be seeing much of each other for some considerable time… again."

"What on earth do you mean?"

"I don't know. We'll have to wait and see." Dick gave his friend a glance that portended mystery.

"You do know…"

"Really, I don't, I… I have my suspicions, but," he held up a hand to stifle Frank's protest, "we'll both have to wait."

The afternoon passed in pleasant chat. Frank learned that Dick had left Parker's for good. "Yeah, I'm going to a crammer after the hols run by a clergyman who gets a dozen guys at a time ready for the military academy." He looked askance for a moment. "I don't suppose you're for the army any more?"

Frank shook his head. "It costs too much and—"

"You haven't got enough," Dick finished for him. The both laughed at the old joke.

A servant brought them a superb meal at about eight o'clock, and a little after nine returned with a message, saying that Sir James wished Richard and Frank to go down to the dining room to discuss the cases of stuffed birds which had arrived earlier. Frank was not shy, but he felt it rather a trial when he entered the room. Eight men stood around the table—the ladies having already withdrawn—engaged in examining and admiring the cases of stuffed birds and animals.

"This is my young friend Frank Hargate," Sir James announced to the room. "It's his work you're admiring. This, Frank, is Mr. Frederick Addington Goodenough, the famous explorer and naturalist. With your interests, I expect you have heard of him."

Frank blushed deeply as he looked up into the man's penetrating gaze with something approaching awe. "Oh, yes, I certainly have. I've Mr. Goodenough's *The Tropical Passerine Family* at home."

Goodenough's eyebrows raised slightly as he leaned back. "An expensive book," he said, "not to mention esoteric. It's hardly about house sparrows."

"I know, sir. My father bought it, not me. He was very fond of natural history and taught me all I know. He had a marvelous library, which a friend is keeping for me at Deal, until I have some place where I can put the books. I was thinking of getting them sent to me soon."

Goodenough turned to his host. "Sir James, will you object if I drag young Hargate to your library for a chat?"

"Please be my guest," Sir James replied, and Frank followed the eminent explorer, not knowing what to expect, but certainly surprised by what occurred next. Goodenough sat him down, pulled out several volumes dealing with natural history, and then put him through what Frank felt was one tough examination as to his knowledge of their contents.

As he answered the barrage of questions, Frank studied the

naturalist firing them at him. Frederick Goodenough, descended from a family that counted ancestors as far back as Saxon times, was in his mid-thirties, he supposed. Not overly tall—Frank, above average height for his age, had only to look up half an inch when they were stood facing each other—Goodenough was solidly built, with piercing gray eyes under bushy brows that matched his neatly trimmed moustache and clipped beard. His lean face duplicated his sleek but well-muscled build and his eyes, ready to smile, could quickly look stern with the slight squint of one who has spent a lot of time shielding them against the tropical glare. His demeanor was typically that of a well educated aristocrat, but years abroad had stripped away any haughty upper-class mannerisms. He exuded supreme confidence in manner and movement, and Frank's only observation of any weakness was the slightly sallow look around his eyes, no doubt the result of tropical fevers, he thought.

"I feel really obliged to you, James," Goodenough said when he returned to the dining room and Frank had gone back upstairs with Dick. "The lad has a genius for natural history, and he is modest and self possessed. From what you tell me he's done things for himself rather than beg for assistance. When I put all that together with the stories you've already told me, I end up with a young man of stamina who's more than capable of coping in many situations. With his pluck and resolution, he will make a perfect traveling companion."

"I'm pleased you think so, Frederick, and I'm happy to be of service to you while at the same time giving the lad a hand, which he's more than owed."

"I feel quite relieved. It's so difficult to find a someone who will exactly fit. Clever naturalists are rare, and you can never tell how you'll get on with a man when you're thrown together. He may want to have his own way, may be irritable and bad tempered, may in many respects be unpleasant. With young Frank Hargate I feel sure of my ground. We shall get on very well together, I'm convinced of it."

* * *

Frank's heart sank when the footman reappeared with a request for them to return downstairs. "I wonder what now, Dick?" he muttered uncertainly.

"Ah, there you are Hargate," declared Mr. Goodenough as they came through the dining room door. "I've seen from your work that you're not only a very skilled taxidermist and preparer of specimens, but also a close student of the habits and ways of wild creatures. But I was hardly prepared to find your scientific knowledge so accurate and extensive. I was inclined to hesitate when Sir James Ruthven made me a proposal last week. But I don't any longer.

"I'm on the point of starting an expedition to the Guinea Coast of West Africa in search of specimens for the new Natural History Museum in Kensington, which we all fervently hope will be opened soon. Sir James has proposed that you should accompany me on this expedition, and has offered to pay the attendant costs."

Frank managed to remember his manners enough to shut his mouth, which had just dropped open.

"I anticipate being away for two years," Goodenough went on. "You'll be my assistant, and have every opportunity of learning whatever I know. It won't be a pleasure trip, you know, but tough work, with all sorts of hardships and, perhaps, some danger. There's a saying that the Guinea Coast is 'the white man's grave'. At the same time it would be a fine opening in a career as a naturalist. Well, what do you say?"

For a moment Frank couldn't think of anything to say.

"It is a great opportunity for you," Sir James prompted.

"Oh, sir!" Frank almost gasped, then recovered his composure, but still clasped his hands in an unconsciously boyish gesture. "Of all the things in the world I can think of, it's what I want the most. How can I thank you enough? And you, Sir James, how can I possibly repay you?"

"Payment doesn't come into it, Frank. We are far from being quits, not yet by any means," Sir James said kindly, patting his protégé on the shoulder.

On his return to the shop on Ratcliff Highway Frank found Mr. Horton sitting up for him, so he immediately told his employer what had happened. Once he'd gotten over his surprise, the old naturalist was sincerely glad.

"I'll miss you sadly," he said. "I'll feel very dull for a time, but this is the best thing for you. I never expected to keep you long. You were made for better things than this shop, and I've no doubt that you have a brilliant career ahead. You may not become rich—natural history's not a lucrative profession, trust me, but you may become famous. Now, off to bed and dream of your future."

First thing next morning Frank went over to see Jekks and found the porter too busy to stop and talk beyond a hurried congratulation. "I'll hear all about it this evening," he promised.

Next Frank made his way to Jermyn Street, where he had arranged to meet the explorer, and went with Mr. Goodenough to Silver's, where he ordered an outfit suitable for West Africa's hot, humid climate. The clothes were simple: shirts made of thin soft flannel ("Must have something to absorb the perspiration and which washes easily..."), knickerbocker-style trousers ("To go with calf-length leather boots. Don't need trousers dragging in the thick undergrowth, or snakes snapping at your ankles...") and Norfolk jackets of tough New Zealand flax ("There's nothing like it. It's the only stuff which has a chance with the thorns of an African jungle, not to mention the constant humidity...")

"Now you'll want a revolver" Goodenough pronounced. "I recommend a Beaumont-Adams. Much better than a Colt for its stopping power. A Winchester repeating carbine and a shotgun. My outfit of boxes and cases is ready, so beyond two or three extra nets and collecting boxes there's nothing further to do in that way.

"For your head you'd better have a soft felt hat with a wide brim.

Place a leaf or two inside and they're as cool as anything, far lighter and more comfortable than those daft pith-helmets so many people seem to think are essential wear in the tropics."

"As far as shooting goes," Frank said, "I think I'll do much better with my blowgun than with a regular one. I can hit a small bird sitting nine times out of ten."

"Hmm, for birds there's nothing better, I agree. They have the advantage too of not breaking the skin. But for birds in flight a shotgun with its scatter-shot is infinitely more effective. I recommend a cavalry carbine over a long-barrelled rifle because they're handier in thick jungle. The blowgun will be fine for specimen collecting, but there may well be more dangerous animals afoot, including the natives. Will you want any knives for skinning?"

"No, sir. I've got several."

"Are you going back to Eaton Square? I heard Sir James ask you to stay there until we're ready to set out."

"Not until tomorrow," Frank replied. "I asked his permission to stay where I am until then. I didn't want to appear like I'm abandoning Mr. Horton in such a hurry. He's been extremely kind to me."

"Mind, you must come back here in three days for a fitting in case any last-minute alterations are needed. I particularly asked that they're to be made easy and comfortable, larger, in fact, than you actually require right now, because we must allow for growing. Two years may make a difference of some inches to you, especially in the shoulders. Now, let's see… we've only the bootmaker's and then we're done."

When the orders were completed they split up. Mr. Goodenough intended going to his country house that afternoon and only returning to London the day before they were due to depart for Liverpool. That evening Frank had a long chat with his two friends, and was much pleased when Mr. Horton, who had taken a great liking to Jekks, offered him the use of a room, saying that he would be more than paid back by the pleasure of his company in the evenings.

Jekks was now happy to accept the offer, and Frank was glad to think that his two friends would be sitting chatting over an evening meal together instead of being shut away in their solitary rooms. The next day he bid adieu to the dubious charms of Ratcliff Highway, Eastcheap, and the East End, and took up his temporary residence in elegant Eaton Square, Knightsbridge.

Chapter 8: To the Dark Continent

February–March 1872

Frank stared sadly at the little house where he had lived, now occupied by complete strangers, and shed a quiet tear for the loss of his dear mother. Then he pulled himself together and went to say goodbye to his sister Lucy and the good doctor, who handed over to him the watch and chain that had belonged to his father, and the other items he had taken care of: the blowgun, skinning knives, and taxidermy instruments. His books he left with the doctor until his return from Africa.

The same evening he returned to London, and spent some days very pleasantly at Eaton Square. "Will you be putting in at Sierra Leone?" Dick asked Frank, one afternoon, as he lay on his stomach on his bed, knees bent and his feet idly tapping together in mid-air, as he read a book.

"I think so, why?"

"It says here that in 1826, of the 1,576 troops sent there, 950 died within two years, mostly from the fevers caused by *mal aria*, the 'bad air.'" He glanced up. "That's not good, is it?"

"I've read that fevers are common on the coastal regions, 'the white man's grave', whereas for the most part we'll be much further inland," Frank replied carelessly. "Still, I will let you know in due course. One the tasks Mr. Goodenough has handed me is to keep the expedition log up to date."

Three days later, the questions of fever had become academic. It was time to depart. Dick accompanied him in the cab to Euston station, where a minute or two later Mr. Goodenough arrived. The luggage, a modest case each, the heavy duty boxes and trunks having been sent ahead the day before, was placed in a carriage, and Frank chatted with Dick at the door, until the guard's cry, "Board!" caused him to jump in. There was one last handgrip with his friend through the lowered window, and then the train chugged out of the station.

They reached Liverpool at midnight and stayed at the Station Hotel. In the morning it was a struggle to get through the lobby for the huge heap of baggage piled up. Goodenough told Frank that this was a daily occurrence, as six to eight large steamers sailed every week for America alone. At twelve o'clock they went on board the African Steamship Company's 'mail boat' *SS Niger*.

The first three days sailing down the Irish Sea and across the Bay of Biscay were grey, rainy, and with high seas. Frank didn't mind, the waves held no terrors of sea sickness for him, and after that the *Niger* left winter behind. Four days later the vessel anchored in the port of Funchal. Frank's eyes would not open wide enough to take in the sight before him. "What a glorious place to ramble about."

"It would be difficult to imagine a greater contrast than between mountainous Madeira and the country where we're going," said Goodenough. "This is one of the most delightful climates in the world, the coast of West Africa one of the worst. Once we're in the interior, the swamp fevers, the curse of the shores, disappear, but African travelers are seldom long free from attacks of fever of one kind or the other. However, quinine does wonders, and we shall be far in the interior before the bad season sets in."

"Have you explored where we're going now before?"

"Yes, twice, but only short distances from the coast. This time we're going into a country which is altogether unknown."

"Have you suffered with fever attacks, sir?"

"Two or three little ones. A touch of African fever, during what's called the good season, isn't any worse than a feverish cold at home. It lasts two to three days, and then there's an end of it. In the bad season the attacks are extremely violent, sometimes carrying men off in a few hours. I consider, however, that dysentery is a more formidable enemy than fever, especially if it occurs during a bout of fever."

"Are we hiring porters at Sierra Leone?"

"Certainly not, Frank. The men of Sierra Leone are mostly returned slaves from the Americas, which means they are the most indolent, the most worthless, and the most insolent in all Africa. It's the last place in the world to hire followers. We'll get carriers when we reach the Gabon, and at each place we arrive at afterward we'll take on others, only keeping one of the previous lot to act as interpreter.

"The natives will let white men cross their territory, but are exceedingly jealous of men from other tribes. However, we'll want to hire some Hausas as a bodyguard, say six. They're Muslims and usually very reliable, hard-working and honest. They're also the best fighting men on the coast.

"Now we'll go onshore for a few hours. I want to buy a couple of hammocks here. They're lighter and more comfortable than those sold on the Guinea Coast. I'll get a couple of their cane chairs, too. They're light, they let the air circulate when you're seated, and they're very comfortable."

After several days' further sailing, they arrived off Freetown, the main city of Sierra Leone, and Frank was soon on deck in the afternoon sun. "What a beautiful place," he breathed. "It's not a bit what I expected."

"No," Goodenough said. "No one looking at it could suppose that this bright and pretty town is the place that gave us the phrase 'the white man's grave.'"

Freetown stood some fifty feet or so above the sea, with its British barracks on a green hill three hundred feet higher up and a quarter mile back. The town, as seen from the sea, consisted entirely of the houses of the merchants and shopkeepers, the government buildings, churches, and other public and European buildings. The houses were all large and bright with yellow-tinged whitewash, and the place hurt the eyes with the intense green of its palms and spreading tropical hard-wood trees.

A score of small boats approached the ship. They remained at a short distance until the harbor master came on board and pronounced the ship free from quarantine. Then they made a rush for the side with shouts, yells, and screams of laughter.

Goodenough and Frank got ready to go ashore, but this was not easily accomplished amid the battle royal among the boatmen whose craft thronged at the foot of the ladder. Each boat had about four hands. Three remained on board while the fourth stood on the ship's ladder and hauled at his painter to keep the boat to which he belonged alongside. Since no more than two could be at the foot of the ladder together, the conflict was a desperate one.

All the boatmen shouted, "Here, sar. Dis good boat, sar. You come wid me, sar," at the top of their voices, while at the same time they worked hard at pulling each other's boats back and pushing their own forward.

"They're just like children," Goodenough told Frank, as they struggled to climb down the ladder. "They're always either laughing or quarreling. They're good natured and passionate, generally lazy, but will work hard for a time—a short time."

On landing the greenness of everything delighted Frank. The trees were heavy with luxuriant foliage, the streets were viridian with grass as long and bright as that in a country lane in England. The town was alive with a chattering, laughing, good-natured, excitable population, all black, but with some slight variation in the strength of the hue. Shivers of exhilaration shuddered through his body every minute as he realized anew every time that he really was in Africa. He had to keep shaking himself to stop the excitement overwhelming his system. He almost fainted with joy at the first sight of a large purple and orange lizard clinging lazily to the bole of a palm tree nearby.

Sierra Leone was such a fun place. Everyone was brimful of it. The inhabitants laughed as they spoke, and everyone standing nearby joined freely in the merriment and conversation. And the display of fruit in the market… Oh, it was all too marvellous. There were massive piles of delicious big oranges, green but perfectly sweet, and of equally refreshing little green limes; pineapples and bananas, green, yellow and red plantains; guava, custard apples, pears, melons, breadfruit, paw-paw, sour-sops, and many other strange native goods.

Goodenough purchased a large basket of fruit, which they took with them on board the *SS Niger*. The next morning they started down the coast. The ship passed Liberia, the republic formed of liberated American slaves, and the next day they anchored off Cape Palmas, the homeland of the Kroomen.

"A magnificent tribe," Goodenough informed Frank. "They provide sailors and boatmen to all the ships trading along the coast, but they're notorious cowards, and no offer would tempt them to penetrate more than a mile inland in the kind of country we're going to."

Stopping a few hours beyond the coastal breakers at Cape Coast Castle, Accra, and Lagos, they crossed the mouths of the Niger river and at last arrived at Bonny.

Frank looked disapprovingly over the railing at the flat, grey-green smudge. "It's certainly not tempting in appearance," he observed glumly.

"Neither is it in the experience," Goodenough replied dryly. "Bonny is one of the most horribly unhealthy spots in Africa. As you see, the white traders don't dare live onshore. They stay in those floating thatched-over hulks, which serve as homes and storehouses. I've a letter from one of the African merchants in London, and we shall stay on his until we get one of the coastal steamers to carry us down to the Gabon. I hope it won't be too many days."

The bulky luggage was soon transferred to the retired vessel, where Frank and Goodenough took up their temporary residence. Any break in the monotony of life at Bonny was eagerly welcomed and the resident agent was overjoyed to see them. In spite of the sun's rays he was pale and unhealthy looking, but then, he had just recovered from an unusually bad attack of fever.

"Like so many of the traders on the coast he has an immense faith in the power of spirits," Goodenough confided to Frank, who gave his mentor a puzzled look.

"Wh... what, the natives' witch-doctor stuff?"

"No, no. Alcohol. It's the ruin of them. Five out of six of the men here ruin their health with spirits, and then fall an easy prey to the fevers."

"But you've brought alcohol with you, sir, I saw some of the cases were labeled Brandy."

"Brandy's useful when taken as a medicine, and in moderation. A little mixed with pre-boiled water at the end of a long day of exhausting work acts as a restorative, and frequently lets a worn out man sleep. But I've brought it along for the use of others rather than myself. One case is of the very best quality for our own use. The rest is common stuff intended as presents. Our main drink will be tea and chocolate—much better for the white traveler than spirits."

"I'm sure you're right, sir. For myself, I have tasted beer once, and thought little of it. Though I must admit to enjoying the small glass of red wine Dick Ruthven offered me. But what of the other large cases?"

Goodenough smiled. "In some of those, large quantities of calico, brass stair rods, beads, and powder. This is the currency of Africa. With these we'll pay our carriers and boatmen, and purchase the right of way through the various tribes we meet. Anyway, it's necessary in Africa to pass as traders. The natives understand that white men come here to trade, but if we said that our object was to shoot birds and beasts, and to catch butterflies and insects, they wouldn't believe us in the least, and would suspect us of all sorts of hidden designs. Now we must go ashore with the agent and pay our respects to the king."

Frank raised his eyebrows in surprise. "Do you mean to say that there's a king in that wretched-looking village?"

Frederick Goodenough gave a barking laugh. "Oh yes, my boy.

You'll find that kings are as plentiful as peas in Africa… but you won't see much royal state."

Freetown had given Frank an exalted idea of African civilization, but this was quickly dispelled by Bonny's appearance. The houses, constructed entirely of black mud, lined streets narrow and filthy beyond description. The palace was composed of two or three hovels surrounded by a mud wall. In one of these miserable huts they greeted the king, seated on a carved wooden stool, a purple-black skinned man of impressive fatness. The agent introduced them and the king indicated they should sit and share his meal.

As they ate a stew consisting of meat, vegetables, and the hot peppers traders from the Americas had introduced to West Africa, the king asked Goodenough what he had come to the coast for, and was disappointed to find that he was not going to set up as a trader at Bonny, as it was the custom for each newcomer to make a handsome present to him.

On their way back the agent asked Frank, "Do you know what you've just eaten?"

"I've no idea. It wasn't bad. What was it?"

"Dog flesh," the agent answered with the touch of a magician pulling a rabbit from a top hat.

"Not really?" Frank forced down an uncomfortable sensation of nausea.

"Yes, indeed," the agent replied. "It's considered a luxury in Bonny, and dogs are bred specially."

"You'll eat stranger things than that before you've done, Frank," Goodenough continued, "and will find them just as good, and in many cases better, than the food you're used to. It's strange why in Europe certain animals should be considered fit to eat and others rejected, and often without the slightest reason. Here sheep, cows, horses, and donkeys would be dead of the sleeping sickness within days of being born and the natives very wisely make the most of those animals which can survive."

At Bonny, with the agent's assistance, they hired the service of six men of the Hausa tribe. These people lived far to the north in the grasslands and some had concentrated around Lagos, but they wandered about a good deal. The men had formed a guard in one of the hulks, but with trade poor and the merchant who had hired them had gone home, they were glad to take service with the newcomers. They spoke some English between them and rejoiced in names which had been given them by sailors. Frank noted them carefully in the log: Moses, Firewater, Ugly Tom, Bacon, Tatters, and King John. *Fortunately, they are eager to leave this dismal Bonny and have no objection to a long expedition with us,* he wrote.

Frank quickly tired of Bonny and longed to be away, especially from the clouds of biting insects, and was glad when three days later they found passage on a sailing ship bound for the Gabon. After the comforts of a fine steamer the accommodation on board the little trader was poor. *She stinks horribly of palm oil and the cockroaches, some more than three inches in length, run riot over everything below decks, so we Englishmen brought up our mattresses and sleep topside.*

On the sixteenth day after leaving Bonny they entered the Gabon. On the right shore of the long but narrow estuary stood the fort and dwellings of the French. A little farther up stood the English factories and, on a green hill behind, the church, school, and houses of an American mission. On the left shore stood the wattle town of the king of Gabon. Goodenough landed and made enquiries for accommodation. He succeeded in finding a house consisting of three rooms, built on piles, an important point in a country in which it was known that the *mal arial* fevers rose up from the saturated soil during the night.

The Hausa contingent were put to work for the first time, and the goods were soon transported from the smelly brig to the house.

"Is anything the matter with you, Frank?" asked Goodenough that evening.

"I don't know, sir. My head feels heavy, somehow, and I'm dizzy."

The explorer reached out and felt his pulse.

"Mmm, you have your first touch of fever," he said. "I'm surprised you've been so long without it. You'd better lie down at once."

A quarter of an hour later Frank was seized with an overpowering heat, every vein felt filled with liquid fire, but his skin, instead of being as usual in a state of perspiration, was dry and hard. Soon after that he collapsed and had to be put to bed.

Chapter 9: The Start Inland

Gabon, March–April 1872

"Now, Frank, sit up and drink this. It's only some mustard, salt, and water. I'm a strong advocate for a powerful purgative."

The horrible drink soon took effect. Frank threw up violently into a large halved gourd his mentor had thoughtfully provided for the purpose, and the perspiration broke in streams from him.

"Here's a cup of tea. Drink that and you'll be as fit as a fiddle in the morning."

Frank woke up still weak, but otherwise well.

"How are you feeling?"

"Much better, Mr. Goodenough, sir, thanks to your doctoring."

"I know there are strict rules of etiquette back home in England, but we're now in the jungles of Africa, Frank, and I think—despite our age differences and the deference usually accorded to the elder by the younger—you must call me by my name—Frederick. I insist."

Frank flushed, and promised to try his best, then Goodenough administered him a strong dose of quinine, and after he had eaten his breakfast he felt quite himself again.

"Now," Goodenough said, "we'll go up to the factories and mission and try to find a good personal servant. Everything depends on that."

In a short time he hired a man of the Mpongwe tribe, who inhabited the region around the Gabon estuary. His name was Ostik and he spoke understandable English, as well as being competent in three other native dialects. He had been with the only other white man to travel into the interior before them.

Ostik is tall, powerfully built, and very ugly, but with a friendly, honest face. I was sure immediately that I would like him.

"You understand," Goodenough explained, "we're going through Fang country, far into the interior. We may be away from the coast for many months."

"Me ready, sar," the Mpongwe answered with a grin. "Make no odds to Ostik. He got no wife, no piccanniny. Ostik very good cook. Master find good grub. He catch plenty of beasts."

"You're not afraid, Ostik, because it's possible we may have trouble on the way?"

"Me not very much afraid, massa. You good massa to Ostik he no run away if fightin' come—but no good fight whole tribe."

"I hope we won't have to fight at all, Ostik, but we have six Hausas who will all carry the latest Snider breech loading guns, so I think we should be a match for a good sized tribe, if necessary."

Ostik looked thoughtful. "More easy, massa, to go without Hausa," he said. "Black man not often touch white traveler but no like his own color."

"That's true, but I must take trade goods for paying my way and hiring carriers. Without any arms I'd be at the mercy of every petty chief who chose to steal the goods. I'm going as a peaceful traveler, ready to pay my way, and to make presents to the different kings through whose territories I may pass. But I won't put myself at the mercy of any of them. I'm not saying that eight men armed with breech loaders can defeat a whole tribe, but we'd be so formidable, that any of these kings would be better off taking our presents and letting us pass peacefully than trying to rob us."

Ostik bowed to this logic. "What do next, massa?"

The explorer stepped firmly to the edge of the ridge on which they had gathered and gazed out over the tidal expanse of the Gabon below. "First, we must hire a large canoe. Two if necessary. The rowers must promise to take us up into Fang country, at least as far as the rapids on the Komo. Then we shall take carriers there, and the boat and rowers can return."

To this point Frank had seen the goods to be carried in the context of larger vessels. Although Ostik had found a boat large enough to carry the whole expedition, it paled into insignificance compared to the massive pile on the river bank. Ten large tin cases, each weighing eighty pounds, contained cotton cloths, powder, beads, tea, chocolate, sugar, tinned meat, vegetables and fruit, and hard-tack biscuit. Three bundles of brass stair rods, also eighty pounds each, were done up in canvas. Further tin-lined wooden cases contained a score of cheap Birmingham muskets as *dashes*, or presents, for chiefs, plus weights of powder and old-fashioned ball shot.

Then came six great chests made of light iron. Four of these were fitted with trays with cork bottoms, for insects. The other two were for the skins of birds. All the boxes and cases had strips of India rubber where the lids fitted down, to keep out both damp and the tiny ants which plagued samples in Africa. The tent made of double canvas weighed fifty pounds, and two light folding trestle beds weighed fifteen pounds apiece. Finally, there were the ammunition boxes containing six thousand rounds for each of the Sniders, besides the cartridges for Goodenough and Frank's revolvers, carbines, and shotguns.

Once out of the canoe, fourteen porters would be required for the main baggage and another ten to carry plantains—the staple food—and other provisions, together with the personal trunks, rugs, and waterproof sheets of the explorers.

It took four more days of hard bargaining and persuading to get together the needed porters because the Mpongwe were terrified of the Fang—with good reason; they were cannibals. Goodenough promised that they would not be forced to proceed unless a safe conduct for their return was obtained from the chief of the Fang. Finally, twelve paddlers were hired after bartering over the size of the dash, and the goods taken down and arranged in the transport.

The Hausas had spent the days with their Snider rifles being shown how the breech system operated, which thrilled them with its ease of use and speed of loading. The men practiced firing at targets set up at a hundred and fifty yard distance. They were delighted with the rifles' accuracy and the rapidity with which they could fire them. However, Goodenough impressed on them that unless attacked at close quarters, they should aim as slowly and deliberately as if using their old guns. "On such long a journey ammunition is precious and must, on no account, be wasted," he warned them. "Besides, in a dangerous situation, it's best to deceive the enemy as to the rifles' real power and speed of use until the last minute to make them most effective."

In order to give their guards as imposing a look as possible, each of the Hausas received a pair of knee-length pants of New Zealand flax specially brought from London. They were several sizes too large, but the men soon set to work with rough needles and thread and took them in. In addition, each man received a red sash to wind several times around his waist. These kept the trousers up and added a distinctive look to the uniform. Moses, Firewater, Ugly Tom, Bacon, Tatters, and King John were very proud of their appearance. In addition to their rifles all of them carried medium-length swords, weapons which they wielded with frightening skill.

The expedition started early in the morning on the first day of April, and passed Konig Island, an abandoned Dutch settlement, after four hours' paddling. After an hour's rest here, a sea breeze sprang up, a sail was hoisted, and the boat made good time to the French guardship which marked the settlement's boundary at the Boqui tributary. They stopped there on the little island of Nenge Nenge, formerly a missionary station, where the natives were converts to Christianity.

The Hausas soon had the tent up. It was a double poled affair, some ten feet square, and a waterproof ground sheet large enough to cover the whole of the interior prevented damp rising up. The beds were soon opened and fixed, two of the large cases formed a table, and two smaller ones acted as chairs. With a lamp lit, the comfort and snugness of their abode charmed Frank.

Two of the Hausas fastened all their weapons around the tent poles to shelter them from the damp night air. As soon as the Hausas had the tent pitched, Ostik set to work. He quickly had a fire blazing and from his saucepans served up rice with slices of salt meat. Goodenough had purchased sufficient from the captain of the sailing brig to last them the canoe journey. This unexpected addition to their staple put the men in high spirits, and their songs rose merrily around the fire in the steamy night air. Frank found that he had become gradually acclimatized to the humidity. At first, it had seemed strange that, after the heat of the day, the nights often seemed even hotter as soon as the evening breeze died away. If the fetid air was cloyingly still, the night was not, alive with the cries, hoots, and squeals of invisible animals, all accompanied by the never-ending *shreek-shreek* of the millions of cicadas in the grass.

In the morning, the tide assisted the paddlers for a further twelve miles before the pressure of water from the mountains ahead overpowered it and they entered the river proper. Six hours from Nenge Nenge they arrived at Olenga, the first Fang village. The villagers crowded around as the canoe pulled in, full of curiosity and excitement, for only once before had a white man come up the river.

Frank's initial nervousness at being in the presence of men known to enjoy the flesh of other men soon abated at the evident friendliness or their hosts. He recorded that, *The Fang look very different to the Mpongwe, with their longer, thicker hair, slighter figures and a complexion a paler shade of coffee. Their projecting upper jaws give them a rabbit-mouthed appearance. They wear coronets on their heads decorated with the red tail feathers of the common grey parrot. Most of the men sport beards, divided in the middle, with red and white beads strung on the tips of each fork. Some wear only a strip of goatskin hanging from the waist, or the skin of a leopard, while others have short kilts made of cloth woven from the inner bark of a tree.*

The travelers were led to the chief's hut, where they were surrounded by a throng of the cannibals. The Hausas had been strictly ordered to leave their guns in the bottom of the canoe to avoid the appearance of an armed force at all costs.

The chief demanded of Ostik what these two white men wanted. "Have they come to trade?" he asked

"No, great king," Ostik replied. "The white men are going upriver into the country beyond to shoot elephant and buy ivory. They do not want to trade for logwood or oil, but they will give presents to you and other chiefs of the Fang."

The chief looked disgruntled until Goodenough produced one of the Birmingham muskets, together with some powder and ball. He added three bright cotton handkerchiefs, some gaudy glass beads, and two cheap brassy mirrors for his wives. The Fang's turned-down mouth brightened into a broad smile. This was considered perfectly satisfactory.

"Have we staved off the threat of being served up as the main course this evening, do you think Mr. Good… er, sorry, Frederick?"

"Levity has its place, Frank, in the right place and at the right time," the explorer admonished him. Then he gave an impish grin. "Tonight, you'll see, we shall have some fun."

The crush around them threatened to overwhelm, and at Goodenough's dictation Ostik informed the chief that if the white men were left in peace until the evening they would show his people many strange things. On hearing this the crowd thinned out. But when at sunset the two white men took a turn through the village, the excitement bubbled up again. The Fang stood their ground and stared at them, but the women and children ran screaming away to hide themselves.

"In my experience," Goodenough informed Frank, "the people of the Guinea Coast—that is from Cape Palmas to Bonny—are long familiar with the white man, but those of Central Africa know little of us. They think we white men are few in number, that we live at the bottom of the sea, and that we are very wealthy, but that we have no palm oil or timber, and are, therefore, forced to come to land to trade for these vital articles. They believe that the strange clothes we wear are manufactured from the skins of sea creatures."

When night fell Goodenough fastened a sheet against the outside of the chief's hut, and then placed a magic lantern projector in position ten paces from it. The villagers were then invited to gather around and take their seats on the ground. A cry of astonishment greeted the appearance of the bright disk, followed by a wilder yell when this darkened and an elephant with some men sitting on its back was seen to cross the house.

The Fang warriors leaped to their feet, and seizing their spears brandished them at the screen. The women screamed, and Ostik, who was himself somewhat alarmed, had great difficulty in calming their fears and persuading them to sit down again, assuring them that they would see many wonderful things, but that nothing would hurt them.

The next view was at first incomprehensible to many of them. It was a ship tossed in a stormy sea, but the few who had been downriver to the Gabon were able to explain what they were seeing. The show included twenty slides, all of which were provided with movable figures. The last two, which were of the Brewster chromatrope design, elicited screams of delight from the astonished Fang at the dancing abstract shapes and their colors. For hours after the performance ended the village rang with a perfect babel of shouts, screams, and chatter.

They are in awe of the white man's powers, Frank congratulated himself.

The expedition stayed two days at Olenga, while word was sent to Itchongue, the next town, asking the chief there for permission to enter his territory. The people had now begun to get over their first timidity, and when Frank went out for a walk after breakfast he was somewhat embarrassed by the young women and girls crowding around him. They touched his hands and face to assure themselves that they were real, and ran their hands all over his clothing. When bolder hands explored the front of his pants amid a gale of giggles, his discomfiture turned to alarm.

To distract them from pursuing their tactile examination to an intimate level, he delighted them by taking off his Norfolk jacket and rolling up his shirt sleeves to show them that his arms were the same color as his hands. His admirers were so elated with this exhibition that he had a struggle preventing them from undressing him entirely. In the end Ostik came to his rescue and carried him off from the laughing crowd which surrounded him.

After dinner Frederick Goodenough invited the villagers to sit down in a large circle holding each other's hands. Through Ostik, he told them that he would speak a magic word which would make them all jump to their feet. Then taking out a small but powerful galvanic battery, he arranged it and placed wires into the hands of the two men nearest to him in the circle.

Looking at Frank, he said loudly, "Now!"

Frank turned on the battery, and in an instant the two hundred men and women, with wild shrieks, either leaped to their feet or rolled backward. In another minute not a Fang was to be seen, with the exception of the chief, who had not been included in the circle. It took Ostik some minutes to persuade the chief to call back his subjects. Eventually he shouted loudly to return, saying that the white men would not harm them, but it was a long time before, slowly and cautiously, they crept back.

As soon as his audience had settled down the naturalist showed them several simple but astonishing chemical experiments, which stupefied them with wonder, and concluded with three or four conjuring tricks, which completed their amazement.

"Advance word should ensure us a good billing at the next venue, Frederick," Frank said with a conspiratorial wink.

A long day's paddling took them to Itchongue, where the bush telegraph had indeed speeded news of the show with advance rave notices, and they were as well received as at Olenga. Here they stopped for two more days, and the lantern worked its magic again, and Frederick repeated the other tricks with equal triumph.

With the first rapids only another day's paddling away, Goodenough began negotiations to obtain porters from the Fang to replace the Mpongwe. After great palaver and the dash of three Birmingham muskets to the chief, thirty men were engaged. These were each to receive a yard of calico a day or one brass stair rod every five days, and were to stay with the expedition until men of another tribe would substitute for them. Only at this point, would they receive their wages and be discharged to make their own way home.

The new recruits paddled upriver in another canoe. Several villages were passed on the way. The Gabon river, also called at this point the Komo, became a series of rapids, against which the canoes made slow headway. They had now entered the mountains which rose steeply above them, clothed in dense rain forest. Two days of hard work brought them to the foot of the major falls. After unloading the canoes, the men hired on the coast received their pay and turned their boats' bows downstream. The Fang canoe went with it, and the explorers remained with their bodyguard of Hausas and their Fang carriers.

"Well, Frank," the explorer said with satisfaction, "we are now really on our way. We'll start operations at once. I've heard the song of a great many birds I can't identify, so I'm hoping for a good harvest. We may remain here for some time. The first thing to do is to find food for our followers. We've got six sacks of rice, but that won't be sufficiently nutritious. The men would soon collapse on that diet alone."

"But Mr. Goo…, Frederick, how do you propose to feed forty people?"

"That shouldn't be a problem. Do you remember me pointing out hippopotamus tracks on the riverbank? We can feed all our men for a week on one hippo."

Frank grinned inwardly as his thoughts wandered back to Jack and his famous hippypotybus. Now, it seemed, he was going to see one close up.

"There were also crocodile eggs on the banks, and crocodile steaks are very tasty. Your rifle won't be much use against their armor-plated hides, but a Snider firing an explosive shell should do the trick."

After dinner Ugly Tom and Moses accompanied them with their rifles, together with three of the Fang, to a place where the hippo tracks had been seen. As they approached the spot they heard several loud snorts. Signing the Fang to hang back, the two white men crept on, the two Hausas close behind. At this point the river widened a good deal and became shallow near the bank, and there they saw two of the great beasts standing in the stream playing together. The noise the animals made prevented their hearing the stealthy approach of their enemies.

"Take the one nearest shore, Frank, I'll take the other. Aim at the forehead between the eyes. I'll make a slight sound to attract their attention."

Frank knelt on one leg and took a steady aim. Goodenough then gave a shout, and the two animals turned to stare at the foliage barely a dozen yards away, which concealed the hunters. The guns flashed at the same moment and, as if struck by lightning, the hippopotami fell in the stream. As he fired, Frank had taken another rifle which Ugly Tom held in readiness for him, but there was no need. The explosive shells had done their fatal work. The Fang came running up, and on seeing the great beasts lying in the water, gave shouts of joy before dashing off to fetch the rest of the men.

"That should give us food enough for more than a week," Goodenough said with satisfaction. Within the hour portions already sizzled over the fires, other cuts were wrapped in leaves and set aside for the next two days, and the rest cut in strips to be dried in the sun. Ostik cut the tongue of one hippopotamus and fried the great luxury for the white men's supper.

"It's not often that the natives of equatorial Africa are able to enjoy meat," Goodenough told Frank. "In spite of appearances, the jungles are not home to many eatable beasts, and those that are, like this hippo, are too large or dangerous for their weapons."

It was evident that the Fang carriers were happy at this unexpected supply, and the prospect of further good eating raised their spirits to a near delirium. Lively song soon broke out as the cooking embers died down.

Next morning at daybreak the naturalists set out from the camp. Each carried a double-barreled shot-gun, while King John and Bacon, who went along with them, shouldered their rifles and a butterfly net each. Three hours later they returned to the camp for breakfast and compared their spoils. "An excellent beginning," Frederick announced.

Nearly a score of birds, of which several were very rare, and five pronounced by Goodenough as entirely new, had been collected, and many butterflies netted. Frank had been most successful in this respect, after coming across a small clearing in which he found several deserted huts. As he knew well, although many kinds of butterfly preferred the deep shades of the forest, by far the greater numbers loved the bright sunlight, and the glade was just the place for them.

After breakfast they again set out, Frank this time keeping along the edge of the river, where he had observed many butterflies as they came up, and where he had also seen several kinds of kingfisher. He collected a good number of specimens and was walking along by the edge of the water with his eyes fixed on the trees above where a minute before he had heard the call of an unknown bird, when a weird whizzing sound alarmed him. At the same time Ugly Tom, who was a few steps behind him, gave a loud shout of fright.

Instinctively, Frank sprang back and ducked at the same time, and it was well he did so. On the instant a dark object lashed past within an inch of his head. Frank gasped with horror as he recovered and swung round to confront a huge crocodile at the edge of the stream, slightly below him. As he did so, the giant reptile tensed, its triangular jaws gaped hugely, and the beast rushed up the short bank at Frank.

Chapter 10: Lost in the Jungle

Gabon, May 1872

The crocodile's first assault had been a strike with its tail and had it not been for his own uncanny sixth sense and Ugly Tom's warning cry, the monster would have swept him into the river.

As it waddled up the bank at an alarming speed for its monstrous size, Frank's instincts took over and almost without knowing he had done it, he raised his shotgun and gave the crocodile both barrels straight down its gullet. He had enough time to notice with a shudder the gaping maw's satiny pink prettiness, horridly at odds with its ghastly purpose. The animal rolled over onto its back, slipping down into the water. Then, horrifyingly, it turned and struggled to regain the bank.

There was no time to eject and bang in two more cartridges, as the scaly leviathan once again opened what must have been aching jaws, but no less lethal for that. Then Uncle Tom ran up and, placing the muzzle of his Snider within a foot of its eye, fired. With a fire-hose hiss, the creature rolled over dead and was swept away by the river current.

Uncle Tom gave a loud shout in his own language which was answered in the distance. He then shouted two or three words, and turning to Frank said. "Men get crocodile, good eating," and proceeded on his way without concerning himself further in the matter.

In the evening Frank found that the croc had been fished out of the water, and that its steaks were indeed, very tasty. "I told you," Frederick managed between bites, "that some bush-meat is very good. I've no doubt before we're through you'll have acquired a taste for snake. Some varieties are better flavored than chicken. Better to eat your crocodile than to be eaten by it." He gave a hoarse bark of a laugh somewhat at variance with his more normally taciturn appearance.

Frank joined in. What had been a terrifying experience suddenly seemed funny now he was safe. His companion gave a harumph, and turned serious again.

"Still, Frank, it's been a good lesson on keeping your eyes to the watch at all times. Crocodiles frequently carry off the native women when they're washing, and almost invariably the beasts sweep them into the river with a blow of their tails. Once in the water the hapless victim is carried off, drowned, and eaten at leisure."

Frank couldn't repress a shudder at the memory of his own close shave. "If a crocodile attacks, what's the best thing to do? I don't mean to be caught napping again, but still I'd like to know what to do if I am."

"Men have been known to get away by driving their thumbs or fingers into the creature's eyes. If it can be done the crocodile will let go, but it demands speed, accuracy, great presence of mind, and guts. When a reptile's tearing at your leg, dragging you under water, you can see that the nerve required to keep perfectly cool, to feel for its eyes, and thrust your fingers into them is very great. The best plan, Frank, distinctly, is to keep out of their reach altogether."

After remaining two weeks at their camp they prepared for a move. Another hippopotamus was killed, cut up and dried, and the flesh added to the porters' burdens. The six Hausas struck the tent rapidly and the expedition proceeded farther into the mountains. Two days later they stopped again, choosing a site beside a little mountain rivulet.

Above the camp the hills marched away in chains to the north of the Komo and Gabon, parallel with the Gulf of Guinea to their west. Here, at this elevation, Goodenough hoped entire new species of butterflies and insects would be discovered and collected. They had scarcely pitched camp when Frank looked up with a puzzled frown and said, a touch accusingly, "You said that African dogs don't bark, Frederick, and yet that's definitely barking I can hear in the distance."

"They may yelp and howl, but they never bark like European dogs. I think that's the bark of some sort of large monkey or baboon."

Ostik soon established from the Fang that this assumption was correct. Goodenough rubbed his hands together. "We'll mount a raid against them immediately."

"I don't like the thought of shooting monkeys," Frank muttered, as he took up his Winchester repeater.

"They're also very good to eat," his companion continued, "better in my opinion to any other meat—and in that many explorers agree. We won't find many other kinds of animal fit for food up here. But baboons are mischievous and vicious creatures, so we'd better take four of the Hausas with us."

Following the direction of the whoops and barks, the hunters cautiously rounded a bluff that had hidden a troupe of great baboons. It was a curious sight. The males, as big as large dogs, were sitting sunning themselves on rocks, others were being scratched by the females. Many of these had babies clinging to their necks, while others were playing about in all directions.

There was something very domestic and familiar about the animals' antics that pricked Frank's teenage conscience. "I'd rather not shoot at them, Frederick."

The naturalist gave his apprentice a look that mixed fondness, amusement, exasperation, and perhaps even a touch of contempt. "You'll be glad enough to eat them," he answered and, selecting a big male, he shot it. The baboon fell dead. Instantly the loud chattering ceased. The others all sprang to their feet. The females and little ones scampered off. The males, with angry gestures, rushed at their assailants, barking, showing their teeth and making menacing gestures.

Goodenough fired again, and Frank, seeing that they were likely to be attacked, also opened fire. Six of the baboons were killed before the rest broke off the attack and went screaming after the females. The dead baboons were brought back to camp, skinned, jointed, and two were put to roast over the fire, while the Fang hung the rest from tree branches. It required a great effort on Frank's part to overcome his repugnance to eating baboon flesh, but when he did so he had to admit to its tenderness and excellent taste.

That night they were disturbed by a cry of terror from the Fang carriers. Seizing their rifles they ran out from the tent.

"There are two leopards, sar," Ostik said, "they have smelt the monkeys."

Shouts scared the cats away, but the natives kept up a large blaze until morning light.

"We must get the skins if we can, Frederick." After a pause, he added cheekily, "I take it leopards aren't good eating?"

"You're right—on both counts. The skins of the equatorial leopard are rare. If we can get them both they'll make a fine group for you to stuff when we get back."

"Are we going to follow their trail?" Frank asked.

"We're not trained hunters," Goodenough answered. "In soft swampy terrain we might track them, but up here on more open and drier rocky ground it'll be difficult. We'll be better off setting a bait and luring them to us."

Terrified that the leopards would not have gone far from the camp, the Fang refused to venture out and two Hausas went with each of the naturalists as they searched for butterflies. Their vigilance proved unnecessary as nothing was seen or heard from the leopards during the day. At nightfall Goodenough had Ostik suspend a haunch of baboon meat from a tree branch, so as to swing within four feet of the ground at a hundred yards outside the camp. The hunters took their seats in another tree a short distance off.

Unlike recent nights, which had been cloudy, the stars shone clear and bright, and provided just enough light to illuminate the bait. Instead of his little Winchester, Frank had one of the Sniders with explosive shells. The Hausas were told to keep a sharp watch in camp, in case the big cats, approaching from the other side, might be attracted by the smell of meat there, rather than by the bait. The Fang needed no telling to keep up a good fire all night.

Soon after dark the watchers heard the leopards' coughing barks—from the other side of the camp.

"Damn," Goodenough said. "We've pitched on the wrong side. However, they'll probably be deterred by the fire from trying to cross the camp, and will circle around. We should hear them before long."

In answer to the roars of the leopards the natives kept up a continued shouting. For some hours the roaring continued at intervals, sometimes nearby, sometimes at a distance. Frank had difficulty in keeping awake and was beginning to wish that the cats would move off altogether. Two or three times he nearly dozed off, and his rifle almost slipped from his nerveless grip.

All at once he was aroused by a sharp nudge from his companion. Fixing his eyes on the bait he made out something immediately below it. Directly afterward another feline form stole forward. They were far less distinct than he had expected.

"Take the one on the left," Goodenough whispered.

They fired so much in tandem that only one great shot thundered out. One leopard immediately bounded away into the dark. The other rolled over and over, and then, recovering its feet, darted off after its companion, apparently unwounded. Frank fired his second barrel.

"I'm afraid you missed altogether, Frank."

"I don't think so, Frederick. I'm sure I saw the flash of the shell as it struck him, but where, I haven't a clue. I couldn't make it out clear enough, just a dim shape, and I fired as well as I could at the middle. Back to camp now?"

"Yes. They won't return now," Goodenough replied. "You can tell by the noise they're making that they're already some distance away. In the morning we'll just have to try tracking them."

The rest of the night passed quietly, although throaty bellows and howling could be heard from time to time in the distance. Early in the morning they left camp with all the Hausas.

"We must be careful today," Goodenough said, "a wounded leopard is a really formidable beast."

There was no difficulty in picking up the traces. "One of them at least must be hard hit," Goodenough remarked. "See the traces of blood every yard."

They had only traversed a short distance of the rocky savannah when one of the Ugly Tom gave a sudden grunt, and pointed to something lying at the edge of a clump of bushes.

"Careful now, Frank, be ready to fire instantly."

The cautious group edged forward slowly. Frank observed no movement in the spotted tawny skin and closer inspection revealed that the leopard was quite dead, of two bullet wounds. The first had struck his shoulder, the other had entered near the tail and burst inside. Seeing the damage, Frank, was astonished at the tenacity of life shown by the animal. "I wonder whether I hit the other?"

"I've no doubt you did, although I didn't think so before. I thought I only heard the howls of one animal in the night, and assumed it was the one I'd hit. But as this one must have died pretty quickly, it's clear that the ruckus was made by the other."

They began to scout around for the other leopard's tracks. Firewater and Bacon in tandem soon found traces of blood not far from the tree, running off in a line diverging from the tracks of the dead animal. For an hour they followed the spoor, sometimes losing sight of it for a while, but then picking it up again. At last they seemed to lose it altogether.

Goodenough and Frank stood together, while the Hausas split up and started scratching around for a sign. Suddenly there was a sharp rasping cough, and from the bough of a tree close by a great body sprang through the air and landed within a yard of Frank. In his surprise, he jumped back, stumbled and fell, but in an instant the report of a shotgun rang out. In a trice Frank was on his feet again, ready to fire, but Goodenough's shot had killed the second leopard.

"You've had another narrow escape," the naturalist said as he bent over the spotted corpse. "I see that your bullet last night broke one of its hind legs. That spoiled its leap, otherwise it would have reached you, and," he cheerfully added, "a blow with its paw, given the weight and impetus, would probably have killed you on the spot."

Frank lowered his barrel with a visible shudder at his near escape. Africa was proving every bit as exciting as he'd hoped… he thought.

Goodenough turned and began to examine the tree branch from which the leopard had launched itself. "Hmm, this bough is only about four feet from the ground, so that even with a broken leg it was able to climb up without difficulty." He glanced back over his shoulder. "Well, thank God, you've not been hurt, my boy. It will teach us both to be more careful in future."

Frank nodded and smiled bravely for the Hausas.

That afternoon Frank went down with a second attack of fever, a much more severe one than the first had been. Mr. Goodenough's favorite remedy had the effect of inducing a high sweat, but two or three hours afterward the hot fit again came on, and for the next four days Frank lay half-delirious, one minute consumed with heat, the next shivering as if plunged into ice water.

Copious doses of quinine gradually overcame the fire, and on the fifth day he was much improved. It was, nevertheless, another week before Frank felt up to the rigors of traveling and was sufficiently recovered to be able to resume his collecting expeditions. For three weeks they made short stages, traversing a variety of terrain: open savannah, light bush, and sometimes thick tropical jungle. Goodenough allowed half a day at each campsite to collect birds, butterflies, and many other fascinatingly strange insects.

On one of these occasions Frank was out with the Hausa Moses in fairly dense jungle when he caught a glimpse of a butterfly of a kind he had never seen before. It flitted gaily across a gleam of sunshine which streamed in through a rift in the overhead canopy.

"Take my blowpipe and wait here with the guns while I chase it," he told Moses, taking the butterfly net from him. The insect fluttered away with Frank in full pursuit. It seemed to take an impish delight in tantalizing its hunter, dancing here and there, settling on a spot where a gleam of sunlight caught the tree bark, until Frank had stolen up to within a couple of paces, and then darting away again at a pace which defied his best attempts to keep up with it until it chose to play with him again. Intent only on his chase, Frank thought of nothing else.

At last, with a shout of triumph, he enclosed the creature in his net, shook it into the wide pickle bottle containing a sponge soaked with chloroform, and then, after tightly fitting in the stopper, he looked around... and uttered an exclamation of dismay. The angle of the bands of light coming through the trees told him the sun was about to set. He knew that he must have been chasing his quarry for at least an hour and now he had no idea of which way he'd come. He had, he knew, run uphill and down, but in circles or a straight line? He might be within a hundred yards of the spot where he'd left Moses. He might be three or four miles away.

Frank drew his revolver, always strapped to his belt, and fired the six chambers, waiting for half a minute between each shot, listening intently for an answering signal. None came. Beyond the sibilant mantra of innumerable insects the stillness of the jungle was unbroken. *Oh God, I've obviously wandered far from my starting place and now I'm utterly lost.* He curbed the panic which wanted him to run off in any direction. Besides, the short tropical twilight would overtake him within minutes. He decided it would be safest to pass the night tucked into the crook of a tree, well above the ground.

The stray knew an active search would be made for him in the morning and that, as every step he took was as likely to lead him away as toward the camp, it was better to stay where he was. He soon found a tree with a branch which suited his purpose and, climbing up into it, prepared for a disagreeable night. *While it might sound adventurous to be perched in a large tree*, Frank thought ruefully, *no one ever told you that in Africa the bark is alive with large and very busily nipping ants.*

Time passed slowly. The jungle amplified a constant discord of grunts, howls, barks, and shrieks, and although Frank didn't expect to be attacked, the incessant noise made sleep impossible. Uncomfortably reminded of the leopard, he had reloaded his revolver, which made him feel more confident that if anything tried climbing his tree, it would not get him. Besides, Frederick had told him that leopards seldom attack men unless themselves threatened.

Bullets, however, were no answer to the damned ants, but then again, sleep was out of the question anyway. His position was not so secure that he would not fall out of the tree if he did nod off. He did doze, now and again, always waking up with a jolt and a feeling that he'd just saved himself from dropping off his perch.

As soon as the dawn light enabled him to see his surroundings Frank climbed down, stiff, weary, and pin-pricked red all over from the ant and other insect bites. "Well Hargate," he said aloud to the jungle as he relieved himself against the base of the tree, "this is a fine pickle you've got yourself into. This is the second time a butterfly's got me into deep hippypotybus pooh. Now, which way?"

He knew his position lay to the south of the last camp, and that by keeping the sun on his right until it neared midday he must eventually hit the little stream on which it was pitched. As he walked he listened intently for the sound of guns. Once or twice he fancied he heard firing, but his judgment of the direction was quite uncertain. He had been out with Moses about six hours before he strayed off in the pursuit of the pesky butterfly, and they had been walking toward the camp for some time, in order to reach it by nightfall. So he thought that at that time they would only have been some three or four miles distant from it. Supposing that he had run due south, that would put him about eight miles from the creek, or about three hours' walking.

Unfortunately, his reasoning proved faulty. In fact, after leaving Moses the lepidopterous insect (he didn't feel kindly enough toward it to grace it with the name butterfly) had led him in a southeasterly direction and, as the stream—one of the Gabon-Komo's upper tributaries—took a sharp bend to the north a little distance above the camp, he was many miles farther from it than he thought.

After walking for two hours the character of the landscape changed. The high trees grew farther apart, and a thick undergrowth began to make its appearance, frequently causing him to make long detours and preventing his following the line he had marked out for himself.

This made him uneasy, because he knew that he had passed through no such country on his way from the camp. Frank began to face the unpalatable thought that he now had no way of finding the camp. The extent of his danger began to press in on him.

Chapter 11: Tribal Trickery

Gabon, Late June–July 1872

The outlook was cheerless. Frank's progress was now very slow. Dense bush, thorny plants, and innumerable creepers continually barred his way, and the necessity for constantly looking up through the trees to catch a glimpse of the sun made his neck and head ache.

Checking his watch, which he had remembered to wind on descending from his tree, he saw it was almost eleven o'clock. He came to a standstill. The sun, too high overhead, no longer acted as a reliable guide. He had been walking for nearly six hours and felt utterly worn out and hungry, not having eaten since midday the day before. Worse still, his thirst, barely slaked by rinsing his mouth in the foul black water of the swamps he had crossed, drove thought from his brain, and his swollen tongue made breathing difficult. His sleepless night, too, had told. He was bathed in perspiration, and for the last hour had scarcely been able to drag one foot in front of the other.

He now lay down between the Gothic-like buttresses of a great ebony tree, and for three or four hours slept heavily. An afternoon tropical downpour woke him. Eagerly, he turned his head up to let the fat drops fill his mouth. As suddenly as it would have begun, the rain stopped and the canopy lightened as clouds fled. Somewhat refreshed, Frank went on his way, the sun serving as a guide again. In two hours' time he had reached higher ground. The brushwood was less compacted, and he again turned his face to the north, and stepped forward with renewed hope.

It was late in the afternoon when he came across a native path. Frank had observed that the Africans tended to walk in single file on major pathways, eventually wearing them well down below the natural ground level. Seeing this one made him think, and he sat down on its sharp edge, his feet barely touching the bottom of the foot-worn gully. He had no recollection of seeing a path on the day before. Perhaps it crossed the tributary river at some point above the encampment, so it would serve as a guide. Clearly, well-used paths joined up places, so he might come on some native village where he could get food and water. By following it far enough he must arrive somewhere. After a fifteen-minute rest he started off in a northwesterly direction.

After about an hour he was arrested by a sudden outcry ahead. He peered ahead to see a troupe of baboons scampering along the path in his direction. Frank at once jumped up into the bush to avoid them—he had no wish to test their ferocity again on his own with nothing but a revolver. They were of a very large species, and several of the females had infants clinging around their necks. In the distance Frank could hear the shouts of some natives, and supposed that the monkeys had been plundering their plantations, and that they were driving them off. The baboons passed without paying any attention to him, but Frank observed that the last was carrying a little one rather oddly in one of its forearms.

Frank glanced at the baby monkey and saw a string of blue beads around its waist, and then the penny dropped. Most of the children of the local tribes wore nothing more than a single strand of beads until they reached the age of ten. The baboons were kidnapping a native child, which had probably been put down by its mother while she worked in the plantation. Without a moment's thought, Frank leaped down from his hiding place, drew his Beaumont-Adams and fired a single shot at the retreating ape. It gave a cry, dropped the baby, and turned to attack its aggressor.

Frank waited until it was within six feet, and then shot it through the head, showing no further reluctance to firing at monkeys. He sprang forward and seized the baby, but in a moment he was attacked by the whole party of baboons, who, barking like dogs, and uttering angry barks, turned and charged him. Without any hesitation, Frank tossed the child up over the path's lip where it dropped into a thick clump of bushes and then turned to stand his ground. He gave the apes the four remaining chambers and dropped two, but then the rest, hurtling pounds of furious brown fur and slavering lips revealing frighteningly sharp teeth, were on him. He struck out with the butt end of his pistol, but in seconds their combined weight bore him to the ground.

One baboon seized him by the leg with its teeth, while another bit his arm. Others struck and scratched at him. He tried defending his face with his arms, kicking and struggling to the best of his power. With one hand he drew the long skinning knife, which he wore at his belt, and struck out fiercely, but a baboon seized his wrist in its teeth, and Frank felt that it was all over, when suddenly his attackers left him, and the instant afterward he was lifted to his feet by some men.

His first thought was for the screaming infant, but a woman had already picked it up, and was crying and fondling it. At that point, his vision narrowed to a tunnel and then blinked out.

He came to staring up at the underside of a palm-thatched roof. He was naked and lying on his back, on a bamboo palette, covered from the waist down by a colorfully woven blanket. His wounds had been dressed with poultices formed of bruised leaves of some plant, and he felt comfortable.

He turned his head to the side and saw a woman with a child in her lap. Frank recognized her as the one who had picked up the baby. She sat on a low stool by his side. On seeing his eyes open she took his hand and put it to her lips, and then raised the baby triumphantly and turned it around to show that it had escaped without hurt. Frank pointed to his lips and she brought a cut pineapple to quench his parched throat.

Frank then tried explaining that there was another white man in the jungle, but she shook her head and went to fetch the headman and two others. When they were gathered Frank held up two fingers. Then he pointed to himself and shut down one finger, keeping the other erect, and then pointed all around to signify that he had a friend somewhere in the wood. A grin of comprehension stole over the face of the older man, and Frank saw that he was understood.

That afternoon fever set in, and for the two next days Frank tossed and turned in the storms of delirium. He kept seeing Frederick's face as if at a distance, but the image always retreated when he reached for it. When he recovered consciousness he found that the explorer really was kneeling beside him.

"Don't try to talk, Frank lad. Here, drink this down. The quinine will soon kick in."

"What… what about the expedition log?"

Goodenough inclined his head and smiled. "Don't worry. I've recorded the main events and soon you'll take it up again. Now, rest."

Comforted by the familiar grey eyes gazing calmly at him, Frank fell into a deep slumber and it was not until the following day that he learned what had happened in his absence. Moses had not returned until long after nightfall. He reported that Frank had told him to stay with the guns, and that he had waited until it grew nearly dark. Then he had fired several times and had walked about, firing his gun at intervals. Hearing no answering shot he had made his way back to the camp, where his arrival alone caused great anxiety.

For the next two days the Hausas and half the Fang went out to search for Frank, but with no success. They had returned to the camp disheartened and worn out, amid fears that a leopard had killed him or left him for dead, in which case, ants would have done the rest. On the third day all of the carriers were sent out with instructions to search for native paths, then to follow them to villages. One of the Fang had met a villager who in turn was seeking a party with a white man.

* * *

In another three weeks they descended the hills, and then there was trouble with the Fang, who suddenly decided to go no further. Goodenough faced them down calmly. "You promised to go on until I can hire other carriers," he told them quietly through Ostik. "If you desert me now you will be paid nothing. We should expect to meet people of another tribe any day now, and as soon as we do you will be allowed to depart... with your pay."

Despite the controlled voice, Goodenough's stance was imposingly aggressive, and seeing that he was firm, and having no desire to forfeit the wages they had earned, the Fang reluctantly agreed to go on.

The very day after this little mutiny, Frank pointed out smoke curling up from the forest. Ostik and two of the Fang, each of whom could speak several native dialects, were sent forward to announce the expedition's arrival. They returned in an hour saying that the village was of considerable size, and that the news of the coming of two white men had created great excitement. The people spoke of immediately sending a messenger to their king, whom they called Malembe, whose palace, it seemed, was a day's march off.

They entered the village in some ceremony. Ostik led the way with great dignity, followed by two of the Hausas. Goodenough and Frank came next, their guns carried by two Fang striding behind them. Then tramped the long line of bearers, two of the Hausas walking on either side as a guard. Villagers packed both sides of the main way to the center, where the village headman sat outside a large hut wreathed in vines covered in luminous scented flowers.

"Best keep our wits about us, Frank. Have you seen, there are no women or children visible. In spite of the lovely blooms, my nose tells me that this place smells bad."

"Perhaps they're afraid of our Fang."

"If you're right, we must reassure them quickly."

A long palaver then took place, made tedious by the need for Ostik to translate English for a Fang, who in turn spoke to the chief in his own dialect and vice versa.

Goodenough gave the chief the usual spiel: white men, friends of his people, come see country; give chiefs presents; wish pass quietly and unmolested; will pay well for chop-chop and other food stores; wish hire bearers who will receive pay in cloth and brass rods; etc.

The chief looked frowningly at the Fang bearers, and Goodenough assured the man that they would be returning to their own country as soon as he had his replacements. Suddenly, the headman gave them a beaming smile and answered, expressing his pleasure at seeing white men in his village, saying that, when he heard, the king would no doubt carry out all their wishes. One of the boxes was opened and Goodenough presented five yards of brightly colored calico, a gaudy silk handkerchief, and several strings of bright beads.

"No like dat black bastard," Ostik said. "Tink we hab big trouble. All women and children gone. Dat bad."

That day and the next passed quietly. As usual, the baggage had been piled in a circle in an open space outside the village, with the tent pitched in the middle. Ostik warned the white men to sleep there instead of in the settlement. In that time no women or children turned up. Toward evening a great drumming rumbled up into the heavy air at a distance.

"Here's his majesty at last," Goodenough sighed. "We'll soon see what his mood is like."

Shortly the village filled with a crowd of men all carrying spears and bows. The drumming grew louder and nearer, and then, carried in a chair on the shoulders of four powerfully muscled, glistening black slaves, guarded by ten warriors armed with ancient muskets, King Malembe made his regal appearance. Even seated on his sedan, it was possible to see that he was a tall man. The bearers lowered the king's chair under the shade of a tree, and two attendants with palm leaf fans at once began to cool his majesty's brow. His expression was clouded and savage.

Ostik and the Fang translator stepped forward with the English naturalists. Ostik gave the same speech he had given the village chief.

As the Fang translated, the king became increasingly ill-tempered. "Why do the white men bring enemies into our lands?" he shouted.

"We have come up from the coast," Goodenough said, "and as we passed through the Fang country we hired men there to carry our goods, just as we wish to hire men here to go on into the country beyond. There were none of the king's men in that country or we would have hired them."

"Let me see the white men's presents," the king snapped, flicking his fingers imperiously at a retainer.

A box was opened, a bright scarlet shirt and a handsome cap of the same hue, worked with beads, a blue silk handkerchief, and twenty yards of bright calico were taken out. To these were added twelve stair rods, five pounds of powder, and two pounds of shot.

Malembe's eyes sparkled greedily as he looked at the treasures.

"The white men must be very rich," he said, pointing to the piled up baggage behind them.

"Most of the boxes are empty," Goodenough said. "We have brought them to take home the things of the country and show them to the white men beyond the sea." To prove the truth of his words, a Fang opened up two of the empty cases and one already half filled with trays of butterflies and beetles.

The king looked at them with surprise. "You eat these?" he queried.

"No, no, we collect them."

After listening to the translation, he raised his eyebrows in confusion, then shrugged his ample shoulders.

"And the others?" he asked, pointing to them.

"The others contain—some of them—food such as white men are accustomed to eat in their own country, the others, presents for the other kings and chiefs I shall meet when we have passed on.

"The fellow is not satisfied," he said to Ostik, "give him two of the trade guns and a bottle of brandy."

Malembe appeared pleased by these additions and, saying that he would talk to the white men in the morning, he retired into the village.

"I don't like the way he looked at our other boxes," Frank muttered.

Goodenough nodded. "I think that the presents we've given him have only made him greedy for everything. However, we'll see in the morning."

When night fell, Bacon and Firewater were placed on sentry duty. The Fang slept inside the baggage circle. Several times in the night the Hausas challenged anyone they heard approaching, but these ran off immediately.

In the morning a messenger presented himself from the king, saying that he required many more presents, that the things which had been given were only fit for the chief of a village, and not for a great king.

Goodenough placed his arms firmly at his sides, then raised his right arm and pointed at the trembling messenger. "I have given the best I have," he said, as Ostik and his Fang translator repeated the words. "The dash was fit for the greatest king, and you can tell Malembe that he can have no more."

Frank frowned deeply. "If we're going to have trouble it's far better to have it now while we've still got the Fang than alone with no one but the Hausas. I'll bet we can hold this encampment against any number of savages."

"I fear we shall see the truth or not of that soon enough." The naturalist smiled grimly, and then took Ostik with him to explain the impending situation to the Fang.

A quarter of an hour later the drums began beating furiously again, including the unmistakable deep bass of war drums. A loud clamor began in the village, and the warriors could be seen moving excitedly about. Then they all vanished.

"Now fight," Ostik said quietly.

"You'd better take down the tent, Ostik. It will only get in our way."

The Mpongwe speedily lowered and stowed the canvas. The Fang grasped their spears and lay down behind the circle of boxes and bales. The six Hausas, the two white men, and Ostik, who had been given a trade musket, took their places at regular intervals around the circle, which was some twenty feet in diameter. After a short pause the beat of the drums again broke the silence, and a shower of arrows, coming apparently from all points of the compass, fell in and around the circle.

"Open fire steadily but slowly as though we only had muzzle loading muskets," Goodenough ordered. "We must tempt them to show themselves."

The lackluster answering fire worked, and a few minutes later the king's bodyguard opened up with old muskets. While the bowmen in the vegetation remained largely invisible to the besieged, the puffs of smoke from the muskets revealed the positions of those firing them.

"Fast fire, Frank!"

The Sniders began their rapid barking as Frank and Goodenough replied so accurately that in a very short time the enemy's musketry ceased altogether. The rain of arrows continued, the yells of the natives rose louder and louder, and the drums beat more furiously.

Soon the sound of a war horn blared out, and from the trees all around them a crowd of dark figures dashed forward, uttering appalling yells. On the instant the Hausas switched to rapid fire, peppering the natives with an almost continuous fusillade.

Yells of astonishment mingled with groans of the dying broke from Malembe's warriors, and a minute later, leaving nearly a score of their comrades on the ground, the rest ran back into the jungle undergrowth.

There was silence for a time and then the war drums started up again.

"They try again hard dis time, massa," Ostik said. "King tell 'em he cut off deir balls den deir heads dey not win dis battle."

This time the natives charged forward with reckless bravery, in spite of the holes made among them by the rapid fire of the defenders, and rushed up to the circle of boxes. Then the Fang leaped to their feet and, spears in hand, jumped over the defenses and fell on the king's warriors.

The counter-attack was decisive. In the face of the feared cannibals, uttering cries of terror, the natives fled, and two minutes later not a sound was to be heard. The forest was silent for long moments before the wildlife resumed its chorus.

"I tink dey run away for good, sar," Ostik said. "They have nuf of him."

Nearly fifty of the warriors had fallen between the trees and the encampment. When an hour passed it became nearly certain that the enemy had retreated. The Hausas stripped off their finery before crawling into the bush to reconnoiter. They returned in half an hour in high glee, bearing the king's sedan and all the presents that had been given to him.

"Dey all run away, sar," Moses shouted across the clearing. "Ebery one, de king an' all, and leab his chair behind. Dat great disgrace for him."

The Fang were so delighted with the victory they had won that they expressed their readiness to remain with their white companions as long as they chose, given a guarantee that they would be sent home at the end of their service. Goodenough readily promised this, and then the explorers turned to the question of what next.

"After this last encounter I don't think it would be prudent to continue pushing further into the interior of Central Africa," Goodenough suggested.

Frank's cheeks were still flushed with exaltation at the battle's outcome. "It does provide a lot of excitement, Frederick, but on the other hand fighting interferes with our collecting. Will it get worse farther in, do you think?"

"I think it will. There'll be continual battles to fight and large numbers of natives killed because of the greed of their chiefs. I think we should cut to the north now and then turn west with the sweep of the coast and keep at about the same distance as we are now from the sea. Then in Ashanti we can turn south and head for Cape Coast or Elmina. The trip will take a considerable time, crossing almost unexplored territory, but we'll be able to send our specimens down to the coast by one or other of the rivers cutting across our path."

"Then what are we waiting for?" Frank clapped his hands together enthusiastically and laughed with the sheer animal joy of being alive and in Africa.

Two days later it was Frederick Goodenough's turn to take to his bed prostrated by fever, and for several days he lay between life and death. When he became convalescent he recovered strength very slowly. Frank penned his concerns.

The heat is prodigious and the mosquitoes render sleep almost impossible at night. The country is low and swampy, but weak as he is, Frederick is determined to push on. It is clear to me that in his current state he cannot walk.

For the first time, they unpacked a hammock. This was slung from a long bamboo pole and overhead a thick awning kept the sun off the passenger. Across the ends of the pole, boards some three feet long were fastened. Four of the Fang wrapped lengths of cloth into fat cushions, placed these on their heads, and then took their places, two at each end of the pole, with the ends of the boards on their heads. In this fashion, they could trot along at the rate of six miles an hour for great distances, often keeping up a monotonous song. Their action was perfectly smooth and easy, and soon the patient, with his eyes closed, likened the motion to swinging in a cot on board a ship on a quiet sea.

After two days journeying they reached higher ground, and away from the unhealthy swamps camped for some time. As Goodenough slowly recovered Frank busied himself in adding to their collections. With nothing else to do, the Fang assisted him in the work. The men entered into the spirit of specimen hunting with enthusiasm, accepting that their paymasters were clearly mad. Frank fashioned several nets from the expedition's supply of muslin, in which the Fang captured large quantities of butterflies. His principal problem was to convince them that only a few of each species were required. The Fang were more valuable in grubbing about in the decaying trunks of fallen trees, under loose bark, and in broken ground, for beetles and larvae. The task suited them better than running about after butterflies, which they often spoiled by their rough handling. Frank was thereby able to devote himself entirely to the pursuit of birds, and although all the varieties more usually encountered had already been obtained, the collection steadily increased in size.

Frank didn't escape severe bouts of fever either, but none as bad as the one he suffered on the day of the leopards' deaths. At the end of a month Frederick Goodenough had recovered his strength, and they again moved forward.

Chapter 12: Stolen and Sold

Cameroon, July 1872

For the next three weeks the expedition trekked through the mountains of the Cameroon, but continual downpours of rain rendered specimen collecting impossible. *It is the middle of the West African rainy season and sometimes it comes down in torrents for hours on end,* Frank recorded. *The thick canopy of trees protect us to some degree, but after a week everyone is drenched through and thoroughly miserable.*

So it was to everyone's huge relief when they descended in improving weather to the lower and less hilly country to the east of the great Niger river, and some hundred miles due north of Bonny. *A pleasant region of open grassland broken frequently by thickets of trees*, Frank noted. One day they arrived at a large village which struck them for its far greater appearance of neatness than any they had so far seen. The plantation plots were neatly fenced, the street clean and tidy. As they entered the cluster of neat huts village elders came out to meet them, headed by a white-haired man.

"Me berry glad to see you, white men," he greeted them. "Long time since I see white men."

"And it's a long time," said Frederick Goodenough, shaking hands with him, "since I've heard the sound of my own tongue outside my party."

"I, Samuel, am chief of dis village. Make you berry comfortable, sah. Great honor for dis village dat you come here. Plenty eberyting for you, fowl, and eggs, and plantain, and sometime a sheep."

"We've fallen into the lap of luxury," Goodenough said to Frank and they followed the chief to his hut. "I suppose the old man has been employed in one of the factories on the coast."

The interior was comfortably furnished and clean. A low divan covered with neatly woven mats extended around three sides. In the middle sat a very reasonable attempt at a table. A double-bore gun and a rifle were suspended over the hearth. A small looking glass and several colored prints in cheap frames hung on the walls. A large wooden chest, with what looked like a book resting on it, stood at one end of the room, while on a shelf above it were a number of plates and dishes of apparently English manufacture.

"You forgive, sah, my English is rusty. No need for it here," he said, indicating that they should be seated. A girl came in, bringing in a large calabash full of water and two cloths for them to wash their hands and faces. In the meantime the old chief went to his chest and, to the immense surprise of the travelers, brought out a starched white cloth which he laid on the table, and then placed knives, forks, and plates on it.

"You must scuse deficiencies, sah," he said. "We berry long way from coast, and these stupid Africans dey break things most ebery day."

"Deficiencies, Mr. Samuel?" Goodenough answered graciously. "All this is most unusual."

The man smiled, his luxuriant silvery eyebrows and close cropped snowy hair in strong contrast to his black skin. "You berry good to say dat, sah, but this chile know how things ought to be done. I libed—lived—in good American family. I know very well how tings ought to be done. An' it's fine to speak English again… it is practice makes perfect, no?"

"Did you say America?" Frank queried.

"Yes, sah, I travel great deal. Live in Cuba long time. Then the Confederate slave states, then Northern state, also Canada under Queen Victoria. I travel bery much."

The dinner consisted of two chickens cut in half and grilled over a fire, fried plantains, and, to their delighted surprise, green peas, followed by cold boiled rice over which honey had been poured.

This was finished, again to general astonishment, by small cups of excellent black coffee.

Once they had satisfied their host's curiosity about their reasons for being there, Sam—as he called himself—obliged by telling his own story. Frank was soon charmed by the lilting voice and by the way the story-teller's English rapidly improved as he told the tale.

I was born in this village somewhere 'bout sebenty years ago. I not know for sure within two or three year, for when I young man I no keep account. My father was the chief, just as I am now, but the village was not like dis. It was not so big, bery dirty and bery poor, just like the other African villages. Those were bery bad times. Everyone fight against eberyone else. Ebery... everyone take slaves and send 'em downriver, and sell to white men there to carry over sea.

When Sam grow up to seventeen, I s'pose, he take spear and go out with the people of this village and the other places of this part of country under king, and fight against other villages and carry the people away as slaves. But Sam, he tink nothing, and just do the same as other people. Sometimes other tribes come and fight against us and carry our people away. So it happens to Sam. Jus' when he about twenty years old we come back from a long 'spedition. This village got its share of slaves, and we drink and sing and make merry wid the palm tree wine and tink ourselves very grand fellows. Well, sah, that night great hullabaloo in the village. The damn dogs bark, the men shout and seize their arms and run out to fight, but is no good. Another tribe fall on us ten times as many as we. We fight hard but no use. All the ole men and women and the little babies that no good to sell they kill, and the rest of us, men, women, and the boys and girls, we are tied together and marched away wid the people that had taken us.

Very bad time that, sah. The dry season and no water. We make long march every day, and get very little food. They beat us wid sticks and prod us wid spear to make us go. A good many of the weak ones they die, but the most of us arrive at the river mouth—don't know which one—but we are nearly two months in getting there. By this time Sam arrive at the strong conclusion that the burning of villages and carrying off of slaves very bad affair altogether. Sam has changed his mind about a great many things, but about dat he's fixed right up to this time.

Well, at the mouth of that river Sam sees the white man for the first time, and me tell you fair, sah, Sam no like him no way. They are Spanish men, and the way they treat us poor slaves is something awful. We huddle up night and day in a big shed they call a barracoon. They give us very little food, very small water. They beat us if we grumble. These men belong to ships, and have bought us from those who take us down from up country. They waitin' for their ship to come, and for a long time we wait in the barracoon, wishing to die. At last the ship comes, and we are dragged on board to huddle down below. Law, what a place it is to be sure! Not more than three feet high, just enough to sit up, and there we're chained to the deck. The heat, sah, is something terrible. Some of us yell out and scream for air, but they only come down and beat us wid whips.

The day after, the ship sets sail. Three hours after there's a great running about on deck, and a shouting by the white men. Then we hear big gun crash overhead that make us jump out of the skin with the noise. Then more guns. Then there is a huge bang, and before we knew what is the matter there is a big hole in the side, and six slaves are killed dead. Everyone shout very loud. We think for sure that the last day has come. For a long time the guns keep firing, and then everything goes quiet again. No one knows the meaning of all this—now I know it was probably an English cruiser chasing us and that the slaver got away.

Awful voyage, sah. At first the ship is smooth and goes along straight. Then she start to toss about jus' as villager does when he's taken too much palm wine, and we all feel very bad. Everyone groaning and crying and thinking that they been poisoned. For three days it is a terrible time. The hatches are shut fast and no air comes to us, and there we are all alone in the dark, and no one knows why the great house on the water roll and tumble so much. We cry and shout till all breath gone, and then lie quiet and moan, till jus' when everyone think he's dead, they take off the hatch and come down and undo the locks and tell us to go up on deck. That very easy to say, not at all easy to do. Most of us are too weak to walk, and say that we dead and cannot move with the heavy chains 'round our ankles. Then they whip all about, and it is astonishing, sah, to see what life that lash put into dead men!

Somehow people feel that they can crawl after all, and when we get up on deck and see the blessed sun again and the blue sky everyone feels better. But not all. In spite of the whip many have to be carried up, and there the sailors lay 'em down and throw cold water over them till they opens their eyes and come to life. Some never come to life. About six hundred when we start, of these pretty near a hundred are dead already.

After that things improve. The weather stays fine and as there are no more English ships, we are allowed on deck for a quarter day each morning. We are given more food too to fatten us up. We talk this over among ourselves and s'pose they are going to eat us when we get to land again. Some refuse to eat, but that gets them the lash, and they conclude that if they must be eaten, they might as well be eaten fat as lean.

At last we come in sight of land and we are all sent below to stay there till night. Then we are brought on deck, and find the vessel lying in a little creek. We all taken in boats, land, and march up country all night. In the morning we halt. Four white men come on horses and look at us. They separate us into bunches, and each march away into country again. Then we separate again, till at last me and twenty others arrive at a plantation up in the hills—I learn later is near Santiago de Cuba. Here we range along in line before a white man. He speaks in very fierce tones, and a black man like us by his side tell us that this man is our massa, that he say if we work well he give us plenty food and treat us fine, but that if we not work with all our might he whip us to death. After this it is clear that the best thing to do is work hard.

Sam is young and strong, sah, and soon he get the name of a willing hard working nigger—that's what the white men and the black overseers call us Africans. The boss-massa he keep his word. Those who work well are treated well, plenty of food and a piece of ground to plant vegetables and to raise fowls for ourselves. So we pass two or three year, plenty hard work, but not much to grumble at.

Then me and a gal of my own village, who had been bought in the same batch with me, ask the boss if we can marry, and he says, "You is a fine strong nigger and work well, so go ahead." He gives the gal four yards of bright cotton for a wedding dress, and a bottle of rum to me, and in a week we's man'n'wife.

Two or three more years pass, and my wife has two piccaninnies. Then the boss goes home to Spain, and leaves the white overseer de Soto in charge. De Soto's a very bad man. Before, if a slave works badly he not beaten. Now he beaten whether he work or not. For two months we take it, but things get worse. De Soto is always drunk and acting like a wild beast. One day he passed my wife hoeing sugarcane and he give her a cut with his whip, jus' out of amusement. She turns and asks, "What dat fer?" He gets mad, lashes her again, knocks her down with the stock, and then, seizing the youngest piccaninny fastened to her back, he catches him by the leg and smashes chile's skull against a tree. Then, sah, I rush at him with my hoe and chop him down, cut his skull clean in half, and he drops down dead.

The chief's two listeners sat, rapt at the story. At a quiet signal from Goodenough, Ostik went and fetched a bottle of brandy from their stock and Sam's eyes lit up when he saw it. He quickly arranged glasses and as soon as he settled again, taking an appreciative sip of his brandy and water, recommenced his tale.

The other slaves they danced and sang with joy to see the overseer dead, but I knew it was no place for me. The other Spaniards they never rest until de Soto was revenged. I ran all day among the hills, skirting other plantations, running in the streams to throw off the hunting dogs that will come for sure. Eventually I had to stop to sleep and jus' as I sit down, four black men, runaway slaves I knew straight away, came cautiously to me. When I told 'em my story, they said to follow them to where they had a camp with some twenty others, a few huts and some patches of yams.

I waited a month before sneaking back down at night to see what happened to my wife. Took two days and on the third night I hid until a slave came walking along the edge of the bush. I called out and asked him to tell my wife to steal away that night, with her things and my other chile, and meet me there.

That night she managed to get away. I was very afraid for her because she was not strong, hurt by de Soto's blow and fretting all the while 'bout me. Anyway, we followed the way I went before and I helped her and the chile up into trees over the streams, and after three days we make it back to my hut in the mountains. There, we lived happily for more'n a year, trading with plantation slaves the baskets we wove to exchange for cotton'n'cloth. We had our own fowls, taken from various plantations over time, and all things considered, we did very well.

As the word got round, more'n'more slaves joined us. We always hid away from the occasional band of soldiers sent to hunt runaways—they never found us—but then we heard tell of a big expedition. When they came there were as many as three thousand. They formed a skirmishing line some six miles long and went over every mountain like a fisherman's net, reeling in every runaway. Any who didn't surrender at their call was shot dead.

My wife and me, we decided to slip around 'em and hide next to our plantation, the last place we thought they'd look for us. But it didn't work. Just when we thought we got around safely, all at once we came on a lot of soldiers in a camp. I called to my wife to run when they fired. A ball hit the baby on the back and passed right through both their bodies. I didn't run no more, but jus' stood looking at my wife and chile as if my senses had gone. The soldiers took me, standing there, roped me, and dragged me away.

"You were lucky to escape execution," Goodenough said kindly, as Frank topped up their glasses.

Sam laughed. "No luck, jus' greed. The new overseer didn't want to waste a good slave, so he told the authorities how it happened, and they let me off with a hard flogging. They chained a log of wood to my legs to stop me running away again, but I didn't care if I lived or died, so I jus' worked. After six months, the log was taken off because it hampered my work, and p'raps they thought I had had enough of the mountains."

Sam took an appreciative sip of his refreshed drink and then took up his story again.

The very next night, I ran away again, this time determined to get to Santiago de Cuba in the hopes of getting on board an English ship, for I heard that the English did not keep black men as slaves. In fact the opposite, that they tried to stop the Spanish from getting them away from Africa.

It was four days' journey down to the town by the sea. I s'pose they only looked for me toward the hills because I got there safe, walking at night and sleeping in the bushes by day. There were some ships lying near the shore, some of them with the Spanish flag—oh, I knew what that looked like all right—other flying flags I didn't know. When it was dark I walked boldly into the town. No one asked me any questions, and I made my way through the streets down to the shore. There I got into the water and swam off to a ship—one that I had noticed had a flag made of lots of stars'n'stripes. It must be English, I thought. There was a boat alongside and I clambered into it and then shinned up the tethering rope to the deck. But, even though it was very late in the night, there were some whites on the deck, and they seized me and spoke in a language I didn't understand but I s'posed was English.

They pulled me into a cabin and said something to the captain man seated behind a desk. I don't know what they said, but it made the captain laugh, and I didn't like the sound of that laugh at all. However, they gave me something to eat and then took me down to the ship's hold and told me to go to sleep on some sacks of sugar, throwing some empty sacks to cover me. This put my mind a little at rest and let me go to sleep after my exhausting journey.

Next morning, when I came up on deck, the land was gone and the vessel sailing. I'd been so tired and slept so deeply I hadn't heard or felt anything. I couldn't ask anyone anything, I only spoke a little Spanish, and no one on board spoke that language. We sailed for some time that day and at last came in sight of land again. We reached a port and when I signed that I wanted to land, they shook their heads.

Next day the captain signed to me to follow him down the gangplank. I was happy and went with him to my freedom. We walked along the shore to an open space in the town, where a man stood on a raised platform. He had a black woman at his side and several white men went up close and looked at her. The man gave a loud shout. Other men said something short. After a minute of this exchange the man banged a small hammer on the table. A man told the woman to follow him and she walked away. Then a young boy was put up, then two more women, and every time the same thing happened.

Then the man called out in our direction and the captain pushed his way through the crowd with me, and told me to climb up on the platform. I got up and looked around quite surprised. Everybody laughed. The man began to holler again, loud in my ear and several men came up and felt my arms and my legs, looked at my teeth. Then the man who was shouting banged his hammer on the table again, and a white man in the crowd, who had several times shouted back, came up and took me by the arm, signing me to go with him.

Suddenly, I understood—that bad captain had sold me, and the flag I had seen was not the English flag. Now I know it was American, but then I knew nothing. I had jumped from the blinking cooking pot straight into the blooming fire."

Chapter 13: A Fugitive Slave

Cameroon, July 1872

Work on a plantation in Cuba and Virginia is very much the same, as far as the slaves are concerned. But the slaves are much merrier in America when the master is a good man, and my new master was a very good man. We were all well treated and not worked too hard. At night there was much singing and dancing. Then I married again, this time to Sally, one of the girls working in the big house. She was a favorite of the master's young daughter, so as a wedding present, the master had me taken off the fields and put to the garden.

Sam gave a long sigh, and for a moment paused his narrative to stare into the distance, looking at something only he could see.

Fine garden, that was. Jus' three others worked there, peaceful. I was as happy as could be. More'n'more I got called in to dress in finery and help in the house when there was a party—that's how I got to know how things should be done properly. The young masters were also fond of me, and when they went out coon-hunting or fishing, it was always Sam they cried out for to go with them.

So fifteen happy years passed by, then the master died; old missy, too, soon after. There were two sons, and the younger went to West Point to become an army officer. The new master was not like his father. I was fond of him, but he had been spoiled as a chile and youth. He wasn't cruel, but he liked pleasure too much—going to the races, stopping in town for two weeks at a time, playing too much with the cards. After the death of the old people the house changed a lot. Where we kept good company, grand balls for the first families of Virginia, now the young master brought back six to eight young rakes from Richmond, and they laughed and drank and played cards all the night.

The young missy spoke to him to mend his ways and there was an argument and she went off to live with an aunt in the city. After that, things get worse. One day, the young missy came back and gave my wife Sally her papers of freedom. She told her that a bad time was coming, that her brother was ruining the plantation and that one day soon all the slaves would have to be sold. "But you're the wife of a slave, which might make for difficulties. You'll be better off up in the north," she said to Sally. "I will write to friends of mine up there and recommend you as a fine nurse. If Sam gets a good master, you can come back to him again."

"Don't you think," my Sally asked, "that the master would give Sam his freedom too? Sam's waited on him for many years and saved his life when he fell in the river." But the young missy shook her head sadly. "It's too late, Sally. My brother borrowed money against the plantation and the slaves, so they're no longer his property to sell or to make free. Best you come with me to the city now before they foreclose and come down to seize everybody."

Well, sah, you can guess it put me in a state when I heard this. I'd often grieved that Sally and I had not had any children, now I was thankful that there were no piccaninnies, for they would have been sold off, one here, one there, and we would never see them again. Now I made a great effort and told Sally to do jus' what young missy told her and that one day I would join her in the north. "Better to be parted for ten years," I told her, "than take the risk of being seized and being sold to one master and me to another."

Only a week after Sally left the bust up came. The officers came down and seized the place, and a little while after they sold all the slaves. It was terrible to see the husbands and the wives and the children separated and sold to different masters. The young master wasn't there at the sale. They say the business pretty near broke his heart—but he should have thought of that before.

Well, we were all sold anyways and everyways. I fetched a high price and sold to a planter in Arkansas. That was a terrible blow. Virginia was close to the border with the northern states, while Arkansas was a long, long way off. For three years I worked on the plantation and then I was sold again to a man who owned boats on the Mississippi at New Orleans. There I worked at loading and unloading boats and working on the barges—and that's where I learned what for sure the Union Jack flag looked like.

Then times went slack, and my master hired me out as a waiter in a saloon. It was a bad place, with gambling and most every night fights, sometimes with pistols drawn. Ships' captains frequented the bar for dinner, and one young fellow came very often. He was always friendly to me and gave me a tip every time. One day I saw four men I knew were Texas horse dealers talking with him, which worried me—they were not good men—thieves, really. I was sorry to see they got a hold on him, and after three days began playing cards.

They thought they were going to cheat him, but in fact he had the devil's luck. They would have cleaned him out for sure if they'd got him to themselves, but that night the place was crowded and they weren't able to cheat easily. It turned out he won all the money. Drinks had been flying about, and when they called the bank closed the young fellow could hardly walk steady on his feet—and his pockets were stuffed full of cash. I said to him, "Why not stay here?" But he laughed and replied, "No Sam, I may be a little fresh in the wind, but I think I can make the boat."

I jus' knew by their scowling looks what they were planning, so I decided to act. I ran to my little room, pulled up the floorboard under which I stashed all my money I was saving to buy my freedom, then ran down again to the kitchen to pick up a heavy poker and a long knife. Then I went out the back, ran up the alley to the main street. I was jus' in time, for the young captain had separated from some other men he'd left with and was now alone and vulnerable.

I ran as fast as I could to the end of the street, which was badly lighted, jus' a lamp here and there. I stole quietly along in the shadow of the houses. Then, of a sudden, I saw four men run out. I leaped forward like a leopard and shouted to warn the captain. He turned around jus' in time to take a heavy blow and he fell to the ground. I was there in a second and brought my heavy poker down with a crunch on the top of one of their heads. They turned on me, but, law bless you, sah, what was the good of that? A strong black with a heavy poker in one hand and a long knife in the other was more than a match for three partly drunk Texans.

I think I killed two outright with the poker and wounded the other with a knife thrust. He fell down groaning anyway. Then I caught up the captain and ran along the wharf. After some feet I heard a hail. "Is that you, captain?" someone cried out. "I've got a captain here," I shouted back. "You come'n see whether he's yours." The men came down and looked into the captain's face.

"'Hullo.' they say, "the captain's dead." "He's not dead," said I, "he had a fight and I came to his aid and beat the bandits off. You'd better get him on board."

The result was that the young captain recovered by morning, and thanked me for saving him. He asked what he could do in return for me, and I said, "Take me out of this country and I will be grateful." This he instantly agreed to do, saying they were sailing for England in three days when a cargo was finished loading. In the meantime, however, they would have to hide me as there was bound to be a posse out looking for the killer of the Texan rustlers, and anyway, there would be a pilot on board until the river mouth, and they were as watchful as cats for any stowaway slaves.

As quick as possible they bored some holes in a big sugar cask for air and then placed me inside with water and some food to last a few days, then piled more casks on top. "They're likely to come aboard to check the cargo when we go past the forts," the captain told me.

There I remained for three very cramped days. I heard some men come below and make a great noise, moving the cargo about near the hatchway, and they hammered at all the casks on the top tier to see if any of them sounded empty. I felt very glad when it was all over, and the hold was quiet again. I slept a great deal and didn't know anything about time, but at last I heard a noise again, and the moving of casks, and then the lid was taken out, and there were the sailors and the captain. He shook me by the hand as he helped me out and told me that the ship was safely out at sea and that I was a free man.

The crewmen were very kind to me, and I lived like a gentleman as good as my old master. And when we got to Liverpool the kindness didn't stop. The young captain took me to a big steamship bound for New York, paid for my passage across, and gave me a present of fifty pounds. I'd already saved about as much myself so I felt that I was a rich man. As I sailed away, I thought to myself what very fine people the English must be if this was anything to go by.

"Did you find your wife in the north of the American states?" Frank eagerly asked.

Sam's wrinkled face creased up even more as he grinned at the young man seated opposite him. "Hah! Not first, no, no, not New York, nor in Philadelphia, the city where the young missy gave me a card with a name and address I could go to and ask where Sally was living."

He sighed deeply at the memory.

You could have knocked me down with a parrot feather when I found a great sign in the window, saying that the house was to let. I asked around everywhere—servants, shopkeepers, everyone, and then finally I found out that the family was traveling in Europe and might be away for years. I nearly went out of my mind—I might have been closer to my Sally in Liverpool than I was in Philadelphia.

Nevertheless, I never gave up and searched about Philadelphia, looking at every black woman I saw walking about. But I never saw anyone looking like her. I got a job as a waiter at a hotel, and wrote to missy at Richmond, to ask if she knew Sally's address, but I never got an answer, and s'posed that missy was either dead or gone away.

After a few months it occurred to me that stuck in one place, at a fine hotel, I wasn't going to find her, so I went out on the road peddling books. I must've walked thousands of miles, saw thousands of black people, but never Sally—but I did make a great deal of money. Every few months I returned to Philadelphia and asked around again. One day a woman, dressed very plainly, came up to me and said, "My nurse tells me you've been looking for your wife." I must've looked hopeful, for she was quick to say, "Oh, I know nothing about her, but I was interested in you. You're an escaped slave, aren't you?"

I agreed that I was, but a free man in the north, and then she told me that I might, like her, be interested in helping free slaves in the Confederate slave states. "Have you heard of the underground railway?" she asked, and I said I had, the brave people who smuggled slaves across the frontier. And she near floored me when she said she was a part of it. "Now," she said, "we want two or three more earnest men, men not afraid to risk their lives, or what is worse their freedom, to help their fellow souls. I thought that you, having suffered so much yourself, might be inclined to devote yourself to freeing others from the horrors of slavery."

And so I was recruited. She told me there was no money to be earned and only the chance of martyrdom. But my mind was made up and I felt ready to undertake any work they liked to give me. My life was of no value to anyone and any spark it might have had was lost with my Sally. "Sam's ready, ma'am," I told her. "It may be that the Lord never intends me to see my Sally again, but if I can be the means of helping to get other men to join their wives I shall be content."

Over the next few days I learned how the underground worked. There were people living in the south whose lives were no different no way from their neighbors—in lonely places, in woods, in villages, and towns—except that at night fugitive slaves would come secretly to their houses, guided by those from the previous station. The fugitives were concealed for twenty-four hours or more, and then passed on at night again to the next station.

Then there were others who lived in the swamps, scattered

through the country. Their homes were known to the slaves of the region, but the plantation owners had no suspicion that agents of the underground were so near. Any slaves could go to these agents for advice and practical help in escaping to freedom. Such brave souls held their own lives in their hands. If any suspicion fell on them, the white folks would lynch them for certain.

On the fifth day, I started for the south.

My share of the business was to make my way down south and settle in the extensive swamps of Carolina. I was taken down by trading schooner, secretly landed on the coast, and made my way to the middle of a big swamp where an old former slave, named Joe, had been working for four years. He had sent to say that he was very ill with swamp fever.

Well, sah, it took me time to find the secret place, so well guarded was the location, and all the slaves I asked were at first suspicious, but one took me into his trust, and so I arrived at my new post. Poor Joe had died of the fever. I buried him and took my place in the hut, and there I lived for three lonely years. It was my duty when I found that a case met the criteria given to me to arrange a flight for the man or woman, I would guide them through the bottoms, twenty-five miles away, to the house of a clergyman, which was the next station. I would jus' knock his door in a particular way, and when it was opened, leave the fugitive there and go straight back to the swamp. The white men got up hunts and my hut was burned down twice, but the slaves always gave me notice in time, and I went and hid in the thickest part of the marshes until they gave up.

Then a time came when I was very busy, passed three men away in two weeks. One night I heard barking dogs and jumped up jus' in time to see a gang of men coming out from the little path toward my hut. I ran for the swamp. They fired at me and one ball hit me. Then I ran into the mud, the dogs followed, but I got farther and farther away, and the quagmire became deeper.

I thought I had lost them by jumping from tuft to tuft and sat down on a stump when I heard something splashing in the water, and all of a sudden a big hound sprang on me, fixing his teeth in my shoulder. The beast growled and bit deeper, holding on like death. I could only see one option and fell forward into the morass with the hound underneath me. And there I lay, with my mouth sometimes above the surface sometimes below, until the dog drowned under my weight.

I was badly off, hit in the hip and gnawed on the shoulder, so it took me three days to crawl to the next underground station, half alive when I got there. I made the special knock and when the door opened, tumbled inside in a faint. They told me later that I was out for almost two weeks, part unconscious, mostly in a fever, dreaming of my Sally. She was talking softly to me, saying good things I remember from the past…

When I came around, the dream was reality after all. Law! There was Sally, sitting beside the bed comforting me! I couldn't believe I was awake, but she soon convinced me. Over the next day or so I learned her story. She had stopped a year in Philadelphia with the family whose house was to let, and there she learned of the underground railway. She was told that a clergyman, who was going south to work a station, wanted a black nurse for his children, who would help in the work.

Sally volunteered, and there she had been living ever since, hoping all he time that I would pass through there or that she would hear from Philadelphia that I had gotten there. She used to guide runaways to the next station, and every man who came along she asked if they knew me. So for the past three years I'd been guiding slaves to the place where she was living without either of us ever knowing about each other.

"An amazing Story, Sam," Goodenough said. "What did you do after that?"

Sam took a sip of his drink. "Well, sah, I stopped there until I was well again. Then I said to Sally that I should like to live under the British flag, so we made our way to Canada and there we lived very comfortably for ten years together. Sally did laundry and I kept a barber's shop, and we made plenty of money. Then she died, sah, and the thought came into my mind that I would return to Africa and teach those poor Africans here the white men's ways, and," he added, pointing to a Bible standing on the chest, "the ways of the Lord which I had learned in all my time in America. So here I am. I came across the Atlantic, and stopped a little while on the coast, for I had pretty much forgotten the language.

"I came back home with plenty of goods, presents, and twenty muskets. It took time for people to remember me, but some of the elders did. As I had plenty of goods, and they didn't like the man that was in charge here, they threw him out and made me chief as my father had been. I told them that if they would behave and mind what I said to them, I would make them comfortable.

"The slave trade's jus' about finished around here, still, the twenty muskets help and make other villages respect us. They come over to visit the village and see that the houses are comfortable, the gardens are very well looked after, the people are well dressed and they are happy and contented. They see that they no longer believe in fetish worship any more, but that every evening when the work is over, they gather under the big tree and listen for half an hour while I read to them and then we sing a hymn.

"When I landed here ten years ago I had eight hundred pounds. I've still got five hundred, which is more than enough to last me if I live to be a very, very old man. There are some good men in the village who, when I'm gone, will carry on the work of the Lord and that's all, sah, that I have to tell you about Sam—other than to thank you for bringing back my English!"

Chapter 14: Abeokuta Under Threat

Cameroon and Nigeria, July–August 1872

Frederick Goodenough and Frank remained at the village for a week, pleased with the hard-working but obviously happy people. At the end of that time they said goodbye to their kind host, giving him a large amount of cloth for distribution among his people. But their greatest gift, he insisted, was English conversation. After the expedition had resumed its path toward the Niger river, Goodenough glanced across at Frank. "I see you are deep in thought."

Eventually Frank turned to the naturalist. "I feel humbled by Sam."

"He's certainly an admirable character."

"It isn't that so much, as everything he went through. I thought I'd had it pretty hard, losing my father and then my mother so quickly, being made a pauper unless I shifted for myself. There were times in London when I just thought of giving up—"

"But you didn't," Goodenough pointed out.

"No, but by comparison, I had it comfortably. Sam went through things that no one should have to suffer, so much sadness too, yet he came back stronger than ever. I hope, one day, I shall be able to stand up and be counted like him."

He fell silent, and they walked on.

The eastern approach to the Niger was lightly inhabited, but what tribes lived there were used to trading with the coast and so proved friendly. At the first large village they came to Goodenough no difficulty in obtaining a fresh relay of bearers. This pleased the Fang, who wanted to go home, and eased their hosts who regarded the Fang with extreme animosity because of their culinary preferences. As soon as arrangements had been made to substitute the Fang, they were paid the four months' wages they had earned. They also received a large dash of beads, three sacks of rice, and six of the Birmingham trade muskets, which would not do much damage to any enemies but the simple possession of the weapons might make other tribes think twice about attacking them.

In crossing the low country to the Niger the white men were objects of lively curiosity, and the exhibition of the magic lantern, the chemical experiments, and conjuring tricks created an equally satisfying effect as they had done among the Fang. They reached the great river at a village called Onitsha, where Goodenough hired a canoe and a crew of paddlers. The boat—loaded with all the specimen cases so far filled—was put in charge of the Hausas Moses and King John, who had been seized with a fit of homesickness.

They were to see delivery of the cases to an English agent at Lagos, to whom Goodenough wrote requesting him to pay the sum agreed to the boatmen on the safe arrival of the cases, and also to pay the Hausas. Moses and King John would then be free to return to their northern homeland near Kaduna.

"If any chief should stop you between here and Lagos," Goodenough instructed them, "you must open up the cases and show them that they contain nothing but birds' skins and insects, which will be absolutely valueless in his eyes."

Frederick has already sent an embassy from Onitsha to the other side to negotiate with the headman of the village on the opposite bank for a fresh troop of porters, Frank recorded in the log.

As the precious freight started out down the Niger with Moses and King John, the explorers crossed over to a smaller village on the western bank. Because the portage was now considerably lighter, twenty men were sufficient to carry the provisions, ammunition, gifts, and collecting equipment.

"We will make a future economy by utilizing the emptied provisions boxes for collecting our bird and insect finds," Goodenough said to Frank.

* * *

For almost two months they continued the westward journey, now only about a hundred miles from the coast, where the Bight of Benin carved a great bay in the low-lying land after the Niger delta. They halted frequently and added continually to their stockpile of zoological specimens.

The country is well populated and, after convincing the village chiefs that we are not slavers (for in spite of the British blockade, the trade still flourishes), it has proven a simple matter to buy food and hire fresh sets of carriers.

They were approaching the Ogun river, when one day a Yoruba tribesman, his dust-covered skin streaked with rivulets of perspiration which made black tracks down his face and chest, ran into to their camp and threw himself on the ground before Goodenough and poured out a stream of words.

"What's he saying, Ostik?"

"I not know, sah. P'raps Ugly Tom know. He live in Yoruba country, speak Yoruba or Egba, de same ting."

Ugly Tom was called, and after a conversation with the panting native, explained that he was a messenger sent from Abeokuta, that the people there were under imminent threat from neighboring Dahomey's king. Word of the white men and their kindness had preceded them and when the Abeokutans heard these paragons were only a few runs to the north, they wanted to implore them to come to their aid.

"What do you reckon, Frank?"

"I don't know anything about it, sir," Frank said. "You've talked to me about Dahomey and its horrible customs of human sacrifice, but I don't know anything about Abeokuta."

"It's an unusual town," Goodenough said. "Its people were converted to Christianity some years ago by Anglican and Baptist missionaries. Unfortunately, its proximity to Dahomey makes it an attractive target. Dahomey has conquered and enslaved all its other neighbors, but the kings have never yet conquered Abeokuta, although it has been besieged many times." He pinched his lower lip between thumb and forefinger in thought.

"The Dahomey people have every advantage, being supplied with firearms, and even cannon, by the opportunist white traders at Whydah, Dahomey's port. Nevertheless, the Abeokutans have opposed them heroically, and so far successfully. If we answer their appeal it will be a perilous business, mind, for if the town is taken the king of Dahomey will definitely put us horribly to death with the rest of the defenders."

"I think we ought to help them, Frederick," Frank replied hotly. "From what you say they sound a noble people, and with our guns and Firewater, Ugly Tom, Bacon, and Tatters… yes, and you, Ostik… we might really make a difference. There may be risk involved, but we've risked our lives from fever, crocodiles, hostile natives, and in other ways every day since we've been in the country."

Goodenough's grey eyes sparked with enthusiasm. He drew himself to his full height and said, "Very well, my lad. I'm glad that's your decision. Tell him, Ugly Tom, that we're on our way to Abeokuta with all speed, and that they'd better send out twenty men as bearers to meet us." He pointed discreetly over his shoulder at the gathered men from Ife, the last town where the expedition had hired porters. "You can bet your last penny that this lot won't go any farther the minute they hear that the Dahomans are on the warpath. Ask him which route we should take because if our current porters turn tail we'll be stuck until his people come for us. How far is it to Abeokuta?"

Ugly Tom barked out the questions in Yoruba. "He says 'bout forty miles, sah."

"Good. We'll march twenty this afternoon. Where we halt I imagine rumors will be flying about the coming war and I expect the local men will go no farther, so tell him he must get us carriers out to that point."

The Hausa translated the orders, and the Yoruba, the whites of his eyes gleaming in his streaming face, snapped out a reply, sprang to his feet, kissed Goodenough's hand and then a startled Frank's, and then turned on his heels and set off down the pathway at a sprint.

"Says he will be at Abeokuta tonight, sah" Ugly Tom reported drily, "if'n he don' die of runnin' on de way."

Goodenough turned on the Hausa with a frown. "Wonderful stamina some of these men have," he said.

"Yes, sah. If'n you say so, sah."

"Ugly Tom, don't provoke me. I know Hausas hold the Yoruba in low regard, but that man's just done forty miles flat out, and now he's off again fresh as a daisy."

"Don' smell like no daisy..." muttered the disgruntled Hausa as he shuffled off to rejoin his comrades.

"What speed will he go at?" Frank asked.

"Say... six miles an hour. Faster when he's running, but he'll sometimes slow to a walk. Five miles an hour would be the ordinary pace of a native runner, but in a case like this, I'd bet on six."

They broke camp swiftly, the carriers took up their loads, and they started on their way along the indicated pathway through the thickening bush. It was late in the evening when they reached a small village about twenty miles south of their last camp. The inhabitants were in a panicked state. The drums had passed news that a great army was marching to sack Abeokuta, and that the king of Dahomey had sworn on his father's skull that this time the place would be captured, and not a house or a wall left standing.

The villagers knew full well that Abeokuta would close its gates and resist for some time, so they feared that Dahomey's warriors would be sent out to plunder and carry away captives all over the surrounding country. The panic instantly spread to the bearers, who declared that not a pace farther would they go.

"Their fear is understandable," Frank commented as he watched the men drop their loads.

Goodenough sighed his resignation. "I'll pay them off, and let them go back to their homes as soon as the camp's set up properly. Make them understand, Ugly Tom."

The tent was soon pitched and the men from Ife hurried back the way they had come. Ostik prepared a supper of fried plantains, rice, a tin of sardines, and tea. Later on they had a cup of chocolate and turned in for the night.

An excited babble of African voices woke Frank and Goodenough just at daybreak.

Ugly Tom thrust his head through the tent door flap. "Men come for baggage, sah."

"Hell, that's quick." Frank said. "They must have started out the moment the runner reached town."

"They certainly haven't lost any time about it," Goodenough said.

While the Hausas pulled down and packed up the tent Ostik made a breakfast of chocolate with biscuit soaked in it. By the time the explorers had eaten this the Abeokutan carriers had taken up their loads, and two minutes later the little army started almost at a run. Ugly Tom soon explained the cause of the haste.

"Is urgent because Dahomey army now only eight miles west of Abeokuta, sah. Dey 'spect it appear in front of town by midday."

"Although it might be later," Goodenough panted. "The movements of savage troops are unpredictable, depending entirely on the whims of their leader." Frank made no reply to save breath for the slog ahead. It was hard work to keep up with the Abeokutans' pace.

So anxious were the bearers to get back to the town in time, that they frequently went at a trot. They were the better able to keep up the speed because many more than were required had been sent, consequently they were able to shift the heavy baggage from time to time. So great was the speed, that after an hour neither the younger nor the older white man, weakened by the effect of repeated fevers and climate, could keep up. The hammocks were hastily taken out and lifted by men unprovided with loads.

When he recovered from his exhaustion sufficiently to observe what was going on, Frank could not help admire the way in which the Yorubas, with perspiration streaming from every pore, hurried along with their burdens. So fast did they go, that in less than six hours they emerged from the bush into cleared land, and a shout announced that Abeokuta was close at hand.

Ten minutes later the recovered explorers were carried through the gate. The inhabitants shouted in jubilation at the white men's arrival. Frederick Goodenough and Frank were carried in triumph to the town's principal building, an imposing hut where the general councils of the people were held. Here King Ransome Kuti and the leading citizens received them, some Yoruba but mostly men of the Egba tribe. The Abeokutans thanked them warmly for coming to their assistance in the time of their danger. Both Englishmen were struck with the appearance of the people, clad as they were with far more decorum than they had so far encountered among the African tribes—excluding Sam's village. In contrast to the townspeople, the councillors' bearing was quiet and dignified and an air of neatness and order infused everything.

Through Ugly Tom, Goodenough addressed the king. "My young friend and I are willing to take part in the struggle of a brave people against a cruel and bloodthirsty tyrant. Our four men of the noble Hausa tribe are armed with fast-firing guns and I am sure their assistance will be of use."

He asked if they could look over the town's defenses to see if anything could be done to improve them.

In turn they learned that a large store of provisions had been brought into the town, and that many of the women and children had been sent to safety far away.

King Ransome Kuti—an unusually lithe man for a West African king, chiefs generally accounting their status through girth—accompanied them on a tour of the walls.

These are about a mile in circumference, built of clay, and are of considerable height and thickness, Frank noted, *but they will not resist an attack by artillery.*

"We must hope," Goodenough said, his words translated by Ugly Tom, "that the gunners of Dahomey don't possess much skill in managing their cannon, in which case we should succeed in repelling the assault." He turned to Tom. "Inform the king—politely, mind—that all the defenders should be set to work throwing up an earthwork just outside each gate, in order to shelter these weakest points in the defenses as far as possible from the effect of the enemy's cannonballs."

Ransome Kuti listened to the translation carefully, and then frowned. "It would require much less earth, and therefore less effort, if it were just piled directly against the gates, surely?"

"This is certainly so," Goodenough answered him. "But it's essential that we can open the gates to make a sortie against the enemy if the opportunity arises."

The king shook his head, and voiced his doubt that his people had the ability to take such a desperate step as that of attacking the Dahomans outside the walls. Nevertheless, he barked out a string of rapid orders and within the hour the entire male population was at work digging at the nearby laterite quarry. One half carried the stony red earth in baskets and piled it up before the gates. The other half dampened it, shaped it, and stamped it into hard, rising mounds.

Not even when night set in did the men of Abeokuta stop working, and by the following morning the gates were protected from the worst effects of cannon shot by impressive outworks twenty feet high. Now all they had to do was to wait.

Chapter 15: Amazons of Dahomey

Southeastern Nigeria, August 1872

The king place a spacious and comfortable at the disposal of the white men, with one adjoining for Ostik and the four Hausas. As they sat down to eat their simple supper Frank pestered his companion about the enemy they now faced.

"I guess you've come across the Dahomans before?"

"I have, but down on the coast at Whydah on the Slave Coast, where they trade with the French, Spanish, and Portuguese slavers and merchants."

"Slavers?" Frank shuddered at the word, thinking of the tale Sam had told them.

"Yes, unfortunately the biggest traders in African slaves in this part of the world are the Africans themselves, and Dahomey is a great exporter of human flesh. The word is more properly *Da-omi*, which in the Fon language—the major tribe in Dahomey—means Da's belly. Two and a half centuries ago Da was the king of the city of Abomey. It was attacked by Tacudona, the chief of the Fons. It resisted bravely, and Tacudona made a vow that if he took it he would sacrifice the king to the gods. When he captured the town he carried out his vow by ripping open the king, and then called the place Daomi. Gradually the conquerors extended their power until the kingdom reached north to the very edge of the Sahara, and to the south where they obtained the port of Whydah by the conquest.

"The kings of Dahomey have always been despots, Frank, and the current tyrant, King Glele, is a fine example of his kind—even his nobility crawl on the ground in his presence. He lives by heavy taxation. Every slave is taxed and every other article that enters the kingdom. If a cockerel crows it's confiscated and, as it's the nature of cocks to crow, every bird in the kingdom is muzzled. The property of everyone who dies goes to the king, and at the Annual Custom, a grand religious festival, every man has to bring a present in proportion to his rank and wealth. The royal pomp is kept up by receiving strangers who visit the country in splendid state, and by regaling the populace with spectacles of human sacrifice."

Goodenough paused long enough to wipe some *eba gari* around his bowl of okra stewed in a soup of palm oil and stink-fish. When he finished chewing the ball of cassava dough and swallowed, he picked up his discourse.

"Oddly enough, unlike in so much of the rest of the region, women have a high standing in Dahomey. Pretty much everywhere else they're put to work tilling the soil, raising the crops, and cooking the result while raising and looking after the children. In Dahomey many fight as soldiers, and perform all the offices of men. Dahomey is principally famous for its army of women... and its human sacrifices. These take place annually, sometimes more often. In almost all the pagan nations of Africa human sacrifice happens, but nowhere else are they carried out to such a terrible extent as in Dahomey and Ashanti next door, two kingdoms which resemble each other in that respect. The victims are mostly captives taken in war, and it's to keep up the sacrificial supply—as well as the flood of slaves—that Dahomey is constantly at war with her neighbors. And the Amazons—as we have christened the force of women—are always at the forefront."

"Are we going to fight women, then?" Frank asked in a horrified voice.

"Definitely," Goodenough answered. "The Amazons are the flower of Dahomey's army and it's said that they're brave and ferocious killers."

"But I can't shoot at women!" Frank burst out.

Goodenough gave him a teasing grin. "Ah, like your scruples over shooting monkeys—that melted quickly enough I seem to remember."

Frank blushed. "That was a bit different. They attacked us and, after all, they were only animals."

"I assure you, we'll be attacked by these lady warriors, and your scruples are formed from outdated ideas of civilization, Frank. Among the middle and upper classes of Europe a man who hits a woman is considered a brute and a coward. You're used to living in a society that puts women on pedestals, in which they're supposed to depend on men to provide for the family while they look after the domestic duties. But among our own lower classes wife- and woman-beating is not uncommon, nor is such an assault regarded with much more censure than an attack on a man.

"When women put themselves forward to do a man's work they must expect man's treatment. While it's not much so now, there will, I predict, come a time when women will challenge men for their jobs and their social positions. Whether they will then hate the notion of men not giving up their seats for them on buses or letting doors fly back in their faces, we shall see."

"Still," Frank said, a touch petulantly, "I won't like shooting women."

Goodenough barked, "Hah! You won't see much difference between women and men when the fight begins, Frank. These female furies kill anyone who falls into their hands without regret, remorse, mercy, or a qualm of any kind, and therefore in self defense you will have to shoot to kill in return."

The following day the sound of drums and sporadic musket fire played an overture to the appearance of the Dahoman army's vanguard. It moved with considerable order and regularity, Frank observed with a touch of unease. He had anticipated something more like a disorganized rabble.

"Those must be the Amazons," Goodenough said. "They're proud of their drill and discipline. I don't think any other African troops could march so regularly."

The main host of the army now came in view, and that did appear more as Frank had expected, marching as a loose and scattered mob. Then, dragged behind oxen, came twelve old cannon.

"How many are they?" Frank wondered.

"Difficult to judge accurately," the naturalist muttered. "Dahomey is said to have fifty thousand fighting men and women to put in the field, that's to say the whole adult population, except those too old to bear arms. I should think that there are twenty to twenty-five thousand out there now."

The enemy approached within musket shot of the walls, and numbers of them ran forward and fired their weapons. Those Abeokutans similarly armed returned shots, but Goodenough had ordered the Hausas not to fire on any account and give away before time the power of their Snider rifles. After this opening of hostilities, everything calmed down while the besiegers set about cutting down all the plantations around the town and erecting great numbers of little huts. A large central structure with several smaller ones surrounding it went up rapidly for King Glele and those who passed for his nobles. The Dahomans quickly surrounded Abeokuta and by their gesticulating and pointing at the gates it was clear that the new outworks had surprised and irritated them.

The wall was thick enough for men to walk along on the top, but being built of clay and laterite it would not stand much of a battering. To this end Frank had been set to supervise a work party making sacks from rough cloth, which they filled with earth and piled in the center of the town ready to be rushed to any threatened point. Meanwhile, Goodenough organized a stock of timber beams, sharpened at one end. Stakes of six feet long were also cut and sharpened at both ends. That day the enemy attempted nothing against the town.

The next morning the Dahoman artillerymen planted the twelve cannon at a distance of about five hundred yards and opened fire on the walls. The shooting was erratic. Many of the balls fell well short, a few topped the wall and fell in the town, some thudded into the wall and buried themselves in the yielding clay.

"We'll give them a lesson in the modern rifle. Frank, you take my double-barreled gun and I'll take the heavy, large-bored one. Your Winchester won't be very accurate at this distance."

The Hausas were already on the wall, anxious to open fire. "Sighted to five hundred yards, sah," Ugly Tom said.

"Good lads," Goodenough approved.

Ranged in a single rank side by side, the enemy's big guns offered easy targets. A crowd of Fons surrounded them, who yelled and danced each rare time one of their shots struck the wall.

As soon as Frank, Frederick Goodenough, and the four Hausas opened a witheringly accurate fire, the triumphant clamoring of the Dahomans at once changed to cries of surprise, pain, and anger. A high proportion of the shots told cruelly. Many wounded were carried to the rear, and black figures were everywhere stretched out on the ground, their blood spilling onto the orange laterite. Still the enemy's fire continued with unabated vigor.

"They fight with determination," Frank pointed out.

"They have good reason. Cowardice is punished with death, and since the lives of others have scarcely any value among them, they'll be killed where they stand rather than retreat."

The exchange of fire continued. Several Fon commanders, surrounded by cliques of attendants, came down to the guns, but Frank and Goodenough always selected the nobles for their mark, and most of them were killed within a few minutes of their arriving on the spot. At the end of four hours the firing stopped, and the Dahomans retired from their guns. The Abeokutans raised a hoarse cry of triumph.

"I imagine they've only fallen back to give the barrels time to cool," Goodenough cautioned.

While the cannonade had been going on, a brisk attack had been mounted at several other points of the wall. The Amazons advanced inside fifty yards, shooting their muskets loaded with heavy charges of slugs, as the defenders replied resolutely. The artillery bombardment was not resumed that afternoon and the Dahomans contented themselves with skirmishing around the walls.

"They're disappointed with the result of their big guns," Goodenough said with some satisfaction. "No doubt they anticipated knocking the wall down without much trouble. I anticipate a change of tactics tomorrow, for which we should get ready."

Ugly Tom conveyed the suggestion to King Ransome Kuti and soon enough a number of barrels of palm oil were lifted up to the top of the wall, with some of the great iron pots used for boiling the oil and a supply of wood for fuel.

Goodenough grunted with satisfaction. "If they try to storm, it will most likely be at the point where they concentrated the cannon. The parapet has already crumbled in several places so the defenders stationed there will be more exposed. That's where the oil supplies must go."

Everyone spent the night in nervous tension until the fires were lit under the iron boilers an hour before daybreak to be ready in case an assault first thing in the morning. In spite of their concern, the Abeokutan men were in high spirits at the effect of their white allies' rifles, and at the apparent failure of the cannon. Before the previous day's battle had been joined, they had quailed at the power of the big guns. Soon after daylight the Dahomans were seen gathering near the guns. Their drums beat furiously, and presently they advanced in a solid mass against the wall.

"I think they've got ladders," Goodenough observed. "I can see many of them carrying something."

The Hausas immediately opened fire and, as the enemy advanced into range, first the Abeokutans who had muskets, then the great mass with bows and arrows, began shooting at the approaching ranks, while ducking the answering fire. In contrast the central host of Amazons advanced without firing a shot, moving in a block at a quick trot.

The Englishmen were not firing either as they devoted themselves to overseeing the defense. Ostik kept close to them, carrying Frank's

Winchester carbine and a double-bore shotgun. "This is getting hot," Goodenough shouted, as the enemy's slugs and musket balls whizzed in a storm over the edge of the parapet. Many of the defenders took musket balls, and the musketry made it difficult for the expedition party to take accurate aim. This, however, the Abeokutans did not try to do. Stooping below the parapet, they fitted their arrows to the string, or loaded their muskets, and then, standing up, fired hastily at the nearing throng before ducking under cover again.

The walls were about twenty-five feet high inside, but the parapet gave an additional height of some four feet outside. They were about three feet thick at the top, which limited the number of men who could stand there to oppose the storming party. Strong squads were placed farther along on the wall to make a rush to sweep the Amazons off if they gained a footing. Others lined up below to attack any who jumped down into the town, while men with muskets stationed on the roofs of the houses near the walls were ready to open fire at any foe who got a footing on the wall. The din of hoarse yells and banging muskets was deafening.

With their easy access to the sea coast, the Dahomans were armed entirely with muskets, either Birmingham trade guns or old converted weapons, purchased by Dutch, French, or Portuguese traders for a song at the sale of disused government stores. The Africans used much greater amounts of powder than was the case in Europe, ramming down a handful of slugs, or half a dozen small balls, on the charge. This did little for accuracy or the safety of the barrel but it produced a frightening volume of powder flash and noise, which they enjoyed. The Abeokutans, on the other hand, more isolated from ports where arms traders operated, were mostly armed with bows and arrows.

The Amazons concentrated at the foot of the wall, and then a score of rough bamboo ladders, each four feet wide, were thrown up. The moment the focus of the attack was obvious, Goodenough distributed cauldrons of boiling oil and set men to knocking holes through the parapet at distances of a couple of feet apart, and at a height of six inches from the rampart. A line of men with long spears lay down on the footing to thrust through the holes at those climbing the ladders. Another line of holes was made two feet higher, through which those armed with muskets and bows could shoot, for when the enemy reached the base of the wall their fire was so heavy that it became impossible to return it over the top of the parapet.

Immediately the ladders were in place, men armed with ladles began to throw the boiling oil over the parapet. Shrieks and yells from below testified to its dreadful effect, but in spite of the burning agony, some of the Amazons still climbed desperately upward. When a second squad of screaming women mounted the ladder nearest to where Goodenough stood, he called for more oil to be thrown down. He snatched a flaming brands from under a cauldron and hurled it over the parapet. The heated oil exploded in a fireball which engulfed the attackers. Flailing limbs of incandescence hurtled to the ground below amid strangled shrieks of agony.

Farther along, more attackers dodged the spears poked out at them, and when they neared the top the fight began in earnest.

The Fons below ceased firing in order not to hit their own, which allowed the garrison to stand up and defend themselves with swords and spears. The breech loading rifles of the Hausas and Frank's repeating carbine now came into play. The Amazons fought with extraordinary bravery, hundreds fell shot or cut down from above or pierced by the spears and arrows through the parapet.

Fresh swarms of assailants took their places on the ladders. The drums kept up a ceaseless rattle, and the bawls of the mass of Fons standing inactive made the surrounding jungle seem to shudder. Their efforts, however, were in vain. Never had the Amazons fought with more reckless bravery, but the position was too strong for them, and at last, after upward of a thousand had fallen, they abandoned the assault. The Dahoman women retired from the wall, chased by the exulting shouts of the Abeokutan men.

The defenders' losses were small. Some ten or twelve had been killed by musket slugs. Three or four times that number were more or less severely wounded about the head or shoulders with the same missiles. Frank had a nasty cut on the cheek, and Firewater and Bacon were both streaming with blood from superficial wounds.

There was no chance of a renewed attack that day. Sentries were placed on the walls, and a grand thanksgiving service was held in the open space in the town center which every free man and the few brave woman who had remained behind attended.

"What's their next move to be, do you think, Frederick?" Frank brushed a clump of grimy, sweat-stained hair from his brow as they returned wearily to their hut.

"Heavens knows, but these people know something of warfare, and finding that they can't take the place by assault, I think they'll try some more cautious move next time."

For two days there has been no renewal of hostilities. We are concerned about the risk of disease arising from so many Dahoman dead lying at the foot of the wall. But when the Abeokutan generals shouted out that King Glele could send men out to carry off their dead, nothing happened. So yesterday all able-bodied men were set to carrying earth in baskets to the top of the wall and throwing the contents over to cover the mass of decomposing corpses below. There is nothing to be done about the ones lying out of range.

On the third morning daylight revealed that a large number of filled sacks had been piled in a line some fifty yards long and some eight feet in height, two hundred yards from the wall.

"I thought they were up to something," Goodenough muttered. "They've been fetching sacks from Abomey."

In a short time the enemy brought up their guns behind the new shelter, regardless of the injury wrought by the expedition's rifles during the maneuver.

"They're taking position two or three hundred yards to the left of the battery's former position," Frank said. He brushed sweaty dust from his brow and screwed up his eyes against the glare.

A troop of men removed some of the sacks, and in a short time made twelve rough embrasures just wide enough for the muzzles of the guns. The sacks taken away were piled on the others, raising them to the height of ten feet and sheltering the men behind completely from any fire from the walls.

"They'll make a breach now," remarked Goodenough. "We must get ready to receive them inside."

The previously prepared beams were now inserted upright in holes furiously dug at regular intervals in a semicircle a hundred feet across, immediately behind the wall facing the battery outside. When secured, the beams stood about eight feet above the ground, and then workers filled the spaces between with stripped bamboo canes twisted in and out between them. At Goodenough and Ostik's direction the men set to throwing earth up behind to the height of four foot to form a new rampart for the defenders to stand on.

The half circle of ground between the new stockade and the wall was then sowed with the sharpened stakes stuck firmly in the ground with their points projecting outward. All day the men labored at these structures, while the wall crumbled fast under the fire of the enemy artillery, every shot of which, at so short a distance, struck it heavily. By five in the afternoon a gap fifty feet wide had opened up and the army of Dahomey again gathered for an assault. Goodenough, with Bacon and Tatters, took his place on the wall to one side, Frank with Firewater and Ugly Tom faced him across the gap. A large number of the Abeokutans also lined the walls, while the rest gathered on the new stockade.

With the usual tumult of drumming and yells the Dahomans rushed to slaughter their foes. The fire from the walls did not check the onset in the slightest, and with bawls of anticipated victory they swarmed over the breach. A cry of shock broke from the Amazons as they saw the formidable redoubt in front of them, from which came an intensely concentrated rain of arrows. Then, with scarcely a pause, they leaped down and struggled to remove the obstructions.

Regardless of the shafts and bullets pouring like hail on them they hewed away at the sharp stakes, or tried pulling them up with their hands. The riflemen on the walls directed their fire now exclusively at the Amazon leaders. The English rapid-firing breech loaders instantly turned the amphitheater into a bloody execution pit, and soon the Amazons and Dahoman warriors in their efforts to advance had to climb over barricades of dead and dying to their front. For half an hour the battle raged, and then the attackers lost heart and retired, leaving fifteen hundred of their number piled deep in the space between the broken wall and the stockade.

"This is horrible work, Frederick," Frank said, wiping blood from his cheek with the cuff of his jacket as he rejoined Goodenough.

"Awful, Frank. But look at it this way. With this fearful slaughter of their bravest warriors we are crippling Dahomey's power as a curse and a scourge to others around it. After this crushing repulse the Abeokutans may hope that many years will pass before they're again attacked by their savage neighbors, and the lessons which they've now learned in defending themselves will enable them to make as good a stand on another occasion as they've done today."

"Do you think they'll attack again?"

"I hardly think so. The elite of their army must have fallen, and the Amazon guard must have almost ceased to exist. I told you, Frank, you would soon get over your repugnance to firing at women."

Frank shrugged and shook his head slightly. "I didn't think anything about women," he murmured. "We seemed to be fighting a body of demons with their wild screams and shrill yelling. In fact, as you said, I couldn't tell the women from the men most of the time."

However, Frederick Goodenough had underestimated his enemy. At daybreak the enemy cannon crashed out again. In the night the Dahomans had built, with the sacks and earth, platforms some six feet high to raise the guns' muzzles so that they were able to fire over the rubble of the breached wall at the stockade behind it. Throughout the long day, the defenders lowered earth-filled sacks on ropes over the parapet of the barrier to absorb the impact of the cannonballs. As fast as one bag was blown apart they lowered another in its place. In the meantime the rifles opened up from the walls at the gunners, who were now more exposed. Seeing the uselessness of their efforts the Dahomans gradually slackened their fire.

When night came Goodenough gathered two hundred of Abeokuta's best troops and they sallied out carrying wooden plugs carved to correspond with the size of the various cannonballs lying about inside the town. They varied from six to eighteen pounders.

The Dahoman sentries stood facing the breach, but anticipating no attack in any other direction, they had left the flanks unguarded, so the Abeokutans' silent approach went unobserved until they swept around into the battery. Large numbers of the enemy lay asleep here but, taken by surprise, none offered any resistance, and they were cut down or driven away.

Goodenough and Frank went to work on the guns. They filled each nearly to the rim with gunpowder, and then drove the plugs tight into the muzzles with mallets. They placed slow matches, composed of strips of calico dipped in saltpeter, in the touch holes. Then the word was given, and the whole party fell back to the gate just as the Dahomans counter-attacked in force.

In less than a minute after leaving the battery, twelve tremendous explosions followed closely one on the other. The tropically black sky lit up as the guns blew themselves to smithereens. The shrapnel wiped out scores of the Dahomey men who had just crowded into the battery.

In the morning, scouts sent out returned with reports that the enemy, including the king, were in full retreat in the direction of Abomey. The people of Abeokuta were half wild with exultation and joy, and their gratitude to their English allies was unbounded.

The inhabitants were poor, but they would willingly have

presented all their treasures to their white friends. Goodenough, however, would accept nothing save a few samples of native cloth exquisitely woven from the inner bark of trees, and some other items of choice native workmanship. He also begged them to send down the Ogun river to Ikorodu and then across the lagoon to Lagos the cases of specimens collected since the departure of the Fang carriers.

Then a violent attack of fever, brought on by their exertions in the sun, prostrated both the explorers a few days after the end of the siege, and it a week passed before they felt able to renew their journey.

"Where to next, Frederick?"

"I think, my boy, that it's time to turn our feet in the direction of home. I propose we travel some miles northward along the Ogun and then head west, well over the top of the Dahomey area, into upper Ashanti, and then to make our way to Kumasi. From there, we can head south down to Cape Coast Castle and take ship for England. Ashanti is the great rival nation to Dahomey, but as the Ashanti are at peace with Britain, we should encounter no troubles and plenty of help."

Chapter 16: Kumasi Captives

London, August 1872

High above the bustle of horse-drawn cabs and buses rattling the length of Whitehall, five mandarins of the British government, gathered around a long table, its surface polished to a mirror-like finish, were discussing a situation of considerable complexity.

"The problem is, gentlemen," said Earl Granville, the Secretary of State for Foreign Affairs, "that the prime minister does not favor what he calls 'military adventures' in the tropics."

"But the situation in West Africa can't be allowed to deteriorate because of Mr. Gladstone's caution in our overseas possessions," protested Edward Cardwell, the reforming Secretary of State for War and the Colonies.

"We already replaced the merchants with military control," the Marquess of Lansdowne, Under Secretary of State for War, pointed out.

"Wolseley, we haven't heard from you," Granville spoke out.

"I think my position's well understood, Mr. Secretary," replied General Sir Garnet Wolseley, who as adjutant-general at the War Office, was Cardwell's assistant and fervent supporter of the reforms being introduced to modernize the British army. "I think it might be helpful if the Military Secretary ran briefly over our recent history of under-achievement along the Guinea Coast."

His words caused a stir around the table. Not all those gathered were pleased to be reminded of failures. Major-General Caledon Egerton stood and shuffled some papers on the table in front of him, then cleared his throat. "A little background might help. The Ashanti empire consists of five petty kingdoms clustered around the Volta river, all of which pay tribute to the Asantehene, or high king. The current incumbent ruling from his capital of Kumasi is…" Egerton coughed quietly at the quaintness of the savage name: "Kofi Karikari."

He shuffled his notes briefly before resuming. "The geography and background to the current situation is simple enough. The European powers have always traded with the coastal tribes, the interior largely being an unexplored region of impenetrable jungles. In the region of the so-called Gold Coast, the coastal tribe is the Fanti—actually a confederation of several sub-tribal groupings. The Pra river, in curling around inland, makes a natural frontier with the Ashanti.

"The Ashanti are not peaceable neighbors. Every four to five years they cross the Pra to war on the Fanti to take captives for their religious rites, which include human sacrifice on an almost industrial scale. Britain has become involved for two reasons: first we're duty bound to offer the Fanti protection, but because that barely extends a mile from the sea, it leads to the second, the fact that the Ashanti have had the temerity to invade right up to the walls of our fort at Cape Coast. Such was the case in 1821—when the African Company, which had failed in its duty—was dissolved and Sir Charles Macarthy appointed governor."

The name sent a perceptible shudder through the meeting. Egerton gave a slight smile.

"As we all know, Macarthy was more pomp and circumstance than substance. He felt he could awe the Ashanti merely by his imperial appearance, and took five hundred Fanti troops with a handful of white officers against the…" he paused to consult his notes again, "ah, Asantehene Osei Yaw Akoto. Macarthy was utterly defeated—though they thought he was so brave that the Ashanti chiefs shared his heart in order to absorb this quality. His bones were given as charms, his jawbones were used as drum sticks, and his skull turned into the Asantehene's drinking cup."

More shudders from the assembly.

"Could we speed this up, do you think Major-General?" Granville snapped out.

Egerton colored and coughed apologetically. "Sorry, Mr. Secretary, yes. As a result, wearied of the whole business, we pulled out but the Fanti region became effectively a British protectorate by default. The tribes' independence was recognized, a situation which remained when the government of the day took over Cape Coast for the Crown again in 'forty-four. In 'fifty-three the Ashanti crossed the Pra again, but were met with firmness and retired. The Ashanti broke the peace ten years later, but Palmerston's government refused to send out the requested troops.

"Up to then our strongholds on the coast were interspersed with the Dutch forts, with the tribes in their region under the protection of the respective nations. This unsatisfactory situation was resolved by giving the Dutch all our forts west of the Sweet river—which falls into the sea midway between Dutch Elmina and British Cape Coast—and the Dutch handed over their forts lying east of the river to us. However, the tribes were never consulted and in the resulting conflict, the Dutch gave up the coast altogether as too much trouble for any return. This effectively left Britain in control of all previous Dutch holdings, including Elmina.

"Two years ago, the British governor in Cape Coast received a note from the new Asantehene—that's Kofi Karikari—protesting the proposed takeover of 'his' possession of Elmina. He insisted that the land on which the forts, English, Dutch, Danish, and French, were built had been originally acquired from the native chiefs at a fixed annual tribute…" Egerton paused for effect… "which we like to think of as a *rent*."

A chuckle ran around the table.

"By the native custom, a chief who conquers another chief who has been receiving such a *rent* inherits the benefit. Asantehene Kofi Karikari claimed right of conquest over Elmina and also over the Fanti, and therefore ownership of Cape Coast. We sent an embassy with presents and a sensible argument, and it seemed the king had given in and agreed with the Crown's position."

Granville spoke up. "You said 'had.' Is that not how matters still remain?"

Egerton plumped his papers down on the table. "Unfortunately not. Kofi Karikari again insists the British government is paying him an annual *tribute* and illegally occupying Elmina. I'm afraid that everything points to the inescapable fact of war."

Near the Volta River, September 1872

"I checked all the latest reports before we left for Liverpool, Frederick Goodenough told Frank. "Matters had been settled amicably by sending an envoy to Kumasi with presents for the king, and he had given up his claims and acknowledged that the money was not paid as a vassal pays a tribute. The last I read was that we had purchased the Dutch forts and stores. The people of Elmina were told that we wouldn't take over without their consent, but that if they refused to accept our protection they would be exposed to the Fanti's hostility as in the past."

"I suppose they agreed, then" Frank said wryly.

"They did, and we offered a safe passage for the Ashanti war-band at Elmina to return to Kumasi. Governor Pope Hennesey told the Ashanti king that Britain only wanted peace and was prepared to pay him twice what the Dutch had paid annually for Elmina. So we should be welcomed with open arms at Kumasi."

"Which will be a great relief after Dahomey," Frank added with a heartfelt sigh.

London, November 1873

"I'm sorry to spoil any plans you might be making for Christmas this year, Wolseley, but this can't wait, I'm afraid." The Secretary of State for War and the Colonies came from behind his desk to shake the general's hand.

"Don't apologize, Cardwell, I'm delighted to hear the prime minister has at last woken up to our responsibilities. What's the latest?"

"It sounded too good to be true, but the peace won't last. The Ashanti have carried off some German and Swiss missionaries from a mission station on British territory near the Volta. The general who did it, with the colorful name of Aboo Boffoo, refuses to give them up without a huge ransom and the Asantehene holds up his hands in resignation—what can he do if his general refuses to co-operate?"

"He's lying, of course."

"Naturally. The king is using it as a tactic to force our hand and give him an excuse to cross the Pra. He says he's concerned for the hostages' health. He also adds a postscript. If we don't leave Elmina he will drink the toast of war from poor Macarthy's skull. So, general, it's time to plan for war."

On the Volta River, late September 1872

With no prospect of trouble, before crossing the Volta, Goodenough sent Bacon, who spoke the Ashanti language, across to enquire of the chief of the town opposite whether two English travelers would be allowed to pass through Ashanti lands.

"It will take several days before we hear anything. These vassal chiefs have to get the permission direct from Kumasi for just about everything," he told Frank.

In fact it took almost two weeks before a canoe rowed over to report that King Kofi Karikari could not wait to see the white men at his capital.

With this happy assurance from the Asantehene they crossed the Volta to be received in state by the local chief, who at once provided them with the necessary carriers. He also provided them with a guard and would not take no for an answer when Goodenough pointed out that they had their own Hausa guard. No, no, he insisted, his own men would prevent any trouble on their way.

On the following day they departed with many thanks for the hospitality. At the end of a day's journey, they stopped at a village. In the morning Frank and Goodenough prepared for a day's collecting in the vicinity. As they were about to set out Bacon ran up, followed at a more leisurely pace by Addo, the warrior in command of their guard.

"Please sah, Addo he say you must get ready to go."

Goodenough drew himself up to his full height and glared at Addo. "Go? Go where?"

"He say his instruction is you must go Kumasi straight, no delay." Bacon looked at the ground in evident embarrassment.

"Tell Addo this will entirely defeat the object of our journey. Tell him we must collect interesting specimens of birds and insects."

Bacon exchanged a flurry of words with the Ashanti, but it was clear to Frank that Addo had no intention of disobeying his orders, even for a day. Addo remained firm. His orders were that there was to be no delay, and if he failed in this, his head would certainly be removed from the rest of him.

"This is serious, Frank," Goodenough muttered worriedly. "If this idiot hasn't blundered about his orders, it's clear that we're more prisoners than visitors." Seeing the look of alarm that Frank failed to keep from his face, the explorer sniffed and said, "Mind, it may just be that the king merely issued the order with no idea that we would want to loiter on the way."

Addo was always civil toward his guests as they made their way in long days' marches. He ensured that they were well supplied with fresh food at every stop and enlisted hammock bearers for both of them when the recurrent fevers struck. He would not hear of their paying either for provisions or bearers, saying that they were the king's guests, and it would be an insult to the king if they were to pay for anything.

Ten days after leaving the banks of the Volta they came to the Ashanti capital of Kumasi. That evening Frank quickly noted his first impressions. *The town lies on rising ground, surrounded by a deep swamp varying between forty and a hundred yards wide. A messenger ran on ahead to announce our coming as we crossed the narrow marshy causeway giving access to the town. I could not repress a shudder as our party passed beneath a great fetish consisting of a dead sheep wrapped up in red-dyed cloth and suspended from two poles.*

Frederick and I took our places at the head of the little procession. On entering the town we were met by a crowd of at least five thousand people, for the most part brightly dressed warriors, who fired their muskets, and shouted. Horns, drums, rattles, and gongs added to the tumult. Men with flags performed wild dances, in which the warriors joined.

The captain-warriors wore caps with gilded rams' horns projecting in front or from the top, and immense plumes of exotic feathers on each side. Charms cased in gold, silver, and embroidery covered their vests of red cloth. These were interspersed with the horns and tails of animals, small brass bells, and shells. They wore loose cotton trousers, with great boots of dull red leather coming halfway up to the thigh, and fastened by small chains to their waist belts, also ornamented with bells, horse tails, strings of amulets, and strips of brightly dyed leather. Long leopards' tails hung down their backs.

Through this crowd the travelers' party moved forward slowly, the throng thickening at every step. Addo escorted them to a house which he said was set aside for their use, and that they would be allowed to see the king on the following day.

"Fascinating, Frederick," Frank said. "These houses are entirely different from anything I've ever seen before on our travels."

Each dwelling was built of red clay, plastered perfectly smooth, topped by beehive-shaped thatched roofs. The outside walls were unbroken by windows or openings of any kind other than the door, which led into an open courtyard of some twelve feet across. On each of the other three sides an alcove built up of clay pierced the wall and projected out from it about three feet from the ground. Each formed a kind of couch, some eight feet long by three feet high, with a thatched roof projecting out to prevent the rain beating into the alcove. Beyond were one or more similar courts in proportion to the size of the house.

In the course of the day Addo supervised the delivery of a sheep and a quantity of vegetables and fruits, which Ostik and the Hausas quickly turned into a meal for the evening. Bacon informed Goodenough of Addo's warning not to show themselves on the streets until they had seen the king.

"I suppose we'll be expected to make his majesty a handsome present," Frank said.

"Hmm, yes, and unfortunately our stores were not intended for so great a potentate." The explorer sighed and cast around for something. "It's no good, I'll have to give him my double-barreled shotgun and your Winchester, Frank. I don't suppose he'll have seen anything like a repeat-fire rifle before."

"Well I hope he appreciates them," Frank grumbled. "I'd better get them cleaned up and polished so as to look as handsome as possible."

"Frank, sarcasm doesn't become you."

"I'm sorry, but I've become quite attached to my carbine."

In the morning one of the captains came and said that the king was ready to receive them. The party of seven made its way through a vast crowd to the marketplace, an open area, nearly half a mile in extent. The sun shone brightly and played over all the colors to make the scene a brilliant one.

Across the space, the king was seated under a conglomeration of sunshades, with his chief warriors and *caboceers*, the vassal kings of his conquered nations, to either side. The huge umbrellas, some of them as much as fifteen feet across, were of scarlet, yellow, and other showy colors in silks and cloths, with fantastically scalloped and fringed valences. They were topped with crescents, birds, model elephants, barrels, and swords of gold and decorated stuffed animals. Members of the crowd carried innumerable smaller umbrellas of striped cloth. They waved them up and down, while a large orchestra of drums, flutes, horns, and other obscure instruments sounded in the air.

The elite all wore robes woven of foreign silk, which had been unraveled for working into native patterns. The *caboceers* sported golden necklaces and bracelets, in many cases so heavy that they had to support their laden arms on small boys' heads, who stood in front of them for the purpose. The crowd of thousands, shone with gold, silver, and shimmering colors.

The Asantehene received them with dignity, standing briefly to shake the two white men in the traditional Ashanti way by the left hand and expressing his satisfaction at seeing them.

Through Bacon, Frederick Goodenough replied that they had very great pleasure in visiting the court of his majesty, that they had already journeyed for many months in Africa, having started from the Gabon and passed through many tribes, but had they had any idea of visiting so great a king they would have provided themselves with presents fit for his acceptance. But as they were simple explorers, catching the birds, beasts, and insects of the country to take home with them to show to the people in England, the only things which they could offer him were a double-barreled breech loading rifle of the best English construction, and a little rifle, which would fire sixteen times without loading in between each shot.

The king examined the guns with great attention, taking each piece in turn, turning them over and running his hand across the sleek finish of the metal parts and the smoothness of the wooden stocks. The small rifle he ordered handed back to Frank and indicated that he wished to see it used.

Frank knew where he would like to use it, but raised the rifle's barrel well over the heads of the crowd and fired off the contents of the Winchester's magazine. Its repeat action caused evident astonishment among the assembled chiefs.

A factotum stepped forward and spoke through Bacon. "The king accepts your dash. He says he will speak more with you on a future occasion. He also says that you are free to move about in the town where you wish, and that the greatest respect will be shown to you by the people. He says you may take your Hausa translator with you, but all the rest of the party must confine themselves to the house the king has graciously given you."

King Kofi Karikari abruptly stood and turned away toward the palace entrance, and a fresh outburst of wild music greeted this dismissal. Addo came forward to escort them all back to their residence.

In the later afternoon, as soon as the sun's fierce heat had dissipated somewhat and the earlier crowds dispersed, Frank accompanied Goodenough for a walk through the town, Bacon following them closely in case his linguistic skills were required. Kumasi was not as large as its initial impression implied, not even as extensive as Abeokuta in terms of buildings, but the well ordered and tidy streets were broad, making it feel like a larger place. There were houses of every size, several much larger than the one the king had allotted to them, but all of them built to the same plan.

"The main population must live in outlying villages, don't you think, Frederick?"

Goodenough looked around and nodded his head. "You're right. There's no way these buildings are sufficient to house so many, so they must be scattered around outside the swamp. I imagine most of what we see are houses of the *caboceers*, generals, and chief warriors. I made a mistake this morning in thinking we were in a market place. Now I think of it, it far more resembles a military parade ground."

Three days passed before a brightly dressed flunky came to inform them that the king wished to see them and he would lead the way to the royal palace. This large building was situated behind and to one side of the 'market place', which was at one end of the town. Constructed solidly of stone, and evidently built from European designs, it was square, with a flat roof and embattled parapet.

They were conducted through the gateway into a large courtyard, and then into a hall where Kofi Karikari sat on a raised throne. Attendants stood around fanning him. "He doesn't look very happy," Frank hissed in Goodenough's ear. They had barely taken their places before the king bellowed out.

"Why do the English take my town of Elmina?"

"Bacon, kindly convey to his majesty that I have been nine months absent from the coast, and that having come straight out from England to the Gabon I am altogether unaware of what's happened at Elmina."

"Elmina is mine," the king thundered and thumped a fist on his knee. "The Dutch were my tributaries, my vassals, and they had no right to hand it over to the English."

"But I understood, your majesty, that the British were ready to pay an annual sum, even larger than that which the Dutch have contributed."

"I do not want money," the king shouted. "I have gold in plenty. There are places in my dominions where ten men in a day can wash a thousand of your ounces. I want Elmina, I want to trade with the coast."

"But the English will give your majesty every facility for trade."

"They keep me from Cape Coast, which is also mine by tribute. Even if they allow trade at Elmina, suppose we quarrel," the king said, "they can stop powder and guns from coming up. If Elmina were mine I could bring up guns and powder at all times."

"Your majesty would be no better off," Bacon translated, "for the English in case of war could stop supplies from entering Elmina."

"My people will drive them into the sea," the king said. "We have been troubled with them too long. They can make guns, but they cannot fight. My people will eat them up. We fought them before, and see..." He pointed to a great drum, from the edge of which hung a dozen human skulls. "The heads of white men serve me as fetishes."

He picked up one and flourished it at them. "This is my drinking cup, I call it the Macarthy cup!"

He then waved his hand to signify the audience's termination.

"Things look bad, Frank," Goodenough admitted as they walked back. "I'm afraid the king is determined to have a war, and if that breaks out our lives won't be worth anything."

"It can't be helped," Frank said as cheerfully as he could. "We must make the best of it. Perhaps something may happen to improve our position." Nevertheless, inwardly he felt uneasy at the development.

The next day the explorers were surprised at the visit of two Europeans, a German, who introduced himself as Herr Kuhne, and Herr Ramseyer, a Swiss. The two missionaries quickly filled the Englishmen in on how they came to be in Kumasi, that although they were held hostage, along with their families—Khune's brother and his wife, Ramseyer's wife and two children—they had been treated hospitably so far. "There is also a French merchant held with us, a Monsieur Bannat, but he's unwell with a fever at the moment."

Their next words gave some hope to the Englishmen that the situation might be more hopeful than the king's words had led them to expect.

"Negotiations are going on for our release, and we expect to be sent down to Cape Coast very soon," Herr Ramseyer said. "So far as we know you English are doing everything possible to satisfy the king."

Frank thought he sounded ambivalent about this.

"I am certain peace will be maintained," Herr Kuhne stated firmly.

The Swiss looked uncomfortable. "It's true we've been treated well enough, but our time in Kumasi has been like living in hell… the horrible rites and sacrifices we have been compelled to witness. At least three thousand people are slaughtered every year."

Frank let out a low gasp of surprised disgust, his eyes widening.

"Oh, it's true," Herr Ramseyer said.

"On an almost industrial scale, Frank…" Goodenough muttered sadly.

The Swiss went on. "You saw the massive tree standing behind the market under which the king sits. That is the great fetish tree. Many victims are sacrificed in the palace itself, but the wholesale slaughters take place there. The bush behind comes up to within twenty yards of the edge of the square and if you turn in there you will see thousands of dead bodies or their remains putrefying together."

"I thought I noticed a foul stench as we were talking to the king," Frank said shuddering. "What monsters these people must be. Who would have thought that all that show of gold and silver and bright colors covered such horrible barbarism."

"It mus' be so sah," Bacon suddenly spoke up. "De Asante have a few meanings for 'Coomassie', but de big big one means 'Death Place.'"

Chapter 17: Invading the Fanti

Kumasi, late September 1872

All too soon Frank discovered for himself the true meaning of savage Ashanti barbarity. On the following morning the noise of a passing crowd attracted their attention, and on going to the house's doorway, to his horror he saw a man being taken to sacrifice.

His hands pinioned behind him, he followed men beating drums. A sharp thin knife had been passed through his cheeks, by which his lips were noozed in a figure 8. One of his guards carried in front of him his severed ear, the other hung from his head by a small strand of skin. Several bleeding gashes marked his back, and under each shoulder blade a long knife had been thrust. He was led along by the man carrying his ear by a cord passed through a hole bored in his nose.

Frank ran horror stricken back into the house, flung himself down on the edge of his bed-alcove and sat for a while with his hands over his eyes as if to shut out the ghastly spectacle.

"Frederick," he said finally, "if they're going to kill us, at least let's die fighting to the last, and blow out our own brains with the last shots we have left. I don't think I'm afraid of dying, but to be tortured like that would be horrible—and why such cruelties?"

Herr Kuhne answered the question when he was consulted later. "Once a man is selected for sacrifice, there are only two ways to evade it. One, he repeats the 'king's oath'—a certain formula of words—before they can gag him. Two, if he can break loose from his guards and run as far as the Bantama-Kumasi crossroad before being overtaken, he is set free. So, in order to prevent their victims getting off by either of these methods, the executioners jump the intended man from behind, and while one binds his hands, another drives that thin knife through both his cheeks and tongue, which stops him from opening his mouth to utter the words.

"The horror doesn't stop there. In all that agony the man awaits his execution, and when the time comes they grab him and force his head over the killing bowl or stool. Then, they don't make a clean execution of it, oh no, one of them, using a large kind of butcher's knife, cuts deeply into the spine, and then carves the head off slowly." The missionary shook his head. "The people here are drunk on blood-lust. To them an execution is as attractive an entertainment as is a soccer match to an Englishman."

The next day a message arrived from the palace informing them that their retaining private guards was an insult to the king, and that the Hausas must remove themselves to another part of the town. Resistance was evidently useless. Goodenough called Bacon, Firewater, Tatters, and Ugly Tom together and told them what had happened.

"I'm sorry I've brought you into this plight, my poor fellows. There are now two courses open to you. Either volunteer for the king's army and then try to escape if an opportunity crops up, or you can slip away now. You're used to the bush, you can all swim, and it won't matter where you strike the Pra. If you travel at night and lie in a jungle thicket by day you should be able to get through. Obviously, if you try to escape and get caught you'll be killed, while if you stop here it's possible that no harm will come to you. On the other hand you may be led to your execution at any moment. Don't tell me your decision. I'll be questioned, and would rather be able to say that I was ignorant of your intentions."

Goodenough, who looked unwell, his eyes shrunken in their sockets, Frank noticed uneasily, explained that he had written out orders on his bankers in England which agents at Cape Coast would cash for them. In thanks for their long and faithful service, he had doubled the agreed rate and would send double that to their families in the event they did not make it safely.

The Hausa men expressed their gratitude for his kindness, gave him the names and means of finding their wives, and then, with tears in their eyes, took their leave.

"Now, Ostik, what do you say?"

"I stay here, sah," Ostik said in a matter of fact tone. "Hausas fighting men, creep through wood, crawl on stomach. Dey get through sure nuff. Ostik stay with massa. If dey kill massa dey kill Ostik. Ostik take the chance."

"Very well, Ostik, if we get through this together you won't regret your loyalty. Now, Frank, I think it would be a good thing if you were to spend some hours every day in trying to pick up as much of the language here as you can. You're quick at it—I've noticed you talking with Bacon these past weeks—and were able to make yourself understood by our bearers far better than I could do. You already know a great many words in four or five of these dialects. They're all related to each other, and I think you'll get along fine in Ashanti within a couple of months. It will help to pass your time and to occupy your mind. I expect the missionaries can point to a man who's worked on the coast and knows some English." His bloodshot eyes held Frank's. "If we get into trouble your knowledge of the language may be the difference between life and death."

As soon as he heard of the Hausas' escape, the king flew into a terrible rage. The next day he sent for the white men. Frank had to lend Goodenough an arm, for the explorer complained of a deep weariness. The court translator knelt tremulously at the king's heaving side.

"I know nothing about it." Goodenough spoke in a tired voice. "They were contented when they were with me, and had no wish to go. Your soldiers took them away yesterday afternoon, and I suppose they were frightened. It was foolish of them. They should have known that a great king does not injure those who come peacefully into his country. They should have known better. They were poor, ignorant men, who didn't know that the hospitality of a king is sacred, and that when a king invites travelers to enter his country they are his guests, and under his protection."

When the interpreter translated this speech the king was silent for two or three minutes. Then he said, "My white friend is right, They were foolish men. They could not know these things. If my warriors overtake them no harm shall come to them."

Hardly believing this assertion but nevertheless pleased with the impression that his friend's words had evidently made, Frank helped Goodenough back to their house. In the afternoon the king sent a sheep and a present of five ounces of gold, and a message that he did not wish his white friends to feel stuck always in the town. They might, he said, walk to any of the numerous villages within a circle of three or four miles, and that four of his guards would always accompany them to see that no one threatened, upset, or insulted them.

They were pleased with this permission, it meant they—or rather more Frank, with Goodenough only up to the rigors on some days—could start collecting again. It took them, too, away from the sight of the horrible human sacrifices which went on daily. Through the German missionary they obtained a man who had worked for three years down at Cape Coast. In the evenings he sat and talked with Frank, who, from the knowledge of native words which he had picked up in his nine months' journeying in West Africa, was able to make rapid progress in Ashanti.

He had one or two slight attacks of fever, but the constant use of quinine enabled him to resist their effect, and he was now to some degree immunized, and thought no more of the attacks of fever than he would have done at home of a violent bilious attack. This was not the case with Goodenough. Frank watched with increasing concern as he lost strength rapidly with recurring fever attacks. He was soon unable to accompany him on his walks at all. One morning he appeared desperately ill.

"Is it the fever again, Frederick?"

"No, Frank, it's worse than that, I think I have dysentery. I had an attack last time I was on the coast, and know what to do with it. Get the medicine chest and bring me the bottle of ipecacuanha. Now, you must give me doses every three hours."

Frank, wracked with worry, nursed his friend closely, and for the next three days hoped that he was winning over the illness. But on the fourth day a fever set in.

"You must stop the ipecacuanha, now," Frederick said shakily, "and Frank, send Ostik to the missionaries, and ask them to come here as soon as they can."

When they arrived the English naturalist asked Frank to leave him alone with them. A quarter of an hour later they went out, and Frank, returning heavy with foreboding, found two sealed envelopes on the table beside him.

"Frank, my boy, I've made my will. Fever and dysentery together are fatal nine times out of ten. Don't cry," he said gently, as the tears welled in Frank's eyes. "I would like to live, but if it's fated otherwise, so be it. I've no wife or near relatives to regret my loss—none, my poor boy, who will mourn for me as sincerely as I know you will do. You've become, over these months, the son I never had, and you'll find that I haven't forgotten you in my will. I've written it in duplicate. If you have an opportunity send one of these letters down to the coast. Keep the other yourself, and I trust that you'll live to carry it to its destination. If, for any reason, you don't make it, I hope it will console you in your last moments that I've not forgotten the little sister you've told me about so often—in case of your death she will be provided for."

An hour later the naturalist dipped into a state of delirium, in which he remained all night, falling toward morning into a dull coma, gradually breathing his last, without another word, at eight in the morning.

A deep grief utterly prostrated Frank, from which he roused himself to send to the king to ask permission to bury his friend. The king responded by saying how grieved he was to hear of the white man's death. He ordered Addo and many warriors to attend the funeral. Frank had a grave dug on a rising spot of ground beyond the marsh.

In the evening a hundred Ashanti gathered, and four strapping warriors bore the body of Frederick Addington Goodenough to his last resting place. Frank, the German and Swiss families, and a recovered Monsieur Bannat followed the Ashanti mourners. Herr Kuhne read the service over the grave as Frank, eyes burning, clutched his broad-brimmed tropical hat and recalled how Frederick had saved him from buying a ridiculous pith helmet all those months ago. Then he went back heartbroken to his house with Ostik, who also felt terribly the loss of his master.

At Elmina, a hundred and fifty miles south of Kumasi, Colonel Harley, the military commandant sent from Cape Coast to govern affairs there, lost his temper with the people he was supposed to look after. With almost incredible idiocy, and in spite of the agreement which had been made with the Elmina tribes, he summoned their king and chiefs to a council, and abruptly told them that they would no longer be allowed to celebrate their customs, which consisted of firing guns, waving flags, dancing, and other harmless rites.

The chiefs were rightly indignant at this breach of the agreement they had solemnly entered into with the British. As soon as they had left the council chamber they gathered around their king who declared in no uncertain terms, "I will send to Kumasi, to the Asantehene of Ashanti, begging him to cross the Pra and attack the English."

Two days after the funeral Frank planted a wooden cross over the grave. On this he had carefully carved the name of his friend. Hearing a week afterward that the king was sending an embassy to Cape Coast, Frank asked permission for the envoy to deliver Goodenough's letter, which the king agreed to after being convinced by the terrified court translator that the contents were not controversial.

At the end of December, when Frank had been nearly three months at Kumasi, he received an unnerving warning from Herr Ramseyer. "The king is spinning his words like a top—he seems intent on the negotiations, but secretly he's preparing for war. An army is collecting on the Pra. I hear that twelve thousand men have been ordered to assemble there."

Frank thumped a fist into his other palm. "That explains it. I've noticed that there have been fewer men about than usual during the last few days. What will happen to us, do you think?"

The missionary shook his head. "No one can say. It all depends on the king's whim. I think, however, that he's more likely to keep us hostage to get money for us at the end of the war, than to kill us. If all goes well with his army we're probably safe, but if he hears of any defeat…" a forefinger drawn across his throat told eloquently of their likely fate.

"Will he be defeated? They've done well before."

"Who knows, but it seems probable that the Ashanti will turf the English off the coast. The Fanti are no use. They may have been brave once, and united might have made a successful resistance, but you English have made women of them. You've forbidden them to fight among themselves, you've discouraged them in any attempts to raise armies, you've reduced the power of the chiefs, you've tried to turn them into a race of farmers and traders instead of warriors, and so you can't expect real help from them now."

Frank took the attack personally. "That's a bit strong, sir. I'm sure under their British officers the Fanti will bear up well."

Ramseyer gave a faint snort of derision. "They'll melt away like snow before the Ashanti. The king's spies tell him that there are only a hundred and fifty black troops at Cape Coast, trained and led by Englishmen but, after all, still natives, no braver than the Ashanti. What chance have they of resisting an army outnumbering them by nearly a hundred to one?"

"Is the fort at Cape Coast strong?" Frank asked.

"Yes, against savages without artillery. Besides, the warships anchored in the roads will cover it."

"Well," Frank argued, "if we can hold that, they'll send out troops from England."

The missionary looked dubious. "So you say, but your government has refused to do so in the past. Even if they do, what could white troops do in the fever-haunted jungle which extends from the coast to Kumasi?"

"They'll manage somehow," Frank replied, with more confidence than he felt. "Besides, after all, as I hear that the greater part of the kingdom lying north of Kumasi is plain and open country, so the Ashanti themselves can't be all accustomed to bush fighting. They'll also suffer from fever in the low, swamp land."

Three days later the Asantehene sent for Frank. "The English are not true," he began, scowling darkly. "They promised the people of Elmina that they should be allowed to retain all their customs as they enjoyed under the Dutch. They have broken their word. They have forbidden the customs and trampled on their feelings. The people of Elmina have written to ask me to deliver them. I am bound by oath to do so."

Frank could only say that he knew nothing of what was going on at the coast, and could only think that his majesty must have been misinformed, as the English wished to be friendly with the Ashanti people.

"They do not wish it," the king spat furiously. "They are liars."

A buzz of approval sounded among the *caboceers* and warriors standing around. Frank, who naturally thought he was about to be instantly executed, felt his bowels loosen, but got a grip on himself as the hand stuck in his right pocket grasped his revolver. He was firmly resolved to shoot the king first, and then to blow out his own brains, rather than to be put to any horrible tortures.

After a laden pause the king suddenly spoke to him in a surprisingly moderate tone, "My people tell me that you can talk to them in their own tongue."

"I've learnt a little of the Ashanti speech," Frank said in that language. "I can't talk well, but I can make myself understood."

"Very well," the king said. "I shall send you down with my general, Amanquatia. You know the ways of English fighting, and will tell him what is best to do against them. When the war is over and I've driven the English away, I will send you away also, weighed down with more gold than you can carry. You are my guest, and I don't wish to harm you. Tomorrow you will start. Your goods will be of no more use to you. I have ordered my treasurer to count the cloth and the powder, and the other things which you have, and to pay you for them in gold. You may go."

Frank left the palace, phewing in relief at his narrow escape from death but distressed at the task laid on his shoulders. He vowed in his heart that he would not tell anyone about the best way to attack his own countrymen. On the other hand, he was pleased at the order in the degree that a means of escape might present itself. Such was also the opinion of Ostik when Frank told him what had taken place.

An hour later the king's treasurer arrived. The whole of the trade goods were appraised at fair prices, and even the cases were paid for, as the treasurer said that these would be good for storing the king's state robes. Frank only retained his own trunk with clothes, his bed and rugs, the journals of the expedition, a supply of ammunition for his revolver, his medicine chest, tent, and a case with chocolate, preserved milk, tea, hard tack, rice, and a couple of bottles of brandy.

In the morning came the rumbling thunder of many drums. Four slave porters were appointed to Frank's service, and these came in, took up his baggage, and joined the line. Frank, brushing flies from his eyes, waited patiently for Amanquatia. He was vaguely acquainted with the Ashanti general, having seen him several times at the palace. Eventually his procession snaked its way along the broad road. The great man was carried in a hammock, with a paraphernalia of attendants bearing chairs, umbrellas, and flags. Frank fell in behind these accompanied by Ostik. The whole population of Kumasi turned out and shouted their farewells as they paused in the parade ground while a hundred victims were sacrificed to the success of the expedition. Frank kept in the thick of the cheering warriors so as to avoid witnessing the horrible spectacle, but he could not keep out the squelchy sounds of the butchery, nor the screams of delight from the massed crowd.

As they passed the king he said to his general, "Bring me back the head of the military governor. I will place it on my drum by the side of my Macarthy cup."

Then the army crossed the swamp and started on its way south to the Pra. Three miles farther they crossed the river Ordah at Agogo, where the water rose up to their necks. The road was little more than a track through the thick bush, and there were many small streams to be crossed. Leeches were an ever-present problem, but by this time Frank had mastered the technique for getting rid of them before they could do much damage.

Frank thanked his lucky stars that he hadn't suffered a recurrence of fever for some time because on that first day they marched nearly thirty miles without a stop to reach the large town of Fomanse. Many of the houses were built in the same style as those at Kumasi, and a stone building housed the petty king's palace. That night Frank slept in a native house which the general allotted to him close to the palace. The army slept on the ground.

The next morning they crossed the tall but narrow range of the Adansi hills before dropping down into the dense jungle beyond. Late in the afternoon the column reached the Pra, where the main army lay encamped along the banks in roughly-made huts of branches and oil-palm fronds. For a week, the army paused while innumerable carriers brought in provisions.

Having assiduously kept up the expedition's journals, Frank knew that the Ashanti crossed the Pra on January 22, 1873. At this point the river was about sixty yards wide. Great canoes of cottonwood tree trunks, hollowed out by the troops who had arrived first, conveyed the army into British territory. If he expected an immediate reaction to the crossing, the emptiness of the forests disappointed him.

"The way to the coast lies open," Amanquatia boasted. "The white governor has upset the Elminas and they will not attack former allies. His entreaties to the Fanti fall on deaf ears and they are of no worth. The Assim, who have been our enemies many times, entreated the white soldiers for arms and ammunition, but a curt refusal offended their king. He has just informed me that he will remain neutral."

In spite of these brave, but to Frank dispiriting words, he noted that the general seemed to be imbued suddenly with a spirit of prudence after crossing the river, and the army moved forward with the greatest caution, sometimes halting for weeks at a time.

Amanquatia had Frank pitch his tent next to his own shelter at every stop. Four 'honor guards' were appointed, but really, as Frank knew, to keep a watch on his porters and prevent him from making his escape. These men kept guard, two at a time, night and day over the tent, and followed him if he left it, even when he went to relieve himself.

The first morning after crossing the Pra Frank had sent Ostik into Amanquatia's hut with a cup of hot chocolate. The general enjoyed the drink so much that he made a point of visiting Frank's tent to thank him. After that, seeing as how he still had a large supply of tins of preserved chocolate and milk, Frank sent him a cup every morning. In return the Ashanti general showed Frank many little kindnesses, sending him in birds or animals when any were shot by his men, and keeping him as well provided with food as was possible under the circumstances.

Frank never attempted to leave the camp. The bush—extremely thick, tangled with undergrowth and creepers—made it almost impossible to make any headway. The majority of the trees were of only moderate height, but above them towered the cottonwood, teak, mahogany, and ebony giants, rising with straight trunks as tall as two hundred feet. Many of the trees had shed their foliage, and some of these were completely covered with brilliant flowers of different colors. The woods resounded with the cries of various birds, but butterflies, except in the clearings, were few.

The army depended for its food partly on the cultivated patches around the Assim villages, partly on supplies brought up from the rear. In the jungle, too, they found many edible roots and fruits. In spite of the efforts to supply them with food, Frank saw before many weeks had passed that the Ashanti soldiers were suffering from hunger. The flesh dropped off them, many shook with fever, and the enthusiasm so evident at the Pra had entirely evaporated.

The first resistance they encountered came on April 8, when the road into Dunkwa, a British outpost fifteen miles inland from Cape Coast, was barred by a force of fifty Hausa troops brought from Lagos, together with some companies of the 2nd West India Regiment and a large body of Fanti police, all under the command of a Lieutenant Hopkins.

The Ashanti attacked, but the Fanti, boosted in confidence by the presence of the Hausas, fought with unexpected bravery. The skirmish was typical of the region—neither side attempting any vigorous action. Instead, the combatants took shelter behind trees and kept up a heavy fire at a distance of a hundred yards. Consequently, great quantities of powder and slugs were fired with few casualties on either side. At nightfall both attack lines drew off.

"Is that the way your English soldiers fight?" the general asked Frank that night.

"Yes," Frank said vaguely, "we fire away at each other."

Amanquatia snorted in irritation. "And then I suppose when one side has used up its ammunition it retires."

"Of course it would retire," Frank said. "It could hardly resist without ammunition, you know."

Frank carefully avoided saying that one or other of the hypothetical

European sides would mount a charge well before its opponents' ammunition was expended. He had no intention of encouraging the Ashanti to adopt tactics which, with their superior numbers, would give them a victory. The Ashanti were not dissatisfied with the day's work—as far as they were concerned they had proved themselves equal to the English troops.

On April 14 the Fanti police unit took the initiative and attacked the Ashanti position. The battle was a mere repetition of the fight of a week before, and about midday the Fanti, having exhausted their ammunition, turned and fled to Cape Coast. Hopkins and his Hausas and West Indians had little alternative but to join them in a retreat against vastly superior numbers.

"Now that we have beaten the Fanti," Amanquatia said to Frank, "we shall march down to Elmina."

Leaving the main road at Dunkwa the army moved slowly through the bush toward Elmina, less than thirty miles away, halting in the woods some eight miles from the town, and twelve from Cape Coast. To Frank, it seemed he was so close to safety and yet still as far away as ever.

Chapter 18: Assault on Elmina

April–September 1873

"I am going to look at the English forts," the general announced. "My white friend and his Ostik will go with me."

With fifty of his warriors Amanquatia left the camp, crossed a stream, and came down to the sea a short distance to the west of Elmina. With them were several of the local tribe, who had visited the camp to welcome the Ashanti war band. The group approached to within three or four hundred yards of the fort, which was separated from them by a river. Frank viewed the British stronghold with great interest. He saw at once that the fort was not built to withstand major artillery, presumably because the local natives had none, and assumed many others like it on the coast were similar in this respect. Elmina was surrounded by high walls sufficiently thick to allow men to walk in single file along the top and to fire over the parapet. At intervals, jutting casements housed field guns. The castellation along the top of the walls lent them an appearance of great strength, which he suspected they did not really possess. Still, the structure was of considerable size, no doubt to house a barracks, officers' quarters, commissary, weapons store, and all the other installations typical of a military establishment within it.

"It is a wonderful fort," the Ashanti general admitted, impressed by its scale and threatening presence.

"Yes," Frank replied. "And there's artillery on the top, those great black things you see sticking out. Those are guns, and each carries cannonballs enough to kill a hundred men with each shot."

The general looked for some time attentively. "Do you have castles in the white men's country?"

"We do."

"How do you take them?"

"We bring a great many cannon throwing balls of iron as big as my head, and so knock a great hole in the wall and then rush in."

"But if there are no cannon?"

"We never attack a castle without cannon. But if we had no cannon we might try to starve the people out. But you can't do that here, because they can land food and even stored water from the sea."

The general looked puzzled. "Why do the white men come here to our land?"

"They come to trade," Frank told him.

"And they have no other reason?"

"No. They don't want to take land, because the white man can't work in so hot and humid a climate."

"Then if he could not trade he would go away?"

"Yes," Frank agreed, rather disingenuously. "If he could do no trade there would be no point in remaining here." Frank himself was not at all sure this would be true, but he had no intention of revealing this to the Ashanti general.

"Then we will let him do no trade," Amanquatia said, brightening up considerably. "If we cannot take the forts we will surround them closely, and no trade can come in and out. Then the white man will have to go away. As to the Fanti, we will destroy them and the white men will have no one to fight for them."

"But there are white troops," Frank said.

"White soldiers?" the Ashanti asked surprised. "I thought it was only black soldiers that fought for the whites. The whites are few, they are traders."

"The English are many," Frank replied firmly. "For every man that the Asantehene can send to fight, England can send ten more. There are white soldiers, thousands and thousands of them, but they're not sent here. They're kept at home to fight other white nations, just as the kings of Africa fight against each other. And they're not sent here because the climate kills the whites too quickly, so to guard the white traders here we hire black soldiers." He fixed the general with a steely gaze. "But when it's known at home that the Asantehene is fighting against us, the white troops will come, sure as eggs is eggs."

"Eggs is eggs...?" Amanquatia pondered the unfamiliar phrase which Frank had thrown out in English. He turned away to stare into the bush and was thoughtful for some time. "If they come," he said at length, "the fevers will kill them. The white man cannot live in the swamps. Your friend, the white guest of the king, died at Kumasi."

"Yes, but he had been nearly a year in the country before he died. Three weeks will be enough for an English army to march from Cape Coast to Kumasi. A few might die, it's true, but most of them would get there—and back again."

"Kumasi!" Amanquatia threw his head back and laughed in three harsh gusts. "The white men would be mad to consider marching against the city of the great king. We should make a great fetish, and they would all die as soon as they had crossed the river."

Frank quickly suppressed the smile that almost broke out. "General, the black man's fetishes don't have any effect on white men. A fetish only has power if it's believed in. A black man who knows that his enemy has made a ju-ju fetish against him is terrified. His blood runs like water and he dies of fright. But the whites don't believe in this magic. They laugh at fetishes, and then they can't hurt them."

The general growled, but said no more. He turned away from the view of the fort and, muttering to himself, retired to his camp.

It tantalized Frank to see the Union Jack waving within sight, and to know that friends were so near and yet he couldn't even stretch out his hand to them.

In Kumasi the king had insisted Frank dress more like his nobles so the people would take less notice of him, and had fitted him out in native garb. In consequence, had the reconnaissance party been seen from the castle walls the soldiers would not have noticed a fellow countrymen among them.

Three days later the general with a similar force crossed the Sweet river at night, and proceeded east along the coast to within a few hundred yards of the fort at Cape Coast, whose appearance pleased him no more than that of Elmina had done. Nor did the sight of several ships anchored close to shore. "Warships," Frank told him shortly.

The Ashanti were now better supplied with food, as they were able to depend on the Elmina tribes who cultivated a considerable extent of ground. To build the store, the Ashanti warriors were set to work to aid in planting a larger tract of land than usual, a proof in Frank's mind that the general contemplated making a long stay, and blockading Elmina and Cape Coast into surrender if he could not capture them by assault.

Having returned to Elmina, Frank noted in his journal that on June 7 the arrival of *HMS Barracouta*, a very serious addition to the British naval force, but in no way a troop carrier. The government is dragging its feet, he thought with some anger. His dismay was allayed to some extent when he saw marines landing and entering the fort. At a distance, it was hard to tell the number, but he thought about a hundred men.

When Amanquatia saw the marines in their bright red coats Frank informed him of their nature and that some of them would be light artillerymen, as well as some others dressed in blue, sailors from the *Barracouta*. As these numbers failed frighten the Ashanti, he detached some three thousand of his force and closed in. Shortly afterward came news that the natives in and around Elmina town had all been ordered to lay down their arms. They rebelled and came over to the Ashanti. As they were about to attack, Festing ordered the anchored naval ships to open up a bombardment of the native town, which lay to the west of the European fort.

The sound of such heavy guns, differing widely from anything they had ever heard before, caused the Ashanti to pause in consternation.

Then came the shriek of the incoming shells, which exploded in rapid succession in the village, from which flames began immediately to rise. After a few minutes' hesitation the Ashanti and Elmina soldiers again advanced.

The general, carried in a chair on the shoulders of four men, took his post on rising ground near the burning village. "There," he said to Frank, "the red and blue soldiers are coming out of the fort. Now you will see."

The little squad of marines and the *Barracouta*'s blue jackets, accompanied by a unit of black soldiers, deployed in line. The Ashanti opened fire on them, but the British force was out of range of the slugs. As soon as the red and blue line formed the men opened fire, and the Ashanti were bewildered at the incessant rattle of rifle-fire from so few men. Amanquatia urged his men forward but the force of their enemy's Sniders swept the warriors backward, mowing them down in considerable numbers. In two minutes the Ashanti turned and ran.

The general's bearers, in spite of his shouts, hurried him off along with the others, and Frank would have taken this opportunity to escape had not two of his guards seized him by the arms and hauled him along, while the other two kept close behind.

As soon as they had passed over the crest of the rise, and the British fire ceased, Amanquatia leaped from his chair and threw himself among his flying troops. He struck out right and left with his staff, and hurled obscenities at them. "If you do not stop and return against the whites I will send every one of you back to Kumasi, and there you will be put to death as cowards!"

The threat worked. The fugitives rallied, and in a few minutes were ready to march back again. In an aside to Frank, Amanquatia asked, "What kind of weapon is it that shoots so fast, so long? It was the surprise of the sustained fire, rather than the actual losses they inflicted that caused my warriors to fright."

Frank grinned inwardly, but kept his face serious. "The white soldiers have the latest rifles, the breech-loading Snider. They do not have to wait to recharge them and load a ball. The bullets go in at the side of the rifle and eject once fired, ready to slam another in."

The general scowled and beetled his brow. "They will feel our spears when we get in close among them and their weapons will no longer count. Look! Even now they retreat."

Frank saw it was true. From their concealment he watched as, the naval contingent went back to their boats and the infantry returned to the fort. *They must think the savages have fled.*

Amanquatia made a detour with his troops, and marched against the town from the east where the cluster of buildings sheltered them from the fort's guns. But someone must have seen the maneuver, for immediately the marines and black soldiers marched out again met the Ashanti just as they were entering the town. The fight was a brutal one, and for a time neither side appeared to have the advantage. Frank, under the care of his guards a few hundred yards to the rear, was filled with dismay at seeing how the Ashanti, in spite of heavy losses, suddenly gained ground and pressed forward bravely.

At that point he saw something still hidden to the fighting warriors which gave him hope for his countrymen. On a low hill on the Ashanti flank the sailors of the *Barracouta* reappeared. The instant these took up their position they opened a withering fire. Amanquatia's men lost heart at this attack by fresh foes and soon fled again. In the two engagements they had lost nearly four hundred men. Frank retreated with the beaten Ashanti, and that evening Amanquatia told him that the weapons of the white men were too good, and that he would not attack them again in the open.

"Their guns shoot farther, as well as quicker, than ours," he muttered gloomily. "Our slugs are no use against the heavy bullets… at a distance. But in the woods, where you can't see twenty paces among the trees, it will be different. If I do not attack them they must attack me, or their trade will be starved out. When they come into the deep bush you will see that we shall eat them up."

"Oh, yes sah," Ostik muttered within Frank's hearing, "munch, munch, munch."

In spite of Cardwell and Wolseley's pressure on the government, they had so far only managed to persuade Prime Minister Gladstone into a small stiffening of the British on the Coast, which had resulted in the *Barracouta*'s arrival with its complement of one hundred and ten marines under the command of Lieutenant-Colonel Festing. He assumed command of all the British and West Indian troops on the Coast and the warship's Captain Freemantle became the senior naval officer on the station.

In the next few weeks there were further hostile encounters, usually inconclusive and frustrating for Colonel Festing and his officers. A packet steamer headed for Liverpool took dispatches making it clear that without a proper British field force, there was no way of making any headway against the Ashanti army.

The reply in mid-August brought great relief with the news that Sir Garnet Wolseley would arrive soon, with a cadre of officers to plan for a full scale assault on the Ashanti empire. Several newspaper correspondents also arrived with the steamer, among them the explorer-hero Henry Morton Stanley, reporting for the *New York Herald*, and George Alfred Henty, representing the London *Standard*. "At last," Festing said, "the situation's being taken seriously."

And not before time. Fevers were taking their toll and with few exceptions the marines first sent out were invalided home; but a hundred and fifty more arrived to take their place. Some detachments of the 2nd West Indian regiment were sent from Sierra Leone to join their comrades and a complement of Hausas brought from Lagos, and the situation remained unchanged. In late August Commodore Commerell arrived from the Cape of Good Hope aboard *HMS Rattlesnake*.

"Commodore, can you take some of your boats up the Pra?" Festing asked him. "Apart from being a useful reconnaissance, we might reach some diplomatic accord with the chiefs on the river's lower reaches."

Commerell quickly began to organize the mission, but it was hard to keep anything secret from the Elmina tribesmen.

A messenger arrived in Amanquatia's camp. There was an immediate stir. "Now," the general said to Frank, "you are going to see us fight the white men on our own terms. Some of the big ships have gone to the mouth of the Pra, and we believe that they are going to land in boats. You will see. The Elmina tribes will launch an attack, but I shall also go with some of my warriors to help… and you and your man will come with me."

Taking fifty picked Ashanti, Amanquatia set off immediately, even though dusk was approaching. They marched all night toward the west and at daybreak joined the Elminas. These hid themselves in the mangroves and bush lining the river. The general with a dozen men, taking Frank, went down near the river's mouth to reconnoiter. The ships lay more than a mile offshore. They watched as six boats were lowered, filled with men, and taken in tow by a steam launch. It was clear they were heading for the Pra.

"We will go back," Amanquatia said. "You will see what we can do."

Frank felt a thrill of alarm. He saw the British running into an ambush. *If it costs me my life I have to warn them.* Within minutes the sharp puffs of the steam launch grew louder and the boats were within three hundred yards, the steamer's bow wave riding along the narrowing banks.

Frank stepped forward and was about to give a warning shout when Amanquatia noticed the movement and the expression on his face which betrayed his intention. As quick as a striking snake the Ashanti reached out and hurled him to the ground. In seconds a dozen hands seized Frank. He was gagged and then tied to the trunk of a small tree, from where he could witness the coming slaughter.

Frank struggled, but the knots and coils were too tight for him to loosen his bonds. Faithful Ostik, he could see, had also been pushed to the ground and trussed to keep him quiet. With growing frustration he heard the panting steam launch coming nearer and nearer. Then he glimpsed it through the bushes as it came toward them, the boats towed behind. The Elmina men and the Ashanti lay stretched on the ground with their muskets in front of them.

The boats were only forty feet from the bank when they came abreast of the Ashanti position. Amanquatia shouted the word of command, and a stream of slugs belched out from the thick bank side cover.

In the boats confusion reigned. Several men died instantly, still seated on the boards, and many others slumped wounded by the deadly volley. Frank watched in horror as the commodore in command and two captains slump fro sight. The launch tried turning around, and the marines in the boats opened fire on their invisible foes, who replied steadily. In five minutes from the first shot being fired it was all over. The launch steamed downriver with the shattered boats in tow, followed by the exulting shouts of the natives ringing in the ears of those on board.

Frank's position had been perilous while the fight raged as the British rifle bullets sang close by him in quick succession. One struck the tree an inch from his cheek and drew blood from the flying shards of bark. He was doubtful, too, as to what his fate would be at the outcome of the battle. Fortunately Amanquatia was in the highest of spirits at his victory. He ordered Frank set free.

"There, you see. The whites are no use," he boasted. "They run with their eyes shut into danger, and then like women they cannot fight. It will be the same if they attack us on the land."

He slapped his thighs in appreciation and took the praises of his men. Then he swung back on Frank. "You were foolish. Why did you want to call out? Are you not well treated? Are you not the king's guest? Am I not your friend?"

Frank gritted his teeth before letting out a quiet sigh. "I am well treated, and you are my friend," he answered guardedly. His lips formed a firm straight line as he thought of his response, and then, with a severe expression, he said, "But the English are my people. I'm sure that if you were in the hands of the English, and you saw your countrymen marching into danger, you would call out and warn them, even if you knew that you might be killed for doing so."

"I do not know," the Ashanti answered candidly. "I can't say what I would do, but you were brave to run the risk, and I'm not angry with you. Only, in future when we go to attack the English, I must gag you to prevent your giving the alarm."

"That's fair enough," Frank breathed, pleased that the matter had passed off so well. "Only another time don't stick me upright against a tree where I may be killed by my own people's bullets. I had a narrow escape this time, you see," and he pointed to the hole in the trunk of the tree and wiped away the blood smear on his cheek.

"I'm sorry." Amanquatia appeared to be genuinely concerned as he examined the superficial wound. "I never thought of your being in danger," he said contritely. "I only wanted you to have a good view of the fun. Next time I'll put you in a safer place."

The following day a distant cannonade rumbled around the bush, and at nightfall reports reached Amanquatia that the British fleet had bombarded and burnt several Elmina villages at the mouth of the Pra.

"Ah," the general said, "the English have great ships and great guns. They can fight on the seaside and around their forts, but they cannot drag their guns through the forests and swamps."

"No," Frank agreed. "It wouldn't be possible to drag heavy artillery through the swamps and the thick bush."

"No," Amanquatia gloated. "When they are beyond the shelter of their ships they're no good whatever, begging your pardon. We will kill them all. Sorry."

The rainy season was in full fling and the suffering of the Ashanti became extreme. Afflicted by swarms of flies, mosquitoes, and tsetse flies—tik-tik to the natives—and accustomed to the savannahs and the high-lying lands free of jungle, the swampy miasma was just as fatal to them as it was to Europeans. Thousands died, and many of the rest were worn by fever to mere shadows of their usually splendid physique.

One day Amanquatia came up to Frank and asked a strange question. "Do you think it is possible to blow up a whole town with powder?"

"It might be possible if there were enough powder," Frank replied, wondering what on earth lay behind the question. The general quickly enlightened him.

"They say that the English have put powder in holes all over Cape Coast, and my people are afraid to go. The guns of the fort can't shoot over the whole town, and there are few white soldiers there, but still my men fear to attack in case they are blown up in the air."

"Yes," Frank said gravely, "I can see that it's dangerous. It would be best for the Ashanti to keep away from the town. But if there are more cases of fever, at the rate we're going at the moment, the army will melt away without help from the explosions."

"Ten thousand more men are coming down when the rains are over. The king says that something must be done. There is talk among our Elmina spies in the English forts that more white troops are coming out from your country. If this is true I will not attack the towns but wait for them to come into the bush for me. Then you will see."

This was the first Frank had heard of reinforcements. "Do the spies say how many troops?" he asked anxiously.

"No. They say only some white officers are coming but this is foolishness. What could white officers do without soldiers? The Fanti are cowards, they are only good to carry burdens and till the ground. They're women and not men."

During this time, the damp rose so steamingly thick that everything became saturated. Frank had a sharp attack of fever, which laid him low for a week. He then returned to the work he had been carrying out for some time—administering to the natives who were sick. He still had plenty of quinine, which did not prevent the fevers but certainly helped to reduce the severe effects, and with its aid he saved a great many Ashanti lives. The men received his doctoring gratefully and in return his patients gave him many presents in the way of fruit and birds after their return to health.

He also made some headway in persuading his African companions to keep food covered with cloth to prevent the plagues of flies from contaminating it with the miasma of the swampy ground they infested.

"I wish I could let you go," the general said to him one day. "You are a good white man, and my soldiers love you for the pains you take going among them when they are sick, and giving them the medicine of the whites. But I dare not do it. As you know when the Asantehene is angry even the greatest tremble, and I dare not tell the king that I have let you go. Were it otherwise I would gladly do so. I've sent a message to him telling him that you have saved the lives of many here. It may be that he will order you to be released."

Frank thanked him and prayed fervently that Kofi Karikari would look kindly on his general's request.

Chapter 19: They Come to Fight

October–November 1873

"It's certainly been useful that the merchant community of the entire coast petitioned the government, otherwise I wouldn't be here," Sir Garnet Wolseley told the newspaper reporters. He didn't hold hacks like the two men sitting opposite him in high regard. The Yank with an oddly Welsh lilt was, of course, famous for finding Livingstone, but Stanley's reputation was tainted by accusations of violent behavior toward his porters and the natives. As for the Englishman, Henty, he seemed sound enough, but it was always sensible to keep war plans away from gossipmongers.

"My biggest problem has been to decide which piece of advice I received in London I should listen to. The war office was flooded with recommendations and warnings of all kinds from certain persons who claimed to know the Coast. As you may imagine, it varied considerably. Some pronounced the climate to be deadly. Others said that it was really not so bad. Some warmly advocated a moderate use of spirits. Others declared that in the tropical heat alcohol is poison."

Polite laughter greeted this and Stanley broke in to say that a modest use of brandy diluted with clean water harmed no man in the tropics. Wolseley frowned at the interruption and continued as soon as the American newspaperman had shut up.

"One man advised me that any exercise should be taken between five and seven in the morning, while another insisted that on no account should anyone be out until the sun had been up for an hour, which meant that no one should go out until half past seven. Then one recommended taking exercise to excite perspiration as another urged that any physical exertion should be avoided.

"After one consistent gentleman had written some letters to the papers strongly advocating the use of white troops on the coast instead of West Indian regiments, I wrote to him for his advice on what type of articles should be taken. He replied that the only item which he could strongly commend would be that each officer should take out his coffin."

The African Company's steamship *Ambriz* had left England on September 12, and after brief stops at Madeira—where they heard of the disaster to the naval expedition up the Pra—and at the various towns on the coast on her way down, arrived at Elmina on October 2. The ship had brought Wolseley with it and thirty-five officers, ten of whom belonged to the commissariat and medical staff. Captain Redvers Buller, who had served before under Wolseley, acted as his chief intelligence officer. Among the fighting men, Lieutenant Colonel Evelyn Wood and Major Baker Russell were each to form and command a Hausa-Fanti regiment, with the other officers as their assistants.

From many of the points in the bush held by the Ashanti the sea was visible, and when a large steamer anchored off the town Amanquatia was concerned to know what it meant. Spies in Elmina and Cape Coast informed him that the ship had brought an English general with many officers. The news that thirty-five men had come out to help to drive back twenty thousand was received with outright derision by the Ashanti horde.

"They'll do more than you think," Frank warned. "You will see a change in the white soldiers' tactics. So far they've done nothing much, simply waited. Now you'll see they'll begin to move. The officers will drill the natives, and even a Fanti, trained and commanded by British officers, will learn how to fight. You've seen that the black troops in red coats can fight. What are these? Some of them are Fanti."

Ten days after the British general's arrival, the bush telegraph communicated to the Ashanti camp that the Fanti kings had been ordered to raise contingents, and that a white officer had been allotted to each chief to assist him in this work. This report had little effect on Amanquatia. The thousands of Fanti who occupied the country south of the Pra had all been driven from their homes by the invaders and—scattered among the towns and villages on the sea coast—vast numbers had died from the ravages of smallpox. The chiefs had little or no authority over them, Amanquatia insisted, and he was confident that no native force could be raised that would in any way be capable of facing the Ashanti army.

Thanks to the bush telegraph Frank now knew who was in command of the British troops and the names of the officers under him. General Wolseley he knew by reputation and his presence on the Coast suggested that the government was taking the situation seriously, but the other names meant little, including Colonel Festing, in command of the marines. He had garnered that Festing and his men were now in support of the fifty Hausas who had held Dunkwa against the main force of Amanquatia's army.

For his part, the Ashanti general remained close to Elmina, where a regiment of Hausas arrived to reinforce the black troops holding the fort. This development still gave Amanquatia little concern, Frank noted in his journal.

That changed on October 13. At six in the morning a runner panted into their camp at the village of Essarman, some three miles from Elmina, with information that two of the English war steamers from Cape Coast now lay off Elmina, and that many troops had been landed in boats. Amanquatia was furious with his spies in Cape Coast for not having warned him of the movement.

"You should expect more of this," Frank warned him. "The British are good at keeping maneuvers secret when they need to."

"You mean sneaky!" the angry general retorted.

"No damn sneaky like 'shanti bastards," Ostik muttered at the retreating general's back.

"Shut up, or he'll have your tongue cut out," Frank reproved with a chuckle.

The few Ashanti keeping a close watch on Elmina retreated as soon as a strong column was seen to march from the fort. Frank, now familiar with the various uniforms, identified the West Indian troops brought from Cape Coast, a force of Hausas, some two hundred men of the West Indian regiment, fifty-odd sailors, and two companies of marines and marine artillery, each about fifty strong.

"What are those long poles some men carry?"

Frank turned to Amanquatia with some excitement. "I'm sure they are rocket tubes and the missiles are carried in the boxes following behind. I also see a small three-pounder Armstrong gun—"

"And they take their beds with them?" Amanquatia said, a tinge of contempt mixed in with his amazement.

"No, general. Those are hammocks for the wounded."

"Pah, then they don't have enough. Come. Time to fight."

His guards ensured Frank kept close to the general as Amanquatia advanced to take up position in the bush behind a small village some three miles from Elmina. The Hausas, skirmishing in front of the column, entered the deserted village and set it on fire. Then, as they advanced farther, the Ashanti opened fire. To their surprise the British, instead of falling back, returned fire and engaged them. The sailors, taking the Armstrong and rockets, made for the upper corner of the bush facing them to their left and a company of marine artillery took the wood on the right. Frank watched anxiously as the Hausas and a company of West Indians moved along the path in the center.

The Ashanti kept up a tremendous rate of fire with their muzzle loaders, but the marines and sailors pushed their way steadily through the bush on either side. Eventually, the sailors gained a point where the Armstrong and rockets could play on Essarman, which lay in the heart of the bush.

The Ashanti were gradually driven back to Essarman, and then out beyond that as well, and a great many were killed by the British fusillade. Then came a lull in the fighting, but any hope in Ashanti breasts that the enemy would now retreat shattered when the assault renewed. Frank knew that his countrymen had only taken a rest and tended to any wounded.

The British moved on, after first burning down Essarman. A great quantity of the Ashanti powder was stored there, and each explosion forced shouts of rage from the African warriors. Amanquatia was especially angry that two large war drums had been lost. Then the conflict heated up and the British fire was so tremendous, pouring into every thicket as they advanced, that Amanquatia was forced to see the sense of withdrawing in the direction of his main army near Dunkwa instead of further disputing the way.

The results of the day's fighting dispirited the Ashanti. All their theories that their enemy could not fight in the bush were roughly upset, and they found that the whites' superiority was as great there as it had been in the open. The heavy bullets, even at the distance of some hundred yards, crashed through the thick foliage with deadly effect, while the Ashanti slugs wouldn't hurt a fly at a distance much over a hundred and fifty feet.

Amanquatia was depressed that evening.

"The white men who come to fight us," he started, "are not like those who come to trade. These men march as well as my warriors. They have guns which shoot ten times farther than ours, and they never stop firing. They carry cannon with them, and have things which fly through the air and scream and set villages on fire and kill men. I have never heard of such things before. What do you call them?"

Frank thought for minute before telling the general, "Congreve rockets. Named after the inventor."

"What are they made of?"

"Coarse gunpowder, I think, mixed with other stuff, and rammed into an iron case."

"Can't we make some too?"

"No, at least, not without knowing what things you mix with the powder, and I don't know that. Besides, the rockets require great skill in firing, or they may come back and kill the men who set them off."

"Why didn't you tell me that the white men could fight in the bush?"

Frank looked indignant. "I told you that there would be a change when the new general came, and that they wouldn't remain any longer in their forts, but would come out and attack you."

A few days after this skirmish the Ashanti broke camp at Mampon, twelve miles from Elmina, and moved eastward to join the main force camped in the jungle near Dunkwa.

Amanquatia told Frank, "I am going to eat up their advance posts at Dunkwa and Abrakrampa. We will do better this time. We know what the English guns can do and won't be surprised."

With ten thousand men Amanquatia halted at the little village of Asianchi, where a large clearing rapidly filled with the little leafy bowers the Ashanti ran up at each halting place.

Two days later they heard that Sir Garnet Wolseley had marched out from Cape Coast to Abrakrampa with a strong force, halting on the way for a night at Assaiboo, ten miles from the town. On the same day the camp at Asianchi came under a surprise attack. The first Frank knew of it was a crackle of rifle fire and his four guards grabbing him up and dragging him off at the side of Amanquatia. The Ashanti, panic-stricken at the sudden assault, fled instantly from the camp into the jungle. The general quickly recovered his composure and ordered the war drums to begin sounding, and Frank was surprised at the speed with which the Ashanti fighters recovered from their fright. Within minutes, the lithe Ashanti fighters were slipping back through the undergrowth to encircle the British. Five minutes after the surprise a tremendous fire opened from the whole circle of bush on the British position. This stood on rising ground, and the British force answered with great rapidity and effect.

By their composition, it became clear that their enemies were Colonel Festing's from the garrison at Dunkwa, West Indians, Hausa, and allied Fanti from Annamaboe under their king. The Annamaboe men stood their ground gallantly, and the West Indians fought with great coolness, keeping up a constant and heavy fire with their Sniders. The Hausas, who had been trained as artillerymen, worked their field gun and rocket tube with furious energy, yelling and whooping like schoolboys as each round of grape or canister was fired into the bush, or each rocket whizzed out.

Notwithstanding the heavy loss they suffered, the Ashanti stood their ground bravely. Their wild yells and the beating of their drums never ceased, and only rose the louder as each cone of grape scythed bloody avenues through them. But they would not advance beyond the shelter of the trees, and as the British were not strong enough to attack them there, the artillery and musketry duel continued relentlessly for an hour and a half. Then Colonel Festing fell back unmolested to Dunkwa.

"You see what I told you was true," Amanquatia bragged. "The white men cannot fight us in the bush."

"You lost a lot of warriors," Frank pointed out. "I counted few wounded and I don't think many, if any, were killed." But the excited general would not be put off.

"We held our ground and the English dared not attack us in the bush. At Essarman the trees were thin and gave us poor cover. Here, you see, they dared not follow us. Still, it might be prudent to fall back on the Pra and consolidate."

The sick and wounded had already been sent back—but he was absolutely determined before retiring to attack Abrakrampa, whose king had sided with the British, and where a garrison had been posted.

On November 2 Frank wrote in his journal: *Colonel Festing again marched out today from Dunkwa to attack us with the West Indian regiment, perhaps as many as a thousand native allies, and some Hausas with rockets. This time Amanquatia was alerted and attacked them in thick jungle before they reached our bivouac. This second reconnaissance in force was, like the first, unsuccessful.*

But he saw that its effect on the Ashanti was significant. Their losses were great, while they could see no dead enemies. The rockets appalled them, one having killed four chiefs who were in a huddle talking together, and two of their staff. True, the British had failed to force their way through the bush, but if every time they came out they were to kill large numbers without suffering any losses themselves, they must clearly be the victors in the long run.

The Ashanti could not understand that their tactics were faulty. *Were the warriors to charge down on the British troops and fire their pieces when in close range, they would quickly overpower their opponents by sheer superiority of numbers. Instead, they halt to fire at a range at which their lead slugs are ineffective.*

Frank refrained from hinting this to Amanquatia. He had already learned, though, that the tribesmen would never assault a foe who was prepared and well armed.

Their general may have been in high spirits, but his men were by now thoroughly demoralized. Their sufferings were immense. Fever and hunger had ravaged them and, although with the wet season over foraging was again possible, the losses which the white men's bullets, rockets, and artillery had inflicted had broken their courage. The longing for home became greater than ever, and had it not been that they knew that the Asantehene's guard stationed at the Pra would prevent any fugitives from crossing the river, they would have deserted in large numbers. Already one of the divisions had fallen back.

Amanquatia spent hours sitting outside his hut talking to the other chiefs. Frank was often called into council, as the general had developed a high opinion of his judgment, which had proved invariably, and sadly, correct so far.

"We're going to take Abrakrampa, kill its king, and then fall back across the Pra," he announced.

"I think you'd better fall back now," Frank suggested. "When you took me with you to the edge of the clearing yesterday I saw that preparations had been made for the defense, and that there were also white troops there. You will never capture the village. The English soldiers have thrown up earth breastworks, and they'll lie behind them and pick your men off as they come out of the jungle."

"I must have one victory to report to the king," Amanquatia snapped back. "Then he can make peace if he chooses. The white men will not wish to go on fighting. The Fanti are eager for peace and to return to their villages. What do you think?"

"If it's true that more white troops are coming out from England, as the Fanti prisoners tell us," Frank answered, "you will see that their leaders here won't make peace. Not until they've crossed the Pra and marched on Kumasi. Forgive me, general, but your king is always making trouble. The British won't be content with letting you retreat. They will invade Ashanti territory."

A round of raucous laughter from the chiefs stopped Frank in his tracks. When Amanquatia recovered his breath he said, wiping the tears from his eyes, "They won't dare to cross the Pra. If they enter Ashanti they will be eaten up."

"They are not so easy to 'eat up', Frank retorted spiritedly. "You've seen how a hundred or two can fight against your whole army. What will it be like when they're in thousands? Your king has not been wise. It would be better for him to send messengers to the coast at once and make peace at any price."

Chapter 20: Enter the Newsmen

November 1873

Two days after being laughed at Frank, a sudden bellow woke him. He leaped from his bed of branches, seized his revolver and, rushing to the door, saw that a band of about twenty men were attacking Amanquatia's hut. In a matter of a second, he saw the two guards stationed there cut down. Frank shouted to his four guards and Ostik to follow him. The guards had been standing irresolute, not knowing which side to take, but their young charge's example decided them. They fired their muskets into the knot of natives, and then charged, swords in hand.

Ostik drew the skinning knife he was permitted to wear and followed close on his master's heels. Frank did not fire until he was within two yards of the assassins. Then his revolver spat out and six shots smacked home with deadly effect. He snatched a musket from the hands of a collapsing man he had just shot, grabbed it by the barrel and fell on the surprised and already hesitating conspirators. Two slumped to the ground at his clubbing.

Fortunately for Frank, the others had not loaded their muskets. Their intention was to kill their general and then to disperse instantly before aid could arrive, believing that with his death the order for retreat across the Pra would be given sooner. Several of them had been killed by the slugs from the muskets of Frank's guard, and his pistol had completed their confusion. The weapons fire alerted other troops, and these came running up on all sides. As one, the remaining conspirators took to their heels and fled into the dark bush.

Amanquatia himself, sword in hand, had just sprung to the door of his hut prepared to fight to the death when Frank's guard fired. The affair was so fleeting that he had hardly time to understand before the survivors of his would be assassins were in full flight.

"You saved my life," he said as Frank caught his breath. "They would have killed me if it hadn't been for your action. You won't find me ungrateful. When I've taken Abrakrampa I will arrange for you to return to your countrymen. I dare not let you go openly—the king would never forgive me, and I have enough to do already to pacify him when he hears how great our losses have been. But rest content. I will manage it somehow."

An hour afterward Amanquatia issued orders that the army should move to the attack of Abrakrampa. For three days the bush around the town had swarmed with Ashanti, and their war drums thundered day and night and day to instil fear into the garrison and wear down the men.

The post was held by a mixed Hausa-Fanti regiment, some marines and sailors, a hundred West Indians, and the native troops of the king of Abra.

Abrakrampa stands on a low hill, surrounded for a distance of a hundred and fifty yards by cleared ground, Frank wrote. *At the upper end stands a church converted into a stronghold. They must have built a platform inside for the men to fire from the high windows, which are partially blocked with sandbags.*

The walls of the houses on the edge of the village are loopholed and connected by earth breastworks. I can see other defenses thrown up further back in case the outworks should be breached. The mission house in the main street and the huts which surround it form, with the church, an effective stronghold.

Amanquatia wanted Frank at his side, which gave him an opportunity of seeing how an Ashanti assault on a fortified position was conducted. The war drums suddenly changed rhythm and gave the signal... and then ceased. For a long moment the jungle was so silent the blood sang in every ear. Then ten thousand voices raised the war song in measured cadence. The effect was very fine, rising as it did from all parts of the forest. By this time the warriors had lined the perimeter of encircling bush.

At a piercing cry, three volleys crashed out, tremendously loud because of the heavy charges of powder used. Before the echoes had dissipated the king of Abra, a splendid looking man standing nearly six feet four in height, stepped out from behind the breastwork and shouted taunts. The Ashanti replied with loud hoots, and with the opening of a continuous fire around the edge of the bush. The slugs pattered thickly on walls and roofs of the village, but their force was spent and the defenders all under cover. In reply, from breastwork and loophole, from the windows and roof of the church, the answering Snider bullets flew out straight and lethal.

Several times Amanquatia tried to get his men to attack. The war drums beat, the great horns sounded, and the men shouted, but each time the British bullets flew so thick and deadly into the trees wherever the sound rose loudest that the warriors' courage failed them.

At five o'clock the fire slackened, but shortly after dark the attack recommenced. A full moon lit the cleared area brightly. Frank feared that the Ashanti would try to crawl a part of the distance across the clearing before making a sudden rush, but they had no clue about effecting a silent attack. Several times when large groups gathered for an assault, their shouting and the drums gave warning to the besieged, and so concentrated fire hit them as they emerged from the shadow of the trees into the moonlight. The British troops repulsed every charge and the Ashanti fell back to leave the ground strewn with the slain.

The Ashanti broke off at midnight and fell back to their camp. To Frank's amazement, considering their losses, they renewed the battle the next day, but it was a repetition except for the inspired defenders, who began to make dangerous sorties into the bush in selected spots. This novel approach disconcerted the Ashanti at the points of penetration and left gaps in the encirclement through which on the subsequent day General Wolseley arrived with two hundred men from mixed regiments.

When Amanquatia saw the reinforcements enter Abrakrampa, he began to fall back with most of his troops. He ordered a handful of snipers to remain in the vicinity to keep the British pinned within the region of the town.

"It's no use," the Ashanti general said to Frank, a mile off at the main encampment. "My men cannot fight in the open against the English guns. Besides, they don't know what they are fighting for here. But if your general should ever cross the Pra you will find it different. There are forests all the way to Kumasi, as you know, and the men will be fighting to defend their own country. You will see what we shall do then."

He paused briefly, as Frank waited anxiously to see what he would say next. He didn't dare bring up his freedom in case the very mention of it might make the general change his mind and go back on his earlier promise. But Amanquatia's next words came as balm to his ears.

"And now, what I told you." He gave a deep sigh as he nodded his head, his penetrating gaze taking in his white captive. "Tonight I will have a potion given to your guards which will make them sleep hard. One of the Fanti prisoners will come to your hut to guide you through the jungle to Assaiboo. Goodbye, my friend. Amanquatia has learned that some of the white men are good and honest and..." he smiled, "make good chocolate. He will never forget that he owes his life to you. Take this in remembrance of an Ashanti friend."

And he presented Frank with a necklace composed of nuggets of gold as big as walnuts and weighing nearly twenty pounds.

This surprising generosity abashed Frank and he wracked his brain to think of something he could offer in return. Then it came to him and he turned over the only article of value which he now possessed, his faithful Beaumont-Adams revolver and a tin box of cartridges. He told Amanquatia that he hoped he would never use it against the English, but that it might be of value to him should he ever again have trouble with his own men. Frank made a parcel of the necklace and of the gold he had received from the king for his goods, and warned Ostik to be ready.

For some time Frank heard his guards pacing outside, and occasionally speaking to each other. Then these sounds ceased and all was quiet. After what felt like an interminable time, the front of the tent gaped and a voice hissed, "Come, all is ready."

Frank stuck his head out and looked around. The Ashanti camp was already largely deserted. Amanquatia had moved away with the majority of his warriors, although the musketry fire around Abrakrampa was being kept up. A Fanti stood at the door of the hut with Ostik. The four guards slept peacefully. Noiselessly, the little party stole away. A quarter of an hour later they struck the path, and an hour's walking brought them to Assaiboo. They met not another soul along the way, but Frank hardly felt that he was safe until he heard the challenge in unmistakable English….

"Oo goes there?"

"Good grief, and what do we have here?"

"Hargate, sir, Frank Hargate."

Captain Bradshaw's jaw dropped at hearing English. The officer commanding the few sailors and marines holding Assaiboo looked astounded. Frank understood his surprise at seeing what appeared to be an adolescent Englishman, bronzed by the African sun in full Ashanti regalia standing before him. Tall for his age and well set, all wire and muscle from the African diet and hard marching, Frank looked back with a steady, open gaze.

"I'm very happy to be here, sir, it's a long story."

His arrival created quite a sensation, and for some hours he sat talking with the officers, who had divvied up some spare clothes for him, while Ostik made an equal subject of curiosity among the sailors. The news that the Ashanti army was in full retreat relieved the small garrison from all further fear of attack, and Frank went to sleep before morning. He was only roused at noon.

Sir Garnet Wolseley, with the greater portion of the force from Abrakrampa, arrived during the afternoon, and Frank was introduced to the general by Captain Bradshaw. In turn, Wolseley introduced the two civilians in his company as the illustrious explorer Henry M. Stanley and Mr. George Henty, special correspondents for *The Herald* of New York and the *Standard* of London respectively.

The second name meant nothing to Frank, but the first left him tongue-tied. Remembering his manners, he shook both men's hands firmly, but with a glazed stare at Stanley. The explorer gave him a tight, rueful smile and said, "Yes, yes, young man, that's the very same hand as Mr. David Livingstone took when I met him at Ujiji. But it seems to me that you have a tale of your own to tell."

"Indeed," Wolseley broke in, "and Hargate may tell it to us on the road. I'm anxious to press on at once to Cape Coast, so that the sailors and marines might sleep on board ship tonight." Frank's story enlivened the two-hour journey and gratified him to see how the somewhat dour Stanley warmed to his words. He blushed with pride when the explorer suggested he join his next expedition. "If I can persuade anyone of its necessity," he added grumpily.

Mr. Henty, who had remained largely silent during the narration, broke into a broad smile and exclaimed, "My word, young Hargate, it's a yarn of great pluck, no doubt about it. I can see your account making a marvelous story of adventure. I hope you won't mind if I borrow your experiences in the future for a novel."

"Oh, n-no sir, I should be thrilled," Frank stammered.

Wolseley asked him to spend the night at Government House, an invitation which Frank accepted; but he found sleep hard to come by. For almost two years he'd slept on the canvas of his little camp bed or a crib of rushes on the ground, and the novelty of a bed with sheets banished sleep. At some point, wrapping himself in a rug, he lay down on the floorboards and finally fell into a deep dreamless slumber.

"What are your plans, Hargate?" Sir Garnet asked Frank over breakfast. "I'm sure you're eager to get home to your family?"

The words reminded Frank that he was after all an orphan, and although a part of him wanted to return to England, something stronger held him. Stanley looked shrewdly at him.

"Does that, y'know, Africa." He held out a hand and clenched it into a fist. "Grabs you somewhere inside and won't let go... not until it kills you, of course." The explorer gave a short laugh. "Henty here knows, he's been about the Dark Continent as well."

The general turned to Frank again. "I see you hesitate. Well if you're in no extreme hurry to return to England it would be a great help if you acted as guide to the campaign, which will start for Kumasi as soon as the troops arrive from England. You've had invaluable experience of the Ashanti methods of war, of the country we have to cross, the rivers to be forded or bridged, and the points at which the Ashanti would probably make a stand. Also, you know this head warrior of theirs, Amanquatia, is it, better than anyone."

Frank smiled. "I'm sure two or three months longer won't make a difference, and there's nothing particular calling me urgently back."

As a member of the general's staff Frank was immediately assigned officers' quarters in the town, with rations for himself and Ostik. He found little difficulty in getting hold of a proper uniform. Many of the officers were already invalided home, and one about to sail was glad to dispose of his, which consisted of a light brown Norfolk shooting jacket, knickerbocker, and helmet (suspiciously pith-like in shape). "They'll be no use to me back home," the man said cheerfully as he nursed his damaged arm.

Next, Frank went to the agent of Messrs Swanzy, the principal African merchants of the Coast. Here he cashed one of the orders on the African bank which Frederick Goodenough had given to him. With this, he paid the long arrears of wages owing to his faithful servant.

"And now, Ostik, if you're ready, you can find a passage to the Gabon and your home."

But Ostik shook his head firmly. "Oh no, sah. I stay with you as long as you stop in Africa."

"Thank you." Frank shook the Mpongwe's hand. "But if that's the case, I suggest you deposit your money for safe keeping with Swanzy's agent, with instructions to send it to your village in case anything should happen to you during the expedition."

The troops coming out from England were not expected for several weeks, and while the officers of the engineer corps supervised the construction of a great military road through the thick bush to the Pra, there was little to do at Elmina and Cape Coast. So when the two journalists told Frank they had been offered a trip along the coast to the mouth of the Volta to see how preparations were going there, he jumped at the chance to go with them. The general approved the arrangement and asked Frank to make any notes he thought might be useful about how the native levies were being equipped.

Two days later Frank, Henty and Stanley clambered aboard the steamer *Decoy*'s boat with their servants bringing their small traveling cases and shortly after the warship got under way.

"This should be an interesting few days," Henty intoned, making some notes as the *Decoy* breasted the long swells.

"Who's in command on the Volta, Mr Henty?" Frank asked the journalist, who quickly consulted his notes.

"Captain Glover, who serves as the government's administrator at Lagos. He has, I hear, done a remarkable job in raising a force of some ten thousand native levies and in marching them along the coast to assemble on the Volta, from where they will make a flank attack on Kumasi."

Aboard the warship Frank found it delightful to be sitting in a large wickerwork chair in the shade of the awning, watching the unvarying line of the grey-green distant shore slipping by and chatting with the officers. The *Decoy* made only about six knots average cruising speed, but no one was in a hurry, and the eastward trip along the coast made a pleasant change after the long monotony of hacking through jungle undergrowth.

The hours passed pleasurably. The beautiful neatness and order prevailing on board a man-of-war were a striking contrast to the rough life Frank had so long led, and the silence and discipline of the men presented an equally strong change to the incessant chattering and noise kept up by the African porters.

The next morning the ship lay off Accra. The captain had to land with some dispatches for the colony, and invited his guests to accompany him. They did not, as Frank expected, land in the *Decoy's* bumboat, but in a surf boat. These large and very wide and flat craft were paddled by twelve natives, who sat on the gunwales. At the stern stood a steersman with a long sweep, who kept up a monotonous song, to which the crew replied in chorus, always in time with their paddling.

Frank held his breath on sighting the heavy surf through which they had to make way. After waiting for a favorable moment, the steersman gave the sign and the boat darted in at lightning speed on the top of a great wave, and ran up on the beach in the midst of a whirl of white foam. He wiped salty spray from his eyes and cheeks to find his companions all smiling broadly at the feat.

While the captain went up to Government House, Frank accompanied the American explorer and his English colleague in a stroll through the town, enjoying the dazzling colors of the clothing and the cheerful chaos of a typical West African town.

The next morning they weighed anchor off Addah, a village at the mouth of the Volta. The ship's bosun whistled for a surf boat, but it was some time before one put out. The surf was much heavier here than it had been at Accra and when it was launched it looked impossible that the boat would make it through the roiling water. Each mounting roller threw the boat almost perpendicularly into the air, so that only a few feet of the end of the keel touched the water.

Still the paddlers struggled on, and at last they got through the breakers. The men waited for a minute to recover from their exertions. Frank suffered a thrill of apprehension at the coming trip to land. None of the officers had ever been here, and several of them obtained leave to accompany the captain, correspondents, and Frank onshore. After seeing the surf boat's struggle to reach them everyone looked nervous, albeit with tight lips. Frank stared anxiously at the approaching line where the great smooth waves rolled over and broke into boiling foam.

The steersman stood on the stern seat, in one hand holding his sweep, in the other his cap. For some time he stood half turned around, looking attentively seaward, while the boat lay at rest just outside the line of breakers. Suddenly he waved his cap and gave a shout. The crew answered with a great shout. Every man dashed his paddle into the water. Desperately they rowed, the steersman encouraging them by wild yells. A gigantic wave rolled in behind the boat. It looked for a moment as if its towering crest would break over them, but the keel rose on the wall of water just as it turned over, and for an instant they were swept along amid a cataract of white foam, with the speed of an arrow. The next wave was a small one, and before a third reached it the boat grounded on sand. A dozen men rushed out into the water. The passengers threw themselves anyhow on to their offered backs, and in a minute were standing almost dry on the beach.

The normally imperturbable Henty looked flushed with excitement. "My, that was a bit thrilling. It will make a great moment in a one of my reports."

Captain Glover's camp lay half a mile distant, and on the way they passed hundreds of Africans, who had arrived in the last day or two, and had just received their arms. Some squatted on the ground cooking and resting themselves. Others examined their new weapons, oiling and removing rust spots, and occasionally loading and firing them off. The balls whizzed through the air in all directions, causing a most dangerous nuisance.

"I should have thought there were orders against it."

"Nothing, my dear Henty, can repress the love of Africans for firing off guns," Stanley declared.

The party soon arrived at the camp, which consisted of some bell tents and the little huts of a few hundred natives. This was only a receiving bivouac where the native recruits were kitted out before being sent upriver in the expedition steamboat to the large camp some thirty miles higher.

Under Captain Glover's command there were only seven British officers and this compact cadre had all the work of drilling and keeping in order some ten thousand men. They were, in effect, generals, colonels, sergeants, quartermasters, storekeepers and diplomats all at once. Squabbles between the dozen petty kings and between them and the officers were by no means the smallest of Captain Glover's difficulties. At the merest perceived slight each of these announced himself ready to march away in a huff with his followers. The most disciplined and reliable soldiers were some two hundred and fifty Hausas, and as many Yorubas.

The new recruits' bewilderment over the issue of some articles in their army kit amused Frank highly—and noted it down. A haversack, water bottle, belt, cap, and ammunition pouch were handed to each, and it was easy to foresee that at the end of the first day's march all of these, to them utterly useless articles, would be thrown away. They brightened up, however, when they were handed their guns.

After spending an enjoyable day on shore, the party returned on board ship. The tide thankfully having turned, the lower surf meant a less hair-raising trip than the inward bound adventure. Two days later, after a pleasant and uneventful voyage, the *Decoy* came in sight of Cape Coast.

Frank had nothing to do until the army began its northward march, and spent a good deal of his time watching the carriers starting with provisions for the Pra. Thousands of men, women, and children were press-ganged from the entire region. Small shopkeepers who had never supposed that they would be called up to labor for the defense of their freedom and country, found themselves with a barrel of salt pork or ammunition on their heads.

When all the men had gone, the turn of the women came. Some three hundred, who had been seated against the fort walls, now came forward and stooped to pick up the bags of hard-tack laid out for them. Unlike so many of their indignant menfolk, the women were in the best of temper, and had enjoyed dancing and singing, continually clapping their hands, before being put cheerfully to work.

After the women set off, chattering and laughing, four hundred boys and girls, aged between eleven and fourteen, followed them, armed with small kegs of rice or meat weighing from twenty-five to thirty-five pounds. When these had first arrived, the small kegs had been a cause of great annoyance to the quartermaster's office, for no man or woman could balance two of the long narrow barrels on their head. At last the happy idea struck an officer of the department that children might be used for the purpose.

As soon as it was known that boys and girls could get half men's wages for carrying up light loads, the juvenile population made a dramatic rush. Three hundred applied the first morning, another hundred the next in a great screaming melee of exuberance. All were accustomed to carry weights, such as great jars of water and baskets of yams, far heavier than those they were now called to take up country. And the novel pleasure of earning money and of enjoying an expedition deep into the interior excited every one of them.

Bullocks arrived from other parts of the Coast, and although the animals would not survive the climate and conditions for any time at Cape Coast, it was argued they would do so long enough to afford the expedition a reasonable supply of fresh meat to supplement the dried Australian jerky and salt pork.

By the end of six weeks the engineers' road approached the Pra just as the very last Ashanti warriors crossed to the other side. Reports suggested that as many as seven thousand fresh warriors had swollen

Amanquantia's army shortly before crossing the river. They brought commands from the king that they were not to return until they had driven the English into the sea. Amanquatia's army, however, though still numbering nearly twenty thousand, positively refused to do any more fighting until they had been home and rested, and their tales of the prowess of the white troops so checked the enthusiasm of the newcomers, that they decided to return with the rest.

Chapter 21: Advance to the Pra

December 1873–January 1874

Mr. Henty was more than happy to fill Frank in on events to the north when he returned from a three-day visit to the front with Mr. Stanley and several others of the news corps who had recently arrived.

"A large force of Africans is now kept at work under the watchful eye of the Royal Engineers on the road up to the Pra. It's about twelve feet wide and either the swamps have been drained off or it crosses them on causeways of bundled brushwood. All the streams have been bridged as well, and every tree root in the way dug out. Rest stations have appeared at easy marches, with six bamboo lattice huts for seventy men each."

"I was most impressed," drawled Stanley, "with the iron tanks holding filters and charcoal to purify stream water. A good invention which should help prevent some disease among the men. But for both of us," he added with a conspiratorial wink, indicating Henty, "the most important item is the telegraph wire strung alongside. It means we can get our dispatches through to the coast immediately they're written."

Frank gave a short chortle. "I imagine General Wolseley will find it most useful too."

Troop ships bringing more than two and a half thousand men began to arrive between December 9 and 18. The men were kept on board for health reasons until the first day of January. By this time Colonel Wood and Major Russell were on the Pra with the native regiments they had raised and trained. The bulk of the soldiers were Hausas and other Islamic tribes who disliked the pagan Ashanti, together with companies from Bonny, some Yorubas, and some of the best of the Fanti. The rest of the Fanti forces were disbanded, as being utterly useless for fighting purposes, and now toiled as porters.

On December 26 Frank started with the general's staff and the news corps for the front. Thanks to the supreme efforts of the engineers the journey to the Pra could even be called a pleasant one, except for the flies. Sir Garnet Wolseley, borne along seated in a wicker chair suspended from two large poles carried by four bearers, traveled in comfort except than—raised above all others—he was more bothered by the multitude of flies than those tramping on foot.

"Damn nuisance," the general was often heard to mutter, flicking his fly whisk at the irritants.

Redvers Buller, walking alongside, related that a German officer he once knew had told him that the trick was to have the bearers run fast with the chair and so keep ahead of the flies.

The general slowly turned his head and glowered. "That's damn stupid, Buller. For sure there will be more flies ahead to run into at high speed."

"Quite right, sir. Sorry."

Wolseley returned to attacking his tormentors with the whisk. "Damn flies," he grumbled, "almost as much a nuisance as the damned Germans."

Passing through Assaiboo they entered the thick bush. The giant cotton trees had now shed their light feathery leaves, and looked like the bones of some primeval beast rising above the sea of foliage below. White lilies, pink flowers of a bulbous plant, and clusters of yellow acacia blossoms occasionally brightened the roadside, and some of the old village clearings were covered with a low shrub bearing a yellow blossom, and convolvuli white, buff, and pink.

The first night the party slept at Akroful, and the next day marched through Dunkwa. The next halting place was Yancumasi and then Mansu, Suta, Assin, and Baraku. After Mansu the nature of the jungle changed. The undergrowth disappeared and the high trees grew thick and close. A wilderness of parasitic climbers clustered round and around the trees, twisting in a thousand fantastic windings, and finally running down to the ground, where they took fresh root and formed props to the tree their embrace had killed.

There were no flowers now, but luxuriant ferns grew by the engineers' roadside. The plantain, the cooking banana which was a staple of the natives and had sustained the Ashanti army during its stay south of the Pra, grew no farther to the north. Frank noticed that there were few butterflies, but dragonflies darted along like sparks of iridescent fire.

It was a relief to emerge into the little clearings where villages had once stood, a respite from the gloom and quiet of the great forest which weighed on the spirits. The monotonous *too too* of the doves—not a slow dreamy cooing like that of the English variety, but a sharp quick note repeated in endless succession—alone broke the hush. The heavy silence, the apparently never ending jungle, the monotony of rank vegetation, the absence of a breath of wind to rustle a leaf, oppressed the column. A damp heaviness of the air and the richly cloying odour of rotting vegetation rising from the swamps only intensified the feeling.

Beyond Suta the smell of the jungle became much more unpleasant, for at Foso they passed the scene of the conflict between Colonel Wood's regiment and the retreating Ashanti. In the forest beyond were the remains of a massive enemy camp which extended for miles, and from there to the Pra large numbers of Ashanti had dropped by the way or had crawled into the forest to die, struck down by disease or rifle fire. The odor of their decay thickened the air.

Everyone, from the general in his airborne chair, to the lowliest porter felt the pleasure of entering the large open camp at Prasu on the first day of 1874.

At twenty acres in extent, the clearing occupied an isthmus formed by a loop of the river. Off the central square stood the range of huts for Wolseley and his staff. Huts for the white troops formed two sides of the square. On the fourth were the hospital, the huts for the brigadier and his staff, and the post office. On the river bank beyond the square were the tents of the engineers and a battery, and the camps of Wood's and Russell's native regiments. The river, some seventy yards wide, ran round three sides of the camp, thirty feet below its level.

"You can't deny the level of achievement," Mr. Henty commented to Frank as they admired the encampment's fresh neat lines. "To carve out an eighty-mile road through thick bush riddled with streams and marsh, especially considering most of the trees we've seen are teak and mahogany—extremely hard wood—is surely outstanding. But I'm damned glad to be off that road all the same."

During the eight days which elapsed before the white troops came up from the Coast Frank found a lot to interest his youthful curiosity. The engineers were at work, aided by the sailors of the naval brigade, who had arrived two days after they had, in erecting a two hundred-foot bridge across the Pra. The sailors labored stripped to the waist in the muddy water of the river, which was about seven feet deep in the middle.

When tired of watching the construction work he would wander into the camp of the native regiments, and chat with the men, whose surprise at finding a young Englishman able to speak their language—Ashanti differing only a little from Fanti and Hausa—was boundless. In these days, Captain Buller, as head of the intelligence department, put him to work translating the statements of prisoners brought in by the native scouts, who had penetrated many miles north of the Pra. One man had interesting information to provide Buller.

"He says they're finding corpses by the side of the road, showing the state to which the Ashanti army was reduced in its retreat," Frank interpreted. "He also says that news of our advance to the southern bank of the Pra has created a sensation in Kumasi. The king blames Amanquatia for his conduct of the war, and for the great loss of life among his army."

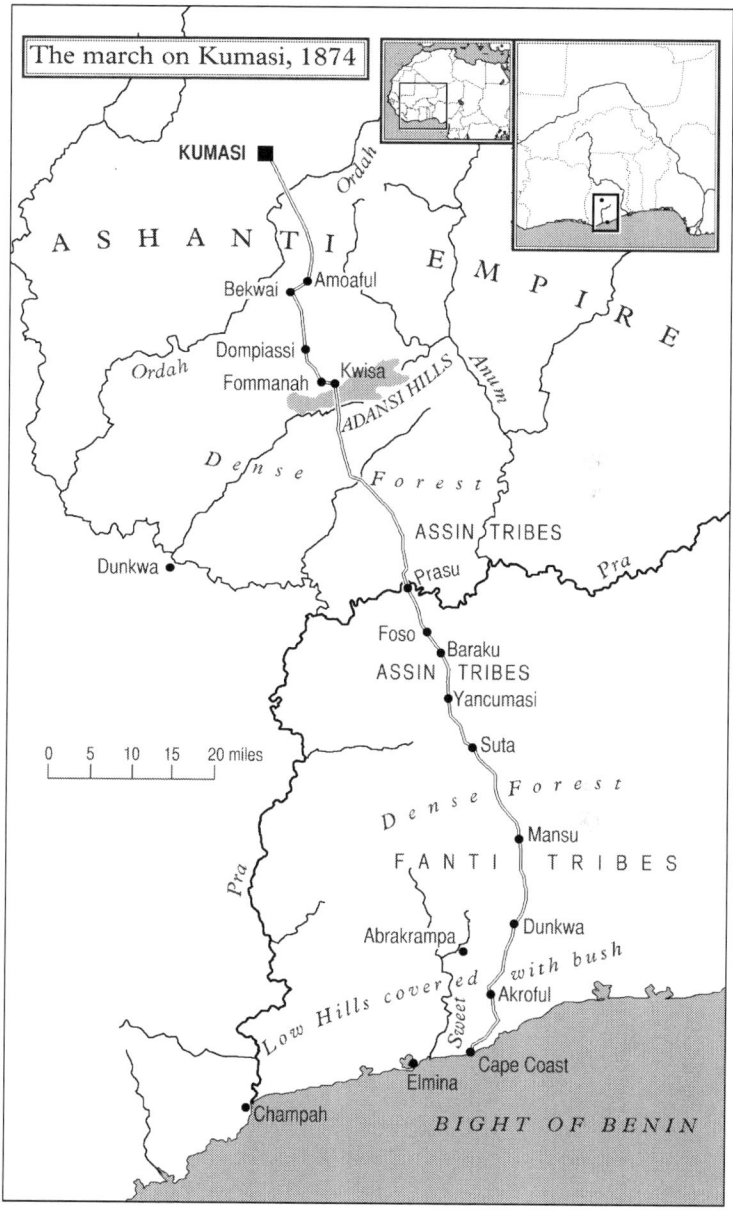

Frank paused to listen to the prisoner's next words.

"There have been many strange disturbances in the city, bad portents, he says. A great flaming rock fell from the heavens to land in the parade ground. Still more strange, a child was born which was at once able to talk fluently. In the morning, however, it was gone, and in its place there was only a bundle of dead leaves. He says that the witch-doctors declare this signifies that Kumasi itself will disappear, and will become nothing but a bundle of dead leaves."

"Is that all?" Buller demanded.

"It seems enough, sir," offered Frank hesitantly.

Buller leant back in his chair and let loose a great guffaw. "I'll give 'em a bundle of leaves before we're done with the evil bastards. Don't have much time for omens, myself, but if it gives them the shivers, so much the better."

As usual, Frank went down at sunset to bathe in the river. On this particular day he had just reached the bank when he heard an outcry among some white soldiers bathing there. He froze in horror to see one of them pulled underwater by a crocodile, which had seized the unfortunate soldier by the leg. The sight immediately brought back his own encounter and Frederick Goodenough's tough advice. Frank never even hesitated. Throwing off his Norfolk jacket, he ran the last feet down the steeply sloping bank and plunged into the river. He dove toward the spot where the eddy on the surface indicated the struggle taking place beneath.

The water was too muddy to see far through it, but Frank speedily came up to the crocodile, just to the side of its scaly head. The violent disturbance of the water caused by the beast's thrashing almost thrust Frank away, but he managed to grasp the sharp armour plating with one hand and hung on grimly. As the crocodile bucked back against him, Frank brought his other arm up and, finding its nearest eye, wasted no time in shoving his thumb into it.

In an instant the creature let go of its prey and made off. Frank turned topsy turvy in the powerful backlash of its tail as it powered away into the murk. Terrified the monster would quickly return, Frank flailed about and found the soldier's arm. He seized the wounded squaddie and swam desperately with him toward the bank, where several others kept up a furious racket and splashed the water surface to scare the crocodile away.

Two burly soldiers waded in to help Frank drag his burden to the bank amid loud cheers of the bystanders. The soldier—in fact a marine—lay unconscious. His leg was nearly severed above the ankle. Three medics rushed the injured fellow to the camp, where a surgeon amputated his leg below the knee. Soon afterward, he was taken back to the Coast.

Wolseley promptly forbade any further bathing in the river and it seemed the men had no argument with the order. It had been thought that the noise of building the bridge, and the constant movement on the banks, would have driven the crocodiles away. The affair made Frank a great favorite in the naval brigade, and at night after dinner he generally took himself over to the great bonfires which the tars kept up and joined in the jovial choruses of bawdy songs they enjoyed.

Two days after the crocodile incident, an ambassador from Kofi Karikari came into camp to ask why the English had attacked the Ashanti troops, and why had they advanced to the Pra. Sir Garnet Wolseley's answer was a demand that all hostages be immediately freed and the king pay an indemnity for having caused the Crown such cost.

On January 12 messengers returned with a familiar figure. "Herr Kuhne," Frank shouted with unalloyed joy at seeing the German again. Sir Garnet was less happy with the news the missionary brought.

"The king's temper was explosive at the loss of probably half his warriors to your weapons and swamp diseases. He fined or otherwise punished all the chiefs who accompanied the army and he was not happy with the contents of your letter. The question of peace or war was hotly contested at a council. The chiefs who had been in the late expedition were unanimous in wishing to avoid further conflict.

Those who had remained at home, and therefore in ignorance of the horrors, were for war rather than surrender."

Wolseley grunted in irritation. "Was there any indication, sir, of the outcome of this debate?"

"I'm sorry, none that I know of. I'm sure I've been sent as a sort of peace offering. Kofi Karikari assumes that because he still holds my brother and his wife among the other white captives, that I will urge you strongly to halt here and make peace."

The general raised his head and stared out across the Pra, looking at the finished bridge, and slowly shook his head. "My orders are to take Kumasi, rescue hostages and put an end to the king's filthy, murderous practices."

Frank left Prasu several days before the main force of British troops were due up from the Coast. He was placed at the side of the young lieutenant commanding the native scouts, Lord Edric Gifford, the 3rd Baron Gifford, detached from the South Wales Borderers. Frank's knowledge of the country and language proved very valuable to Gifford. The scouts did their work well. The Ashanti were in considerable force, but fell back gradually without fighting.

With Russell's native regiment and the Hausa gunners under Captain Rait of the Royal Artillery in support, they pressed forward to the foot of the Adansi hills—a familiar sight to Frank. Here, on the steep slopes which were clear of undergrowth and only lightly clothed in trees, it seemed logical to Russell that the Ashanti would make their first stand.

Gifford led the way at the head of the scouts, Frank at his side, and Major Russell's regiment following behind. As they neared the crest a shamanic witch-doctor with five acolytes startled them. The wizened ju-ju man waved his arms and shouted to go back, that five thousand men waited there to destroy the invaders. Gifford paused for a moment to allow Russell's regiment to come within supporting distance. "Hargate, what do you reckon?"

Frank thought briefly and shrugged. "Probably safest to assume he tells the truth."

Lord Gifford nodded curtly. "Fix bayonets!"

The scouts made a rush for the crest.

It was deserted. The ju-ju man and his followers turned and fled when they found that neither their fetish curses nor the imaginary force hurled at the British-native soldiers prevented them from advancing.

The crest of the main hill was very narrow, little more than a saddle, with some eight or ten yards only of level ground between the steep descents on either side. From this point the scouts could see Kwisa. "It's the first town in the territory of the king of Adansi, one of the five petty kings of Ashanti," Frank said.

"Nice view," breathed Lord Gifford, "but I wonder why they really didn't have a strong force here to oppose us? A hill clear of trees is of immense advantage to men armed with rifles and supported by artillery."

"But that's the point, sir," Frank replied. "To men armed only with muskets firing slugs a distance of fifty yards, the advantage is not that much, especially when, as is the case with the Ashanti, they always fire high."

The next morning the scouts skirmished toward Kwisa. Although the beating of a war drum came clearly from the town they encountered no opposition. Gifford, however, thought it best to halt at the foot of the hills until more troops came up. While the scouts kept guard, Russell's men and the engineers labored, as they had done all the way from the Pra, in advancing the military road over the Adansi range for the following troops and guns.

On the fifth day a scouting party found Kwisa deserted and Major Russell moved his regiment into it. To Frank, the town's architecture was familiar enough from Kumasi, but the red clay houses, with their alcoved bed places, and their little courts one behind the other, surprised the white officers at their sophistication.

Five days later the Naval Brigade, Wood's regiment, and Rait's battery marched into Kwisa. The same afternoon the whole force marched the bare half mile to deserted Fommanah, the capital of Adansi, a big town capable of housing some eight thousand inhabitants, with similar architecture to Kwisa. The king's palace, a large structure of royal apartments, harem, fetish room, and execution chamber, still smelled horribly of the blood which sprinkled the floor and walls.

Blood apart, Fommanah was the most pleasant station the troops had reached since the Coast. High above sea level, it enjoyed a temperature lower than that of the stations south of the hills. A nice breeze sprang up each day about noon and the dawns were usually free from the steamy morning jungle fog.

An eager debate broke out among the officer corps as to whether the Ashanti would soon stand and fight. On the one hand some urged that if they had meant to attack they would have disputed every foot after the crossing of the Pra.

"If they had," Russell opined, "they could have stopped us dead. Their policy should have been to avoid a pitched battle, but to harass us from either side. They could have stopped the men working on the road and made it impossible for the carriers unless protected on either side by lines of troops. Let's face it, even without opposition, it's difficult enough to keep the carriers from constantly deserting. If they'd been exposed to continuous attack there would have been no possibility of keeping them together."

The lack of opposition argued the case in favor of a desire for peace. In the other case no ambassadors had brought further messages from the Asantehene. His silence was ominous; nor were other signs wanting. Threatening fetishes pointing toward the Pra stood in the track. Several kid goats were found buried in calabashes in the path pierced through and through with stakes; while a short distance outside Kwisa a freshly killed and mutilated slave hung upside down from a tree.

Frank thought there was still hell waiting ahead.

Chapter 22: The Battle of Amoaful

January–February 1874

Beyond Fommanah the country hit the British hard. The terrain and flora gave all the advantage to the Ashanti. Thickly covered with tall trees, festooned with creepers below, the pioneer forces had to cut a way through dense clinging brushwood before the troops could push on. Spies brought intelligence which suggested that the main force of the Ashanti army was indeed preparing to make a stand between the neighboring towns of Bekwai and Amoaful, some ten miles ahead. Frank experienced a thrill of mixed emotions to learn that Amanquatia had the command.

The rest of the troops came up to the scouts' forward position, and on January 25 Russell's regiment advanced to Dompiassi. Wood's regiment and Rait's battery joined him the next day. Lord Gifford led the way with the scouts and Frank went with them. The sweat on every man's brow was not only due to the steamy heat but reflected the fear of running into an ambush at any moment. A well-founded concern, since only half an hour of cautious advance faltered when the hidden enemy opened fire as soon as the scouts came within range. There was an immediate response. Above the scattered firing, Lord Gifford's voice rang out and the scouts, with the Hausas of Russell's regiment, charged impetuously into Dompiassi. The Ashanti fighters took to their heels.

The pioneers pushed ahead through two more tiny hamlets— Kiang Bossu and Ditchiassie. And then, about five miles from Amoaful, ambassadors arrived from Kofi Karikari finally declining to accept Wolseley's last offered terms. The two native regiments marched forward to within half a mile of the enemy's outpost, another hamlet called Quarman. The white troops came on to within three miles behind. Quarman was stockaded to resist attack, so a halt was called. For the rest of the day the engineers cut a wide path for the advance of the troops to within a hundred yards of the enemy-held village.

Before dusk, Sir Garnet Wolseley outlined the battle plan for the next day, January 31.

"The area is riddled with these wretched little habitats of a few huts, which pose a problem. They must be cleared. The 42nd Highlanders of the Black Watch will go into the first in our way, Quarman, and will then form the main attacking force, with the artillery. Straight through Quarman, gentlemen and immediately on to the next place, Agamassie, driving out the enemy's scouts.

"The 42nd will then extend in line to the right and left and, if possible, advance in a skirmishing line through the bush. You will go with your guns, Rait, in their center and advance along the road itself. On the right I want a column of half the Naval Brigade, with your native regiment Wood. I know your numbers have been severely reduced through leaving garrisons behind, but you should have enough. The right column is to cut a path out to the right and then turn parallel with the main road, so that the head of the column should touch the right of the 42nd's skirmishing line.

"On the left the mirror reverse from the other half of the naval Brigade and Russell's regiment. That way, the two columns will make a hollow square to protect the Highlanders from any of those flanking movements that Mr. Hargate tells us the Ashanti are so fond of. The 23rd Fusiliers will proceed with my headquarter staff, and the Rifle Brigade are in reserve."

The general turned to Frank. "Mr. Hargate, would you be so good as to accompany Major Home and the Highlanders. I feel the Black Watch could do with your knowledge of Amanquatia's tactics, and you can translate any orders issued to the Ashanti fighters that you may overhear."

* * *

In the utter confusion of battle, even more so in thick bush, Frank only understood the events in which he was not directly involved afterward. Before seven in the morning Major Home cut the road to within thirty yards of Agamassie, where there were less than a score defenders. Gifford circled around the village and discovered the Ashanti army camped on rising ground across a stream behind Agamassie.

The 42nd's point men experienced no opposition until they issued from the bush into the little clearing surrounding the village, which consisted only of four or five small huts. The Ashanti fired their muskets hastily as the first white men showed themselves, but the fire of the leading files of the column quickly cleared them away. The Black Watch pushed on through the village, and then formed in skirmishing line to advance through the thick bush. At Major Home's side, Frank felt more nervous than he had at any time before. One hundred, two hundred, then three hundred yards and still no opposition. Then suddenly all hell broke loose.

Everyone ducked as they came under a tremendous rattle of fire from an unseen foe in front. The left column had not gone a hundred yards before they too came under another fusillade. Captain Buckle of the Engineers, who was with the laborers cutting the path ahead of the advancing column, was shot through the heart. The right column ran into a similar hail of Ashanti slugs.

The roar of the shooting was so heavy that all sound of individual reports went lost and the noise became one hoarse, hissing howl. Even the crack of artillery vanished in the general uproar, although Frank made out the distinct sound of rockets whooshing off from the two launchers accompanying each wing.

The Black Watch were brought to a complete standstill, unable to make any headway against the storm of musketry, and the flanking columns also juddered to a halt. Owing to the extreme thickness of the bush and their ignorance of the nature of the ground the two columns were unable to keep in their proper position, and diverged considerably. Fortunately, the Ashanti made no effort to infiltrate between them and the Highlanders.

Like all those around him, Frank had flung himself to the ground. Not a single foe was visible, but the enemy fire cracked out incessantly from the bushes some twenty yards ahead. The air above was literally alive with shards of lead and a perfect shower of shredded leaves continued to fall on the path.

So bewilderingly dense was the bush that the men soon lost all idea of the points of the compass, and fired in any direction from which the enemy's shots came. Wolseley soon received complaints from the sailors that the 23rd and 42nd were firing at them, while the 42nd and 23rd made the same complaint against the Naval Brigade. The general, who had made Agamassie his headquarters, repeated instructions to the commanding officers to warn their men to avoid this error.

For two hours the firefight went on. Then the column to the left found that the Ashanti in front of them had fallen back; they had, however, altogether lost touch with the 42nd. They were ordered to cut a road to their right, the northeast, until they made contact with them.

In the meantime the 42nd Highlanders were having a hard time of it. They had fought their way to the edge of the swamp, beyond which lay the immense Ashanti camp, and here the fire was so appallingly heavy that the advance again came to a standstill. And still the Ashanti remained concealed, but from every bush of the opposite side puffs of smoke came thick and fast, and a perfect sleet of lead ball swept over the ground on which the men lay.

Eventually, Rait brought up one gun—the pathway was too narrow to bring more than one into position—and, advancing boldly in front of the line of the 42nd, poured round after round into the enemy. The effect of grapeshot was devastating and the enemy fire slackened a little. The Black Watch promptly leaped to their feet, struggled across the knee-deep swamp, and step by step won their way through the camp and up the hill. Everywhere dead Ashanti lay in heaps, attesting to the terrible effect of the Snider fire as well as the determination with which they had resisted.

On the hills beyond the camp the bush was thicker than ever, and here, where it was impossible for the white soldiers to skirmish, the Ashanti made a last desperate stand. Again, Rait's artillery cleared the lane ahead leading to Amoaful. The gun stopped firing and with a rush the regiment went up the narrow path and out into the open clearing beyond. For a short time the Ashanti kept up a fire from the houses, but the 42nd soon winkled them out. Then a single artillery shot down the wide street which divided the town burst in the midst of a group at the farther end. The explosion killed eight and drove all further idea of resistance in that direction from Ashanti minds.

With a shock, glancing at his pocket watch, Frank realized they had been fighting nonstop for almost four hours. It was midday. The Ashanti had lost their camp and village stronghold, and had suffered terribly, but they were not yet finally beaten. They moved the main part of the forces which had engaged the British left around to the right, and now pressed hard on the column there, cutting in between the 23rd Fusiliers and the Black Watch.

However, luck played a part in defeating the attackers. Through the disorientation in the thick bush, the main and subsidiary columns had actually turned slightly and come into contact with each other and been reinforced by a company of the Rifle Brigade. The front, therefore, had swiveled to face east instead of north, and the Ashanti were unable to break this stronger line.

Just as the firing died down at about a quarter to one it broke out from the rear of the column. Amanquatia was making a last and desperate effort to turn the British flank, and to retake Quarman and Agamassie. Three companies of the Rifles went back to strengthen the line, and for three quarters of an hour the roar of musketry was as heavy and continuous as it had been at any time during the day. Then, as the enemy's fire slackened, Sir Garnet Wolseley gave the word for the line to advance and to sweep around from the rear so as to drive the enemy northward before them.

The men from Bonny—Wood's regiment—who had fought silently all the time that they had been on the defensive, now raised their shrill war cry, and slinging their rifles and drawing their swords—their favorite weapons—hurtled forward like so many panthers let loose. By their side, skirmishing as quietly and steadily as if on parade, the men of the Rifle Brigade searched every clump of brush with their bullets, and in five minutes from the commencement of the advance the Ashanti were in full and final retreat.

The battle of Amoaful ended at about half past one, having lasted five and a half hours.

"It adds up to Ashanti losses of well over two thousand," Henty agreed with Stanley. "Although it's hard to be accurate, as they quickly carry off their dead, at least where they can."

Many of the slain enemy still lay in the bush where they had fallen, left by their comrades because of the ferocity of the fighting, but many other bodies were being laid out for identification. Several heavies from the Black Watch conducted this grim business by taking prisoners along the line to see if they could identify anyone important among the corpses. As the journalists looked on, with several illustrators sketching in a fury to capture the detail for the newspapers back home, a kerfuffle attracted attention.

After a moment, a sergeant marched up smartly, snapped a salute and addressed Frank.

"Mr. Hargate, sir, if you please, one of the Ashanti prisoners has apparently pointed with some excitement at one of our bodies, and I'm told you might be able to help identify if this was a personage of some importance or not."

"Of course sergeant," Frank replied reluctantly. He glanced briefly at his companions, and Henty and Stanley went with him to the line of dead, stretched out like cordwood ready for stacking. Frank immediately recognized three. Among the bodies, lay his foe and his friend, General Amanquatia. For a long time he simply stared down at the lifeless figure of someone who only an hour before had been so alive. And he was unsure of his feelings. Of course the man was an enemy, but he had also been an honorable man after his own customs… and Frank's friend.

When he finally spoke, not looking particularly at anyone, it sounded like an irrelevance. "I saved his life once, you know."

The sergeant wanted to know who it was and Frank told him it was the man in charge of the Ashanti army. He also identified, with rather more enthusiasm, the body of Aboo Boffoo, whose grasping ways had started the whole business when he seized the Volta missionaries, and the body of the king's chief executioner who had been pointed out by some of the prisoners.

Henty laid a comforting hand on Frank's shoulder. "I'm sure he was a fine man, lad, but he has caused the deaths of many British fighting men and held us up from our objective."

Frank blinked back the gathering moistness in his eyes, well aware that this was no place to make a scene of any kind, and in a quiet, choked voice he said, "You know, he liked chocolate so much."

On the British side, the losses were amazingly slight, all things considered: eight killed and just over two hundred and fifty wounded, most only slightly, including Frank himself, who had taken two slugs at the same time Major Home was hit. While painful, his strikes were really more bad bruises than open wounds, and he was able to sit around the camp fire later and enjoy a glass of rum and water. Two kegs of rum were the only stores that came up from the rear that night, thanks to the consideration of a quartermaster, whose name was ever after revered by the rankers gagging for a drink after their long and fatiguing day in the tropical heat.

Amoaful's population of some three thousand had plenty of

food stores, among which the soldiers found large bundles of grain and coarse flour packaged up in dried plantain leaves. These were requisitioned by the quartermasters as an abundant supply of excellent food for the porters. The troops were in high spirits that night. They had won a battle fought under extreme difficulty, and that with a minimum of losses. There were therefore few sad recollections to dampen the pleasure of victory.

At about a mile and a quarter from Amoaful lay Bekwai, capital of one of the most powerful of the Ashanti petty kings, and a place to which many fugitives had fled. In the morning Lord Gifford, Russell's regiment, Rait's guns, and the Naval Brigade were again engaged in a tough but short battle, after which they burnt the town to the ground. The 2nd West Indian regiment was brought up from the rear to garrison Amoaful and free up the frontline troops for the further advance.

Wolseley now faced a problem. With his lines so extended, should he play safe and wait for the trailing supply column to catch up or should he throw caution to the winds and press on toward Kumasi? After weighing up the risks, he went for broke. Each man received four days' rations and each regiment was ordered to take charge of its own provisions and baggage.

The push started at seven in the morning with Russell's regiment, Rait's battery, and the Rifle Brigade. Then came the headquarters staff followed by the 42nd Highlanders and the Naval Brigade. The hammocks and rations went on with the troops. The rest of the baggage remained behind. They were, effectively, a flying column.

However, the rate of progress was slow—the country had to be thoroughly searched by the scouts on point duty. There were numerous streams to be crossed, each causing a delay. At one village a sizeable camp housed about a thousand men, who made a stand. However, their defense was feeble, and it was evident that their defeat on the first day of February had badly demoralized them. Russell's regiment charged the enemy, who fired wildly at targets well beyond the range of their ancient weapons. Several died and the rest soon disappeared in the bush.

On reaching the village of Agamemmu, after having taken six hours in getting over as many miles, the column halted, and orders were sent for the baggage to come on from Amoaful. The troops were set to work to cut the bush around the tiny village and throw up a breastwork to defend it.

That night unpleasant news arrived from the rear. There had been attacks made again on Quarman, but more of more concern also on Fommanah, where the garrison had, after some hours' hard fighting, repulsed the assault. Several convoys had also been attacked, and the whole road down to the Pra was unsafe.

"The indications are clear," Stanley told Frank. "Unless the great king is brought down and the vassal kings freed of his influence so that the empire collapses, this region will remain unsafe. The general has no choice to press on since he can't garrison this country effectively. The Asantehene must be brought down."

The next morning, after waiting until the large convoy from Amoaful came safely in at about nine o'clock, the column marched, Gifford's scouts, Russell's regiment, and Rait's battery in the vanguard as usual. The resistance increased with every step, and the head of the column was constantly engaged. Ahead, Kumasi's final protection, the Ordah river, lay six miles away and by mid-afternoon the column made its banks.

"What do they want?" Henty wondered, taking out his notebook as he peered across the forty-five feet of river separating the British from the colorful assembly that had appeared on the other bank. Under a flag of truce, the envoy shouted out to the general that the king regretted he had not yet been able to send the hostages Wolseley had demanded in his last message because many of them "were away." He added that the king could not agree to give over the queen or the heir apparent.

Sir Garnet—a naturally tall man—drew himself up to his full

imposing height and, without shouting, nevertheless made himself clearly heard.

"Unless the indemnity money and every hostage I have asked for arrives here before sun-up tomorrow, tell the king I shall be pleased to meet him in Kumasi later in the day."

Chapter 23: Kumasi Captured

February–March 1874

Ostik attracted Frank's attention and pointed at the gathering clouds. "Big rains come soon, sah. Bad."

Frank glanced up at the lowering sky visible through the overhanging branches and remarked to Henty, who was with him watching Russell's native regiment beginning to cross the Ordah, "It's much too early for the rainy season but that certainly looks like a bad storm."

"It doesn't look good," the journalist replied. "You're more of an expert on the Guinea climate, Stanley, what's your opinion?"

The explorer squinted at the low clouds and pursed his lips grimly. "I would say that the quicker we're in Kumasi and finished with it, the better." He looked back at the river and the men up to their waists toiling in its sluggish current. "How's the bridge coming along?"

The Ordah was only three feet deep in the middle and as the Hausa-Yoruba regiment waded across to clear the bush on the other side and cover them, the Engineers had started driving timbers into the riverbed for a bridge. As the night began to close in, Russell's men hastily built themselves shelters, as the first fat drops of warm rain began to fall.

For the troops stranded on the southern bank, this was the first night that—due to traveling light and the speed of advance—tents were unavailable, and it turned out tremendously wet. The rain came down incessantly, hammering soaked helmets as lightning flashed and thunder crashed. The Engineers worked tirelessly through the awful night and, tired as the troops were, there were few who slept, even under the hurriedly erected rush huts which soon became waterlogged and dripped on their occupants just a bit less heavily than on the posted sentries. The storm, however, made an Ashanti attack unlikely since the rain rendered their ancient flintlock guns useless.

The rain stopped a little before daybreak, and the sky turned clear when at six o'clock Wood's Bonny men, who had come up by a forced march the evening before, led the advance over the completed bridge. An artillery piece followed them with the Rifles in support.

Before the Bonny men had gone half a mile they were hotly engaged for two hours in a fight as tough as that of Amoaful. Eventually, the first gun—a seven-pounder—was brought up through the bush path to the front, and a few rounds of grape cleared its sides of the enemy. The respite was short and again the Bonny men became bogged down and their forward movement halted. Wolseley sent the Rifles ahead and the stiffening of the white troops did the trick. Very slowly, they made headway until the clearing around some huts could be seen fifty yards away. Then the Rifles gave a cheer and with a sudden rush swept through to the open and took the village without a check.

In the meantime the whole column had been following in the rear as the Rifles advanced, and was hotly preoccupied in repelling a series of flank attacks in which the Ashanti bravely persisted, at times in such masses that the undergrowth swayed and moved as they pushed forward. Their losses were large from the overwhelming power of the British Snider rifles. At the same time the native road, like almost all in the country, was sunk two to three feet in the center below the level of the surrounding ground, and consequently the men had some shelter, as though in a trench, while they kept up their tremendous fire on the foe.

Using the same cover, the noncombatants, crouched double, could run along behind the troops. Frank and Ostik observed the carnage alongside the several journalists furiously committing the scenes to memory for later writing up.

Six hours from the first advance the rear guard entered the village, and only a mile and a half had been covered with Kumasi still six miles away.

"This is proving harder than I'd anticipated," Henty observed. "If the Ashanti continue this resistance with the same desperation, and if the baggage has to be carried on step by step from village to village, we won't get halfway to the objective by nightfall."

As if he'd heard the remark, Wolseley switched tactics again and this time progressed with the Black Watch in the van.

The opposition was very heavy and the 42nd went on slowly with two flank companies covering the center, but after twenty minutes' work they had pushed the Ashanti over the brow of a hill, and thereafter advanced rapidly. Officers to the fore, the men dashed forward, at times at the double, to the skirling bagpipes. The enemy fighters, alarmed at the sudden onslaught and probably, Frank thought, terrified of the awful wail of the pipes, gave way altogether and literally fled as fast as they could. Village after village fell. Hastily discarded war drums and horns, chiefs' stools, and umbrellas told how sudden and complete had been the stampede.

Well after midday a despatch from the front came back to announce that all the villages except the last were taken, that opposition had ceased, and that the enemy was in complete rout. This also proved to be so further back, where the Ashanti had kept up a furious onslaught on the Naval Brigade bringing up the column's rear. When news from the front was known, whether scared by British shouts of triumph or because they too had heard the awful truth, the black warriors' efforts ceased, and not another shot was fired.

At half-past three the baggage was sent forward and the staff officers and Rifle Brigade followed. The Black Watch Highlanders entered Kumasi without another shot being fired in its defense.

Frank noted: it was February 5, 1874.

Sir Garnet Wolseley arrived soon after, amazed that the Ashanti seemed in no hurry to leave Kumasi. The troops formed in ranks and gave three cheers for Queen Victoria while their former opponents crowded around and even shook hands with some of the soldiers.

It turned out that the inhabitants had been told by the king that peace was, or would be, made. They seemed in no way alarmed, but watched the activities of the white troops as amused and interested spectators. Things changed rapidly when the order passed to disarm any Ashanti carrying a weapon of any kind. Alarm spread rapidly and in a short time the town was almost entirely deserted.

Dusk settled over the town. The troops bivouacked on the parade ground. Frank shuddered in recollection as he looked around the shrouded square and at the gap to the forest at the back where, already mercifully lost in the shadows, stood the fetish tree and its gruesome freight of bones and freshly sacrificed bodies. The charnel house exercised a hideous fascination for the white soldiers, unable to believe such horrors existed.

Although Kumasi was well known to Frank he was still ignorant as to the character of the interior of the *caboceers'* houses, and the next day he wandered about in the company of Henty and Stanley with almost as much curiosity as the soldiers themselves. The insides were filled with dust and litter, which could not be accounted for by the bustle and hurry of picking out the things worth carrying away prior to the evacuation.

From the roofs hung masses of spiders' webs, like ancient shrouds, thick with dust and insect remains, while sweeping a place out before occupying it brought down an accumulation of dust, the result of years of neglect. The principal apartments were lumbered up with drums, great umbrellas, and other paraphernalia of ceremony, such as horns, state chairs, wooden maces, decorative helmets, and many elaborate objects whose purpose remained a mystery.

In front of every street door stood a tree, at the foot of which were placed little idols, calabashes, bits of china, bones, and an extraordinary jumble of strange odds and ends of every kind which acted as fetishes. Over the doors and alcoves were suspended a variety of charms, old stone axes and arrow tips, nuts, gourds, amulets, beads, and other glittery articles.

After wandering through several nobles' houses, the two Englishmen and the American reporter came to the palace which was in all respects exactly as the king had left it. The royal bed and couch were in their places, the royal chairs occupied their usual raised position. Only, curiously enough, all had been turned around and over.

The storerooms upstairs were untouched, and here they found an infinite variety of articles, for the most part mere rubbish, but many interesting and valuable. "Good heavens," Henty exclaimed at the sight. "It looks like the sales room of Sotheby's on an auction day." At their feet sat piles of silver plate, gold masks, gold cups, clocks, glass, china, pillows, guns, cloth, caskets, and cabinets.

Signs that human sacrifice had been carried on up to the last minute were evident. Several stools were thickly coated with recently shed blood, and a horrible smell of gore pervaded the whole palace. The building was as full of ju-ju objects as the humblest cottage. King Kofi Karikari's private sitting room was, like the rest, an open court with a tree growing in it, covered with fetish objects, and thickly hung with spiders' webs. At each end a royal chair occupied a small but deep alcove, so the monarch could always sit in the shade no matter the time of day. Along each side of the little court ran a narrow veranda which provided shelter to a large assortment of little figurines and magic idols.

From one of the verandas a door opened into the king's tiny bedroom, which was about ten feet by eight. A small window about a foot square, which opened into the women's rooms, provided the only light in the dark chamber. At one end stood the raised royal bedstead with curtains, and on a curious low ledge, over which the king would have had to step to reach his bed, the explorers found a number of pistols and other weapons, among them an English general's sword, bearing the inscription, "From Queen Victoria to the King of Ashanti."

"This must have been presented to his predecessor," Henty suggested.

"And this is my Winchester!" Frank shouted as he spotted the repeater he had given away. He was immediately reminded of Frederick Goodenough. "I must visit his grave," he said, suddenly feeling guilty for having so far in the excitement forgotten to pay his respects. The others went with him to the place where the naturalist lay in his grave.

After a few minutes' reverent silence, Stanley murmured, "He was a fine scientist and an interesting writer. I particularly enjoyed *The Passerine Family*."

"You read that?" Frank burst out in surprise.

Stanley gave one of his rare but warming smiles. "I'm painted as the murderer of innocent natives, though Lord alone knows, Livingstone has killed more, so don't dare let my secret out of the bag that in my spare time between shooting my porters I do a bit of exotic bird spotting."

The famous explorer's words lightened their mood, and the three returned to the town. Frank headed for the field hospital, where he helped with washing and binding wounds with dressings. His experience with the Ashanti sick and wounded outside Elmina fitted him well for the task of helping the overworked medical staff.

All day Wolseley expected the Asantehene's arrival—a runner had said he would be in early. At two o'clock a tremendous rainstorm broke over the town, lasting for three hours. In the evening it became evident that the king was again playing for time and, indeed, word soon came that Kofi Karikari was deep in the interior, not at the tombs of the kings, three miles away, where he was supposed to be.

Another torrential rainstorm threatened, and with the weather breaking for an early rainy season, the general considered it unwise to linger. He gave orders to burn the town and to start for the coast next morning.

All night Major Home with a party of Engineers mined the palace and prepared to blow it up, while a prize committee selected and packed everything which they considered worth taking down to Cape Coast. In his search for local color, Mr. Henty had gained information from a few of those citizens who hadn't run off, and informed the others that a large amount of treasure might be discovered at the kings' tombs. The prize money would have been welcome, but several officers warned the general that their men were rapidly becoming exhausted. Battling the foe and the capture of Kumasi had kept up spirits, but now the campaign had achieved its principal aim the usual sense of anticlimax after great exertion followed. Every hour added to the number of fever-stricken men who would have to be carried down to the Coast, and each man, as he saw his comrades fall out from the ranks, felt that his own turn might come next.

At six in the morning the advance guard and the baggage began to move out of the town. The main force left by seven. The Black Watch remained as rearguard to cover the Engineers and the burning party.

Frank, Henty, and Stanley stayed behind to witness the town's destruction. A hundred laborers were supplied with palm leaf torches, and in spite of the outer coats of thatch being saturated by the recent rains, the flames soon spread. Volumes of black smoke poured up, and soon a huge pall over the town told the Ashanti of the destruction of their blood-stained capital. The palace and nobles' residences were blown up, and when the Engineers and the Black Watch marched out from Kumasi not a house remained untouched by the flames.

The troops had not gone very far before they had reason to congratulate themselves on retreating when they had. "Thank God these thunderstorms didn't set in three days earlier, otherwise we'd be spending the next three months trapped in Kumasi," Stanley shouted above the rattle of a fresh downpour.

The swamp surrounding the town quickly rose a foot in depth, while the next stream, before a rivulet two and a half feet deep, had now swollen its banks for a hundred and fifty yards on either side, with over five feet of water in the old channel. Across this the engineers managed to throw a large tree, over which the troops crossed precariously, while in order to keep up the native carriers had to wade across. Only the eyes of the taller men showed above the water, while the shorter disappeared altogether, seen only by the boxes carried on their heads. Fortunately, in the deepest part—some three or four yards wide—the current remained sluggish and by taking a deep breath the porters were able to struggle across.

There was an even longer delay at the Ordah, where the swollen river had topped the bridge by two feet or more. Some of the cross planks had been swept away, and each man had to feel every step of his way over. It was taking so long to get the men across that by five in the afternoon it was clear that night would overtake them before everyone was safely over.

The river was still rising and no one wanted to be left on the wrong side in case the Ashanti mounted a counter-attack. So the order was given for the white troops to strip and to wade across wearing only their helmets and holding their guns above their heads. The clothes bundles were carried over by natives swimming, while others took their places below the bridge in case any of the men should be carried off their feet by the now swift current. Everyone got over without any accident.

However, it was quite dark before the last men were over, and the natives collecting the clothes missed those of a soldier who had undressed at the foot of a tree, which meant he passed the night, a very wet one, in a blanket. On the morning everyone had a good laugh as this worthy paraded smartly with his regiment in nothing but a helmet and rifle. A Fanti porter offered to swim back over and brought back his uniform.

The newspapermen were now eager to get back to file their reports, at least to Prasu where they could use the telegraph. As the stages were necessarily slow and tedious, owing to the quantity of baggage and sick being carried, Frank decided to join Henty and Stanley and push straight on down to the Coast.

Sir Garnet Wolseley shook him firmly by the hand as he gave his consent to Frank's departure. "You have been an enormous help, Mr. Hargate and I'd be glad to recommend you to a commission on my return—you'd make a fine officer."

Frank thanked the general for his kindness, but replied that—having perhaps had his fill of African adventure for the time being—he thought his mind was now set on becoming a medical doctor. And, bidding goodbye to Sir Garnet and the many friends he'd made during the expedition, he set off for the Guinea Coast. The two reporters and Frank hired bearers to carry them in hammocks, including one for Ostik, which made their journey pleasant and—at the speed the bearers carried them—a great deal quicker than if they had been on foot.

There was some risk as far as the Pra, for straggling war bands of Ashanti often intercepted the convoys. Frank and his traveling companions, however, met with no obstacle and, after a brief pause at Prasu, made Cape Coast ten days after leaving the army.

Frank's first mission was to discover from the agent whether the Hausas Firewater, Ugly Tom, Bacon, and Tatters had made it safely back from Kumasi. The man confirmed that they had and received the agreed payment from him and sailed for their homes.

Now Ostik implored his master to take him with him across the sea to England. "But Ostik, you wouldn't be happy for very long in England. The customs there are so different to your own, and in winter when the rain turns to ice flakes you'd feel the cold terribly." In the end Ostik gave in to the arguments and, having earned enough to purchase for years the small comforts and luxuries dear to the African heart, he agreed to return to the Gabon immediately Frank left for England.

Three days after their arrival at Cape Coast the African Steamship Company's mail boat *SS Freetown* arrived off the fort, and Frank booked his passage for England. Three days he sailed, watching the green smudge of African coast fade into the morning haze as he leaned on the rail alongside George Henty, who had a complete set of detailed reports on the war to write, and Henry Stanley, who, after doing the same for the *Herald*, intended haranguing his sponsors for a trip to explore the Congo.

During a stop at Madeira, they all heard of the death of Dr. David Livingstone in Africa. It left all of them in a pensive mood for days, especially Stanley, who had come to like and admire the Scotsman during the time he had spent with him at Ujiji.

It felt very strange to set foot in Liverpool. Nearly two years and a half had elapsed since Frank had sailed with Goodenough, and he had gone through adventures sufficient for a lifetime. He was only just eighteen, but his experiences in Africa, fending for himself and doing a man's work made him feel far older.

The next day, in London, the three travelers shook hands and said their goodbyes to each other. Stanley restated his offer of a place on his next expedition if Frank wanted it. Henty gave his young companion an appraising glance, as though burning his appearance into his memory. "I shall feature you as a character in one of my stories, Hargate, if you've no objection."

"No Mr. Henty, I shall be flattered… I think."

"Oh, you will be."

As the two older men went their separate ways, Frank went and booked a room at the Charing Cross Hotel before sorting out his next steps.

He wanted to go first of all to visit Jekks who had been his earliest friend in London, and then drive to the Ruthvens', where he was sure of a warm welcome. He had written several times, whenever it had been possible to send letters, to his various friends, first of all to his sister and the doctor, to Dick Ruthven, to the porter and to the old naturalist, Mr. Horton.

At London Bridge Station he learned that Jekks had been off for a week after straining his back lifting a heavy trunk, so he took a cab to Ratcliff Highway. The shop was closed, but his knock brought the naturalist to the door.

"What can I do for you, sir?" Mr. Horton asked civilly.

"Well, in the first place, you can shake me by the hand."

The old man started at the voice.

"Why, it's Frank Hargate! Grown and sunburnt out of all recollection. My dear boy, I'm so glad to see you. Come in, come in. John's inside."

Frank received another hearty greeting. "John?" he asked, as he shook Jekks by the hand.

The porter grinned back, "Well'n I haven't used it in an age, but that's as I was christened, John Jekks, but the monika at work's always been simple Jekks."

They sat for a couple of hours chatting over Frank's adventures. He found that had he arrived a fortnight later he would have missed both his friends. In a week's time Jekks was to be married again to a widow who owned a small but very successful shop. Mr. Horton had sold his naturalist business, and was moving to the country to live with his sister.

After taking his leave Frank took a cab to Eaton Square and the Ruthven town residence. A servant showed him into the drawing room, where he sat down on a sofa. A minute later the door opened with a terrific crash and his old schoolfellow rushed in.

Frank had barely reached his feet before being swept off them in a crushing bear hug. After a second, Dick let him go, stood back to take his hand and wring it. "My, my Frank Hargate, look at you. How thin you are, and as black as a native African! I wouldn't have known you if I'd passed you in the street, and... I don't know, but there's something in your eyes. Yes, I believe you look older than I do."

Frank finally got a laughing word in, as the young men let go of each other's hands. "The sun's effect will wear off in time, and I've no doubt I'll put on a bit with some decent English food. As to looking older—"

"But it's no wonder after all you've gone through. You must fill me in on the last few weeks, which are a blank at the moment. When did you arrive, and where are your things? Why haven't you brought them here?"

Frank said that he had left them at the hotel, as he was going to Deal early the next morning. He stayed, however, and dined with his friend, whose father also received him with kindness and condolences on the loss of his mentor and Sir James' personal friend. "I shall pay for the erection of a stone at Brompton Cemetery in memory of Frederick Goodenough, and let you know, young Hargate, when it's to be unveiled."

On leaving the hotel next morning he had his luggage sent to Eaton Square and then took the first train to Deal. There he found his sister Lucy suddenly grown up, very well and happy. She was almost out of her mind with delight at seeing him. Frank stayed two or three days with her and then returned to town and took up the offer of his own room in Eaton Square.

"Well, my boy, what are you thinking of doing?" Sir James Ruthven asked next morning as the family sat at breakfast. "Have you had enough of travel?"

"Quite enough, sir," Frank answered. "I've made up my mind to become a doctor. The gold necklace which I showed you, the one General Amanquatia gave me, weighs more than twenty pounds of the purest gold. Properly sold, it will keep me in some comfort and pay my expenses until I've completed the course and passed my examinations. And Mr Goodenough's left me, I believe, something in his will. I sent home one copy to his lawyer and have the other with me. I must call on the solicitors this morning. I've also some thirty pounds' weight in gold which was paid me by the king for the goods he took, but this, of course, belongs to Mr. Goodenough's estate."

The solicitor was clearly excited to meet Frank when he called in on the firm later that morning.

"Congratulations on your safe return," he effused. "I'm delighted to tell you that the many specimen cases were safely delivered to port here and are now at the new Natural History Museum premises. "I understood from my client that you are an accomplished taxidermist. The museum, I've no doubt, would welcome your expertise, especially with the rare specimens you found."

Frank smiled politely and explained that, while the task would please him enormously, he was now determined on a medical career.

"You've called, of course, in reference to the late Mr. Goodenough's will which was sent from Kumasi. Are you acquainted with its contents?"

Frank gave the slightest shake of his head. "No, beyond the fact that Frederick told me he had left me a small legacy."

"Then I have pleasant news to give you." The lawyer smiled broadly. "Mr. Goodenough died possessed of about sixty thousand pounds. He left fifteen thousand each to his only surviving nephew and niece. Fifteen thousand pounds he has divided among several charitable and scientific institutions. Fifteen thousand pounds he has left to you."

Frank's eyebrows rose in surprise.

"The will is a just and satisfactory one," the lawyer said, "because he hasn't had much contact with his relations, who live in Scotland, and they had no reason to expect to inherit any portion of his property. They are, therefore, delighted with the handsome legacy they've received. I may mention that Mr. Goodenough ordered that in the event of your not living to return to England, five thousand pounds of the portion which would have come to you was to be paid to trustees for the use of your sister, the remaining ten thousand to be added to the sum to be divided among the charities."

"I don't know what to say," Frank stuttered. "I'm quite taken aback. I never for a moment thought when he said 'legacy' that he meant so much. It's an absolute surprise." Then he recovered a little and addressed the lawyer. "Sir, would you draw up for me papers to sign to settle the five thousand pounds on my sister. Whatever happens then she'll be well provided for."

* * *

The acquisition of the most unexpected fortune to add to his own in no way altered Frank's views as to his future. He applied for a student position at Guy's Hospital, and was pleased to be accepted toward the end of the year. He also read with interest in the *Daily Telegraph* that the newspaper, together with the *New York Herald*, had agreed to sponsor Mr. Henry Morton Stanley in an expedition to find the sources of the Congo and Nile rivers. A letter from the explorer invited Frank to join him, but he wrote to thank Stanley for remembering him and declined his invitation to join the party.

For three years he worked hard and steadily before passing his first medical degree with high honors. He spent another three years as a junior doctor in hospital work, where he met Joyce Rainbow and married her the year after. Frank purchased a partnership in an excellent West End practice and soon became known as one of the rising young physicians of the day.

For a while, until his marriage to Joyce, his sister Lucy kept house for him in Harley Street, but the last time Lieutenant Richard Ruthven was at home on leave he persuaded her of her duty to make civilian life bearable for him when he attained the rank of captain and, in accordance with his father's wish, retired from the army. They became engaged and then married a few months later.

Dick often laughed and told Frank that he was a good soldier spoiled. "It's a pity a man like you should settle down as a doctor when you made your way in life by sheer pluck," he used to tease.

"Oh I keep my eye on things African in the paper," Frank replied, but I think that was adventure enough."

"They say," said Dick gazing steadily at his friend, "that once you've been in Africa, she never lets you go."

Epilogue

London 1896

In the gloomy light, the squat buildings with their beehive thatch roofs form a black backdrop framing the ghostly fingers of the great fetish tree. In the twilight, the mountain of human skulls and dismembered limbs of fresher death glows palely, silhouetting the massive trunk of the tree, its branches draped with ju-ju fetishes. And yet, in the dark brightness flares in brilliant color from the rows of giant umbrellas of the little kings and the chiefs.

Beneath the voluminous parti-colored segments of the largest umbrella the face of the king is lost, formless, menacing. He can't make it out but he knows the hidden eyes are watching with fanatic glee.

Now he sees a line of kneeling men, pathetic figures, hands brutally bound behind their backs, their mouths squeezed grotesquely into figures of 8—"noozed" the Swiss had said. He can see the cruel thin-bladed knives driven through their cheeks to secure their tongues. There's a reason for this cruelty, but it eludes him.

And there it is, as he knew it would be, pulsing slowly in the dying light as though throbbing to the rhythm of the chanting crowd, the large brass bowl. Even though he knows, somewhere deep inside, that he's dreaming, he can begin to smell the putrescent stench emanating from the dish of death. It is ornamented with four small lions, and a number of round knobs all around its rim, except at one part, where there is a space for the sacrificial victim's neck to rest on the edge.

This is a filthy dark part of Africa. He doesn't want to be here. There were other places, of light, of grace, of honor, even when the natives contemplated how to persuade you to part with more for less. Where the hell's a good Hausa when you need one?

Suddenly he's forced to his knees, head pushed down, the bowl's rim bites into his Adam's apple. He struggles but his arms are bound. Beneath, the bowl is inches deep in sloshing blood, from which rises a malodorous stink, the smell of death, of countless deaths, a smell of Africa which he can't get out of his head, a scent of decay so awful his head reels.

Slowly, slowly, catchee monkey, West Africa's slogan. *Once you've been there, Africa will never let you go...*

His hands are useless, but his mouth is free.

Frank screams, filling his lungs with a shuddering gasp.

And screams again...

"Darling, wake up! You're dreaming again."

He became aware of Joyce's firm grip on his drenched, shuddering shoulders.

"That's the third nightmare this week. What on earth's the matter?"

Dr. Frank Hargate calmed down. "A nightmare," he said hoarsely. "I'm sorry, I woke you up."

"Can't you tell me about it, Frank? Sometimes it helps to talk over a dream while it's still fresh."

"Fresh!" Frank barked. "That's the last word you could use to describe this."

Joyce bit her lip in concern. "Is it always the same nightmare?"

He nodded slowly. "Yes, and it's all the fault of Monday's *Standard*. I picked up a copy on the way back from the clinic."

Balancing her busy life between the household, looking after their two sons and her charity nursing work among the poor, Joyce Hargate had little time for reading newspapers. She looked at him enquiringly.

Frank sighed. "I can't believe he brought it back, that evil thing, back here to London."

"Who brought back what?"

"Colonel Baden-Powell, the man put in charge of the assault on

Kumasi. He was sent to enforce the treaty signed with 'King Coffee,' the one signed just after I was left there." Frank turned to look at his wife in the dim light of the bedside oil-lamp she had lit. "You see the new Asantehene, called Prempeh, had refused the payments and no doubt adopted the practice of sacrifice again. Baden-Powell went out last year to command the march and do all over again what Sir Garnet Wolseley did twenty-two years ago."

"But what's so upset you, Frank?"

He gave a deep shuddering sigh, feeling the shackles of the dream sloughing away like a dead weight. But Frank could not tell her about the sacrificial bowl, even think of it in his own mind. But he knew that the nightmares had a deeper meaning than simply bringing back foul memories. The news reports of the recent march on Kumasi had awakened a sense of things undone for far too long.

Africa will never let you go…

Next day, he took Joyce—who had never been before—and their youngest son James to Brompton Cemetery and to a small, elegant stone monument.

"Oh, how lovely!" Joyce leaned from the waist to read the inscription. "This is dedicated to your friend, isn't it? 'Frederick Goodenough,'" she read out.

James peered at a second, lower line in smaller text, then looked up at his father questioningly. "But what does this mean, daddy?" he asked, pointing to the word. "A… man… whati?"

"Amanquatia. Ah, that's a long story. I'll tell you one day soon."

Joyce stared quizzically at her husband, reading his face like a book. "You want to go back…? I think I've known for some time."

Frank gave a sigh, then smiled. "So many exciting discoveries about the marsh fevers in the last few years. I could do research as well as doctoring where it's really needed. A cure for *mal aria* is just around the corner, I know it! There must be something better than quinine. And we need to discover what causes it."

His wife took his arm, the slightest of smiles playing at the corners of her lips. "Then for Mr. Goodenough and Mr. Amanquatia, let's go!"

"You mean it?"

"I do. It will be an experience for the children, a chance for them to be as plucky as their father."

Frank glanced at the pale English sun and grinned happily. "Stanley and Henty both said I'd go back one day. Seems like they were right after all."

Historical notes

Taxidermy, the process of stuffing dead animals for the purposes of display, either for decoration or for serious study, was extremely popular in the Victorian era. London's Natural History Museum holds hundreds of Victorian exhibits. The Natural History Museum first opened on Easter Monday in 1881, later than Frederick Goodenough had hoped for, since its site had been chosen as early as 1862. Before the museum officially opened, the natural history exhibits were a part of the British Museum's collection. The new museum had a great need for animal stuffers, or taxidermists.

The value of money in the past is always difficult to calculate accurately, but in Chapter 5, Frank is certainly correct in saying that £25 will keep him in reasonable circumstances if he's careful with his spending. It would approximate to £13,000 (US$20,000) in today's earnings. On his return to England, Frederick leaves Frank £15,000. In today's earnings that sum is worth £4.9 million (US$7.9m). The two lots of gold given him by the Ashanti king and General Amanquatia added up to 800 ounces. In 1874 an ounce of pure gold was worth £4.25, so Frank could have realized a total of £3,400 on selling it, which in today's earnings would give him a further £1.7 million (US$2.53m).

Toward the end of Chapter 9, Goodenough delights the Fang with slide shows on his magic lantern, which was a kerosene-fired slide projector. Victorian lantern slides were large and complex creations, often with built-in mechanical features using crank-pinion and gear wheels with operating handles, so that a limited form of animation was possible, such as the storm-tossed ship described. In 1817, Sir

David Brewster patented the kaleidoscope—very much still with us today. Chromotrope lantern slides were made up from two glasses, each painted with geometric patterns, which when revolved in opposite directions projected fabulous displays of ever-changing colors like a kaleidoscope.

In Chapter 17, the ipecacuanha medicine mentioned comes from the root of a Brazilian plant and is a powerful emetic. Over several centuries its uses—depending on dosage—included inducing vomiting in people who had been poisoned (a sort of early stomach pump), inducing sweating (in malaria fever sufferers when they became over-hot), and most powerfully to treat dysentery.

All the tribes referred to in the story are real, although variable spellings may be found (Asante for Ashanti; Fante for Fanti, etc.). This is largely due to the fact that none of the West African and Central African tribes had a written language until the coming of Europeans, so names were rendered differently depending on the language used and the way the Europeans wrote down the sounds they heard. So, for instance, at the time the story is set, the spelling for Kumasi was usually Coomassie. The port for Dahomey (now Republic of Benin) in the story is given as Wydah, but appears today on maps with its more French-sounding spelling of Ouidah.

The military units and participating officers in the Ashanti War are all based on real characters who were there at the time, as are the characters of the Ashanti general, Amanquatia (or Ammon Quatia), and the Asantehene, or king, Kofi Karikari.

Every town/village named in the story is a real place. Note that Sam's village is not given a name and is fictitious although its circumstances are entirely authentic, as indeed are the circumstance of his tale.

On the military road built between Cape Coast and Kumasi, the engineers constructed a total of 273 bridges across streams, swamps and rivers, including the largest, at over 200 feet, at Prasu.

As described in the story, the famous explorer Henry Morton Stanley really was present at the Ashanti War as a newspaper reporter. And so indeed in the same capacity was the famous novelist George Alfred Henty. Henty did write his story. His real inspiration for the character of Frank Hargate was Anthony Bannister Swinburne, Stanley's sixteen-year-old traveling companion, described as his "hero-worshipping clerk and valet."

While Henty may have been obliged to defend himself, we are told that Stanley took an active part in the climactic battle at Amoaful. General Wolseley, "strolling" through the battle, noted with approval the coolness and accuracy with which Stanley ("a thoroughly good man") picked off the enemy.

At the start of Chapter 19, General Sir Garnet Wolseley (who also appears as the overall commander of the failed Nile river campaign to relieve Khartoum in *Storm Over Khartoum*) refers to Stanley as "the Yank with an oddly Welsh lilt." The famous explorer passed himself off as an American, but in reality he was born John Rowland, the illegitimate son of an impoverished farmer, in Denbigh, North Wales. His grandparents raised him until he was about six, when he was sent to a workhouse, where he remained until he ran away and made his way to the USA. His fascinating story has been covered by several biographies, none better than Tim Jeal's *Stanley: The Impossible Life of Africa's Greatest Explorer*.

Tim Jeal also wrote a terrific biography of the founder of the Boy Scouts, Robert Baden-Powell, who crops up at the end of this story in the Epilogue. Baden-Powell led a native levy against Kumasi in the war of 1896 across almost exactly the same ground as Wolseley before him—although the engineers' marvellous road of 1874 had fallen into disrepair by then and so much of the work had to be repeated. The Asantehene Prempeh put up no fight, which greatly upset the vigorous Baden-Powell, who had been looking forward to a good scrap and a name-making victory. (Prempeh was exiled to the modern holiday hot-spot, the Seychelles Islands, so you might wonder who came off best...).

The origin of the Boy Scouts' left handshake is often attributed to Baden-Powell's time among the Ashanti. It's said that when B-P entered Kumasi, he was surprised when a warrior chief offered his left hand to shake. The man told B-P that the brave shake with the left hand because a warrior uses his right hand to hold the spears and his left to hold his shield. To show your trust in someone, you put down the shield and greeted them by holding out the left hand. Now, hundreds of thousands of Scouts worldwide greet each other with the left handshake.

Read an extract from

Prologue

El Obeid, Sudan, Early November, 1883

An ochre haze hangs in the large square, its dusty particles stirred like a thick pottage by the clamoring throng of jubilant Arabs. Constant chants overpower the groans of tethered camels and distressed lowing of coraled cattle terrified by the stench of blood. The great and the humble of Kordofan express their exuberance with shouted slogans and ululation. From every mouth praise sings out for the Mahdi's great victory over the hated Turks and their British infidel commanders.

Two of the nonbelievers stare sightlessly from severed heads mounted on poles close to the center of the square. Colonel William Hicks—known by his Egyptian title of Hicks Pasha—and Baron Seckendorf, distinguished by his full, light-colored beard, have fought their last battle and paid the price of defying the Mahdi's Dervish army. Their blood stains the tangerine and burnt umber soil beneath the heads a clotted black.

To the side of these grisly trophies stands a slightly raised platform on which it is eagerly anticipated the Mahdi, his Khalifa, and his leading emirs will soon appear. Two British officers kneel before the dais, heads bowed as much in shame as from their terrible battle wounds. Kneeling beside them in a row, some twenty black Nubian Sudanese survivors of the battle await their dread fate.

The harsh call of an *ombeya* and the rattle of drums heralds the appearance of Mohammed Ahmed, the Mahdi, chosen of God, conqueror of Kordofan and, according to his own prophesy, soon of all the Sudan and Egypt. His avowed mission is to sweep away the hated Turks and their infidel white allies. For this, God has placed him on earth. He strides from his humble hut and mounts the platform. His beautifully washed, short quilted *jibba* is perfumed with sandalwood, musk, and attar of roses, a perfume his disciples call *Rihet el Mahdi*, the Scent of the Mahdi.

The Mahdi is a tall, powerfully built, broad-shouldered man of light-brown skin tone. He has a broad forehead above sparkling black eyes. His nose and mouth are well shaped, and he likes to smile a lot—as he does now—to show off his white teeth and expose the V-shaped gap between the two front incisors. This *falja* is a sign of good fortune in the Sudan, which it is for the Mahdi, for women flock to share his luck and he reserves the prettiest for his harem.

A step behind the Mahdi stands his Khalifa, handsome Abdullahi ibn Muhammad, in his *jibba* covered with the small square patches of different colors that mark him out as a Mahdist warrior. His sympathetic Arab face belies a ruthless nature in pursuit of the Mahdi's spiritual aims. His son Yakub stands at his father's side, shorter and with an ugly countenance. The unworthy fear him, for he is known to resolve disputes efficiently with the executioner's sword. Much of his recent handiwork litters the square's extremities.

The Mahdi raises his arms in greeting. The crowd falls silent. But there is no silence.

In the sudden absence of screaming ululation the moans of Yakub's victims taint the powdered air. Men hang from wooden frames, dead and dying, their flesh in tattered shreds from the flaying lash. Others are suspended from beams by their thumbs, legs twitching in their agony, or lifeless from the torture of inexpressible pain. Here and there, slumped against mud walls, are men caught in thieving, now missing their left hands and right feet. At the end of the square a score of men bound to a rail suffer torments from recently inflicted wounds to their arms, legs, and torsos, into which interrogators pour a strong solution of salt and water well seasoned with Sudan pepper. This desperate but muted chorus becomes the background to the Mahdi's words. He starts quietly, slowly.

"O Beloveds of the Prophet!" His voice, a deep baritone but sibilant, rings out. "In the name of God the most compassionate and merciful, swear to renounce this world and look only to the paradise to come through the glories of our religious war. The war the Turks have brought down on their unbeliever heads through their greed, their adultery, their theft, and their deception."

A collective sigh gusts from bearded lips…*alalalalalala!*

The voice begins to resound. "O Beloveds, know that I am the Mahdi! The Chosen of God!"

He stretches his arms to heaven, head tilted back into the gaze of God.

Ayayayayay!

His black eyes flash beneath hooded lids as he returns his mesmerizing stare to the adoring crowd. He lowers a hand slowly to point at the kneeling prisoners and his voice mounts toward crescendo. "See before you those who defy the word of God. See the infidel dogs who would claim this land in the name of Shaitan."

Aaahhhhh… "Kill them," shouts a warrior.

The Mahdi's smile narrows to a cruel slit which allows only a glint of teeth between his lips. "O Beloveds, let their just punishment be a lesson to those who cower in Khartoum. It is the will of God. He has spoken to me. Let the words of the Mahdi be taken to Gordon Pasha in Khartoum that *jihad* is coming…" His voice rises to an unearthly shriek of spitting passion. "The desert whirlwind will wipe him and his soldiers from the face of our Sudan…" he slams out his right hand… "and then we take Egypt!"

Allahu Akbar! Allahu Akbar! Allahu Akbar!

The seven executioners begin their work, striking heads from shoulders of the kneeling men. They start with the two European officers. Massive sweeps of their curved swords carve through flesh and bone as easily as reaping grass. White and black bodies fall to their sides, fountaining life blood into the sand, and the joyous screams of the crowd sound like the end of a colonial dream.

Chapter 1: The Lineup

September 1882

Colonel James Clinton (retired), eyed his two sons fondly. "Everything packed and ready, boys?"

Rupert got in first. "Yes, father, I think so."

"Make sure you're ready in time. I don't want you missing the train. Well, did you enjoy your vacation?"

"Oh yes," Edgar replied, ever ready to please.

"Definitely," Rupert echoed. "Most enjoyable."

Edgar's enthusiasm lit up his earnest face. "Brittany was the best, though we've always enjoyed our holidays," he added hurriedly. "But it's much more fun staying in out-of-the-way places, and stopping at little old inns without the crowd and fuss of that great big Swiss hotel we went to last summer. It might have been Switzerland but everyone was English, and you had to eat at set times and fight to get anything."

"I hope we can go to Norway next year, like you said yesterday, Father," Rupert broke in. "Different scenery, different language, and different people." He turned on his younger sister. "Madge, you'll have to learn Norse so you can interpret for us."

"You're lazy, you are. I did all the talking in Brittany and you've been doing French longer than me."

Her words scandalized Edgar. "That's not fair! I spoke French the most—"

"No one cares about French," Rupert butted in. "At least Latin and ancient Greek are dead languages, so you never have to use them. Talking foreign makes no difference to your status in school. That's why no one bothers with it."

Edgar chuckled at his brother's lofty disdain. "You never know when the ability to learn a language quickly will come in useful."

"It's all right for you, Ed, you're a natural at picking up the local lingo, whatever it is. Makes me sick!" Rupert made a move toward the French window. "Come on, let's take a turn around the lawn. We've an hour before we have to leave."

The two boys and Madge, two years their junior, went out into the mid-afternoon sunshine, which turned the ancient yew, the lilac and rowan trees a golden buttercup.

Colonel Clinton watched through the window. They were sons any father with a distinguished service in the British army in India might be proud of—well-built, handsome lads of sixteen. Both boys had pleasant open faces and a ready sense of fun which he knew made them popular among their fellow pupils at Cheltenham College. But in no other way could the colonel discern any marked likeness between them: Edgar, with hair a much darker brown than Rupert's and eyes of a deep hazel, while Rupert's pale gray irises lent him the greater distinction. If Rupert had the edge in height, Edgar beat his brother in the breadth of his shoulders. And they shared little in temperament, from Edgar's serious countenance and natural reserve to Rupert's quietly amused cheeriness. Rupert, the more outgoing of the two, generally led the conversation, but Edgar—in attractive contrast to his studiousness—had the livelier sense of humor, and some quiet remark of his now caused a burst of collective laughter.

Apart from a natural and light-hearted sibling rivalry, the two boys were their own closest friends. To avoid the unpleasant arguments that happen sometimes when two brothers go to the same school, Colonel Clinton had organized for Edgar to study "modern" subjects, which suited him, and Rupert classics. This arrangement dampened down any heated debates as to who might be the cleverer.

As he so often did, the colonel reviewed the boys' futures. "I've divided the property as nearly as possible equally between them," he muttered under his breath. "Madge, of course, will be looked after until she marries, but as to the boys... My will says they must draw lots as to who gets the part with the house and park on it, and who is to have a sum of money enough to build an equally good house on his share of the estate. We can only hope that chance will be wiser than we have been, and give the old house to the right boy."

Colonel Clinton curtailed his barely whispered thoughts sharply as he turned around on hearing a sigh from his wife. She walked up behind him and stood at his side to gaze out at the lawn and their children larking about on it.

"Well, Lucy," he murmured, placing a hand on her shoulder, "I know what you're thinking—another summer vacation over, and we're no nearer to the truth. I have to admit—our plan has failed so far."

Edgar grinned secretly at his brother. The twins found themselves unwillingly enrolled in a discussion about weight, taking place in the senior boys' study room of River-Smith's boarding house at Cheltenham College.

Skinner, captain of the house rugby team, spoke heatedly with the tone of indignation that he was prone to. "You see, Wade is a great loss because his weight and strength told in the scrimmage. Hart was a great half-back too, and there wasn't a better half-back in the whole college than Wilson. Three gone to uni and we've no one to take their place. Wade was as strong as a bull—an awful loss to us! Why don't some of you grow up like him?" He looked around reproachfully at his listeners. "Well over a hundred and eighty pounds Wade weighed in at, and there's not one of you above one-sixty."

"Why don't you set us an example?" Edgar avoided Rupert's warning glance; he couldn't help taunting Skinner.

The others guffawed readily—Skinner, all wire and muscle, and well under a hundred and forty pounds.

"I'm not built like that," he said, unruffled at Edgar's jibe. "What about you, Wordsworth?"

"I can run," the boy said defensively.

"Oh, sure, you can run all right, but if someone half your height tackles you, over you go like a ninepin. No wonder, you're like a jointed walking stick. What we want is *heaviness*, and the sooner you put weight on the better—go for more puddings and eat your food more slowly."

Wordsworth grumbled something about his having done his share last year, but Skinner ignored him, pulled out his pocket watch, and glanced irritably at the face.

"Where the hell's Easton got to?"

"He always gets the evening train," Rupert said. "Something to do with the connections not matching up."

"Really?" Skinner's expression made him resemble a snappy terrier. "It takes him an age to fold up his things without a crease, to scent his hankie, and coif his hair to his satisfaction...no wonder he never manages to get going early. Well, at least, since he's not here, we can talk about him. I didn't like having him on the team last season. What do you reckon?"

"Yeah, I don't really like him either," said one called Scudamore. "But I have to admit that once he gets his jersey on he drops all the poncy nonsense and plays a good, hard game."

Edgar could see that Rupert felt disposed to offer support to the absent Easton. "He doesn't seem to mind how muddy he gets either, in spite of moaning about it after. I'd put him in again, Skinner, if I were you."

Edgar nodded his agreement and a mutter of assent came from the others.

"It gets my goat when he saunters up as if it were an accident that he's there, and talks in that *d-r-a-w-l-i-n-g* way," Skinner protested.

"So, if he wants to make an ass of himself at other times," Wordsworth said, "it doesn't affect us so long as he plays well in the team."

Skinner looked incredulous. "The words team and Easton don't go together—there's nothing sociable about him."

Edgar's sense of fairness pressed him to leap to Easton's defense. "That's not true. When that young kid Jackson twisted his ankle badly last term at the high jump, Easton used to go up and read to him for an hour at a time pretty much every day. I don't like his swanky fashions nor his droning way of talking, in fact, I don't care for him at all personally, but he's good-natured in spite of his silly airs."

Just then, the object of their discussion appeared in the doorway, leaned elegantly against the door frame, and regarded the study's inmates languidly. If he'd overheard their conversation, he did not let on. Easton puzzled Edgar. As one of River-Smith's prefects, he seldom asserted his authority or put himself out in any way to perform the duties of the office, yet the juniors obeyed his every command, always voiced as a quiet suggestion. He dressed with scrupulous care and certainly didn't look as though he had just completed a lengthy rail journey—with innumerable missing connections. He nodded all around in a careless manner as he sauntered into the room with none of the boisterousness that had marked the meeting of most of the others on returning to their school boarding house.

"Affected ass!" Skinner hissed to Rupert, who sat next to him.

"You're a prejudiced bugger, Skinner," Edgar heard Rupert whisper in his neighbor's ear. "You know you might've turned out the same if you had nurses and valets who always insisted on your looking like a fashion-plate." He glanced up enquiringly. "So, Easton, what have you been doing with yourself since we saw you last?"

"I've been on the Continent most of the time. Spent most of the time in Germany. Had a week in Munich and the same time in Dresden doing the picture-galleries."

Edgar knew that Easton's quiet, deliberate voice grated the most on Skinner, and he smiled inwardly at the inevitably splenetic riposte.

"That must've been a real treat." Skinner's sarcasm washed over its victim without effect.

"Yes Skinner, it was pleasant." Easton stretched languorously. "Though standing about so long makes your feet ache."

"I'm surprised you didn't have a wheelchair."

"Hmm, not such a bad idea, only I don't think I could bring myself to do it."

Sniggers broke out at his taking Skinner's suggestion seriously.

"And what have you been doing?"

Skinner drew himself up energetically, shoulders back. "Scotland, climbing hills, getting myself fit for the rugby football."

"Ah, rugger? Yes, I suppose it's *that* term."

This brought on an outright laugh from the others, mostly at Skinner's angry growl which greeted Easton's indifference to what everyone knew was to Skinner the most important feature of the year.

Easton looked around the gathered faces as if unable to understand what so amused them, "I wouldn't mind, if it weren't for the dirt. If you could get the kit properly laundered after a match every time it wouldn't matter so much, but it's disgusting to have to put on things that look as if they'd been rolled in mud."

"Why play at all, Easton?" Skinner snapped.

"Well, I wonder myself sometimes. I suppose it's a relic of our primal savage nature, when men didn't mind mud, and lived by hunting and fighting and that sort of thing—"

"And never wore starched shirts or had a tailor, and didn't part their hair in the middle, Easton…and never used soap."

Easton maintained his grave expression. "No, it must have been dreadful. I'm so glad that I didn't live in those days."

Skinner's patience broke. "Oh, never mind what you think! Let's go for a walk. It's a fine afternoon. You're all out of condition. The sooner we begin work the better. Are you coming, Easton? After lolling about looking at pictures a twelve-mile spin will do you good."

"Thanks, Skinner, but I'm not sure I want any good done me. Besides, when you say 'walk' you generally mean rushing across plowed fields, jumping into ditches, and getting hot and uncomfortable. If you don't mind, I'd rather a game of tennis."

With a politely apologetic smile, Easton walked insouciantly from the study room and disappeared along the corridor.

Skinner gasped and went red in the face. "He drives me around the bend. Arrogant pri—"

"Oh, come on!" Rupert loosed a chuckle. "Easton puts most of it on just to get you worked up. I'm sure I saw the amusement on his face when he was talking so seriously."

"He'll regret messing with me." Skinner put his hands up in an aggressive boxer's pose.

Edgar exchanged a quiet smile with the others. Tall and well built, Easton had the reputation of being the college's best boxer and Skinner, although tough and wiry, would have stood no chance against him.

Skinner's gloom proved correct when River-Smith's house lost almost all their trial matches to the much heavier players of the nine opposing boarding houses. It was a bitter blow for the house that had previously carried tournaments year after year. Skinner took the matter personally in a chronic state of disgust and fury. As Easton observed to Edgar, "He's becoming positively dangerous. Like a bull-terrier with a sore ear, snapping at everyone."

"I don't see anything's to be done," Skinner moaned, after they lost to rival house Green's. "It's not our play. The Greenites must average at least twenty pounds heavier, so we can't stand up to them. I suppose no one's got any bright ideas?"

"Well, yes, I have a few words to say." Easton's drawn-out words matched the elegant nonchalance of his cross-legged pose where he perched on the edge of a table in the study room.

"Well, say away!"

Easton ignored Skinner's waspishness. "It seems to me that weight's not the only thing. We might make up for it by stamina. It could make the difference—we might lose in the first half, but if we're in good training and can stay the pace better than the others, we'll win in the second. I know you always said we ought to keep ourselves in good condition, Skinner, but I mean strict training—up early for a three- to four-mile run every morning, taking another in the afternoon, cutting out deserts and fatty food, and going at it for heart and soul."

A stunned silence met this pronouncement, and then a clamor of agreement. Finally, Skinner tried manfully for graciousness. "Well, there's no reason not to train for rugby just as one does for rowing or running. You're the last person I'd have expected to hear it from, though, but if you're ready to train so will we."

And so the program began immediately. The hard-earned benefits began to show as River-Smith won some matches. The improvement became a topic of conversation in College, which explained the huge gathering at the side of the pitch for the Green's–River-Smith's rematch. Edgar saw in the enthusiasm radiating from packed touchlines that—as the under-dogs—the school's sympathies were for the most part with River-Smith's. The loud shouts of applause and encouragement whenever they defended their goal added to the irritation of the Greenites. With a half-time score of nil-nil, as they changed ends all the players showed weary evidence of the games' tremendous pace.

"Now's our time," Skinner urged his team. "They're more done in than us, and our training's going to tell more and more every minute."

But the Greenites displayed equal determination and kept the ball at River-Smith's end of the field. Then Skinner got it and made a run. The heaviest of the Greenites charged full out, but Easton checked him. Then came a scrimmage which, with their weight, favored the Greenites, but as the ball rolled out Edgar ran around faster than his opposite and scooped it up.

"Well done, Clinton! Go for it!" shouted some boys from the touchline, and a score of others joined in chorus.

"Which one is Clinton?"

One of the younger boys standing at the side of the pitch looked up to see a woman, quietly dressed in an obviously new, glossy black outfit. He turned back to the game. "They're all mixed up now."

"There are two of them, aren't there?" Jane Humphries persisted.

"Yes, that's the other—there—Edgar, the one who's just picked up the ball and is running with it."

Having snatched up the ball, the boy identified as Edgar shot off in a moment, dodging through the Greenite half-backs who attempted to block him. The young boy jumped up and down in his excitement. "Look, he's still got his wind, thanks to weeks' of hard training!"

They watched as the Clinton boy neared the Greenites' goal before two of them threw themselves at him.

"There!" the touchline fan shouted out for her benefit. "That's the other Clinton, Rupert, the one who's just charging the Greenite who's trying to stop his brother. Well done!" he shouted, as the other Clinton bowled over his opponent and his brother made a touchdown with barely a minute's play remaining.

The Greenite captain appealed that Rupert Clinton had fouled his player, but the referee upheld the points and the River-Smith's crowd went wild, along with most of the other spectators.

Jane asked no more questions. She concentrated her attention on the two boys her young informant had pointed out and stared intently as the players left the ground. The Clintons walked together, laughing and talking in high spirits. The youngster she had questioned earlier had strolled off, but she turned to another as the boys approached.

"Those are the Clintons, aren't they?"

"Yes, aren't they brilliant!" the fan replied with gushing enthusiasm, barely paying her any further attention as he joined the crowd wanting to pat the team members on the back as they pushed through the throng on their way to the baths.

She stood observing the Clinton brothers until they passed her, then she walked away with her eyes bent to the ground, and made her way to the small hotel room she had taken in the town. For several days she placed herself so that she could see the Clinton boys as they made their way to and fro between River-Smith's and the scattered College buildings, and watched them at sport.

Jane Humphries was uncertain as to what her next step should be. Which boy should she select? She changed her mind several times, and at last decided to leave it to chance, and whom she next met.

"Who is that woman?" Rupert asked Edgar one day. "I constantly see her hanging around, and she always seems to be staring at me."

"She's been staring at me too. I've no idea who she is. I can't recall seeing her face before this week."

"She asked me whether you were Clinton the other day when you were playing Green's." The brothers exchanged neutral glances at this surprising news delivered by one of the juniors from their house, who had evidently eavesdropped on them as they all walked down the path.

"It was just after you'd made a run with the ball, and someone shouted, 'Well done, Clinton!' And she asked me which was Clinton, and whether there weren't two of you. I pointed you both out," he added helpfully.

Rupert frowned. "That's weird. I wonder who the hell she is, Ed, and what she finds so interesting in us?"

Edgar strolled by himself along the pathway between his classroom and the school library, head down in an exercise book. He looked up in surprise as the strange woman stepped out in front of him. After a second's stab of alarm irritation took over.

"Well, what is it? You've been stalking us for the last week. What d'you want?"

"It's Edgar, isn't it? I want to speak to you about something very important," she began with apparent hesitancy, but noting her cold eyes, Edgar suspected an inner core of something more steely. He never bothered asking her how she knew his first name, he knew she knew it.

"Oh, rubbish!" he said. "There's nothing important you've got to tell me."

"Yes, there is; something of the greatest importance. Do you think I would have waited around here for a week to tell you, if it wasn't?"

"Well, if it's that important, fire away."

"I can't tell you here. It's too long a story. But it will only take half an hour. You won't be sorry for it afterward, I promise you."

Edgar jerked his watch out impatiently. He had nothing particular to do for an hour, and he had to admit that she had aroused his curiosity. "What about now, then?"

"I'm staying at—" she named the hotel, which Edgar knew. "It's not five minutes."

"All right," Edgar snapped, "though I'll bet this is some trick or other."

She walked away rapidly and he sauntered after her, attempting to appear as casual as possible. He followed her to the hotel and into its deserted lounge, where he threw himself down into a chair.

"Now, spill, and be as quick as you can."

She spoke quietly but with a firm voice. "Before I begin, will you tell me if you know anything about your birth?"

He looked at her in astonishment. "No. What in the world should I know about my birth?"

"You know you were born at Agra in India?"

"Of course I know that."

"And your father has never told you the circumstances?"

"How do you know my fa—" Edgar shook his head. "No. I only know that I was born there."

She gave him a small calm smile of assurance in which he detected a certain satisfaction that reminded him of a young schoolboy eager in the playground to impart information only he had. "I would have thought that he would have told you the story. Lots of people knew about it, and I was sure you must have heard it sooner or later."

"I don't want to hear about it." Edgar got to his feet. "If my father wanted me to know something, he'd already have told me. I don't know what you're going on about." He shouted the last words as he made for the door. Her next words froze him to the door frame. "Then, Edgar Clinton, you don't know that you are not his son."

* * *

Read the thrilling adventures of Edgar and Rupert in *Storm Over Khartoum*, and they appear again in the sequel, *Avenging Khartoum*, available in print and as ebooks.

1884
Deep in the deserts of Sudan a crazed fanatic spawns violent bloodshed...

Available as ebook or paperback

As members of the British force engaged in a desperate bid to save heroic Gordon of Khartoum, besieged by the frenzied armies of the Mahdi, teenagers Edgar and Rupert Clinton, twin brothers divided by a woman's greed, unravel a past crime
that threatens their futures.

Separated by events, Edgar and Rupert are thrown into their own desperate adventures as the conflict rages on – and both find Muslim allies willing to risk all to see them through.

In a hostile world of searing sun, sand and rocky wastes the two boys discover the wider meaning of what truly is a family.

1896
In the heart of the Sudan, the Mahdiya's despotic rule faces final retribution...

Available as ebook or paperback

As the British and Egyptian armies under General Kitchener mount a massive campaign to free Khartoum from the fanatic Dervish forces, one young man promises his dying mother to set out and seek the truth of his long-lost father's fate. Did he die in battle against the Mahdi's frenzied hordes in 1883? Did he escape and survive against all odds?

Sixteen-year-old Gregory Hilliard stakes his life on discovering the truth, helped by his loyal friend Zaki and two captains, the brothers Edgar and Rupert Clinton. Born and raised in Egypt, fluent in native languages, Gregory is pitched into the heat of war as interpreter for the British command, and through battle and peril unravels a tragic and life-changing mystery with its roots in faraway England.

1857
The terror of the Indian Uprising against British rule...

Available as ebook or paperback

As hell breaks loose, two teenage brothers, Ned and Dick Warrener, and their family are plunged into the maelstrom — hunted fugitives from appalling violence.

On their desperate trek through a mutinous country they must brave extreme perils if they are to survive. Only courage, cunning and sheer tenacity will see them through...

In this action-packed epic about a crucial moment in British colonial history, Ned and Dick are thrown into dangerous adventures that will turn them from boys into men.

1191
In a harsh clash of two faiths, a boy knight destined to be a true hero...

Available as ebook or paperback

Young Cuthbert, hungry for adventure and glory, joins King Richard the Lionheart's army on its way to the Holy Land with French and German allies to free Jerusalem from the grasp of the Saracens.

Even before reaching their goal the Crusaders are torn by jealousy and intrigue, and Cuthbert soon finds that chivalry and honour are little valued.

From the battlefields in Palestine, across Europe and back to England Cuthbert faces desperate obstacles to his quest for knighthood and a castle of his own, and learns that you only truly win what you fight for fairly.

Printed in Great Britain
by Amazon